NEVER
CAME
HOME

An addictive crime thriller with a twist
you won't see coming

GRETTA MULROONEY

Detective Inspector Siv Drummond Book 2

JOFFE
BOOKS

First published in Great Britain 2020
Joffe Books, London

© Gretta Mulrooney

Please join our mailing list for free Kindle books and new releases.

www.joffebooks.com

We love to hear from our readers! Please email any feedback you have to: feedback@joffebooks.com

ISBN 978-1-78931-526-4

To C.A.M.

PROLOGUE

28 July 2013

Adam roamed around the house, trailing restlessly from room to room. Now and again, he rubbed the edges of his trainers on the wood floor because he enjoyed the mousy squeak they made. Usually, his mum would tell him off because it might leave marks, but today she was distracted, so he reckoned he'd get away with it. He made a little noise in his throat as he went, to reassure himself: 'Catchungcatchungcatchung.' There was an exciting, expectant atmosphere like Christmas morning. Everything was unsettled. He liked it and was a bit frightened at the same time.

The house smelled of a cocktail of nail varnish, shower gel, hair products and mingled perfumes. Jeff from next door had popped in to return the strimmer, and he'd laughed and said the place 'ponged like a tart's parlour'. When Adam asked what that meant, Jeff had put his hand over his mouth and then said, 'I'd forgotten small boys have big ears. You know, Adam — like a fruit tart.' When Jeff had gone, his mum had muttered, 'Bloody annoying pest, always turning up when he's not wanted.'

There were six girls filling the house with giddy exhilaration: his older sister Lily and her school friends. They called themselves the Damsels, and they were like brightly coloured, long-legged birds from a rainforest, swooping and chattering before resting on chairs or beds. They giggled and called to each other: 'Oh no, I've got a humongous spot, has anyone got concealer?' 'Help! I've smudged this — I need emergency nail varnish remover.' 'Eye alert! I've forgotten my mascara.' When Tasha wasn't looking, Adam picked up her pearly orange nail varnish and sniffed the acid-drop scent.

The girls were sipping a light, rosy drink that fizzed. Lily had offered him a taste and he'd taken some, then pulled a face because although the bubbles were nice, it was bitter. Lily laughed and told him to scram, to go and play or watch telly because he was being annoying. 'Children shouldn't be seen or heard,' she told him, making the others giggle. He wandered from her room but loitered on the landing, listening to the girls singing along to Olly Murs, Adele and Rihanna. They fell silent only when they delved into make-up bags and gazed intently in mirrors, their mouths open as they concentrated on drawing steady lines around their lips and eyes. He hung in the doorway and watched as they worked magic with wands, pencils, palettes and brushes. They barely noticed him, other than to warn him not to touch their dresses. Except for Izzie, who bent down, caught him under the chin with one light hand and deftly dotted her cherry-flavoured lipstick on his cheeks. 'It's called "Beach Babe" so I'll put some on you, babe.' Her braids tickled his face. She smiled and turned her mirror to him so that he could see the two red spots. He smiled too, at the pleasure of being included. Izzie was nice. She ran her hand through his hair and handed him a Twix, his favourite. She smelled of soap and something else, like the tinned sweets Papu bought in the chemist.

Lily was complaining as he came downstairs. He sat on the bottom step, picking at a scab on his knee, listening to her high, whiny voice and his mother replying in that quiet, level way she had when she was trying to smooth things over. She'd been talking like that a lot lately.

'Mum, stop fussing, will you. Go away!'

'I was just checking your bow.'

'Well, don't! And that's enough photos for now, you're in the way.'

'D'you want a hand with your hair?'

'No, I can manage.'

'Is that a bit too much eyeshadow?'

'No, it's exactly how I want it.'

'It's quite thick around . . .'

'Mum! Just get lost, would you? You're doing my head in. I need to concentrate on my hair. Where's the tongs? Rosie, have you got my tongs?'

Lily had been talking about the prom for weeks. She'd bought her dress online and had then had it altered by Elsa at Quickstitch in town. Pearce, her boyfriend, hadn't been allowed to see it. He was meeting her at the prom and it had to be a big surprise. Mum had said, 'That's usually the custom for a wedding dress,' and Lily had replied, 'Well, we are getting married soon, so this can be a practice run.' His mum's face had gone strange and tight when Lily had said that, and there was that funny atmosphere in the house, as if the roof was pressing down and the walls were squeezing together.

His mother came to the top of the stairs and stared into space for a few moments. She fiddled with her ponytail and sighed, then slumped and leaned her head against the wall so that she was half in shadow. It was a warm evening, and she wore a bright yellow dress with bits of white on the shoulders that were called epaulettes. It was strange, peering up at her with his head back. She was small but from where he sat, she seemed taller and very like Lily.

She glanced down and saw him. 'Okay there, Adam?'

He wasn't but he couldn't explain. He asked, 'Has Dad phoned?'

'No.' She came down slowly, peering at him. 'What's that on your face?'

'Lipstick. Izzie did it.'

'These girls! What'll we do with them? They're a law unto themselves, that lot. Don't pick that scab, it'll never heal and it might get infected.'

He felt sorry for his mum. She was dying to be in the bedroom with Lily, involved in the make-up and hair. She would put photos of herself and Lily on Facebook, saying things like, 'Guess which is the mum?' She loved it when people mistook her and Lily for sisters. Lily would say things like 'Yeah, only when the light's dim,' that Mum was 'sad,' and didn't she realise people laughed at her when she posted stuff like that? If Dad ever heard Lily being horrible, he'd ask her if she'd been sharpening her tongue.

Adam missed his dad. He'd been gone for a while now. He'd heard his mum on the phone, saying Dad might have a disease. He wondered if Dad might be in hospital with no one to visit him. Although he was friends with people who worked there, so they'd probably take him fruit and stuff. When he asked Mum, she said he'd see his dad soon enough, but in a flat, abrupt way that Adam didn't believe. And what did 'soon enough' mean? Next year? Lily refused to talk about him at all and had told Adam to shut up when he had said it would be Dad's birthday soon. If Dad were here, he'd have made a dry comment when Jeff brought the strimmer back. Something like, 'Oh, you've had it so long, I thought I must have sold it to you.'

Adam drifted out to the dusty back garden and sat in his tepee for a while, with the zip closed. He picked up his big sketch pad, laid it across his knees, and drew astronauts and planets. He could hear bees clustering around the lavender. His mum said that they love-bombed it. The air was syrupy. Sweat was pooling on the back of his neck, but he didn't want to open the tepee and anyway, it was just as hot outside. He liked being tucked away inside while everyone else was out there. The tepee smelled faintly of cheesy socks and cat pee. Adam was supposed to leave it zipped up all the time so that cats couldn't get in, but he usually forgot. Last week, he'd found a dead shrew in there and he'd chucked it over the fence into the weeds at the bottom of Jeff's garden. That would have made Dad laugh.

His stomach grumbled, so he ate a malty biscuit from a packet he kept under an old cushion for this kind of emergency. A couple of ants ran out when he picked it up and darted into a corner. Adam had read that an ant could carry up to fifty times its own body weight, so they'd probably hauled a chunk of biscuit between them. He crunched a couple more. It was past dinner time, but his mum wouldn't be able to think about food until the girls had gone. Now and again, he glanced at the shifting shadows on the side of the tepee and heard Jeff whistling softly while he opened his barbecue. It was his pride and joy and had cost nearly a thousand pounds. Mum said, 'He treasures that dual fuel as if it was one of the crown jewels.'

The sun was low on the horizon when he heard his mum call. 'The limo's here, girls! Come on, I want to take photos.'

He ran down the side of the house past the whiffy dustbins to peep at the limousine. He'd never seen one before. It was silver, massive and gleaming, a sleek monster with a huge grille at the front like a mouth. The orange sun sparkled off the shining roof. Pink and white ribbons stretched across the windows. The girls' parents had clubbed together for the evening's hire and his mum had organised it, a special package called 'Perfect Prom.' There would be chilled Prosecco and tiny frosted cupcakes on offer for the journey to Newton High, although Lily had stated that she wouldn't touch a cake in case she got stuff on her dress. The driver got out and doffed his peaked cap to the girls, who were skittering out through the front door, giggling like mad and holding their skirts. Several of the neighbours came out to watch.

'Aren't they lovely!'

'Ah, so beautiful!'

'Just like princesses, all of them!'

'Have an amazing evening!'

'Wish I'd had something like this in my day. I got a Mars bar when I finished school.'

'Jealous? Me? Too right I am!'

'And me. Pea-green with envy!'

Adam's mum got the girls to line up by the limo and snapped away with her phone. Lily was in the centre of the group, in a blue fishtail dress with sequins and a huge bow at the back. Adam had crept into her room and touched the dress when she was out. It hung from her wardrobe door, slippery, scaly, and cool, just like a briny mermaid. He'd pressed his face to it and squirmed at a weird ripple in his guts.

The air was shimmering with heat and blueish smoke from next door. Adam smelled sausages. His mouth watered. Jeff made great hot dogs and spicy chicken wings, too. The girls were jiggling up and down as if they needed the loo but they were impatient, wanting to get going. Mrs Devani from two doors up took a photo and called, 'This'll be a night you'll always remember!'

At last the chauffeur said, 'Are we ready, ladies?' They all climbed into the limo, giggling and settling their dresses. His mum took final photos as they were driven away, waving to anyone watching. The driver tooted his horn as they turned the corner.

'Bloody hell, they think they're royalty,' Jeff said. He was leaning against his gate, holding a pair of tongs and wearing an apron with a picture of sausages in a pan and the caption, *Prick With A Fork*.

Adam saw his mum glance at the apron and frown. Sometimes she said that Jeff was 'a bit much.'

'They are for tonight!' she replied.

'Want to come and have a bite now the girls have flown?' Jeff asked. 'Be ready in about twenty minutes and there's plenty. Judy's coming over with the kids. Forecast says a storm's coming later so might as well make the most of the dry evening.'

Adam was disappointed when Mum said, 'Thanks, but no thanks, I've got something prepared.'

Indoors was silent and flat. Traces of scent lingered in the hall. His mum picked up a tangle of moulted hairs from a corner by the door and rolled them in her hand, looking sad. Adam couldn't smell anything cooking.

'I'm hungry. Can't we go to Jeff's?' He leaned his head against her.

She put an arm around him. Her skin was warm and she smelled of peppermint tea. 'Course, you must be starving. You're an angel for waiting. I'm a bit of a grump these days but things will get better, I promise. We can't go to Jeff's tonight because I've got to pop out in a bit. Just to the shop for a few things. Will you be okay if I do sandwiches?' He didn't reply but she carried on. 'You can have them on a tray and watch a film, stay up late. I'll nip out while you eat, and then when I get back, we can watch the rest of the film together and have hot chocolate. Okay?'

He'd have preferred barbecue food from next door but he agreed. He'd never been left on his own before, and he'd usually rather go out with his mum but he was hungry and excited about staying up. He busied himself flicking through the TV menu and choosing a film. He sat on the sofa with his ham and tomato sandwiches, crisps and a glass of milk and raised a thumb when his mum stuck her head through the door. She'd combed her hair out from its ponytail and it fell in soft, glowing waves around her shoulders. He smelled her peachy hair mousse.

'Mind you don't spill that milk. Back soon. Don't open the door to anyone. Oh good, *Toy Story*, my favourite! I guessed you might choose that.' She crossed to the sofa, kissed the top of his head, and was gone.

He'd seen the film many times before but sat, entranced, chuckling, saying the lines with Woody and Buzz Lightyear and taking a bite of sandwich now and again. Halfway through, he paused it, ran to the window, and peeked out into the violet evening. No sign of his mum. She hadn't taken the car, so she'd only gone to Smart Mart. She must be chatting to someone. Lily said she couldn't leave the house without swapping her life story with a stranger.

When the film ended, he pushed the unfinished crusts into a pyramid in the centre of the plate. He licked his finger and harvested crisp crumbs, enjoying the last taste of vinegar. His milk had turned warm and cloying. It coated the roof of his mouth. The house was quiet, but not in a friendly way. He was suddenly aware of the silence and held his breath for a moment, listening. The sweat on the back of his neck had grown cold and itchy. He crossed to the window again but the street was empty, curtains drawn. Mrs Devani's cat was sniffing at something in the gutter and batting it with a paw. He stared into the dark, willing his mum to walk through the gate. She always pushed it shut with her hip and rested against it for a moment. He closed his eyes tight and counted to ten, but when he opened them, she still wasn't there.

The sky was a deep, brooding blue now. Night loomed against the house and then there was a quick spark of lightning, like someone flicking a torch on and off. He knew that light travels faster than sound waves and that there would be thunder soon, but when the loud roll sounded, it made him start and grab at the curtain. Goosebumps prickled on his arms.

Adam ran to tell Jeff that his mum hadn't come back.

CHAPTER 1

2019

The sprawling building in Orford End had been standing empty for years. It was in the north, less desirable area of Berminster, boxed in by streets of shabby Victorian houses and near the rail station. Trains rattled the crumbling windows as they pounded to and from London and the south coast, and the air vibrated when the fast, non-stop ones raced through.

Steiner & Sons Removals had operated from the cul-de-sac since the 1930s. Bernie Steiner had taken the business over from his father and had hopefully added the '& Sons' when he had redeveloped it. Fate had sent him a daughter, Maria, who took no interest in the removals business and became an agronomist. The business had been in decline towards the end of Bernie's life and when he died Maria had closed it down and put the premises on the market. It was dilapidated and had idled on the agent's books with just one viewing. The prospective buyer had offered for the premises, but had then withdrawn when he couldn't get outline planning permission to convert it into flats. When it had come up for auction, it didn't meet the reserve price.

Maria Steiner led a busy life and had moved away from the town. She was financially secure and laid-back about when she might realise money from the sale, aware that the land would increase in value. So, Steiner's stood empty, gathering dust, visited by foxes, mice and roaming cats. Rising damp climbed up the internal plaster and penetrating damp seeped down from damaged gutters. Cracks and huge, dark stains appeared where they met.

Bored teenagers broke the odd window and climbed in, but there was little of interest in there: an ancient kitchen, an office with a few bits of furniture, empty filing cabinets and stacks of mouldering cardboard boxes stamped with the fading logo of Steiner & Sons. A few youths used it occasionally to hang out while they took drugs, drank or had uncomfortable sex, sometimes all three. A homeless man had camped out there for a while until he'd moved on to a bigger coastal town. He'd had a small dog who'd used various corners as a toilet. Buddleias sprouted from the guttering and ivy had colonised part of the roof. Now and again, local residents who viewed the place as an eyesore that affected their property values raised the dreadful state of the premises in letters to the press or at council meetings. There would be heated debate and then it would die away. No one had the funds to buy the building and so it settled into its inexorable process of decline.

In 2016, Berminster council woke up to two uncomfortable facts. It had a looming budget deficit and the town had a housing shortage. People who couldn't afford to live in London were seeking homes within commuting distance of the capital. A national newspaper had described Berminster in a glowing article: *A secret Sussex gem, easily commutable from Victoria by fast train, with the beautiful River Bere and just five miles from the coast.* Estate agents were suddenly busier. The council had a new financial manager who wanted to make her mark and saw a smart way of raising revenue. It bought the old premises and surrounding land from Maria Steiner, then sold it on at a hefty profit to a Manchester-based developer, who wanted to construct a small estate of eight houses. Work began at Orford End to clear the empty building ready for demolition in autumn 2019.

The clearance crew rolled up at Steiner's at eight on an October morning. Ivor Bass, the gaffer, groaned when he saw who was waiting there, leaning against the splintered fence, listening to music on his phone.

'Sunshine's turned up. That's all we needed.'

He hopped out and spoke to the young man, Grant Haddon, then shrugged to the others, pulling a face. A skip was already lined up. The crew stood outside, taking in the weeds, smashed roof tiles, leaking gutters and jagged glass. A fast train caused a loud *whoosh* and sounded its mournful horn.

'Who'll want to buy a house here, with that racket?' Alec Clements sucked his teeth.

'Plenty of people.' Ivor laughed. 'The estate agent's going to make it into a selling point.' He made quote marks in the air. '"With handy proximity to the station and its frequent services to London." There'll be plenty of suckers who'll fall for that. Anyway, once you'd lived here a while, you wouldn't notice. My sister's got a house over the Central Line in Ongar. The mirror on her living-room wall rattles. Terrifies the life out of me, sounds as if there's going to be an earthquake but she doesn't bat an eyelid.' He stepped forwards. 'Right, this place has plenty of muck in it so make sure you get your gloves on before we go in. If anyone wants one, there are masks as well. There's all kinds in here, including shit — not sure if it's human or dog. I haven't examined it too closely.'

Ivor liked this kind of job. It was straightforward, and there was a deep satisfaction to be had in filling skips. He loved the clunks and crashes as debris was heaved in. Now and again, you found stuff that might be worth something that you could pocket, although he had little hope of any treasure trove in this dump. He undid the padlock on the door and led his crew inside to a long room littered with boxes and rolls of paper, twine and packing tape. An office to one side housed a battered oak desk, an electric typewriter, a mattress and khaki-coloured metal cabinets. A door at the other end of the room led to a kitchen and brick outbuilding with an old chain flush toilet and bits of broken furniture. Ivor checked the order sheet and allocated tasks.

'This'll be easy enough, lads. Shouldn't take us too long. Sunshine, as you've turned up like a bad penny, you can help.'

Two of the men set about tackling the old boxes and Grant and Ivor started on the dim, chilly kitchen. Ivor rolled the heavy-duty trolley behind him and parked it in a corner. Grey light struggled to get through the filthy window and the electricity had been switched off. The terracotta-tiled floor was sticky underfoot.

'This place must be full of germs,' Grant said through his facemask. Of course he'd put one on. He was such a sensitive flower.

'My dad used Steiner's Removals when we came here from Dagenham in the seventies,' Ivor told him. 'I remember him packing stuff in their boxes. Now it's like the land that time forgot.' He ran a hand along the edge of the stained, cobwebbed sink. It was filled with grimed mugs, desiccated tea bags, fag ends, a couple of wine bottles and tarnished spoons. 'There's old spliffs in here.'

Grant stifled a sneeze. 'Kids have been in. What's that smell?' He nudged his shoe against a bundle of newspapers lying on the floor that were charred at the edges.

'Damp, decay and shit. About time this place was demolished, before it rots away and falls down. Wouldn't be surprised if it's full of rats. Could be a nest in those newspapers.'

Grant started and backed away. 'I hope not. I hate rats. They give me the willies.'

Ivor smiled to himself. He'd said that to get a rise. Grant was the boss's son. He'd worked with them over the summer and now that he'd started at university, he helped out on odd days. He was a weedy, dreamy youth who sneezed around dust and spent most of the time plugged into music. He had little energy and looked as if heavy lifting would exhaust him. Because of his easy-going nature, they'd nicknamed him 'Sunshine'. He was willing enough, but if you didn't keep an eye on him, he'd wander off, singing to himself, his hips swaying. He'd been a hindrance all summer, not least because they couldn't skive off early if the chance arose. Ivor was annoyed that he'd turned up unexpectedly today, cancelling any chance of an early finish.

Ivor now eyed the filthy fridge standing by the wall, the kind that had a small freezer compartment at the top. It resembled an antique, if such a thing existed in the fridge world. He remembered his Uncle Harry getting one like it back in the sixties. He had been the first family member to have a fridge and they'd all gone round to his house to stare at it and wonder, especially when he'd revealed the Neapolitan ice cream in the freezer. That ice cream had seemed so exotic, with its strawberry, vanilla and chocolate stripes. Harry had been involved in the liberation of Naples in 1945, and had had his first taste of the ice cream there, handed up to him by a grateful citizen as he sat in a jeep. He'd said it was the flavour of freedom and sheer joy. Ivor used to stare at it in his bowl, trying to work out how the colours stayed separate.

He kicked aside the dusty plug that trailed on the floor beside the fridge and then opened the doors, having to pull hard on the rusting handles. He was half expecting it to contain rotting food but mercifully, it was empty. Fetid air gusted out and blackish-green mould clotted the fridge shelves. He shut it quickly. 'Fuck me sideways!'

Grant recoiled. 'Yuck! That's gross.'

'At least it was turned off and defrosted. Let's get it out of the way.' He reckoned it was the heaviest item and Grant might manage to help before running out of steam or getting a disabling fit of sneezes. 'I'll pull it out a bit and then we'll manoeuvre it onto the trolley between us. Get ready to grab the back.'

Ivor put his hands on either side of the door and pulled with a twisting motion. The fridge was heavier than he'd expected. It resisted and then rocked and screeched on the tiles.

Grant stepped towards the back of it. 'Stop!' He put a hand out. 'Hang on, there's something here.' He took one step closer then shrank away.

'What is it, Sunshine?'

Grant pointed and went to speak, but no sound came out.

'What?' Ivor stared at him. He'd gone as pale as a dustsheet.

'There's . . . there's . . .' He started shaking, fumbled at his mask and vomited profusely on the floor.

* * *

Siv Drummond put her book aside, nestled her back more comfortably against the gnarled trunk of an alder, and raised her face to the pale yellow sun. Make the most of it. The sun's power was waning, the days cooling, the evenings drawing in. The slow dying of the year always made her pleasantly melancholy. The Finnish word for the season was *ruska* and Ed used to say that her autumn gloom came from her Finnish heritage — the awareness that a long, bitter winter lay ahead. She heard him now, teasing. *Have you knitted the socks, salted the herring, stabled the horses, smoked the bacon and pickled the cabbage?* She'd talked to him regularly since he'd died, telling him about her days and her new home and job, and sometimes scolding him for leaving her. Now he'd started making brief comments at odd times, in his dry, humorous voice. She never knew when he might call by. She'd read that the experience was called 'bereavement hallucination' and that it was 'entirely normal and usually helpful.' She wasn't sure about the helpful, because at times she was winded and desolate after hearing Ed and wanted to engage him, but he never stayed around long enough for a conversation. *It's all very well for you, just popping by when you fancy it,* she told him. *Bet you never dreamed I'd be a spectator at fishing!* She listened, but there was no reply.

She glanced down at the riverbank. It was bathed in a delicate, greenish light. Bartel didn't seem to have moved in the last hour. He stood tall among clumps of late-flowering meadowsweet with his legs apart, balanced, contemplating the water. Zenlike. He must have sensed her gaze because he turned and smiled.

She picked up the Thermos and waved it. 'Coffee?'

He propped his fishing rod on the bank and came to sit beside her on the rug.

'Caught anything?' she asked.

'One grayling, one brown trout.'

'Want a sandwich?'

'Not now, thanks. In a while. What are you reading?'

'Le Carré. Spies and treachery.'

'I read one, long time ago. Spy who was cold or something.'

'*The Spy Who Came In From the Cold.*'

'That's it. Very sad. I didn't like the girl dying. They tricked her, treated her badly and then shot her. No, not to my liking.'

She handed him his coffee. 'That's because you're a gentleman and chivalrous.'

'Thank you, *madame*. Really, I'm much too good for this messy, ruinous old world. I should have stayed in the peaceful seminary, with my mind on higher things.'

'Was it peaceful?'

He laughed. 'No, it was just like any other community — the brothers could be spiteful, petty and cruel as well as attempting to be holy.'

'You must have been thrown out for some misdemeanour. Maybe you stole the communion wine, or had liaisons with a convent or went out to nightclubs. I should check back copies of Warsaw newspapers.'

Bartel tapped his nose. 'A man has to have a few secrets, especially when he has a detective for a friend.'

They sat watching the Bere. It was running quietly and smoothly on such a still day. Dragonflies glided above it, swooping together and then parting in a mysterious, glittering dance. *It can't be courtship*, Siv thought. *Too late in the season.*

The sunlight polished Bartel's naked skull and caught the reddish glints in his beard. Bartel Nowak looked nothing like an ex-seminarian who'd studied to be a priest for three years. You'd notice his rough, rumbling voice, his powerful physique, bald head, pointed Viking beard and the three earrings he wore in each ear and take him for a bouncer or a biker, rather than a roofer. They'd met when Siv was investigating three murders, her first case after moving back to the town, and he'd provided a vital piece of information. Now they spent time together at the river or occasionally at Polska, the Polish club, playing backgammon and eating pierogi. She'd been frank with him — 'I can't imagine anyone replacing Ed. I can't bear the idea of it.' Once he'd understood that she wasn't seeking a relationship, they'd settled into this companionable way of getting on. He accepted that she had no interest in fishing, except as a spectator sport. She liked reading while he fished, or just watching him. She'd told him that the slow silence was restorative and her knots unravelled under the ancient trees. Sometimes she made him laugh with a mock commentary in a quiet, David Attenborough voice: 'And here we see the greater Polish Nowak, head gleaming, poised by the riverbank. He can stay here for hours, waiting for his prey and pouncing when his line twitches.'

'Do you ever go back to fish at Lock Lane?' She was pretty sure what the answer would be. Berminster Angling Club owned the site. Bartel used to trespass there. It was where two people had been murdered, including his friend Matis Rimas.

He narrowed his eyes at her. 'You asking as a cop?'

'What do you reckon?'

'Nah. I don't go there, not now I'm mates with *madame* the detective. Have to behave myself. The fishing's just as good here, and free, and I'm not reminded of Matis.' He lay back on the rug. 'This is the life. I can smell the autumn. Fresh, but with a hint of rot. Like those dark, fleshy mushrooms.' He gave the little cough and wave of a hand that meant he was about to tell her a folk tale.

She smiled in anticipation, tucked her hands into her sleeves, and watched the reeds stirring. Listening to him gave her a fleeting illusion of warmth and security. Sometimes he sent her an email with a story attached, 'just to ease the day,' as he put it. When she was absorbed in his fable world, she didn't fret about losing Ed, her nightmare mother Mutsi, her bald patches, or the fact that her boss was a mealy-mouthed bastard who didn't like her.

'There was once a glass mountain with a gold castle at the top. An apple tree with golden apples grew in front of the castle. If you picked an apple, you could enter the castle where a beautiful princess sat in a silver room. Princes from many lands tried to visit the princess but they couldn't climb up the glass mountain. Many died in the attempt and there were bodies lying all around the base of the mountain. The princess waited for seven years and finally, a prince wearing gold armour managed to ride his horse to the top of the glass hill, but just as he reached it, a huge eagle flew down and knocked man and horse back down to the bottom, killing them both.

'Then a young man, a peasant, who'd heard of the princess's beauty decided to try to see her. He caught a wolf in the forest, cut off its sharp claws and fastened them to his hands and feet. Then he started to climb the glass mountain. He climbed and climbed, until his hands and feet were torn and bleeding. Hours went by and the moon came out. The eagle saw the bloodied youth in the moonlight, but when it swooped on him to kill him, the youth held onto its talons and was lifted high into the air. He saw the princess in the window of her silver room. He reached with one hand for his knife as the eagle flew over the apple tree. Then he cut the great bird's feet off and fell into the tree. The eagle dropped to the bottom of the glass mountain and died.

'The boy picked two of the golden apples and entered the castle. He and the princess fell in love and they married.

Soon afterwards, a messenger came to them and said that the blood of the eagle had restored life to all the princes who had died while trying to climb the mountain. There was great rejoicing and feasting throughout the land.'

Bartel sat up and finished his coffee. 'You like that one, *madame*?'

'Food for thought. Life springs from death and you can't have one without the other,' Siv summarised.

'This is true. Or you have to suffer for true love.'

'Hard on the wolf and the eagle.'

'Necessary sacrifices. That's one of my favourite tales.'

'I like all your stories.'

'You've never told me any folk tales. You must have them in England — or Finland.'

'I don't really know any — or only ones from films, like Snow White and Rumpelstiltskin. I didn't have that kind of childhood.' Until she was thirteen and had come with her sister Rikka to live with their father in Berminster, it had been a case of damage limitation. She turned to Bartel. 'I envy you yours. You had a gran who sat you on her knee by the fire, fed you gingerbread biscuits, sang you songs and spun you stories at bedtime. In fact, your childhood sounds like one from a book. I had a mother who was interested in just one story — her own.'

On many evenings when she had been cultivating her latest romantic interest, Mutsi had left Siv and Rik alone with a sketchy supper of cheese and crackers, and an airy kiss blown from the doorway. Rik had coped with their hit-and-miss upbringing through maverick behaviour and defiance. Siv had withdrawn into anxiety and a need to take cover, but she'd often followed her older sister's lead because Rik had been left in charge. Once, in their top-floor flat in Camden, Rik had decided that they'd climb out onto the roof and throw bits of bread and broken guttering at passers-by below. The TV had broken and they were bored and fed up of squabbling with each other. Siv had followed her sister through the window, fretful but swayed by Rik's determination. Someone had called the police and a kind officer had made them cups of tea, and waited with them until Mutsi arrived home, smelling of cocktails. She'd been all apologies, flirty smiles and reassurances with the male constable, spinning a hasty but genuine-sounding story about an emergency and having to visit a relative who was in hospital after an accident. Once he'd gone, the graciousness had vanished. *You're both so selfish. Can't I even go out for one night?* Rik had replied tartly, *It would make a change if you stayed in for a night!* Siv had never forgotten the police officer's kindness. She'd been reassured by his calm manner, his humour. Maybe that early experience had navigated her towards her career choice.

Bartel poured more strong black coffee. 'Your dad didn't tell you any stories?'

'He didn't have that kind of imagination. He was a scientist, a clinical engineer. He'd explain how a clock or a barometer worked with great enthusiasm, and he'd read from natural history or scientific books. He'd have told me that this alder must be over a hundred years old, judging by the major trunk cavities and the fruiting fungus on the bark. I'd hear about the dynamics of jet engines, or the history of Halley's Comet. I got my talent for maths from him. He didn't enter the realms of fantasy. Maybe he'd had enough of that with my mother. She was always as slippery as your glass mountain.' Siv stretched, flexing her back. 'If Mutsi had been the princess, she'd have sized up all the resurrected princes and if she'd fancied one, she'd have dumped the peasant youth for a better option.'

'Have you talked to her recently?'

'Not since she told me that she'd rented a flat by the harbour.'

'You planning to go and see her there?'

'Not if I can help it.'

He struggled to understand her family dynamics. He came from a close clan who bombarded him with emails and photos. His mother sent him boxes of home-baked, sticky cakes: doughnuts, milk candies and angel wings. Rikka was now in New Zealand and communicated rarely. She'd always been clamlike, mysteriously going her own way, and never revealed anything about what she was doing. And with Rik, you didn't ask. Then, after years away, Mutsi had drifted into town from another failed affair in Finland, and seemed to expect that she and Siv would regenerate a mother-daughter bond, like in a Hollywood tearjerker. In her dreams.

Bartel cupped his beard and tugged on the end. He had thick, strong fingers, the skin chapped from working outdoors and in all weathers. 'I'm considering buying a house, a little terraced one. Somewhere around Poets' Piece. Time to put roots down properly.'

She was pleased. 'Despite all the current political firestorms? I read that the Polish government is encouraging its citizens to return to the fold.'

He shrugged. 'Going back would seem like defeat. I've always been one to front things out. I've been here almost ten years now and I like it. Business is good, everyone getting their roof mended or house extended because they can't afford to move, and it makes them feel secure. When the world's full of stormy winds, make sure your roof tiles are tight and snug. Would you come to some viewings with me?'

'Of course. Weekend's best.' Siv's phone rang and she saw it was the station. She stood and moved away to take the call from her sergeant, Ali Carlin.

Bartel went back to his rod and opened his little camping stool. The only times Siv heard him speak Polish were at Polska and when he leaned towards the water and murmured to the fish, '*Chodź do mnie, moje cuda*' — Come to me, my lovelies.

She finished speaking, and glanced regretfully at the river and the box of sandwiches they hadn't yet eaten. 'Sorry, Bartel. I have to go. A body's been found. You'll have to picnic alone.'

He shook his head. His earrings flashed sparks of gold. 'On your day off! That's too bad!'

'Dead people are a bit annoying like that. They spoil a sunny morning.'

CHAPTER 2

DS Ali Carlin was waiting for her at Orford End, chatting to two uniformed constables and turning his head to blow wisps of smoke away from them. He'd have things under control, all the basics sorted. He was a sound, reliable man and she was grateful to have him by her. But like Polly, his wife, she wished he'd give up the twenty-a-day habit. She saw him stub out his cigarette and hitch up his black jeans, engaged in their never-ending struggle to find his waistline.

The cul-de-sac was derelict and abandoned, with huge dandelions and thistles pushing up through the rutted, cracked tarmac. A couple of empty lager cans and chip wrappings skittered in the breeze. It reminded her of one of those deserted towns in a western, and she half expected to see tumbleweed and Clint Eastwood in a poncho. Steiner & Sons was an unlovely, single-storey brick building with peeling window frames. A splintered wooden sign, red leaching to pale pink, drooped over the metal doors that were shielded by a police cordon. She saw a skip near the doors and a grey van with the logo *L. Haddon, General Building* on the side.

'Hi, guv, hope you weren't enjoying yourself too much.' Ali came over. He had a loose, quick walk, surprisingly agile for such a bulky man.

'I was watching Bartel fish at the river.'

'Grand day for it. Steve's inside with his crew and Dr Anand's on his way.'

Good. Rey Anand was her preferred pathologist, unshowy, skilful and direct. 'Who found the body?'

'Two of the guys in the van. There were four of them here from the building company.'

'What were they doing here?'

'The place is being demolished, and new—' Ali stopped as a train thundered nearby and then raised his voice. 'New houses are going up here, so they came to clear the place out. The two guys in the front, Ivor Bass and Grant Haddon, went to move the fridge in the kitchen. That's when they found the body, tied to the back. It's been here a while, according to Steve, and it's mummified. The older guy's taking it in his stride, but Grant Haddon is just nineteen and he's pretty shaken. It wouldn't be a good start to anyone's day.'

She saw the two men in the front of the van. One had his head bent low, earbuds in, and the one in the driver's seat, an older man with sparse grey hair, was smoking. He'd wound his window down, his elbow propped on the frame as he flicked a curl of ash out into the bright, clear air. She saw Ali's nostrils quiver. He'd be longing for another of the Gitanes in his pocket. He started to salivate if he was in sight of fags or sweets.

'Have you seen the body?'

'Aye, just a quick wee check. It's a terrible sight, hanging there.'

'Bass and Haddon need to go to the station and wait until we can speak to them. Ask Haddon if he wants to see a doctor and make sure he's okay. The other two can go for now. Let's go inside.'

Ali gave one of the uniform constables the order. Then she and Ali donned protective gear and went through into the huge, rectangular space with its peeling, stained walls, rambling damp patches and perilous bulges in the ceiling. As soon as they stepped in, the air was chilly and dank.

'We could probably do with hard hats,' Siv joked, eyeing the pitted ceiling and chunks of plaster on the floor.

Ali grimaced. 'This place gives me the willies. Reminds me of businesses back home in Derry that were bombed and left because the insurance wouldn't pay out.'

Steve Wooton, the crime-scene manager had spotted them. 'In here, in the kitchen,' he called.

'Hi, Steve.' Siv's tone was cool. There was an unspoken antipathy between them. She didn't care for his self-importance — he was one of those small, chippy men who liked to flex his muscles. But he was adept at his job, even if he had to make snide remarks at every opportunity.

'I'd say this is a female,' he said, pointing at the filthy fridge-freezer. 'Small mercies — there's no smell from the body because it's been there a while and is part-mummified. Careful of the pool of vomit, though. Mr Haddon threw up when he saw the fridge's hidden secret. It's dim in here and there's no power supply, so we've put up a spotlight.'

Siv wrinkled her nose at the sour smell of sick. The spotlight had the unfortunate effect of making the dingy kitchen resemble the set of a low-budget horror film. She glanced around at the ancient, dirt-encrusted appliances: the tall, wide fridge-freezer, a narrow gas cooker spattered with years of grease and food spills, and a grey cylindrical water heater above a stained ceramic sink, once white, now a tobacco colour. It was full of rubbish. There was one tiny window facing the back of the building with a grimy, torn calico curtain dangling down. Someone had written CLEAN ME on a filthy pane. She could almost taste the dust and dirt.

She approached the trussed body and felt overwhelming pity and anger. It was tied to the back grille of the fridge with thin rope, face forward. The arms had been bound with hands flat against the thighs. Thin leathery flaps of skin adhered to the skeleton beneath, and dried wisps of hair clung to the skull. Strips of yellowing material hung from one of the shoulders, with another band visible under the rope that encased the legs below the knee. Siv caught her breath. It was a shocking sight. Any murder was a desecration, but this killer had been particularly demeaning, hanging the victim up as if they were a carcass.

'I'd say that's remnants of a dress, and our corpse has long hair,' Steve said. 'Unless it's a long-haired male who liked wearing women's clothing, I reckon we have a female.'

Siv and Ali stood on either side of the corpse. The desiccated neck was circled by a band of pale blue cord.

'You're probably right, but let's wait for Rey Anand to confirm the sex. Those might be strands of some kind of cord or nylon twisted around the neck. Seems like this person was strangled and then tied on here.'

'I'd agree strangulation,' Steve said. 'You can see the cord round her neck is different to the rope she's been tied up with.'

'The killer could have brought their own, but I wonder . . . A removal company — there's probably a lot of cord and rope in here somewhere.' Ali gazed around. 'God-awful, minging place to die. I suppose the mummification happened because it's cool and shady in here.'

'Any idea how long this premises has been empty?' Siv glanced at Ali, then Steve, who shrugged.

'That guy Bass said at least five years, probably longer,' Ali said. He was repulsed and mesmerised by the corpse. He'd seen dead bodies and bones, but never anything like this half-human thing that could have come from a case in a museum. He glanced at Siv. As usual, she was giving nothing away.

'Any sign of identification?' she asked.

'Haven't seen anything yet,' Steve told them. 'No phone or bag. No rings or jewellery that I can see from a visual search.'

The floor and windowpane vibrated as another train rattled by.

'It's as if we're on top of the station,' Siv said.

Ali pointed. 'The railway's just over the back there, in a culvert. There's a path near here that takes you to the station in minutes.'

'I wish the new homeowners joy.' Siv turned back to Steve. 'We'll let Dr Anand do his thing in here. We'll go around the rest of the building and then check up on missing persons. What other rooms are there?'

'That brick outbuilding has a revolting toilet and bits of chair legs and such — general junk. There's a grotty office on the other side. We've finished in there for now if you want to see it.'

Ali followed Siv out. They glanced into the outbuilding with its cobwebbed toilet and broken furniture. It stood beside a small patch of garden filled with more junk and an incongruous tall apple tree that was still laden with fruit. Bruised and rotting apples lay around the base, among the weeds and nettles.

Ali nudged an apple with his foot. 'They're Grenadiers. They make a great crumble.'

Nothing dampened Ali's appetite. He could have been one of those Parisians who made a day out of sitting by the guillotine with a picnic. They carried on to the office, a small, square room, just as desolate but a little brighter with a larger window facing south. The graffiti sprayed in dark blue on the wall facing them declared, *The Moving Finger writes, and having writ, moves on.* Below it, someone had selected bright yellow to spray an anatomically detailed, bright yellow penis: *Suck on this, Moving Finger!*

'This is old school.' Ali pressed a key on the Olivetti typewriter, dislodging fine dust. He picked up a bottle of correction fluid, shook it and replaced it.

Siv opened the filing cabinets and the desk drawers. Several of them stuck and she had to wrench at them. 'All empty, except for some sheets of carbon paper.'

'This is interesting. A mucky wee love nest?' Ali gestured at the pale blue single mattress lying behind the desk and wedged against the wall. Rubbish framed it: crisp packets, lager cans, condom wrappers, chocolate and biscuit papers, empty cigarette and chewing-gum packs, a couple of wine bottles and fast food cartons. The mattress was grimy and the quilting stained, with cigarette burns exposing the fabric beneath.

Siv knelt by it and examined the material and the grubby label with the make, RestEasy. 'It's had plenty of use. It's a grim place for romance but I suppose if you're short of a venue . . . Although it's damaged, this mattress isn't that old. Let's make sure Steve checks the age and whether there are local outlets still selling it. God knows how many people have been in and out of here over the years. The forensics will be a nightmare.'

Ali sniffed at his arm. 'I'm sure I can smell vomit.'

Siv was glad that she was wearing old jeans and a sweat-shirt under her protective gear. 'It's just in your nose. Light up once we're outside, that'll cure you.'

'Have you ever seen a body like that one before? Like something that kids would make for Halloween, to sit beside a pumpkin. Those wisps of hair . . .'

'Yeah, I agree. From a distance, you could imagine it's papier mâché. I haven't dealt with a mummified corpse before. It's as if it's caught in an anteroom of death. I'll be glad when whoever it belongs to can hold a funeral.'

'Assuming it belongs to anyone.'

'Yes, there is that. Anyway, we're nowhere near estab-lishing identity yet. Whoever murdered and secured the vic-tim to that fridge knew that this place was deserted, and was likely to be for some time. They chose well.'

Ali scratched his scribble of a beard. Like his hair, it was peppered with premature grey. 'I suppose it was easier than digging a grave. No shovel needed, just enough strength to shift the fridge and support the body. Maybe it was a drug deal gone wrong, or a row between junkies or street people. Who else would be in here?'

'No point in getting ahead of the facts. Let's go back to the station. I'm going to call in at home on the way to get changed.'

* * *

Ali walked back to the kitchen. This was one of the most depressing places he'd been in for a long time. He steeled himself for the reek of vomit. It was a smell that had always made him gag and he hated getting sick. He'd heard people say they were better once they'd thrown up, but it made him nauseous for days.

'Can you not clear the boke up?' he asked Steve.

'If that's one of your quaint Derry expressions for "vomit" — no, not until Rey Anand's been.'

'Oh, aye, right. Just checking in about the mattress. We need to find out how old it is and whether it's available locally.'

'Of course.' Steve waved his notebook under Ali's nose. 'I've got the details and a sample so we can try to establish exactly that information. I suppose DI Drummond worried I might be slacking?'

'Not at all,' Ali said. 'Just making sure.'

'How are you finding her to work with? She's not overfriendly, is she? Pale as a ghost some days, and about as approachable. A smart suit doesn't mean a smart mover.'

Ali took in Steve's shiny complexion and narrow eyes. The guy was a sneaky wee gobshite, and he agreed with DC Patrick Hill's assessment that Steve was the kind of man who'd have been a bully at school — the sort who slyly cornered a victim when no one else was around. 'The guv's fair and she gets results. She's okay by me.'

'Mortimer doesn't like her. He wanted Tommy Castles for the job.'

'Really? I'd no idea,' Ali lied. 'All water under the bridge now, anyway.'

'We'll see. Time will tell. Tommy would have been a good fit for the team. He's snappy, on the ball, and I've heard that he's not too happy with his new job and wouldn't mind coming back this way. The DI's on another planet sometimes, in a different orbit.'

Ali was fed up with Steve's jibes. 'You do know that her husband was killed last year?'

Steve half closed his eyes. 'I heard on the grapevine that something had happened to her in London. I wasn't aware she'd been widowed.'

'Well, she was. A lorry knocked her husband off his bike. Maybe your orbit would be out of kilter if your Mrs was killed, wee man. I'm not sure you'd deal with it as well as the guv does. Now, I see Dr Anand arriving, so I'll leave you to it.'

Before he left, Ali nipped back to the garden and picked some apples, stuffing them in his pockets. He loved a crumble and Polly made a great one, even if she did insist on adding ground almonds and reducing the sugar.

* * *

Siv was hungry when she arrived at the station so she made a detour to Gusto, the Italian delicatessen just round the corner and ordered a chicken salad panini and coffee. As usual, the windows were steamed up and the aromas of garlic and herbs made her mouth water. They made fresh breads throughout the day: focaccia, pane di casa and ciabatta, laced with olive oil and rosemary. If there were a heaven, it would smell like this. If ever the flat above the shop became vacant, she might move in, have a dumb waiter installed, and order all her meals from downstairs.

'You're in here so often, you should buy into the business.' The woman behind the counter laughed. 'The panini's a good choice, I just baked it myself.'

Polly, Ali's wife, would have made him a packed lunch full of healthy foods that he would eat as if he was doing a penance. He was diabetic, and struggled to balance his sugary cravings with the illness. Siv bought him a pot of plain yoghurt with berries, and a small bag of cantucci biscuits to share with Patrick, grabbed her goodies and headed to her office.

DC Patrick Hill — generally called Hat-trick in the station because he once caught three burglars in three weeks

— was at his desk, straw-blond hair sticking up in gelled spikes, working simultaneously on a PC and his phone. He held up his phone to her as she came over and she read the screen.

@DCBerminsterPolice. Three men arrested & charged with dealing heroin after a lengthy & complex investigation. Big shout out to members of the public who gave us vital information. It's good to work together. We always need your support.
#keepingberminstersafe

Patrick's Twitter feed was popular in the town and useful for maintaining good relations with the public as well as information gathering. He was justifiably proud of it. But right now, she needed him to focus.

'Good stuff. Have you heard about our body?'

'Yes, guv, Ali filled me in. The builders have been fingerprinted and he's sorting out hot drinks for them. He said he'll see you in the interview room. He's asked me to find out how long Steiner's has been empty, and then check any mispers in that period.'

Siv took a bite of her panini and stuffed the rest in her desk drawer for later. She rang her boss, DCI Will Mortimer, to update him about the corpse, and was thankful when his PA informed her that he was at a two-day conference in London. Any day that she didn't have to talk to Mortimer counted as a good one. She sent him an email instead, took a gulp of coffee and carried it downstairs to the interview room, a cheerless place with a warped table, orange plastic chairs and a sad ficus plant. Ali was in there with the men from Haddon's, chatting to them about the weather while opening a window. He was good at putting people at ease with his banter and blokeish camaraderie. They both had cups of tea and biscuits and the older man paused mid-dunk while Ali did the introductions.

'This is Detective Inspector Drummond. Ivor Bass and Grant Haddon.'

'You've had a difficult day so far, so we'll try not to keep you too long.' Bass was sturdy with a pockmarked face. Haddon was childlike, wan and sweaty, with a faint whiff of vomit about him. That would be why Ali had opened the window. 'Mr Bass, I understand that you were heading up this clearance operation at Orford End.'

'That's right. We're knocking Steiner's down next week, ready for a new build, so we've got to get all the crap out — and I mean literally. There's dried-up shit in there. Disgusting how people behave — or let their dogs behave. There's someone who's always letting their dog do his business in my front garden. So nice to step out into a pile of steaming turd! I'll catch them one day and when I do, I'll rub their face in it.'

'I wouldn't advise it. That would be assault,' Siv said. 'Can you talk us through what happened from when you arrived in your van?'

'Sure. I met up with Alec and Malik at base at seven forty-five and I drove the three of us to Steiner's. We got there at eight. Grant was waiting outside. I opened up, we had a quick recce and I allocated the jobs. Me and Sunshine — sorry, Grant here — went to the kitchen and I decided we'd start with the fridge. I went to pull it forward,' he demonstrated with his hands held out, 'and I'd eased it out a foot or so when Grant yelled to stop. He'd seen . . . well, what he'd seen. He chucked his guts up. Projectile vomiting, it's called. My youngest used to do it a lot as a kid. We called him "Barfy". Anyway, I stepped round the back of the fridge and I couldn't believe my eyes. At first, I thought it might be some kind of dummy from a joke shop. Then I rang the police. Poor old Sunshine. He wasn't supposed to be with us today, and I bet he wishes now that he hadn't turned up!'

Haddon was still ashen-faced. His tea was trembling in his hand. 'I realise you've had a nasty shock,' Siv told him. 'Have you anything to add?'

He put his tea down, slopping some and licked his lips. 'No, that's what happened.' He cleared his throat. 'Sorry about the sick. It's just . . . I almost touched it because I was going to hold the back . . . It was terrible, like something from a nightmare.'

'Where had you planned to be today?'

'I was supposed to go to London with my friend Jamie, to visit the Design Museum. I'd stayed the night at his place in town so we could make an early start, only he fell on the stairs and sprained his ankle half an hour before we were due to leave. It swelled up to twice its size so there was no way he could walk on it. I didn't fancy the trip on my own, so I decided I might as well head to Steiner's and help out, get an extra day's pay too. Jamie's mum gave me a lift. I arrived five minutes before Ivor turned up.' He shivered and shook his head.

'Sunshine's a bit delicate,' Bass explained in a sneering tone. 'He's a student, into music and drama.'

'That sight could turn the strongest stomach,' Siv said. Haddon did give the impression that manual labour would put him in bed for weeks. 'If you're a student, how come you're working with a builder?'

'Bloody good question,' Bass mouthed.

Haddon turned his watery gaze to her. 'My dad, Lewis Haddon, owns the company, so it's a way of shoring up my bank balance. I've started at Rother College, doing a degree in performing arts. I didn't have any lectures today.'

Bass pulled a face and asked, with a glinting eye, 'So, what happened to our corpse, then? One of them sex games gone wrong? I've heard about that. People get themselves all knotted up and then it's nighty night. Sad way to go when you were just hoping to have fun. But there must have been two playing. There's no way you could tie yourself to a fridge like that.' He nudged Haddon, who flinched and groaned.

Ali said stonily to Bass, 'Had you visited the premises before today? Did you go there to assess what needed to be cleared out?'

'Come again?' Bass put a hand behind his ear.

'Had you been to Steiner's before today? Ali asked again.

'Oh right. It's your accent, a bit broad for me. I'm not much good with accents — Scots, Welsh, Brummie, whatever. Irish goes right over my head. Hurts my ears or something.'

'Oh aye? Maybe you're the delicate one in the room, then.' Ali smiled without warmth. 'So, do you need the question again? I've plenty of time.'

Bass sniffed. 'I went there in April with the boss to give it the once-over, and draw up a list of what needed chucking before we knock it down. We weren't there long. It's not a place you want to hang around. We fitted a stronger padlock to deter the lowlifes.'

'Did you see anything suspicious?'

Bass pulled his earlobe. 'Nah. There was no one there, if that's what you're getting at — except the stiff, that is. Bloody weird to think that was there all the time we were doing a recce. It was a tip in April and it was the same tip today.'

Siv sipped her coffee. 'Have either of you had any other connection with that premises, apart from your involvement in clearing it out this year?'

They both shook their heads. Haddon winced, as if the movement hurt him.

'Who'd want to go in that shithole unless they had to?' Bass asked.

'What about your colleagues?'

Bass laughed. 'They'd be tickled to hear themselves described that way. Neither of them have ever been there before, far as I'm aware, but you'd have to ask them.'

Haddon had closed his eyes and was holding his stomach. Siv didn't want him chucking up in the interview room.

'Okay, that'll do for now. We'll need formal statements in the next couple of days. Please don't talk about the details of this to anyone at the moment. Especially you, Mr Bass.'

Bass sounded wounded. 'I can keep my lip zipped.'

Ali fetched a constable to see them out. At the door, Haddon turned and swallowed.

'Do you know who that poor person was?'

'Not yet, but thanks for asking,' Siv told him.

She met with Ali and Patrick in her office and ravenously attacked her panini. Ali eyed his yoghurt dubiously but made a show of tucking in. He sat with his back to the window, framed by the tall Japanese maples across the road in front of the museum. Their bronze leaves reflected the warm tones of his skin.

Patrick had poured hot water on miso noodles and was stirring them with a fork. 'Guv, I rang the builder and spoke to the boss man, Lewis Haddon, Grant's dad. He oversees all the work, with Ivor Bass as his site manager. Haddon was all genned up about Steiner's. He said that the daughter shut the removals business down in May 2009 and put it on the market. She had trouble selling, so it just sat there deteriorating, and then the council bought it in January 2017. A company called Building Blocks based in Manchester closed the deal for it with the council earlier this year, and then they subcontracted the building work to Haddon's.' He slurped a forkful of noodles, catching broth on his chin with a finger.

'Ivor Bass told us the builders had been into the premises in April. Did Lewis Haddon confirm that?' Ali asked.

'Yeah. He said that he and Bass gave it a once-over in the spring, just to see what needed clearing out and to make sure it was securely padlocked. Given that they're going to knock it down, they weren't too bothered about the state of it.'

Patrick didn't smoke, yet he had a hoarse, scratchy voice while Ali, who was addicted to his Gitanes, had a smooth, jolly baritone.

'How about missing persons?' Siv licked her fingers and dried them on a tissue. Her email pinged.

'In a twenty-mile radius, seven from January 2009 to date. Three women, one in her twenties, one in her early forties, one fifty, a sixteen-year-old girl, a fourteen-year-old boy and two men in their twenties.'

Ali was staring glassily at a spoon of yoghurt as if it was an unsuccessful experiment. 'Bass is a waste of good air but he might have had a point when he talked about a sex game gone wrong.'

'Eh?' Patrick coughed on a noodle.

'The delightful Ivor Bass had a theory that our corpse was the result of a sex game,' Siv explained. 'There is a mattress on the office floor which means that's a possibility, but there's no point in theorising as yet. I've had an email from Rey Anand. He can fit an autopsy in this evening, so we'll have something to work with in the morning. Ali, can you go to that? In the meantime, Patrick, can you check those misper records to see if any of them, especially the females, had a connection to Steiner's Removals. Also, if there have been any reported break-ins at the premises. I doubt that anyone would have noticed, given where it is and the state of the place, but worth considering. Ali, can you make sure we get fingerprints from the other two builders and Lewis Haddon. We need to talk to him in person as well.'

She watched them depart, Ali with his hand concealing his half-eaten pot of yoghurt. He'd once mentioned that he'd been made to finish everything on his plate as a child. Perhaps that was why he was covert about leaving food. She'd never had that problem, as her mother had rarely noticed if she had anything on her plate or not. Mutsi had been a stranger to the cooker and regular mealtimes. Meals had been hasty pick-and-mix affairs, cobbled together from delicatessens and corner shops. She and Rik were the only kids at school who had serrano ham with anchovies and olives for breakfast. They'd forage for bits and pieces to take for lunch. Other pupils had sniggered and elbowed each other as they watched to see what the Drummonds had in their lunch boxes. They weren't disappointed as she and Rik would palm scraps of stuffed vine leaves, crab pâté crackers or aubergine fritters.

When she or Rikka complained about not having enough for dinner, Mutsi would say, *Most people eat far too much and that pattern starts in childhood. One day you'll thank me for your slim figures.* Hunger had driven them to filching money from Mutsi's purse — never too much, and just once a week so that she didn't notice. They kept their stash in an empty tea packet under Rik's bed, and used it for fish and chips and snacks at school. Rik had got the habit, and she'd stolen from their father after they moved to live with him, until Siv — the embryonic cop in the making — threatened to tell him if she didn't stop. Then Rik had turned to shoplifting. Luckily, she'd got off with a caution when she was caught.

Their poor dad. He'd not understood what had hit him when his two hungry, half-feral daughters landed on him, one a bag of nerves, the other mouthy and anarchic. He'd done his muddled, bewildered best and it had been a relief to find that he kept the fridge and cupboards reassuringly full, and turned out basic but regular, filling meals.

She opened a window to let out the mix of food smells and rested her hands on her waist. She'd put some weight back on, eating pierogi with Bartel, but her suit trousers still sat at hip level and her eyes maintained their hollow, faded expression. In one of their brief contacts, Mutsi had said, *You really need to wear some make-up, something to make you less washed out. Grief ages people.* She'd wanted to ask how Mutsi had come by such wisdom, given that she'd never grieved for anyone. Her mother never left home without a carefully applied mask of foundation and mascara — what Ed used to call *full slap armour.*

The trees across the way were glorious, with leaves turning through a spectrum of dark mustard, russet and the deepest conker brown, almost the same shade as the shirt she was wearing.

Some of the older leaves, the ones that would fall first, were the same colour as the tan flesh on the corpse.

CHAPTER 3

At home, Siv headed straight for the fridge, poured a chilled glass of akvavit, and changed into jeans and Ed's sweatshirt. It still smelled of him, all these months later, a faint aroma of citrus and spice. The last time he'd worn it had been the Saturday before he died, when they'd walked in Greenwich Park. They'd talked about the possibility of having children — neither of them convinced — booking a long weekend in Madrid, and the fact that they needed to replace their old, leaking boiler before it broke down.

In the afternoon, they'd gone to a film, eaten popcorn washed down with cool white wine, then gone home and made love before Ed cooked pasta.

Two days later, he was cold and still in the morgue.

She'd never wash the sweatshirt.

She'd hated him cycling around London, aware of all the traps and dangers: the mountainous lorries with their blind spots, lumbering buses and powerful jeeps. He'd been so vulnerable on his bike, encircled by those drivers protected in their tough steel cages. They'd disagreed on this one thing. He'd tried to reassure her, insisting that the exercise was important for him and that he was always careful. 'It's the other lunatics who worry me, not you,' she'd say, knowing she wasn't going to change his mind. When she got the phone call about the accident, it was almost a bitter relief because she'd been imagining the possibility of the moment for so long.

Don't be cross with me, Ed said in her ear.

All right. I'm not really. Just . . . It's crap without you. And you wouldn't listen to me!

She stood at the window, watching the darkening river that ran nearby, and the drifting smoke from Corran and Paul's wood-burner at the other side of the meadow. They were her friendly, helpful landlords. When she'd moved back to Berminster earlier in the year, she'd rented this trim, three-roomed home from them, a circus wagon that they'd bought on eBay. They'd converted it into a bright, comfortable dwelling. Full-length oak doors at the front led down steps to a decked area with a barbecue, table, chairs, and tubs of shrubs and flowers. Inside, there was a living/kitchen area with a wood-burning stove, a shower room and a bedroom. Compact summed it up. It took just a few steps to get from the bedroom to the kitchen, and another couple to the bathroom and the living room.

Corran and Paul's home was a beautiful converted barn, full of light and pale wood. They were busy and productive — they kept goats, made their own bread and preserves, grew their own vegetables, and worked the two acres of woodland they owned bordering the meadow.

Corran was a weaver, and the wagon was decorated with throws and cushions he'd made in contrasting dark pinks and greens. It had taken her a while to get used to the colour scheme. She'd experienced a sense of displacement when she'd arrived from London, and had wondered if she'd regret the move, but she'd adapted and come to relish the cosy space. It was quiet and secure after the grief and turmoil she'd experienced, and Corran and Paul were good neighbours who supplied her with free logs from their woodland.

There was only one snag with her doll's house of a home. Mutsi had found it and doorstepped her in the spring.

At least she hadn't returned since, although that in itself was a puzzle. Siv was now on tenterhooks, wondering when she might be back, loitering by the steps or bothering Corran and Paul. Hopefully, her absence meant that she was busy exploiting whatever prospects Berminster could offer to a relentlessly sociable and well-preserved woman in her sixties.

The warmth of the akvavit was in her throat, the notes of caraway and dill lingering. It was Finland's best export and she had it delivered by the case from Helsinki. She was always reassured when she came home and found the box with the blue fish label on the side. She rolled her neck until it clicked. The sky was an intense span of velvet blue. She opened the door and gazed up, enjoying that quiet pause at the season's turn. Just for this moment, she was at peace. Her skin still felt paper-thin, but it was a while since her scalp had prickled alarmingly. Every day was still a challenge, her sleep troubled and broken, and each morning brought the unwanted reminder that Ed was gone. She rested her face against his sleeve, and then lit the wood-burner and watched the flames hiss and lick.

In the fridge, pickings were sparse. Ed used to do most of the cooking and she hadn't quite got the hang of food shopping yet. He'd been diabetic like Ali, and not being much use in the kitchen herself, she'd gladly handed over chef's duties. Before she'd met him, she'd eaten mostly in police canteens, or created variations on open sandwiches. Corran sometimes knocked on the door around this time with food. He always made too much — enough, Paul maintained, to feed several counties — and he'd turn up with chicken casserole, paella or a stuffed baked potato. No sign of him tonight, though. She cracked eggs, not sure how old they were but when she sniffed them, they seemed okay. She scrambled them with toast, and poured another glass of akvavit to wash them down. While she ate, she checked her emails and saw one from Mutsi that delivered on her expectations.

Darling Sivvi, as you never return my calls, I'm writing to you. I love my new flat and I've already had a drinks party with several of the neighbours round. This is such a friendly town and makes me realise how much I needed to move on. I've hardly had a minute to myself! I've joined a tennis club and made new friends. Their daughters invite them for lunch at weekends. And of course, they've got grandchildren to dote on. Can't see that I'll ever have any, the way things are with you and Rikka. I've told some friends that I have a daughter in town, although I haven't mentioned that you're living like a gypsy in a field. They say it's good that I have family locally. I hoped that would be the case when I moved back, and it's very hurtful that you don't keep in touch. I'm not getting any younger, Sivvi, and I am the only parent you have left. Remember our old Finnish saying: 'Family is not an important thing, it's everything.'

Hope to talk soon, love, Mutsi xx

The usual mix of emotional blackmail, innuendo and self-regard. If Mutsi wanted to trade sayings from her homeland, Siv could send her another one: 'My family is my strength and my weakness.' And why on earth would Mutsi want grandchildren? She'd taken little care or notice of her daughters, and had certainly been missing from the queue when maternal affection was being distributed.

Mutsi had headed back across the North Sea from Finland after a failed affair, one in a long history of such disasters, with yet another man who'd decided not to leave his wife. Siv could imagine that life in Turku had got a tad uncomfortable. Women didn't care for other women who went poaching their husbands. It wouldn't be long before Mutsi had another man in tow, and his being married wouldn't stop her. She had no intention of being caught in her mother's intricate web, and the kind of fallout that always accompanied her machinations. She'd had enough of meeting a string of 'uncles' as a child. She'd liked a few of them, especially Franz, who'd been good at making animal shapes on the wall and had entertained her with talking hippos and swooping vultures. But it hadn't really mattered if she warmed to them or not. They all vanished as soon as she got used to them. She suspected that most of them had ditched Mutsi when she became too demanding, although her mother had always made it sound as if she was the one who'd ended the relationship. Siv and Rikka could take their pick of, *That man was boring, mean, selfish, sarcastic, old-fashioned, cold, unsympathetic.*

Her father had rarely mentioned his ex-wife but had once said, *Your mother is an insoluble conundrum.*

She washed her plate, poured another drink and sat with her feet on the top of the wood-burner, stroking the arm of the sweatshirt. *Still there, Ed? This is as cosy as I can be without you. It's not really getting any more bearable. I'm just more used to the numbness inside. At least I can manage to resemble a functioning detective. I'm confident I can do the job again and it's a distraction. I seem to have conned people into accepting this weird version of me — except for Mortimer, but then I suspect he has his own agenda which is in a file labelled, 'I wanted Tommy Castles and they sent me this pale imitation.' I wish you were around to put Mutsi back in her box. Wish you were around. Wish I'd padlocked your bike and thrown away the key, like I threatened. Not cross really, just so sad.*

She listened, but he'd wandered off. Maybe if there was an afterlife, he was pedalling along the great cycle path in the sky, where you wouldn't need a helmet and you never got blisters or aching calves. She closed her eyes, liking that picture.

An owl's insistent hooting woke her with a start at half eleven. The fire had burned down to fine, glowing ashes. She was parched and drank a glass of water before she staggered the few paces that it took to reach her bed.

* * *

They met with Rey Anand at the mortuary early the following morning. As usual, he'd provided a Thermos of coffee and a sweetener to soothe the bitter taste of death. Today it was a plate of almond croissants. He was a tall, courteous man with a neatly trimmed beard and rimless glasses. Steve could learn some lessons from his civil manner.

Ali reached for a croissant. 'My blood sugar's fine this morning,' he told Siv.

She raised an eyebrow. He'd managed to get coffee on his shirt cuff as he poured it, and his dark tie, which he only ever wore to the morgue as a gesture of respect, was too short at the front. He often looked as if he was still learning how to dress himself. Patrick, on the other hand, was smart but washed out and stifling yawns. As usual, he was fidgeting and tapping, drumming his fingers silently on his thigh. She imagined him as a restless sleeper, constantly shifting and turning, his feet snarled in the bedding.

She sipped her coffee. 'What have you got for us, Rey?' Ali had already given her the highlights.

Rey leaned forward, elbows propped on the table. 'What I have for you is inevitably limited, because of the mummification process. The pelvic bones and rib measurements demonstrate that they are the remains of a mature female of middle years — between thirty-five and fifty, around five feet four in height. There was rapid skin dehydration after death, which means the tissue is brittle, partly because there was no heating in the premises, and also the kitchen is cool and shady. That would have facilitated mummification instead of the usual putrefaction. Hair was darkish blonde. She was bare-legged but fully clothed, wearing knickers, bra and a dress. There were signs of former low-level insect activity present on the body, mainly flies, pupae and maggots, of the usual type found in houses and other buildings. She had been strangled with paracord, a type of heavy-duty commercial nylon, and her body was then tied to the back of the fridge with rope. It's hard to be definite because of the deterioration of the body, but given the lack of any other substances, fibres or materials, my best guess is that she was strangled there. I can't be precise on that point. She could have been murdered elsewhere. Given the time that's elapsed since her death, it wasn't possible to determine if there was sexual activity beforehand.'

He paused to sip coffee. His aftershave was pungent and woody, an effective barrier against the powerful stench of blood, antiseptic and decay. He'd once told Siv that he never ate cauliflower cheese because, to him, the dish smelled exactly like putrefaction. Steve Wooton had eaten two of the croissants and Siv took the last but one. It was warm and soft. She tried not to picture maggots.

'I'm going to ask the predictable question,' she said. 'Can you tell us anything about how long she'd been there?'

'Hmm. That's a difficult one because of variants in temperature and moisture. I'd say no longer than eight years and not less than four. But those are approximations. The woman had been wearing a yellow dress made of a cotton mix and shreds of it were still intact. The label has disintegrated too far to get anything from it.'

'So we can't tell if she was murdered at the scene,' Ali said. 'It might be that she went somewhere else to start with, and then was taken to Steiner's by her killer, rather than meeting him there.'

'Rigor, as you are aware, sets in after about four hours and dissipates after approximately forty-eight hours,' Rey said. 'Therefore, if she was strangled elsewhere, it would have been easier for the killer either to move her quickly, or after two days.'

Steve wiped his mouth with a tissue. 'We didn't find any paracord in Steiner's. The type used to strangle the deceased is widely available in most DIY shops or online. There was an identical bale of rope in the outhouse where the toilet is. There's no ID of any kind.'

'I've not heard of paracord before,' Siv said. 'What's it used for?'

'It was originally used in parachute suspension lines,' Steve told them. 'Then it migrated into general commercial use. Astronauts have used it. Joe Public uses it for anything from engines to pet collars to water bottle straps, bracelets and garage storage. You could say it's ubiquitous and multipurpose, which doesn't help you much if you're trying to track down who might have had it handy for a strangulation.'

Ali groaned. 'Thanks, Steve.'

'We have two missing women in the age range you've given us,' Siv told Rey. 'How soon can you give us a result from their dental records?'

'It should be within twenty-four hours.'

'Guv!' Patrick was checking his phone. 'I made a few basic notes from the mispers files. None of them had any connection to Steiner's but one of those two women was reported as wearing a yellow dress the night she went missing in July 2013. Her name was Lyn Dimas and she was blonde.'

Patrick had sleep crust in the corners of his eyes and he rubbed at it as he spoke. He could be callow and distracted but now and again, he nailed it. Siv smiled at him.

'Good work. We'll focus on her. Do we have any results from the mattress?'

'That's still underway,' Steve reported, 'and we're running checks on all fingerprints found in the premises. We have thirty-five full sets in all, at least four of which presumably belong to our builders. There are also a number of part-prints, just useless smudges. Judging by the spliff ends, empty matchboxes, takeaway cartons, lager cans, wine bottles, used condoms and one pair of knickers we found — size twelve, Primark, pink with a rose pattern — Steiner & Sons has been in regular informal use over the years. Either that, or Mr Steiner was living it large before he croaked.'

* * *

Siv was in her office early. A positive dental match for Lyn Dimas had come through, and she was reading the 2013 records and making notes. She saw that DS Tommy Castles had been active on the case. His name had followed her around since she took this job. Mortimer had favoured

Castles and mentored him for the vacancy that Siv had filled. According to Ali, Mortimer had been annoyed that the appointment hadn't gone his way. Castles had gone off to Kent instead, but she'd heard that he hadn't settled there.

She stood and opened a window wide, pushing against the warped, reluctant frame. The station was a listed building. Bits of it were crumbling and damp but repairs were costly and funds tight. Her office had an uneven, worn floor and was always musty. It had been partitioned off from the main room with a dark wood surround, inset with small windows and beige vertical blinds. Every evening, the cleaners opened the blinds and every morning, she closed them, so that it didn't seem as if she was posing in a shop window.

She'd called a meeting at nine thirty. The team for now was her, Ali, and Patrick. DC Lisa Flore, who usually worked with them, had been seconded to a specialist domestic violence unit and there had been no budget to replace her.

'We've made progress,' she said. 'We've had a positive ID on dental records for this woman, Lyn Dimas. I've done a trawl through the record. She went missing on the twenty-eighth of July 2013. She was forty-three, living with her eighteen-year-old daughter, Lily, and her son, Adam, aged nine. Her husband, Theo Dimas, had moved out of the family home six months previously. He'd come out to his family as gay and was living with his new partner, Monty Barnwell.

'The evening of the twenty-eighth was hectic in the house, because Lily had a bunch of friends round getting ready to attend their school prom. After Lily left with her friends, around quarter past seven, Lyn made Adam a sandwich and told him she was popping out to the shop and she wouldn't be long. According to her son's account, she left just after half seven with her shoulder bag. She didn't take her car. Adam watched a film and ate his supper. When the film ended, it was just before nine. Adam was worried because his mum hadn't come back, and he went to the next-door neighbour, Jeff Downey.' She paused to take a sip of water.

'Downey drove with Adam to the nearest shop, Smart Mart, which was the one she'd have walked to for odd things, but they didn't see Lyn. The shop owner knew her well and said she hadn't been in. Downey went home with Adam and phoned Mr Dimas, who said he'd heard nothing from his wife for weeks. Mr Dimas then went to the family home and rang around his wife's friends. Most of them refused to speak to him at first — she'd been doing a good job of denouncing him — but when he explained that she hadn't returned home, they all said that they hadn't seen her, or expected to see her that evening. Mr Dimas phoned the police at 11.30 p.m. Given the circumstances, a search was launched immediately.'

Patrick waved his iPad stylus. 'Guv, were there any major suspects?'

'Not that I've noted so far. All the team members who investigated at the time have either moved elsewhere or retired. That might not be such a bad thing — no toes to tread on. I did read that Theo Dimas said he'd been at home all evening with his partner, who confirmed that. But no one had seen, or reported seeing, Lyn Dimas after she left the house that evening. She vanished into thin air. Her bag was never found, there was no activity on her cards and her passport was at home. She'd left her phone in the kitchen. A trawl through her phone records showed just calls from family members or her work, and none on that day. There was no unusual email activity or arrangements for that evening. Ali, did you get hold of Theo Dimas?'

'Aye, I did. He's living back in the family home. I told him we had news of a development and we'd see him mid-morning. He sounded wobbly.'

'We'll head to see him soon. Patrick, I've started summarising the family structure, who was interviewed at the time, any major leads or suspects, forensics and any arrests. Can you carry on with that?'

'Sure, guv. What are our chances of finding out who murdered her?' Patrick asked. He seemed a bit apathetic and unfocused. He was keen on pursuit and quick results that he could tweet, not old cases with cold trails.

'They're probably equal to our enthusiasm and skill,' Siv said sharply. 'It's not easy, investigating a murder years after the event but there's a woman whose life was taken, a killer still at large and a family that's hurting. My view is that we start from scratch with open minds, a completely fresh investigation, as well as using what information we already have from 2013. We'll meet again first thing tomorrow. I've just got to speak to DCI Mortimer before we leave,' she told Ali.

* * *

'Enjoy,' Ali said, sinking his teeth into a nectarine and dribbling juice on his jacket collar. He shook his head at Patrick when she'd gone. 'You deserved that reprimand,' he said. 'You should have the measure of the guv by now.'

Patrick pulled a mutinous face and danced his fingers across his desk. 'Everyone says cold cases are a nightmare.'

'Yeah, well, don't go tweeting that! Some things are best kept to yourself, wee man. Not always a good idea to say what's going round in your head.' Ali often adopted a mildly paternal air with Patrick. The younger man didn't seem to mind.

* * *

Siv climbed to the top floor and found Mortimer sitting at his desk, staring at his laptop. His narrow shoulders were hunched. He was a bony man with a small head and a prickly manner. His skin had improved recently, the rosacea on his cheeks less inflamed. She told him that the body had been identified.

'I still can't give you any more than two officers,' he said. 'We're thin on the ground, what with retirements and a lid on recruitment. And given that you'll have a lot of information already on file, that should suffice. It goes without saying that the case will be difficult to resolve.'

He and Patrick could form the glass-half-full team together. 'Best not to be pessimistic, though. Three of us will be fine, sir.' She didn't want to hear about how he was having to recruit volunteers to help with forensics, rape cases and checking fingerprints. She was distracted by a painting that had appeared on his wall, just behind his badly dyed hair. He had a number of photos and paintings of boats and seascapes but this was a new one. It was of a silvery blue lake, threaded with ice and with purple hills in the background. It seemed familiar but she couldn't place it.

Mortimer straightened his tie. A leather case with a manicure set sat by his laptop. He was proud of his slim, long-fingered hands and sometimes worked on his cuticles while he was on the phone. 'It will have to be, and let's hope you stick with just one body this time, Inspector. No more multiples if you can help it, and no attempted suicides or murdered witnesses.'

He was referring to the complexities of the first case she'd worked when she arrived. As payback for the sarcasm she said, 'Still, we found our murderers and got a prosecution. I see that DS Castles was involved in the Lyn Dimas investigation. Shame he didn't find her.'

Mortimer sniffed. 'Just get on with the job in hand, eh?'

'Of course. I'll keep you up to speed, sir.'

Fifteen-love today. She smiled to herself on the way back down. Petty but satisfying.

CHAPTER 4

Ali was driving, his seat pushed so far back to accommodate his bulk that he was almost in the boot.

'How are you getting on in your wee wagon?' he asked. 'You must be wild cosy, tucked in there. Snug as a bug in a rug.' What he was thinking was, *How can she stand being in the back of beyond with no one for company?* When he'd said this to Polly, she'd reminded him that Siv was in a strange part of her life, grieving and hurting. Some people coped better alone and when she was back on a more even keel, she'd be more sociable. Ali hoped so, because he worried about the guv, down there on her own by the edge of the river. None of them had been invited to her home. He'd picked her up one day when her car wouldn't start, but she'd been waiting on the lane. He'd just caught a glimpse of the tiny wagon before she was in the passenger seat and telling him to step on it. It was like an illustration from a kids' story — the cover of an Enid Blyton came to mind. At least she'd put a bit of weight on in the last couple of months, but there'd still be more meat on a hamster.

'It took a bit of getting used to, but I like it now. Dead easy to maintain. Just me, the river and trees.'

It wasn't Ali's idea of a good time. He and Polly lived in a snug crescent of twenty houses. He liked being surrounded by neighbours and was reassured by car doors slamming, kids' voices, the odd snatch of someone's music, the general background hum of domestic activities. 'You're not a tad isolated? It'd do my head in, with nothing but the Bere and the owls to listen to.'

'Corran and Paul are just over the way, and don't forget the goats. They get very busy at sunset.'

'Oh, of course. They must be great for the craic. And no one's likely to call by, given where it is,' Ali said.

'There is that.'

He grinned and she smiled too. They were getting used to each other.

* * *

The Dimases' home was a semi-detached on Bishop Close, a residential street to the east of the town. The outside had been recently decorated, with cream cladding from the roof-line to the top of the ground-floor windows. The front door was a matt grey, flanked by large wooden tubs of pristine white dahlias.

'Theo Dimas is a radiographer at the Towers, a private hospital, or was at the time when his wife went missing,' Siv said. 'How long would it have taken Lyn to walk from here to Orford End?'

'I had a wee poke about earlier. A good twenty minutes at a fast pace, I'd say. There are some cut-throughs.'

'She didn't intend to go there, surely — she told her son she wouldn't be long. That would take at least forty minutes, there and back. You wouldn't leave a nine-year-old alone for that long, or at least not without ringing to check on him. And she left her phone — she didn't expect that she'd need to. The records indicate that everyone spoke of her as a devoted mother. Why would a respectable person be hanging out in a filthy, disused building?'

'Not a clue. Unless it was part of a plan for bailing out, running away.'

'With just a shoulder bag and no phone, car or passport? Come on, we'd best not keep this man on tenterhooks any longer.' She got out of the car and braced herself. Delivering this kind of news never got any easier and in some ways, the time lapse in this case made it harder. If this man wasn't responsible for his wife's death, they were about to dash any lingering scraps of hope.

Theo Dimas opened the door before they could knock. He was a short, solid block of flesh, bullnecked with slightly bowed legs and a mass of dark, closely cropped hair. He wore a navy shirt and jeans, teamed with bright red braces.

'Come in, please. This way.'

They followed him into an orderly, comfortable living room lined with bookshelves and framed charcoal sketches. One of them was of Theo Dimas, a good likeness. A home entertainment centre in light oak occupied one wall, housing a large TV, Xbox, an old-fashioned record player with a stack of vinyl records beside it, and an antique rosewood chess set. A pile of school textbooks was on the table beside the chair Siv sat in: *GCSE Guide to Macbeth*, *Combined Science*, *Biology Explained*, and *The Tudor World*.

Siv made introductions. 'I'm very sorry, Mr Dimas, but we have bad news about your wife.'

'You've found her?' He held himself straight, hands gripping his knees, as if braced for a shock.

'Yes. Two days ago, a decomposed body was discovered in an abandoned building in town. The body was tied to the back of a fridge. We've checked against your wife's dental records, and confirmed along with other autopsy results that the body is that of your wife, Lyn Dimas. She'd been strangled. I'm very sorry to have to tell you this.'

Dimas pressed down on his massive knees. 'A fridge?' He shook his head. 'Did you say a fridge?'

'Yes, a large fridge-freezer. She'd been secured to the back grille with rope, and the fridge had been pushed back towards the wall, so that she couldn't be seen.'

'My God. All this time and she's been . . . So she died on the night she vanished?'

'The autopsy couldn't tell us that. Certainly, she must have died on or soon after that night.'

'I didn't really hope . . .' He stopped, cleared his throat. 'I'd given up hope that she was alive. Where was she found?' He spoke slowly, deliberately, as if weighing every word.

'In Steiner & Sons Removals, a disused business premises in Orford End,' Siv said. 'It's been empty for a long time.'

He had wide, full lips. He pressed them tightly together and ran a hand up his impressive neck. 'Orford End. Where's that?'

'North of town, near the railway station. The building is about to be demolished to make way for new housing.'

'I read about that. How on earth did Lyn get there?'

'We don't know that, or if that's where she was killed. Her body might have been taken there soon after she died. We'll need to go through the original investigation step by step and talk to people again. It will be difficult because of the time lapse.'

'Six years,' Dimas said faintly and sat back, rubbing his forehead with agitated fingers.

'Can I get you some water?' Ali asked.

'Hmm? Please, yes.'

He sat gazing at the dark green carpet. Siv said nothing further until Ali returned with three glasses of water on a tray. A breeze shook a blazing Virginia creeper at the back window and the branches tapped at a pane. Dimas took a few sips from his glass. His dark eyes were miserable.

'What happens now?' he asked. 'I mean . . . can I see her or something?'

'Not just yet. We don't need you to identify your wife and her body had deteriorated.' *He's a nurse, he'll know what I mean.*

He shivered and drank more water. 'I suppose after six years . . . Oh God. How was she found? I mean, who found her?'

Ali had been standing, hands clasped behind his back and rocking on his broad feet, studying the sketches. He sat down again. 'The building is going to be demolished by a local builder. The men who went to clear it out found her body hidden behind the fridge when they went to move it.'

'So Lyn was concealed?'

'Yes. As DI Drummond said, you couldn't see her until the fridge was pulled out.'

'Even so . . . surely someone who went in there would have noticed something? I mean, as her body decomposed . . .' He stared at them both in bewilderment.

Siv said, 'The building has been broken into over the years and left in quite a state, with rubbish and other materials left lying around. Your wife's body was mummified as well as hidden.' *I can hardly say that Steiner's reeks of so many unpleasant odours, it would have been hard to detect a decomposing body.*

Dimas took his time mulling this over and then gulped back the rest of the water. 'Was she . . . was she attacked sexually?'

'The pathologist couldn't determine that.'

'I don't get it. How would she have got to Orford End? Why would she go there? She didn't drive that night.'

'Either she walked there, or someone drove her. If she was abducted, she could have been taken there after she died. Did she ever have any business with Steiner's Removals or was she friendly with anyone who worked there?' Ali asked.

'No. When we moved in here, I hired a van and a friend helped us. Lyn was a podiatrist, based at the Brookridge clinic near the harbour. She never had any reason to contact a removal company.'

It was warm in the room, with the autumnal sun throwing thick golden bars of light across the floor. Siv slipped her jacket off.

'Can you tell us a bit about what was happening in the weeks before Lyn disappeared? You'll have been through all this before but it would help us.' Dimas had a faraway gaze. She recognised shock and deemed it was genuine. 'Take your time.'

He put a hand to his mouth and stood. 'I'm having a brandy. Would you like one?'

They both shook their heads and waited while he took a bottle from a sideboard and poured a glass. Ali opened his notebook and crossed a leg at right angles over his knee. He scribbled a note, *HUGE CAKE IN KITCHEN. IT'S HIS PARTNER'S BIRTHDAY* and showed the page to Siv. She gave a little shrug.

Dimas sat, feet pointing outwards. He held his brandy glass in front of him with two hands circling it at the base, like a chalice. 'This is all so hard to take in. Unreal.'

'I understand,' Siv said. *Unless your shock stems from your wife finally being found where you hid her.* 'Take your time and tell us about what was going on in the family.'

He blinked hard. 'What a bloody awful year 2013 turned out to be. I told Lyn that I was gay on the third of January. She said it was a lovely start to the New Year. I'd been trying to tell her for months and finally plucked up courage.' He drank more brandy and sighed.

'How did she react?' Siv prompted.

'Badly. She was angry, shocked, frightened, betrayed. Shouting and crying. I could understand all of that. I expected it. I'd had some counselling when I was working things out, building up to coming out. The counsellor took me through worst-case scenarios. I realised that Lyn would think that the man she'd been married to for twenty years had always been lying to her. When she tore into me, I accepted that was how she saw it, even if I didn't set out to deceive her. But when I considered the worst that could happen, I didn't anticipate that she'd get her revenge by alleging that I might be HIV positive. Even when I told her that I'd been tested and I wasn't, she kept on about it. She told the children and other family and friends that I might have AIDS. She pretended not to know that HIV and AIDS aren't the same thing.'

He'd been somewhat naïve, expecting his emotional, vengeful wife not to strike a low blow. Siv asked, 'Did that make you angry?'

'Sad, more than angry. Lyn turned my father against me, too — it wouldn't have taken much effort, but she made sure she got him in her camp. That was unforgivable. I couldn't get through that kind of spite. She insisted that I move out the next day — threw me out, really — and she wouldn't let me see the kids afterwards. I managed to tell them both that I'm gay just before I left.'

'How did they take it?' Ali asked.

Dimas closed his eyes, the remembered pain clear on his face. 'My son, Adam, was just bewildered, and then in the months after, he was worried that I might die because Lyn was saying I had a disease. Lily, my daughter, was vicious. I was stunned. Young people now are supposed to be inclusive and enlightened, but not Lily. She was worried about being laughed at, losing status. That girl with the queer dad. It was all about her — what her friends would say. Plus her boyfriend, now husband, is homophobic. She's hardly spoken to me since her mother went missing. You spend eighteen years with your child and then she just cuts all the ties, as if you don't exist. Madness. Lily's always been a tough cookie but I didn't realise she could be so heartless.'

Ali raised his eyebrows at Siv. She reached for her water. 'Where did you go when you moved out?'

'I went to live with Monty, my partner. He had a rented flat in town. After Lyn went missing, I moved back in here to care for Adam. I took three months off work. Lily wouldn't stay in the house with me. She went off to Pearce, the boyfriend, and they got married six months later. I wasn't invited to the wedding. Adam went as a pageboy. Then Monty moved in here about two years ago, when . . . when it looked as if Lyn wasn't going to be back.'

The creeper was tapping at the window again. Siv wouldn't be able to stand that on a dark winter's night. She'd imagine it was Ed, out in the cold, longing to come in. She fingered the little scar over her eyebrow. 'What did you think when Lyn was missing? She must have been under a lot of strain, with you leaving in those circumstances. Did you ever believe that she might have run away or committed suicide?'

Dimas shook his heavy head. 'I just didn't have a clue. Lyn would never have left Adam alone, not intending to come back. She was a devoted mum, wrapped up in the kids. And she took nothing with her except her bag. Your colleagues asked at the time if she was having an affair. I had no idea. I'd not seen her or the kids for months. Lily decided she'd committed suicide but I never thought that was likely.'

'Why not?'

He drained his brandy. 'This is going to sound cruel, but you see, if she'd killed herself, that would have left the children with me and Monty. That would have been her worst nightmare, and she'd have seen it as me winning, coming out on top. She'd never have allowed that.'

Siv saw his point. Some people killed themselves out of spite — *See what you've made me do*. She could understand that staying alive to be a thorn in the flesh was another way of getting revenge. 'Adam was young to be left on his own that night, even for a short time. Had Lyn done that before?'

'No, and it was unlike her. I agree that she shouldn't have left him — some shopping can't have been that urgent. Back then, your colleagues believed she must have had another motive for going out, but if she did, they never found it.'

'Where were you on the night your wife disappeared?'

'At Monty's flat. We'd had dinner and we were watching football when Jeff Downey phoned. I came straight round. The weather had broken and there was a massive thunderstorm. The heavens opened as I was driving. I'll never forget it, the way the sky seemed to burst open. It was . . . apocalyptic.'

That was before Siv's father died. There'd been flooding in the town two years running, and he'd had to protect his house with sandbags because of the stream that ran at the bottom of his garden. 'Lily was out at her school prom. What time did she get back?'

'About one in the morning. She flipped when she saw me in the house and heard about Lyn. She was pretty drunk. It really upset Adam, the way she went on. As the days went by, she blamed me for Lyn's disappearance — said I'd driven her into depression and that must have led her to commit suicide.' He linked his hands together, palms up and flexed his fingers.

'Was Lyn depressed?' Siv asked.

'I've no idea, because there was no communication. I'd ring her, pleading to see the children, but she either shouted at me or didn't reply. Anyone can become suicidal, but Lyn was never that type and as I've said, she wouldn't have abandoned the children, no matter how down she was. Lily was being a drama queen and I'm afraid I said that to her at one point, which didn't help. To be honest, I was relieved in a way when she moved in with Pearce. Her hostility was exhausting.'

Siv knocked the stack of textbooks as she put her water down. 'Are these Adam's?'

'Yes. He's studying for his GCSEs.' His eyes creased and he took a breath. 'How in God's name am I going to tell him about his mother when he comes home from school?'

'We can send you a family liaison officer,' Ali offered. 'They're trained to help out in this kind of situation.'

'No, it's okay. I'd rather just talk to him myself. Monty will help. Can you inform Lily? I don't want to do it by email, and she's blocked my number on her phone.'

Ali said, 'Of course. We'll need to speak to her anyway. Is she still in Berminster?'

'Yes, she's Lily Aston now. She lives near Halse woods.' Dimas slumped, exhausted.

Siv stood. 'This has been difficult for you, so we'll leave it there for now. We'll need to speak to you again and to Adam and your partner. Do you still work at the Towers hospital?'

'Yes, in radiography. Monty works at Berminster General. He's a nurse, too — in the maxillofacial unit.'

'We'll advise you when your wife's body can be released, so that you can arrange a funeral.'

He glanced vaguely at her. 'Funeral? Oh, yes — of course. Sorry, I'm a bit muddled right now.' He walked them to the front door and turned. 'Will you be able to discover who did this? I mean, the detectives back then couldn't even find Lyn.'

'We'll do our best, Mr Dimas,' Siv said.

In the car, Ali took a packet of diabetic fruit drops from the glove compartment. 'Want one?'

'No, thanks.' She'd tried them and found them horribly sweet.

'Lily sounds like a dream daughter,' Ali said drily.

'Theo Dimas certainly dropped a bomb on his family when he came out. I wonder if he'd considered Newton's third law at the time. "For every action, there is an equal and opposite reaction."'

'I'm impressed that you remember your school science so well. I've forgotten nearly all of mine, apart from a few chemical symbols.'

'My dad was keen on Newton, especially his research on optics. He'd wax lyrical about him, usually when we were drinking cocoa.' If Rikka was around, she'd indulge in theatrical, mock yawns behind his back. Siv had found herself so delighted to have a parent who stayed in at night and could make proper cocoa in a saucepan, she'd hung on his every word.

Ali laughed. 'My dad would've been studying the form for the next day's horse racing.'

'What did you make of Dimas?'

Ali sucked his sweet, pondering. 'He looked convincingly shocked.'

'Do I hear a "but?"'

'His wife was badmouthing him to everyone and he was facing years of a war of attrition. Not hard to see a motive.'

She gazed at the house. 'If Dimas and his partner killed Lyn, they waited patiently for four years to move in together.'

'That would be a sensible plan, if they'd worked it through carefully. They wouldn't want to draw attention to themselves. Is that a possibility? The team that worked in 2013 must have scrutinised their alibis.'

'I hope so, although there wasn't much to check. They alibied each other. Otherwise, there was just a neighbour who said she didn't hear them go out, which doesn't amount to anything. Dimas seemed stunned but then, if he knew that site was being developed, he'd have had time to prepare for the body being found. Drop me back at the station and I'll go and see Lily Aston, tell her we've found her mother. You work with Patrick on trawling the records and getting the incident board up to speed. That'll make sure he stays awake. Does he have any kind of social life?'

'Patrick? He never says much. It must be hard for him, with Noah at home. He asked Lisa out a couple of times but then had to cancel because of Noah duties and in the end she told him not to bother.'

Patrick lived with his brother, Noah, who'd had a stroke that had left him disabled. Patrick was run ragged at times, because he went home to his second job as a carer. He was stretched taut like a piece of elastic and she worried that he might snap. 'Keep an eye on him. I can tell he admires you.'

'Yeah?' Ali was pleased. 'Okay, I will. It's hard though. He can get defensive if I ask him anything about home.'

A bit like me, then. 'Hmm. Right, we'll leave Theo Dimas alone for a day or two, especially if it's his partner's birthday.'

'They won't enjoy the gorgeous chocolate birthday cake in the kitchen. It said *Happy Birthday, Monty* in white icing. It was amazing, a work of art. I was drooling.' Ali started the engine.

Siv shook her head. 'You and sweet stuff. You're like a moth to a candle. I'm surprised you didn't nick a slice. Do you dream about sugary treats at night?'

'No, I don't.' Ali accelerated sharply, throwing her back in her seat.

* * *

Theo Dimas sat for a while on the sofa, staring into space. His marriage seemed so long ago. It had been a cave he'd spent years hiding in, holding his breath, wondering if he would be found out. Wanting to be found out. That had been another Theo, a timid, confused man and he was glad to be rid of him.

Had he ever loved Lyn? Probably, but he wasn't sure anymore. They'd met when they were eighteen and she'd been so pretty, bubbly and optimistic, he'd buried any half-formed doubts he had about himself. He'd never been a brave man, and it was easier to marry Lyn, please his father and live a conventional life than to hover in the shadows, trying to pluck up the courage to visit one of the few gay bars that were available around Sussex in the 1980s. So he'd dumped his well-thumbed, hidden copies of *Mister*, *Him* and *Zipper*, and deferred to his father's wish for the marriage to take place in the Greek Orthodox church of St Demetrius.

He'd tried to be content in his marriage and had managed to pretend to himself that all was well during his twenties. But in his early thirties, he'd started visiting some of the growing numbers of gay bars popping up around the coast, and discovering the joy and anxiety of understanding his true nature. He had been trying to pluck up the courage to talk to Lyn when she told him she was pregnant with Adam. He hadn't wanted another child, another dab of glue to the marriage, but he'd lost his nerve and buckled down to being a father again. He loved Adam fiercely, and indulged him to assuage his guilt about not having wanted him.

Lyn's face was a blur now, and any affection had been corroded by her vitriolic words and behaviour after his departure. Despite the counselling, he'd been naïve in his expectations when he left. Because the marriage had been stale and lacking in any intimacy for years, he'd never understood that Lyn might end up so despairing and undermined. He'd been astonished and angry when she spat her poisons, and deeply dejected when Monty warned him that she might maintain her flow of venom long-term. He remembered Monty's sombre words: *Lyn can try to make our life together a nightmare if she chooses, and I fear that she will.*

For the last couple of years, things seemed to be improving. He and Monty had been through the fire and they'd achieved some equilibrium. It had been hard forming a new family unit. Adam didn't like Monty, even if he never said so. But each day bonded them together a little bit more, despite tensions. Now this news, stirring up memories, would inevitably take Adam back to a bleak place. And their friend Justin, too — they needed to protect him. He had a fragile core and this might destabilise him.

He reached for his phone and sent a text to warn Monty.

The police have just been here. They found Lyn's body. I'll tell you about it later. There's a new lead investigator, a DI Drummond. She's sharp. Can you tell Justin and advise him to stay calm? We all need to keep clear heads, stick to our story and hold steady.

CHAPTER 5

Lily Aston checked the oven setting and the timer. She was making flaounes for Papu. They were his favourite pastries and he loved them still warm from the oven. She'd left out the sesame seeds, because they might get stuck between his dentures. She didn't do much baking but if she had time, she liked making things for Papu. He had, after all, bought them their state-of-the-art, black glass integrated cooker. He was everything a grandad should be: kind, dignified, proper, doting and generous to a fault. He was a bit of a bore when it came to religion, but he'd given up asking if she'd attend St Demetrius, so she could coast that. He'd paid for her wedding at the five-star Cliffdean Heights Hotel and had given her away, stepping in where her dad should have been. He'd been so elegant in his grey morning suit, with his white hair brushed straight back from his long, regal features — like a face on a coin. She'd swelled with pride at having him by her side. He'd also given her and Pearce fifty thousand towards their house. Pearce called him 'Papu' too, because he'd never known either of his grandads.

She went into the office to check the answerphone but there were no messages. Just as well, because the morning had been frantic and Pearce was already booked up for weeks.

When the doorbell rang, she checked her watch. Too early for Papu. He was always precise about timings. Through the peephole she saw a tall, dark-haired woman in a grey suit and jade green shirt. She was looking straight at the door, as if she was aware that Lily was checking her out. When Lily opened it, she held out a warrant card.

'Lily Aston?'

'Yes.'

'I'm Detective Inspector Siv Drummond. I need to speak to you.' The woman had a solemn, no-nonsense manner.

Lily was alarmed. 'Has something happened to Pearce?'

'No, that's not why I'm here.'

'I'm just baking,' Lily said. She must sound foolish.

'How lovely. I do need to talk to you. It's important.'

Lily let her in and took her into the sitting room. The inspector sat down in one of the matching blue Ikea chairs. Lily sat opposite her. Her finger was sticky with honey and she took a tissue from a box on the table.

'I've come to see you because I have news about your mother. I'm very sorry because it's bad news.'

Lily tried hard not to dwell on it, but she'd always suspected that this day might come. She'd decided that if it did, she'd stay calm and not turn into one of those red-eyed chavs you saw bawling their eyes out when there was a tragedy. 'What's happened?'

'We found a body and we've identified your mother's remains.'

She rubbed the skin through the rip in her jeans, circling her finger. 'How did she do it? Did she take tablets? That's what women usually do, don't they?'

'Your mum didn't commit suicide.'

Lily listened as Inspector Drummond gave her the details. She had a clear, level voice, easy to listen to. Her eyes were an unusual dark blue, almost navy, and Lily wondered if she wore coloured contact lenses. She was saying terrible things about a fridge, strangulation and a disused building. Lily went hot and then cold. She was aware of a hissing in her ears, like a kettle boiling and she pressed them so that the detective's voice sounded far away.

Siv watched the colour drain from Lily Aston's face. She was blonde and fair, very like her dead mother, but with her father's wide mouth. Pretty in a vapid way, and without any spark. 'Are you okay, Ms Aston?'

'Hmm. Yes. I don't understand . . . why would mum have been in a place like that?' She'd painted a picture for herself of her mother lying peacefully, deep in a forest, tucked under the foliage, her hands under her head. Taking a forever nap.

'It's hard to work that out. I spoke to your dad earlier and he couldn't come up with any reason.'

'You've seen my dad?'

'Yes. I've just visited him. I said I'd tell you the news. I understand that you don't communicate with him.'

'That's right. After what he did to us . . .' She resumed rubbing her finger on the tissue, even though the honey was long gone and the paper was starting to shred. 'Strangled,' she whispered.

'Yes, I'm so sorry.'

There was a ring like an alarm clock. Lily scrunched up the tissue.

'That's the oven. I have to check.'

'I'll come with you.' Last time Siv had allowed a woman to head to the kitchen during an interview, she'd been planning to kill herself with scissors and nearly succeeded. She didn't reckon that self-harm was on Lily's mind but she wasn't risking it.

She followed Lily down the short, narrow hall to the kitchen. It was a small house, two bedrooms, she guessed, and unremarkable. There were a couple of sketches in the style she'd seen at Theo Dimas's home, including one of Lily. A white heart-shaped plaque was hanging by the kitchen window. It said, *Love Makes Our House A Home*. Siv sat at the white wood table and watched Lily take a tray of small pastries from the oven and set them to cool. They were golden and gleaming. She was slim, with neat movements, her hair drawn back in a clip. Her pale blue jeans had strategic tears at the knees and backs of her calves, and her white ruffled blouse sat just on top of her waistband. She wore quite a bit of make-up for someone cooking at home — light and subtle, but it would have taken time. She stood, gripping the edge of the work surface.

'Come and sit down.' Siv pulled a chair out. 'Can I make you a cup of tea?'

Lily shook her head but she sat near Siv, clasping her hands to the back of her slender neck and staring out the patio door to the tiny paved garden. Siv followed her gaze and saw a few pinched plants in a narrow border, surrounded by healthy weeds.

'You thought your mother had committed suicide,' Siv said.

'I was sure she had. Pearce, my husband, believed that too, because of all the turmoil she'd been going through back then. You know about what Dad did to us?'

'Yes. He came out as gay and moved out.'

'Mum was in a state. She pretended that she was coping, but it was a front. It sent her mental and horrible. It was really hard living with her. I had a nightmare time back then.' She glanced at Siv. 'You'll never guess one of the last things I said to her.'

'Tell me.'

She gave a high, nervous laugh. 'I told her to get lost. She was getting on my nerves while I was preparing for my prom. It was embarrassing, like she wanted to be one of the girls. She was always doing stuff like that, pretending to be younger than she was.'

'You must have regretted saying that to her. It's hard.' The last thing she'd said to Ed as he strapped on his helmet was, *Be careful, see you later.*

But Lily wasn't seeking reassurance. She was the centre of the story. 'Mum could be *so* overwhelming. She took up my oxygen. That was my day and she was all over it like a rash — and with my friends there! It was ever so selfish of her. Pearce told me I had to forgive myself about saying that because I was stressed and I didn't mean it.'

'I see.' Clearly, feeling stressed trumped being strangled in Lily's world.

Lily took a breath, her expression sullen. 'I just thought Mum had despaired of this life and ended the pain.'

It sounded theatrical, like a phrase she'd said many times. Lily had been eighteen at the time and teenagers could find the idea of suicide romantic — attractive, even.

'Your dad said he'd never supposed that was likely.'

She tossed her head, flicking her hair like a petulant pony.

'He wouldn't want to believe that, would he? Because he'd been responsible for destroying her life. Our lives. He drove her to it.'

Siv said slowly, 'But he didn't, did he? Someone murdered your mother.' *But you liked the idea of suicide because it puts the blame on your dad and piles on the misery.*

Lily reached into the pocket of her jeans and produced a pale pink lip gloss that she drew absentmindedly across her wide, full mouth. 'Did you find my mum's bag with her?'

'No, no bag.'

'Oh. She had a necklace of mine in there. She was going to take it to the jeweller to have it repaired. It was one of my favourites, a gold butterfly. One of the wings was chipped. It'd have been good to have that back.'

Maybe it was shock making her appear so uncaring. Siv silently agreed with Theo Dimas that Lily had chips of flint in her heart. There was an artlessness about the woman, a lack of true centre.

As if to confirm her opinion, Lily said, 'I really like your suit. It's so smart. Is it from Whistles?'

Siv was nonplussed. 'No, it's Zara.'

'Oh, right. I haven't bought their stuff for a while. I've been into Ted Baker recently. I love their skinny jeans. This is one of their tops.'

She might as well follow the clothes route. 'It must have been exciting, getting ready for the prom with your friends in all your special outfits.'

'You bet! We'd been planning it for months, down to every last detail. I had a terrific dress, it cost almost five hundred pounds. All my girls came round about three o'clock — we're called the Damsels — and it was magic. We were all hyper.'

'Did you see much of your mum that afternoon?'

'Too much! I was hoping she'd go out with Adam and stop fussing, but she was doing her hovering thing, getting in the way and commenting on our dresses. I warned her that she wasn't to post any photos of herself online with us. *So* not cool! At least Adam made himself scarce when I'd told him to.'

Poor Lyn, what a kindly daughter Fate sent to her. 'Had your mum gone out before and left Adam alone in the house?'

'I asked him that afterwards, and he said it was the first time it had happened. She'd sometimes pop to Smart Mart in the evening if she'd forgotten something but then I'd be in, so that was okay. She shouldn't have left him on his own like that — it's like child neglect, isn't it? Pearce said it was illegal.'

'It seems out of character for your mother. It's not illegal, but nine is young to be left alone.'

'Adam's never got over it. He's turned into a bit of a sad loner and he's piled weight on, too, around here.' Lily laid a hand on her own flat abdomen. 'If he's not careful, he'll never shift that. Pearce reckons the trauma's given him delayed development, and he should see a psychiatrist.'

The way she declared it indicated that Pearce liked issuing pronouncements, and Lily swallowed them wholesale. 'Do you see much of Adam?'

'No. He prefers to stick around Dad and that revolting man so . . . Haven't seen him now for nearly a year.' She put her hands to her face. 'I've gone a bit weird. We're supposed to eat out tonight, but I don't want to now. It's a lot to take in. Am I very pale?'

'A bit.'

'I hate looking washed out, like when I get a cold.'

Siv didn't have much sympathy after the comments she'd been hearing, and pressed on. 'Pearce was at the prom with you that night. What time did he meet you?'

'All the Damsels went in a limo together and I met Pearce at the school hall about a quarter to eight. It was a wonderful, brilliant evening and then I got home and everything was ruined. It should have been one of the best memories of my life, but then there was this terrible thing and my lovely night was spoiled.'

This young woman was all heart. 'Do you want me to call anyone for you now — someone to be with you?'

'No. Papu — my grandad — will be here soon. He's been wonderful to me.'

'Is that your dad's father?'

'Yeah. Papu's my dad now, really. He stepped in for Dad at my wedding and everything. He's been amazing.' She waved towards the baking. 'That's why I've made his favourite pastries, flaounes. He loves them with black coffee. I don't drink coffee, it stains your teeth. You've got nice teeth, ever so even. Have you had work done on them?'

'Just the usual check-ups and the odd filling.'

'Lucky! I had to have a tooth removed at the back, to make room. I cried my eyes out afterwards but Pearce was lovely, he brought me ice packs and soothing lavender oil and said I was his wounded Lilypad.'

Siv wanted to gag. Lily was adjusting her hair, running her fingers through it and then tying it back in its clip. She got up to check it in the mirror and ran a little finger along her bottom lip. Siv watched her. *What a spoiled brat.* She had no qualms about leaving Lily, who seemed to be recovering quickly from the news about her mother. 'We'll need to talk to your husband. Tell him one of my team will be in touch.'

'Okay, but give him some notice. He's very busy, workwise.'

As Siv opened her car, she saw a tall, elderly man approach the house and wave to Lily, who was standing in the doorway. He walked up the path carrying a bouquet of flowers wrapped with an orange bow. He wore a black suit with a waistcoat on his slim frame and polished black brogues, an elegant crow. He peered down at Lily, head to one side.

'Lilies for my Lily,' she heard him say, flourishing the bouquet, before they vanished inside.

* * *

Ali had pinned a photo of Lyn Dimas to the top of the incident board, and written the names of people in her network on there. Lyn was smiling, her long hair carefully waved and arranged, her make-up flattering. She was slim and fit, with a hopeful expression, as if the future promised good things. The photo had been taken on her forty-second birthday, the year before her marriage had imploded and then, as if to add insult to injury, she had been murdered. Siv had often considered the fact that some people had one bad stroke of luck, and then all kinds of misfortune were aimed their way, as if they kept hitting the jackpot in some cosmic calamity game. In the photo, Lyn could have been in her mid-thirties and the resemblance to Lily was striking. The likeness could have caused either a close bond or friction, and from listening to less-than-devoted Lily, she'd gathered it had been the latter.

Ali and Patrick joined her in front of the board. She'd brought in coffees from Gusto and Patrick was adding chocolate powder to the top of his. Ali talked them through the highlights of the previous investigation.

'There was no evidence to show where Lyn Dimas went when she walked out of her house. No one saw her in the surrounding streets and there's no CCTV around that residential area. There's also none around Orford End. Steiner's had a security camera for a while, but it broke down and it was never replaced. Main interviews were with the husband and his partner, Monty Barnwell; the kids, Lily and Adam; Joe Dimas, grandfather; Pearce Aston, Lily's boyfriend; Trudy Kemp, Lyn's sister; Jeff Downey, the next-door neighbour; and Antonia Santos, Lyn's colleague at the Brookridge clinic. A lot of people said that Lyn had been down because of her marriage break-up. She'd had a bit of time off work after her husband left, and she'd been on antidepressants for a couple of months. Theo Dimas and Trudy Kemp said that Lyn hadn't been too keen on Jeff Downey. She'd told her sister that Downey had tried it on with her earlier that summer, bringing flowers and chocolates around, but he'd backed off when she rebuffed him. He was a suspect.'

Siv perked up. 'So what was his alibi?'

'He said he was at home all evening. He'd started a barbecue for his daughter and her young kids, but she had car trouble and had to ring him and cancel. That was at twenty to eight.' Ali checked his notes. 'Downey was out on the pavement with the neighbours at around seven fifteen, when the limousine arrived to pick up Lily and her friends for the prom. He was in when Adam went to him around nine to say he was worried about his mum. We checked out his car and his home, but there were no forensics identifying Lyn's presence.'

'But he was alone for about an hour and a half. Did the daughter phone him on his landline or mobile?'

'Landline. So, no one could vouch for him for eighty minutes. He didn't make any calls during that time, and he didn't take a taxi anywhere. None of the neighbours could say whether or not he'd gone out. But he could have gone to Orford End and back.'

Siv tapped a finger. 'But why would Lyn have gone there with him? She didn't like him much. Patrick, what other information do we have about the family?'

Patrick licked chocolate from his lip. 'It was full-on dysfunctional. Lyn had been telling anyone who'd listen what a shit Theo was. Lily was nasty about her dad and cut off all contact with him after Lyn went missing. She kept saying her mum must have killed herself. The grandfather, Joe, sided with Lyn and Lily after Theo left. Seems to have been shocked and disgusted by his son's sexuality. He's old-school Greek Cypriot and deeply religious. Pearce Aston is homophobe central. Poor old Adam drifted around amid all of it. Antonia Santos said that Lyn had been worried about Lily, because she was talking about getting married to Aston. She met him when he did some work in her school. Lyn's view was that she was too young and there were rows.'

Siv finished her coffee. 'A bit off, a man in his twenties hitting on a schoolgirl, but she was eighteen and it was only a couple of months before she left.'

'Still cradle snatching in my book,' Ali said.

'Water under the bridge now,' Siv told him. She didn't want them getting bogged down in too much history. 'I can report that Lily still comes across as a shallow young woman. The family was deeply troubled that year. Where you have that kind of trouble, you can have motive. Were there any indications that Lyn had sought comfort in any other relationships or dating?'

'No sign and no one knew of any men she'd been seeing,' Ali said.

Siv said, 'When I spoke to Lily, she was referring to the notion of suicide and the final notes I've read on the record indicate that the SIO ended up deciding that was a possibility — either that, or Lyn had decided to run away. Lily didn't mention that she'd had any rows with her mother, although she indicated that her mum had annoyed her by wanting to be in on her social life a bit too much. Okay, we talk to everyone again and ask for their whereabouts on the evening of the twenty-eighth of July, from 7 p.m. onwards. The previous investigation must have missed something. We now have the context of Steiner's, so we need to check out anyone having a connection to that premises.'

'What if it was a random murder?' Patrick asked. 'That could be needle-in-haystack stuff.'

Siv gave him a frosty smile. He seemed to have decided to take the role of devil's advocate, which could be useful, but not in this case. 'The lone opportunist? Could be, although not likely. So, Patrick, I want you to trawl the databases to see if you can find any similar crimes. Women strangled, tied up and left in disused buildings. But I don't see this as random. This was a middle-class woman on suburban streets. Either she lied to her young son about where she was going and she was aiming for Orford End, in which case we need to find out why, or she was abducted while it was still daylight. How did that happen without anyone noticing or hearing her scream? Why would she willingly get into a car unless she knew the driver? And how did she end up in that dump, Steiner's?' She stood and added 'Maria Steiner' to the board and numbered the names. 'Maria Steiner was aware that the premises was empty so we need to check her, see if she had any connection to Lyn. We take the names in numbered order, where possible. Patrick, you see Trudy Kemp. Ali, you talk to Monty Barnwell and I want you to visit Lewis Haddon with me. We need a full list of his staff.'

Ali pointed to number five. 'What about Jeff Downey, given that he was a nuisance with no alibi?'

'He can stew for now. I'm organising a press release so he'll find out we've found Lyn. If he did kill her, he can wonder when we're going to knock on his door again. And Patrick, can you tweet about Lyn and ask if anyone remembers anything about that night?'

'Who else are you going to speak to?' Ali asked.

'Adam Dimas. He didn't give much information at the time — he was only nine and deeply upset when he was questioned. But he was the last person, other than her killer, to see his mother alive.'

CHAPTER 6

Lily had a terrible urge to bite her nails, like Adam did. Instead, she stuck her hands in her pockets and executed some tap steps on the kitchen floor. She'd been going to tap dance lessons for nearly a year. Papu had bought them as a Christmas present. He'd been a keen footballer in his youth and said she had his control and balance. It was a great way to keep fit and Pearce liked watching her demonstrate to him, said it was sexy.

She thought about her girls as she tapped. She'd always had pole position in the Damsels. After all, she'd named the group after they'd been studying damselflies in biology. She'd kept her position even after her dad had gone weird and got a boyfriend. She'd worried about losing face over that, but it had worked in her favour, causing a lot of gratifying excitement and curiosity. Her place as top dog was just the way things were, and now what had happened to her mum would enhance her status once more. She messaged the Damsels, telling them her tragic news. She enjoyed it, in a way, watching as the responses came back, peppered with hearts and sad face emojis.

OMG hun, no way, that's such a shock!
I can't believe it, that's way too awful.

Babes, it's so terrible for you. We're all here for you.

You poor thing and how awful for your family. RIP your mum, she was a lovely lady.

That last response from Izzie was the least satisfactory, lacking the required drama, but then Izzie had never really fitted in the Damsels, being a bit too earnest. She was tolerated because her dad had committed suicide when she was little and the Damsels relished showing her sympathy.

Lily tippity-tapped over to the kitchen mirror and gazed at herself. She checked her appearance several times an hour, minimum, including her teeth. She needed to verify what other people were seeing. She'd once been mortified to realise that she'd gone around all afternoon with a shred of lettuce stuck to a tooth. Never again. There were times when Lily suspected that she was superficial, but she brushed the idea away as efficiently as she swept her mascara along her lashes. She undid her clip and lifted her long hair at the back, watching it ripple. Her eyes were dry and clear. She'd been upset to hear about her mum, but not overwhelmed. Life had moved on. As Papu had said, at least now people would stop skirting around the subject and it could all be laid to rest. She and Papu were so alike, no crying over spilled milk for them.

She applied fresh lip gloss, remembering the way her mum used to want to check out the new cosmetics that she and her friends were buying, asking about colours and styles. It would get so awkward, the way she muscled in on Lily's life, wanting to go 'girlie shopping,' wearing clothes that were too young for her and putting her oar in about Pearce. Lily sighed. It was so unfair, having two embarrassing parents — a dad who'd dumped his family because he preferred men, and an interfering mother who'd vanished and managed to get herself strangled. Her friends had normal parents who stayed in the background, had hobbies and pottered around garden centres or did voluntary work. That's why she adored Papu so much for being a stable, model grandad — it was a shame about the religious stuff but he didn't flaunt it in public. She'd been worried that he might start spouting prayers at her wedding but he'd been perfect — stylish, mannerly and staying in the background during the reception.

She heard Pearce's key in the door and went to greet him.

'I cancelled the restaurant and I've brought pizzas. Reckoned you could do with your favourite after the news you've had,' he said, balancing the cardboard boxes.

In the kitchen, he drew her into a close hug. 'My poor Lilypad, how awful for you. You should have called me as soon as the police arrived. I wish I could have come home earlier.'

She shut her eyes, sinking into him. He smelled of the Armani aftershave she bought him. 'You had a busy day, I didn't want to interrupt you, that's why I texted. And Papu came round.'

'Are you okay?'

'Sort of. It's so horrible. I can't really take it in.' She made her voice small, injecting more sadness than she felt.

'Poor baby. But at least you don't have to worry anymore.'

'Yeah.' Although she'd rather not have had that peaceful, woodland image replaced by the picture of her mother with cord around her neck, stuffed behind a fridge in a deserted building.

Pearce straightened and stroked her hair back. 'D'you mind if we eat? I'm starving.'

She fetched two beers from the fridge. She watched Pearce tear at his pizza. It was the only thing she found off-putting about him, the way he always attacked his food as if he hadn't eaten for months. Otherwise, she was infatuated with him. The sight of him made her blood beat. It had since the day she first saw him, when he'd come to upgrade the school computers. He was so beautiful, tall and slim, like a film-star. She liked the way he drew women's glances, and then how they envied her. Sometimes, she'd presumed that was why Mum had had a problem with him, and had kicked up such a fuss about her determination to marry him. Mum had been jealous, because she didn't have a man and her daughter had bagged such a fit, gorgeous one. Lily had shouted that at her one evening when they had been rowing, and her mum had slapped her across the face. Lily had slapped her back, and then Adam had come downstairs with tears in his eyes, asking why they were so angry. She picked at her pizza, eating just the olives.

Pearce drank his beer. 'Where did you say they found your mum?'

'A disused place called Steiner's. It's an old removals firm in Orford End, by the station.'

'Orford End? Isn't that where they're building new houses?'

'That's what the inspector said. The men who went to clear it found her. Why, have you been there?'

'No, I just read about the development somewhere. What would your mum have been doing in a place like that?'

'No idea.'

He ripped a piece of crust and folded it over. 'In my opinion, they'll have trouble finding whoever did it after all this time. Evidence will have deteriorated or it'll be unreliable. Has your dad tried to get in touch?'

'No. The inspector saw him earlier today. Do you think he will?'

'Probably. Be careful, Lilypad. He might try to use this as a way of getting back into your life.'

'No way. I'll have to see him though, won't I?'

'How do you mean?'

'Mum's funeral. I can't stand the idea of Monty being there. He'll be gloating, won't he, because her disappearance left plenty of room for him. He didn't have to worry about the ex anymore. A bit like Princess Di dying and then Camilla stepping up.'

'Oh, right.' He put a hand out and took hers. 'Well, in my opinion, you've every right to insist that Monty shouldn't go to the funeral. He's not family.'

She wasn't really listening. She was casting her mind back to that prom night — the excitement, the limo, the warm crush outside the school hall, and then waiting by the door for Pearce without letting on to any of the others that she was anxious. Luckily, they'd been too high on the buzz to notice his absence or her discomfort. She'd started to feel like an ugly stepsister instead of Cinderella at the ball, and eventually she'd gone inside, avoided the Damsels and hovered near the door, talking to some girls she barely recognised. Then Pearce had appeared in front of her, in his tailored blue sharkskin suit and she'd forgotten her worries.

She put a hand on his now. He'd finished his meal and was checking his phone. She'd accepted what he'd said about being delayed at work that night, because he'd been so attentive and amazing once he was there, and she'd never mentioned it to anyone else. When it had all kicked off about her mum, he'd suggested that it would be best to tell the police that he'd arrived at seven forty-five, because it would just keep things straightforward and she'd gone along with him.

Now and again, a tiny worry flickered, and she'd wonder why he'd been keen to cover the fact that he'd been late. But she soon damped it down. Pearce was the best thing that had ever happened to her and nothing was going to get in the way of them staying together.

* × *

Adam Dimas had made Siv an amazingly weak cup of tea. He was drinking from a bottle of something fizzy and cherry-flavoured and eating bacon-flavoured crisps. They sat in the L-shaped kitchen. Theo Dimas was upstairs. He'd said that Adam was happy to see her on his own but to call him if needed. Siv was relieved, because parents often acted as a brake on their children talking.

Adam wore his school uniform. She was a little surprised that he'd gone back in so soon after hearing that his mother's body had been found.

'I went to Newton High too,' Siv told him. 'I see they haven't changed the uniform.'

'Right.'

She'd liked school, unlike Rik, who had regularly bunked off. Siv had found the structure and rules reassuring, and she'd liked getting high grades. She had immersed herself in maths and sciences — you were on safe ground with the immutable laws of physics. When she went to Newton High, it was the first time she'd worn a proper uniform. She'd bought the full kit with her father in town. During the Mutsi years, she'd attended so many schools, there had been little time to acquire the right outfits. She and Rik had been sent home numerous times because of missing items. Mutsi was never in so they had been left to get up to their usual mischief — roaming the streets, climbing on roofs, hanging out in arcades and shopping malls. When Mutsi arrived home and they told her, she'd say, *We never had school uniform in Finland and my education was excellent. What is all the fuss about? I suppose it's the usual British obsession with conformity. This gives me such a terrible headache!* So, all about her as usual.

Adam was a stocky, shy boy, clearly destined to be as bulky as his father when he matured. He had unhealthy skin the colour of lard. His dark hair was floppy on top and shaved at the back of the neck and above his ears. The style didn't do him any favours, but then who was she to talk, with her bald patches strategically covered by careful layers? Grief had brought strange visitors to her life, including alopecia.

'I'm very sorry about your mum,' she told him.

'Thanks. Yeah, crap.' He picked at the label on his bottle.

'Do you remember much about that time?'

He shrugged. 'Bits. Sometimes.'

He was a mouth-breather, which gave him a gormless appearance, and now and again he sniffed and swallowed. Somebody needed to coach him in keeping his mouth closed, at least in public.

'I wanted to see you because you were a little boy back then, and it can't have been easy, talking to the police when you were so worried about your mum.'

'Seems ages ago. I told them about that night. I didn't like the guy who spoke to me. Castles, his name was. He was in everyone's face, throwing his weight around.'

She was quietly satisfied at hearing this negative comment about Tommy Castles. 'Well, it's my team working on this now. We want to find whoever did this to your mum. It won't be easy because of the years that have gone by, but we'll give it our best shot. It would really help if you could tell me about the time around your mum's disappearance.'

He slouched down in his chair. 'Not sure what you want me to say.'

'Your dad had come out and he'd moved in with Monty. Your mum must have been very unhappy.'

'Yeah. She was different. Snappy, a bit out of it. Dinners got burned or we just had eggs on toast or takeaways. She used to cry in the bathroom. My bedroom's next to it so . . .'

'You'd hear her?'

He filled his mouth with crisps and ripped a strip of label. Sadness was leaking from him — Siv could see it in the heaviness of his limbs. It was a marked contrast to his sister's reaction. She studied her acorn-coloured tea with its oily film and nudged it away.

'So you must have been upset.'

'It was all a bit shit.'

'And you were worried about your dad.'

He gulped from the bottle. 'I heard Mum on the phone, telling someone he had AIDS. I didn't know what that was so I googled it. I got really frightened. I worried I might never see him again.' He pushed his hair back. His brows were like dark caterpillars. 'Funny — I fretted that Dad might die before I'd see him again, but it turned out to be Mum who was taken from me.'

He blushed and squirmed in his seat. Whatever confusion and grief Lyn had been going through, she should have considered the impact that such a terrible allegation would have had on her children. Siv wondered if Adam had been angry with his mother for spreading vile rumours, and if he was still. She would be, in his shoes. But then she knew herself to be unforgiving about that kind of malice. Unforgiving in general, if she'd been wronged. Adam was chewing the side of his thumb. Time to take the spotlight from him.

'What about Lily? How was she during those months after your dad left?'

'I'm not sure. She was doing A levels and she spent a lot of time with Pearce. She and Mum had terrible rows.'

'What about?'

'Pearce, mainly. Lily met him soon after Dad left, and they'd decided to get married. Mum didn't approve, because Lily said she wasn't going to uni. She'd got accepted at Brighton. I remember Mum saying that Lily was too young and it was all happening too quickly. Lily was wasting her talents and throwing away her education, that sort of stuff. She said she didn't want Pearce in the house. She went ballistic once when she came home and found him here.'

'How did you get on with Pearce back then?'

'Me? Dunno, really. He was okay, I s'pose. I didn't talk to him much.'

'How did Pearce react when your mum came home and got angry?'

He glanced away. 'I don't like talking about this. Doesn't seem right. I mean, I can't speak for other people and it seems a long time ago.'

She was unsure if the discomfort was about Pearce or a mixture of shock and shyness. She reached for a large pad of lined paper on the table, tore a page out, smoothed it and started to fold creases. Adam watched, his chin cupped in his hand as she made four squash and petal folds, pressed edges together, creased two legs and executed reverse folds. There was silence in the room. She stretched the back legs she had formed and paused. 'Recognise it?'

'A frog?'

'Right. Now watch.' She blew into the slit at the base to inflate the frog's body, and then pressed her finger on the base to make it hop across the table. It was a tad childish but then Adam seemed young for his age and it was just a way of easing the atmosphere.

Adam grinned. 'Cool. How did you learn to do that?'

'I took up origami years ago. It keeps me sane, because I can lose myself in it. Cheaper than seeing a shrink and I have something beautiful at the end of the process. The frog's dead simple — it was one of the first things I learned. I make my own designs now, and I do commissions sometimes.'

'So why are you a detective? Origami must be way more interesting.'

'I like the discipline of an investigation and the process of finding solutions. It's very satisfying. Must be my mathematical brain, and I suppose it's a bit like origami in that you have to see patterns and make sure pieces are in the right place. Adam, when we're trying to find a murderer we have to ask difficult questions. Embarrassing ones, sometimes. Nothing's off limits and we intrude on people's privacy.'

'I get that. It's just . . . everything was so horrible for so long and now it's no way ideal, but sort of like . . . a negotiated truce.'

'But hostilities could break out at any time?'

'Something like that. I don't want to cause trouble for Lily.'

'I understand that. Unfortunately, causing trouble is exactly what I have to do sometimes, and whoever strangled your mum and deprived you of her deserves all the trouble that comes their way.'

He jumped the frog across the table. 'S'pose.'

'Tell you what, I'll make you any shape you ask for now, and you just tell me whatever you can about the situation with Lily and Pearce.'

He hummed. 'A helicopter. I was supposed to go up in one with Dad for a charity jump next week, but he cancelled it after we heard about Mum.'

'Okay, I'll need scissors to make that.' She tore another piece of paper while he fetched them, and then she cut an oblong and started folding.

Adam went back to picking at the label. 'Pearce was okay with Mum that time she was shouting at him and Lily. He stayed calm, said he didn't want to cause trouble and he wouldn't come round again. I remember him saying to Lily that Mum had a lot on her plate, and it was best to back off. He had his own flat so, after that, Lily would just go there. She stayed over sometimes, and then Mum would blow up at her. She went round there once and caused a fuss. Own goals. It just made Lily more determined.'

'Must have been tough for you, all of that.'

'Yeah. Mum would get all emotional over Lily after a row and try to make up with her, but Lily wouldn't have it. Then Lily would go mental when she saw some of the stuff Mum put on Facebook — photos of her and Lily together, saying that people mistook them for sisters. Pathetic, really. Mum was funny in the head because of . . . everything.'

Siv stopped folding. 'Understandable.'

'Yeah. She'd buy a load of new clothes and make-up and stuff. She'd try it all on when she came home, and ask Lily and me for our opinion. Lily usually said something catty.'

'Was your mum dating at all?'

He watched her fingers and then shook his head. 'I don't remember anything like that.'

'Did you — do you like Jeff Downey?'

Adam smiled broadly for the first time. 'Yeah, because he does great barbecues. Dad always calls him a scrounger, because he borrows things and keeps them for ages. He bought Mum flowers once after Dad left, and when he'd gone she put them in the bin. She said some men eyed any woman on her own as fair game.'

'Jeff's still next door?'

'Yeah. He still asks to borrow stuff.'

'There.' Siv launched the helicopter and they watched it spin downwards. 'I believe there's a stand-off between Lily, your grandad and your dad. That sounds complicated.'

He blushed again, picked up the helicopter and fiddled with it. 'I try to stay out of it. I don't see Papu much, or Lily.

Papu's a narrow-minded bigot, always has been, and Lily just believes whatever Pearce tells her. She's always been Papu's favourite. Mum used to say that he idolised her, spoiled her, and it was because she looks like Yaya, my dead grandmother. He's always buying her presents. If she ever told him she wanted something, he got it for her. I once heard Dad ask him not to buy Lily so many things, because it wasn't good for her and it wasn't fair on me. Papu said he was a grandad, he could be indulgent if he liked, and he just ignored Dad and carried on. If anything, the presents got more extravagant — riding lessons, expensive vouchers, a TV for her room.'

Adam didn't sound grudging. Perhaps that was because of the age difference between the siblings. By the time he'd arrived, Papu's gifts to Lily would have been well established. Siv wondered why Lily's parents hadn't been more forceful about the grandfather's behaviour. Maybe Theo had been frightened of his father and unable to stand up to him. That would explain a lot about the family dynamics. 'Sounds like your grandad's a law unto himself.'

'Yeah. So's Lily.' He yawned. 'To be honest, I'd rather not talk about that crap. I'm sorry for my dad. I'm just trying to get on with my own life.'

'Going back to that night when your mum disappeared — have you remembered anything you didn't at the time? Sometimes a shock like that freezes you, and stuff comes back afterwards.'

He drew the frog to him and cradled it in his hands, focusing on it. A row of five bonsai trees stood in pots on a window ledge by the back door. They were clipped and trained into different shapes, some with wire supporting them. Siv had never liked bonsais and found the stunted, twisted forms disturbing, tortured. She recognised a dark green yew in the centre. The branches had been trimmed to a triangular silhouette above peeling bark. She frowned, uneasy, and turned back to Adam.

He rubbed at the creased skin between his bushy brows. 'It was a weird kind of day, because Lily was here with her friends getting ready for the prom. Mum was as wired as Lily about it. She kept hovering around the girls, getting in their way. Lily snapped at her a couple of times. The house was strange, everything on edge and out of place. I didn't like it much. I suppose I felt a bit ignored.' He had a faraway expression, as if he was back in that afternoon.

'I was relieved when Lily and the others left. We were outside and Jeff asked if we wanted to go round for his bar-becue. I was hoping Mum would agree, because I was hungry and it smelled good. She said no, because she'd prepared something for dinner.' He stopped, did some mouth-breath-ing. 'She hadn't, though. That was a fib, because she hadn't been cooking. She made me a sandwich and said she had to nip to the shop. I was watching *Toy Story*. When it finished and she hadn't come back, I got scared so I went and told Jeff. He drove me to Smart Mart but they hadn't seen Mum. It started to pour and I was worried that Mum must be get-ting soaked.' He made a vague gesture. 'Then Dad arrived.'

'Did anyone else call round that day or phone your mum?'

'I don't really remember. I try to keep a kind of photo in my mind of that last time I saw her. When she put her head around the door to say she wouldn't be long, she'd brushed her hair out from the ponytail she'd had it in all day, and she'd used hair mousse.'

These small details that might mean something or noth-ing. 'How would your mum usually have worn her hair to go to Smart Mart?'

'Tied back, out of the way.'

'But she hadn't changed her clothes.'

'No. She was wearing a yellow dress. It was new, from Next. When she tried it on upstairs, she made this comment . . . that if Dad saw her in it, he'd regret what he was missing. She just didn't seem to get it, Dad being gay. I wonder if she hoped he might change his mind. Mental.'

'I suppose she was struggling and trying to boost her confidence.' Siv had kept an important topic until last. 'How about Monty, how do you get on with him?'

Adam grew still and his expression tightened. 'Okay, I s'pose.'

She was picking at scars. It was the part of her job she liked least, but it had to be done. 'It must have been strange when he moved in here — after everything that had happened.'

'Yeah, it was.'

She got the impression he was holding something back. 'I understand that Monty and your dad were at home together the night your mum went missing.'

'Yeah. Watching telly, Dad said.' He rose and gestured at a pile of textbooks. 'I've got homework to do now.'

'Okay, thanks for the talk.' She passed one of her cards to him. 'If you recall anything else, get in touch. What charity were you going to jump for?'

'Cancer Research.'

He spun the helicopter over the table, distracted by it. He seemed so immature. Siv went into the hall and called to Theo Dimas. He came down with a weary tread, carrying a laundry basket.

'Everything okay?' he asked.

'Yes, thanks. How are you?'

'Oh, well . . . I contacted a funeral home today. They were helpful. I wasn't sure that Adam should go to school but he insisted and maybe it was better for him to have the distraction . . .'

'That works best for some people.'

'Do you want to talk to me now?'

'No, that can wait. I'll be in touch. Although, what's your opinion of Mr Downey next door?'

He ran a hand through his hair. 'He's a nerd. I've always assumed he must be deeply insecure because he puts on all that bravura. He's forever borrowing stuff and forgetting to return it. Monty calls it middle-class theft.'

'What did Lyn make of him?'

'She said he was a bit coarse at times, saying off-colour things in front of the kids. We used to dread being invited to his barbecues and having to listen to his heavy attempts at humour.'

She pointed through the doorway, at the sketch of Dimas. 'Who's the artist?'

'My father. Obviously, that was done when he still regarded me as his son, before he decided I was beyond the pale.'

'How did you and Lyn get on with your father?'

He took a breath. 'She had a better relationship with him than me. He prefers women to men in general, although there are exceptions, such as the "properly masculine" Pearce. I've never ticked the right boxes for my dad, even before I was sent into exile as a pervert.'

CHAPTER 7

Ali sat at a table by the kitchen in Nutmeg, the restaurant where his wife was the chef. He made his way through the plate of lemon chicken she'd given him. At the diabetes clinic, they'd told him to eat slowly and savour every mouthful, but he couldn't. When you'd grown up as the youngest of five brothers, you learned to eat fast so that you could get seconds, and your plate had to be cleared before seconds or pudding. He shovelled the food down, licking the fork with relish.

Ali didn't like his own company and got fretful if he went for an hour without talking to anyone. If Polly was on an evening shift and he was home alone, he'd be watching TV while flicking through his phone or, more often than not, ringing one of his family in Derry. Three of his brothers still lived on the family farm, two with their families in houses they'd built on land their parents had given them. When he phoned, he could easily while away the time chatting to them about the sheep and crop yields, or with his mother about her poultry and the gossip from the close-knit rural community. His parents had offered him his own piece of land to build on when he'd got engaged. He'd been based in Belfast then, in a homicide team, but Polly had been set on returning to

Sussex after her restaurant training. She'd had no intention of settling on a farm in a remote area, and told him that if he wanted to stay in the police force, there was no way she wanted him doing that in Northern Ireland, even if peace had more or less broken out.

Truth was, *he* hadn't wanted to move back to Derry. It wasn't an easy place to have his skin colour, especially as a cop. His Mauritian mother had met his father in Derry during her nurse training but had abandoned her studies when she got pregnant. He'd never got on well with his father, who was a tough, pedantic man. He still missed the easy company and chat of a big family, though. If no one was available to talk to at home, he'd spend time on Facebook, popping out to the garden for too many Gitanes, or he'd drift into Nutmeg and sit at the bar with a coffee, reading the paper while Polly bustled in the kitchen.

He and the guv were chalk and cheese. She liked her own company, he was alarmed by silence. Maybe that's why they got on well, although tonight, he was still smarting from the comment she'd made in the car about him craving sweet things. He'd told Polly, who was watching him eat on her break. She did fuss over him but he liked it, really. He didn't understand why she was so besotted with him, though, when he was such a pain with his smoking and his penchant for fattening foods. He was chaotic if left to his own devices. He needed Polly and her unflagging efforts to keep him on the dietary straight and narrow.

'It's not like you to take a daft comment like that to heart,' Polly said. 'I'm sure Siv didn't mean anything by it. She's a plain talker, but I've never heard her being snide.'

'Hmm, well . . . maybe I wasn't in the mood.'

'Or maybe what she said hit home,' Polly said. She pointed at her husband's tubby middle. 'Sometimes, the truth hurts.'

Ali narrowed his eyes at her and changed the subject to what they'd do at the weekend, until it was time for her to get back to the kitchen. He glanced at his watch and saw that he'd better make a move. He wanted to talk to Monty Barnwell on his own, and had agreed to meet him when he came off shift at the hospital at 9 p.m.

He paused by the car to have a fag. He'd promised Polly he'd cut down, but it wasn't going so well. He lit up and sucked in deeply. Happy days!

Barnwell was waiting in the hospital café, which was quiet at this time of night. It had been revamped and was decorated with bright collages done by local schoolchildren. A group of papier mâché monkeys swinging through acid green trees bordered their table. Despite the freshly painted walls, the place had that underlying institutional whiff of boiled cabbage and cooking fat.

'I don't care much for all this,' Barnwell said, nodding at the wall, 'but I suppose it's better than the scabby landscapes that used to hang there.'

They both drank bottled water. Barnwell was tall and hefty with thick, strong forearms. Ali was pleased to see that the man had a bigger gut than he did. He had a long, sweaty nose and short upper lip, which made his face appear out of proportion.

'It must be tough at home at the moment,' Ali said.

'Indeed. We always hoped that Lyn would be found, but not like this . . .'

'Did you know her?'

'No, we'd never met until she came to the hospital one day and confronted me. It will be in the interviews from 2013.'

Ali had read about it. It had been combustible. 'Talk me through what happened.'

Barnwell yawned and pinched the end of his nose. 'Sorry — that was a long, busy shift and an agency nurse didn't turn up.' He sighed. 'It was about three weeks after Theo moved in with me. Lyn found out where I worked, and she came steaming into the unit asking for me. Then she threw a wobbly in front of everyone, called me a home-breaker and a degenerate.'

'That must have made you angry.'

'Up to a point, although I laughed when she said "degenerate" because it was so ridiculous, and that made her madder. The worst bit was when she yelled that I had AIDS. She was telling people that about Theo, too. That was very upsetting. I couldn't get a word in, and I could see that if I did try to say anything, I'd only provoke her more. In the end, one of the doctors pointed out to her that there were very ill patients nearby, and she was causing them distress. He managed to persuade her to step outside.'

The accusation might well give anyone enough of a motive for murder. 'What happened afterwards?'

'I had to talk to hospital managers. They accepted that what had occurred wasn't my responsibility. It was a tough time, though. Most of my colleagues were okay, but there was a chill in the air with some. Even in the health service, where people should be better informed, you still get prejudice about HIV.'

'Did Theo hear about the incident?'

'Oh, yes. I told him that night. He's at a private hospital, but the health community is a gossip web. Word got round so his colleagues were discussing it too. Sometimes I'm not sure how we got through it, but we did. Probably because we're devoted to each other.'

'Did you ever see Lyn again?'

'No, and I didn't want to. That one time was enough.' Barnwell had a habit of twisting his neck, as if scanning the area. He did it again now, flexing his heavy shoulders and giving another huge yawn.

Ali was a bit sleepy himself, full as he was of lemon chicken. It was warm in the café, that dry, intense hospital heat. He took a drink of water. 'You seem very pragmatic about what happened.'

Barnwell straightened up. 'The cops at the time said something like that, as if they were implying that my calmness was a front. I'll tell you what I told them. When you're gay, you're used to having shit shovelled in your direction, and you can never tell where it might come from. You have to pick your battles, or you'd spend your life exhausted. What Lyn did to me and Theo was nasty and cruel, but I understood that she was suffering and lashing out. We accepted it was going to be hard for a while and that there'd be family fallout. The AIDS accusation wounded us both, but there was nothing we could do except get on with our lives. And that's what we did. We believed that eventually, Lyn would run out of steam and get on with hers.'

Except she didn't. She was removed from her life and, handily, Theo and Monty had a comfortable wee home to share, and Theo reclaimed one of his children. 'Was there fallout in your own family?'

Barnwell frowned. 'What's that got to do with Lyn's death?'

'No idea. Just getting a picture.'

'My family are in London. I told them I was gay when I was sixteen. They were happy for me when I met Theo.'

'How did you meet?'

'We both attended a conference here at the hospital. We got chatting on a coffee break and it developed from there. It was so good to meet and fall in love with someone without having to go online or hang around in bars. We were seeing each other for almost two years before Theo was ready to tell Lyn. I hated the skulking around, but I understood that he was worried about how it would affect his children. In the end, I believe that Lyn caused the children more damage with her reaction than Theo did by leaving.'

'It seems that your relationship stood no chance of acceptance by Lily, Pearce and her grandfather.'

'That's right.'

'How do you manage their hostility?'

'I don't. I don't need to. They're homophobic and it's their problem, so I leave it with them. I don't see them.'

Barnwell spoke calmly, but Ali could tell he was agitated. He was turning away again, his eyes scanning the café.

'What about Theo and Adam — how do they cope with the family hostility?'

Barnwell clasped his hands on the table. 'You're being intrusive now. I don't see what current family relationships have to do with an investigation into a murder that happened six years ago. If you want to hear Theo and Adam's opinions, ask them.'

Ali decided to let that go for now. The guv reckoned it was best to just let things roll sometimes. There was a bead of sweat trickling down Barnwell's nose. Was it the heat in the café, or nerves? 'Talk me through the night that Lyn went missing. How did you find out?'

'I was at home in my flat with Theo. We'd been in together all evening, from 6 p.m. It was Lily's prom night, a big occasion for her. I could see how much Theo wanted to call her and wish her well, but of course, he couldn't. He talked about driving to the school, just to watch her going in, but I told him it wouldn't be a good idea. It was her night and if he turned up, she'd see it as an intrusion.' He cleared his throat. 'We were watching football and Theo's phone rang. It was Jeff Downey, telling him Lyn hadn't come home and wasn't answering her phone. Theo headed straight round to the house to be with Adam and try to find out where Lyn was.'

'What did you do?'

'I stayed at home and waited for Theo to call. I wanted to help but, given the situation, my presence at the house wouldn't have gone down too well. Theo rang me around three the next morning to say that the police were investigating, and that he'd have to stay at the house. I took some of his clothes and stuff there the next evening, once Adam was in bed and Lily had gone to Pearce's.' He rubbed his eyes. 'I've said all of this before. Can we leave it there for now? I'm dog-tired and I'd like to get home to Theo and Adam. We need to be together at a time like this.'

Ali watched him walk away. He stopped to speak to a colleague who was on her way in. There were more people in the café now, staff who'd come off shift or on a break. They sat wearily at tables, drooping over snacks, checking phones.

Ali went up to the counter, bought a slice of key lime pie and took it back to the table. The meringue was soft and wobbly, just as it should be. He eyed the clambering monkeys as he tucked in, recalling the proverb his gran was keen on, *Hear no evil, see no evil, speak no evil.* All well and good, but Barnwell had presented an unusually reasonable and understanding front when it came to Lyn's damaging personal attacks.

* * *

Monty Barnwell didn't leave the hospital immediately. He took the lift to an orthopaedic ward on the second floor, and found Justin Desmond in his tiny office near the nurses' station, staring at a computer screen and entering figures on a spreadsheet.

'How did it go?' Justin sounded anxious.

'Fine. All the questions I expected, pretty much the same as last time. Just sit tight, Justin. No need to worry.'

'It's hard, after six years.'

'It's hard for all of us.' *This is all much bloody harder than I ever bargained for.*

'I haven't been sleeping since you told me. I fooled myself that I'd been able to put the past behind me. I can't concentrate here.'

'Just try to focus. We'd better cancel dinner on Saturday night, given the circumstances. We all need breathing space.'

There was silence as they both considered the circumstances, past and present. The past was barging back, like an unwanted guest. Monty recalled the panic and fear in Justin's eyes that July night. His pulse had been racing when Monty had placed his fingers on his wrist.

'Sure, okay.' Justin said thickly. 'How's Theo coping?'

'He's distracted. There's a lot to absorb.'

'And Adam?'

'He's not saying much. Trying to take it in. Eating for England.'

'Well, if there's anything . . .'

'I'll keep you posted. How are things with Scott?'

Justin pulled a face. 'He keeps contacting me. It's like stalking. I'm not responding, but he's not going away. I've managed to avoid him around the hospital, but I keep expecting to see him on the ward.'

'Give it time. Hopefully he'll get fed up. He's always been high maintenance and clingy, which is why you wanted out.'

It started raining as Monty drove home, fat drops smearing the greasy windscreen. He hoped that Adam would be in bed when he got back, so that he and Theo could have some time together. They hardly ever did, unless they went out. He couldn't warm to Adam, especially as the boy was always *there*. When Monty was a teenager, he'd always been busy, hanging out with mates, messing about in youth clubs and getting home late. Adam was a homebird, forever squatting in the nest, with no instinct to spread his wings. He had no interests and apparently no friends. Once he came home from school, he was in for the night, sitting in the living room or sometimes the kitchen, snacking constantly and always gravitating to where there was company. Weren't teenagers supposed to spend hours ignoring their parents and hibernating in their bedrooms? Not Adam, whose ample backside had worn a dent in the sofa. It was as if he was stuck in that evening when his mother vanished, glued to the same spot on the cushion with a sandwich and watching TV, waiting for her key in the door. It was sad but it was also bloody exasperating.

Monty would have liked to sell the house and refresh their lives. He and Theo could afford something bigger and detached, and it would benefit them all to be under a roof where there were no lingering memories of Lyn. They needed a clean start, maybe even in another town or one of the pretty villages nearby. But whenever he raised the subject, Theo demurred, saying that Adam needed stability and moving would disrupt his life and schooling. Theo didn't want to cause him any upset, or risk the chance that the upheaval would damage his son's frail emotional state. Monty had to bite his tongue. He longed to say that Adam didn't have any life to disrupt.

Adam. Everything came back to Adam.

Monty was sorry for the boy, but it was as if Adam had decided to make mourning his mother's loss into a career. A dull rage came over him whenever he walked in and saw Adam's lethargic, lolling shape. It was baffling how Theo had ever expected that his son would summon the energy to jump out of a helicopter. Theo worried about Adam's lack of friends, but he indulged him and never pushed him to socialise. Monty understood that a lot of this was down to Theo's guilt about leaving the family, and of course, he was always trying to compensate for the deep chasm caused by Lyn's absence.

Monty switched the fan on to clear condensation on the windscreen. Bloody Lyn. She'd been a pain in the arse when she was alive, and she'd been a constant source of anxiety for the last six years, like a low-grade headache that wouldn't shift. Now she was causing even more turmoil, bringing the police back into their lives. So far, the sergeant had covered the same territory but there might be new questions next time.

When he let himself into the house, he could hear Theo and Adam talking over the TV in the living room. He sighed, hung his coat up and went through. Adam was sitting next to his dad on the sofa, eating cheese on toast, his legs stretched across Theo's lap.

Theo sipped at a glass of red wine. 'Want one of these? I uncorked it a couple of hours ago.'

'In a minute.' He sat in an armchair. The cheese smelled sweaty, like the hospital canteen. 'More late-night calories, Adam? Never a good idea.'

Adam took another huge bite of toast.

'I spoke to a Sergeant Carlin earlier,' he told Theo.

Theo lifted Adam's legs down and sat forward. 'How did it go?'

'Okay. I popped in to see Justin afterwards.' He gave Theo a meaningful nod.

'That's good. Did you cancel Saturday?'

'Yep. He understood.'

There was a silence while they watched Tom Cruise abseil down a building.

Monty glanced at his watch. 'Must be time for bed, Adam.'

'Dad said I can stay up to the end of this.'

Theo ruffled his son's head fondly. Sometimes, Monty worried that Adam would never leave home, that if he could fast-forward twenty years they'd be sitting like this, a cosy threesome. He and Theo would drift into senility with a middle-aged man-child on their hands. He leaned his head back, exhausted. Next thing, Theo was nudging him awake.

'You'll get a stiff neck. Time for bed, it's half eleven. Is Justin very worried?'

'Yes, but he'll be okay as long as we support him. Grim times ahead.'

'I'm sorry. I realise that this is a lot for you to carry and I am grateful.' Theo waved his hand in a helpless gesture. 'The grim times will end.'

Monty flexed his shoulders. 'Will they? Sometimes I wonder. If I believed in malevolent spirits, I'd think that Lyn was pursuing us and making sure we can never be at peace.'

'Don't. Don't talk like that. You're tired, that's all.'

'Maybe. Theo, it would help if Adam was a bit less babyish and dependent, so that we got more time to ourselves. Sometimes, it's as if we're two childminders rather than a couple. And he really needs to change his diet and get more exercise.' He saw Theo flinch. He hadn't meant to sound so cold and cutting, but he couldn't regret saying what was on his mind.

Theo stepped back. 'Monty, he's just found out that his mum was murdered. This isn't a time to be critical or tough on him. He needs comfort and understanding.'

He's been getting that in spades for six years. 'I can't see that there's ever going to be a time when Adam is independent, the way you carry on with him, treating him as if he's still an infant. He needs to stop stuffing his face, get a grip and start doing something with his life instead of hanging around here piling on the pounds.'

There was a profound silence but Theo's turned back spoke volumes. Monty watched while he cleared away Adam's litter of crisp packets and toast crumbs and was seized by a sudden, overwhelming surge of resentment and self-pity.

CHAPTER 8

Adam was halfway down the stairs, sixth step down, perched on what he'd named the sentry step, listening. He did this often. He'd got into the habit when he'd first heard his parents rowing. He'd listened with a lurching stomach when his mother had phoned everyone she knew, informing them that Dad was diseased, when Papu had shouted at Dad that he was no longer fit to be his son, and when Lily had raved at him about how he'd destroyed their lives. He regularly monitored his father's conversations with Monty, slipping out of bed late at night. The adult world was unpredictable, treacherous and confusing. Eavesdropping gave him a sense of control. If he kept an eye on what was going on, what grown-ups were planning, he could head off any surprises. A while ago, he'd listened to Monty's urgings that they should move house, and made sure that he'd chatted to Dad subsequently about how much he loved where they lived. He'd been relieved to hear Dad standing firm when Monty had broached the subject again.

He leaned his head against the wall and huddled into his dressing gown. He heard Monty call his mum malevolent and dug his nails into his palms.

He'd been okay, living here alone with Dad after Mum vanished. At times, he'd almost felt content. Dad had been easy-going and coming home from school was like putting on comfy old slippers. Adam didn't miss his sister. She'd always hogged the limelight, and he'd been frightened of her sharp tongue and waspish comments. He was relieved that he didn't see much of her.

Then Monty had arrived, and the atmosphere had grown spiky and uncertain and Dad was somehow different, tenser. Adam had heard Monty come out with all the comments before, the criticisms and nitpicking about him, and had been relieved to hear Dad defending him. He'd see Monty giving him evils when he helped himself to more pudding, or decided to make pancakes late at night. He hated everything about the guy, and especially Monty's snarky comments from the sidelines about his appetite, weight gain and lack of social activity. He was always having a dig, especially if Dad wasn't around, his teasing voice snaking through the house: *Having another snack, Adam? Still wearing that dent in the sofa? That's unusual, you staying in tonight. How about adding some tea to all that sugar?*

Monty was the enemy and always had been. Mum had realised that too. He wanted Dad to himself, and tried hard to drive a wedge between father and son. So far, Dad had resisted but Monty was forceful and Adam worried that one day, soon, Dad might buckle and start laying down rules that would make life uncertain.

No matter how many times he'd heard the harsh words, they still upset him and brought tears to his eyes. *Babyish . . . dependent . . . stuffing his face . . .* It was as if Monty was cutting into his skin, probing deeper and deeper with his scalpel. Still, he'd be sorry for his horrible words. He had no idea of the powers being deployed against him.

Adam hoped that Chimera would be online tonight. He needed her calm wisdom and encouragement.

He crept back to his bedroom, took an empty herb jar from the back of his wardrobe and started his preparations.

He had feasted on Harry Potter's adventures for many years. He'd read the books numerous times and had seen all the films. He'd learned the spells, charms, hexes, curses, jinxes and enchantments by heart. When Papu heard of his grandson's fascination with the world of wizardry and magic, he'd told him how archaeologists had found Ancient Greek curse tablets, called *katares* in Kolossi, where the Dimas family came from. *Katares* meant 'curses that bind tight' and were often used to gain advantage in sporting competitions. The curser engraved the intended victim's name on a lead tablet, sometimes pierced it with a nail and then placed it in a grave so that the spirit world could enhance the curse. He could still hear Papu's low, thrilling voice as he described how some of the contestants in the first Olympics were terrible cheats, and would try to place hexes on their opponents. It was one of the few occasions when his grandfather had paid him any attention.

Some months after Monty had moved in and started throwing his weight and his mean comments around, Adam had been filled with a growing desire to torment him in return, repay the misery he caused and force him out of their lives. He'd turned to the Harry Potter books for help at first. He'd tried to do Slugulus Eructo, but Monty failed to vomit up slugs. None of the other incantations worked either. When Adam went for the big forbidden one, which was murder, Monty stayed annoyingly alive, despite repeated efforts.

Adam had abandoned Harry Potter magic and researched curses online. He'd found numerous blogs and websites dedicated to witchcraft, and forums where he could talk to witches. He'd had no idea that there was such a cornucopia of information about the occult out there, and spent hours absorbing its history and practices.

For some time now, he'd been chatting to Chimera, a witch in Idaho and had told her all about his mother and his troubles with Monty. Chimera had rescued him. She understood him and was in his corner. He didn't always comprehend what she said, but he wouldn't have survived without her help. He looked forward to talking to her and whenever he did, he was bathed in a glow of reassurance. He sensed that she was watching over him, and he loved the way she signed off each time with *Merry Meet Again*. She'd been wise and compassionate when he'd first explained his situation.

> Chimera: You poor dear soul. You've been through such torments in your young life. The loss of a mother is a psychic, emotional and spiritual wound and now you have this awful man tormenting you in his own special way. What is it you're seeking from the unseen universe?

> Adam: I just want Monty to go away so that Dad and me can be happy. My mum would be so upset if she knew that Monty was living with us and behaving like he does.

> Chimera: Of course she would, dearest. Your mom would protect you if she was still with you. Mothers weave powerful daily spells of their own without even realizing it.

> Adam: I've tried stuff from Harry Potter but it hasn't worked.

> Chimera: Well, you see, Adam dearest, your spells and charms from Harry Potter are amazing but they're just fiction. I don't deal in wands or potions but I can help you, if you want me to. There's no quick fix, no 'abracadabra.' Our magick doesn't work like that, it's serious and it needs time and concentration. It's taken me years to learn it and increase my powers. Sometimes you have to try different things, depending on what you want to achieve.

He'd liked the sound of serious magick and had asked her to help him. Chimera had said she'd consult her books. He pictured her as tall, with flowing white hair and a wise, ancient face, dressed in grey robes and living in a house full of centuries-old witchcraft manuals. A couple of days after their second chat, she'd suggested curse jars, advising him that it was one of the most effective ways of wishing ill on someone. She gave instructions on how to prepare an effective spell.

Adam had acquired a collection of empty jars. The one he was using tonight had once contained oregano. He took two small plastic bags from a drawer in his wardrobe. Sitting on his bed, he wrote *Monty Barnwell* on a piece of paper, and said the name three times, directing all his animosity towards it. He folded the paper into the jar, added dried chilli flakes and a couple of rose thorns from the plastic bags and sealed it up tight. Then he lay on the carpet and wriggled under his bed, tucking it at the end of the line of twenty or so similar jars neatly marshalled against the skirting board, each one containing Monty's name.

He understood from Chimera that curse jars were a long-term, cumulative project and that the curses' powers darkened and deepened the longer they were sealed. And he'd had some successes, which he'd told her about. After he'd sealed the fourth curse, Monty had come down with flu and a nasty chest infection, and the fifteenth had been followed by Monty rupturing his Achilles tendon when he was playing squash.

Adam lay in the dark beneath his bed for some time, concentrating on the dusty jars and willing them potency.

* * *

@DCBerminsterPolice. Do you remember Lyn Dimas? She disappeared on 28 July 2013. Sadly, Lyn's body was found this week. She was murdered. If you have any information that might

help our enquiries, please get in touch. We will
find who did this. Let's work together.
RIP Lyn.
#keepingberminstersafe

Patrick posted the tweet and sniffed his armpits. They
were okayish but he took some deodorant from the glove
compartment of his car, unbuttoned his shirt and applied
some. The shower had broken yesterday, and he hadn't had
an opportunity to find someone to fix it yet. He really needed
to get a second shower installed and leave the wet room to
Noah, but that took time and planning. When he got home,
he had to focus on Noah and before he could blink, the
alarm was going and he was back at work. He buttoned his
shirt, straightened his narrow tie and headed to where Trudy
Kemp lived.

She owned a pretty cottage in Baronet Street, one of
the sloping, cobbled lanes leading down to the harbour. It
was a pedestrianised conservation area, and the council often
used the view towards the water to advertise the town. The
lane was tranquil, unlike the busy coast road where Patrick
and Noah lived. There, the windows rattled when heavy lorries swept past. The only sound here was the faint clink of
masts in the harbour, carrying like wind chimes on the warm
breeze.

Patrick stood for a moment, appreciating the view.
Berminster was a good-sized town and had once been a
thriving seaport, important for trading from Roman Britain
to medieval times. It was now five miles from the English
Channel. A combination of storms, silt and human interven-
tion had changed the course of the River Bere, and the town
had been an inland harbour since the thirteenth century. It
still maintained a steady, if diminished, fishing industry. Ms
Kemp's cottage had once housed a family of six who had
made their living at sea.

She was in her early forties, plump and dressed in various stripy layers covered by a long, flowing cardigan, all in

shades of lavender. She took him through to a conservatory furnished with a couple of wicker chairs and a white metal daybed covered in cushions. A tall pile of books and magazines and a large box of chocolates were on a ledge that ran along beside it. Patrick had a mental image of Trudy lying against the cushions reading, her stubby fingers dipping into the chocolates.

She gestured to the chairs. 'We'll sit in here, make the most of the last of the sun for this year. Lyn loved this room.'

She had a pleasant, podgy face and a small, rosy mouth. Her voice was deep and loud. He'd read that she was a teacher so perhaps she was always projecting.

'I'm very sorry about your sister.'

'Thank you.' She clasped her hands together and gave him a straight, stern look. 'Why didn't your colleagues find her six years ago?'

Patrick saw that her button eyes were lively and alert. It was a good question and an obvious one. 'I can't really answer that. Your sister's body had been hidden behind a fridge in an abandoned building, Steiner's Removals. There was no evidence Lyn had any connection with the location, so the investigating officers had no reason to search there.'

She was puzzled. 'Did Lyn die straight away, that night?'

'We're unsure. If not that night, soon after. Because of the body's decomposition, it's hard to be precise about other details.'

'You mean like if she was raped?'

'Yes.'

She pulled her cardigan around her. She wore a pair of red and purple glasses on a green string around her neck, wedged on top of her jutting bosom. 'So, what happens now? I suppose you have to trawl back through all the previous records.'

'That's right. Of course, we now have DNA from Steiner's, which might prove useful.'

She crossed her legs and the wicker chair creaked. 'Steiner's. Since I heard that name, it's been ringing a bell.'

'Really? We're anxious to establish if Lyn had any connection with the place. It's near the railway and has been empty for years.'

She clicked her fingers. 'That's it — it's in Orford End, a cul-de-sac. I was there once, quite some time ago.'

'You used it for removals?'

'No, no.' She sounded testy. 'It was after it had shut down and been left to rot. I took a group of students there, just to see the outside and get the context. I teach geography at Minster Academy, and I used the visit as part of an A-level project on urban issues and development potential. We took photos of the building, and used its history as an example of the challenges faced by planners — missed regeneration opportunities, et cetera.'

The sun was directly overhead, turning the conservatory into a greenhouse. The chocolates must be melting. Trudy seemed oblivious to the heat. Patrick shifted his chair further back, where there was a shallow pool of lemony shade. 'When was this?'

'I can't remember exactly. It was a while before Lyn disappeared. I'd have to go back through my records to be sure — that's if I still have them. I expect I will because I never chuck resources away.'

Patrick made quick notes. 'Did you mention Orford End to Lyn?'

'I might have done. I can't remember. We'd chat about our work, so it's possible.' She took the arms of her glasses in both hands and rotated them. 'Why on earth would Lyn have been in that place?'

'That's the question. Can you tell me what Lyn said to you about Jeff Downey, her next-door neighbour?'

Trudy rubbed her stomach and made a face. 'Indigestion — the teacher's enemy. Eating on the hoof.'

Patrick smiled. 'Same for cops, and snacking on crap.'

She pressed her hand against her abdomen. She had a world-weary manner, as if she'd seen it all and nothing would surprise her. 'Downey was irritating. He started popping round a bit too often after Theo left, bringing little gifts. Reckoned he was in with a chance. Lyn wouldn't give him the time of day. He didn't seriously worry her, just got on her nerves. And he didn't try anything on. From what she told me, he was probably working on the principle that if he kept up his profile as a suitor, he might eventually wear her down. The dogged path to romance.'

'So she saw him as a nuisance?'

'Exactly. A minor one.'

Patrick squinted at her through the harsh light, wishing he'd brought his sunglasses in with him. 'How did Lyn manage, after her husband left?'

She gave a dry laugh. 'With difficulty. When he came out it was completely out of the blue. I had no clue and my gaydar's usually pretty reliable. When you're a teacher, you develop an instinct for these things because you see pupils struggling. Lyn was raging with misery and anger. She was harsh about Monty, reckoned he'd "lured" Theo away. She'd come round here and cry for hours. Lots of "he's had the best years of my life" shtick. It was grim. Made me glad I've never been tempted to enter the minefield of marriage. I got her to see the doctor, who gave her some pills that took the edge off and helped her sleep. After a couple of months, she started shopping as if there was no tomorrow, buying clothes and make-up. Retail therapy.' She shook her head at the memory.

'She made some bitter allegations about her husband.'

'Hmm. Said he and Monty had AIDS. I told her that was too much. You can't go around saying stuff like that. I warned her that she should let the kids see Theo too, instead of building walls. She went for me then — said I wasn't on her side and the least I could do was back her up, so I buttoned my lip. Theo rang me at one point, asking if I could get her to stop spreading rumours and negotiate about him seeing the kids, but I told him I'd tried and it was no go.'

'You're in touch with Theo still?'

She gave a wry smile. 'You're fishing as to where I stand in the quagmire of family politics.'

'I just wondered.'

She waved a hand. An amber ring caught the sun, a flash of bronze. 'I'm sure you get to hear and see it all. I've no problem with Theo and Monty. They make a good couple. I'm fond of Adam. He's a bright kid, a bit immature and a Billy No-Mates, but he's had a rough deal, losing his mum. I go there for meals occasionally and they come here. So, given the rift, that means I don't see my niece. It's no great loss to me. Lily's a shallow person, always was. She has a coterie of friends she cultivated at school called the Damsels. She calls them that or "my girls". I've never trusted girls who hang around in self-serving cliques.'

'You're not a feminist?'

She laughed. 'Believe me, that kind of group has nothing to do with feminism. It's all about status and pecking order.'

'Why are they called "the Damsels?"'

'They were supposed to be gorgeous and bright like damselflies. More like witches if you ask me, with Lily as lead broomstick. She's obsessed with her image and she was often nasty to her mum. Not much milk of human kindness. Her grandfather's partly responsible for how she is. He's always spoiled her and given her anything she wants, putty in her hands, so she learned early how to manipulate and control. He undermined her parents — if they refused her anything, she just went to Papu.'

'How did they feel about that?'

Trudy shrugged. 'They weren't always happy about it, but Theo could never stand up to his dad, and Lyn gave up saying anything when she saw that he wasn't going to be firm. Lyn liked to keep the family sweet and Joe Dimas was always gallant towards her so, in the end, she went with it.'

'Were you at Lily's wedding?'

'You're joking! I wasn't invited because I made it clear I wasn't going to freeze out Theo and Monty. Her husband, Pearce — or "IMO," as I call him — '

'"IMO?"'

'For "in my opinion," a phrase he comes out with frequently. Pearce has a view about everything and isn't shy of telling you, despite being exceptionally dense. He is easy on the eye, though. Lily hangs on his every word. The gospel according to Pearce. Someone wise once said, "Better to remain silent and be thought a fool than to speak and remove all doubt." And to add to his attractions, he's a total homophobe. My theory is that's probably because he's been mistaken for gay, with his handsome face and nice clothes, so he's terrified. Or maybe he's just a shit.'

'I gather you don't like him.'

She pulled a face. 'I'd cross the street to avoid him.'

Patrick recalled the previous interview with Trudy. 'Were Lyn and Lily rowing a lot after Theo left?'

'From what Lyn told me, pretty constantly. Lyn didn't like Pearce, said Lily was rushing into a relationship. I could see her point — Lily was talking about marriage within months of meeting him and she withdrew her application for university. Just as well in the end, because she got crap exam grades, courtesy, no doubt, of the handsome Pearce's distractions, so she'd have struggled in higher education. But Lyn could be her own worst enemy. She got on Lily's nerves by trying to muscle in on her life — doing that embarrassing thing of getting down with the young people. Lyn threw Pearce out of the house one time. So, it was all a bit inflammable.'

'When did you last see Lyn?'

'Four days before she vanished. I went round for a coffee. She was talking about Lily's prom, showing me her dress. She'd forked out a fortune for it — madness for something that was probably only going to be worn once, but Lily had had her heart set on it. Of course, if Lyn hadn't coughed up for it, Papu would have put his hand in his pocket. Lyn was so excited about the prom, she might have been going herself! The only downside was that Pearce was going to be there, but Lyn was saying daft things like Lily might meet another boy who'd take her mind off Pearce. As if! I was sorry for her that day. I could see she was floundering, not sure what to do with her life.' She blinked and pressed her eyes.

'Where were you the night your sister vanished?'

'Here, on my own, with my feet up. Term had ended and I always have at least a week of sleeping and doing nothing much at the start of the summer holiday. Theo rang me around eleven to ask if I'd seen Lyn. You'll find that that's exactly what I told your colleagues in 2013.'

Patrick wiped sweat from his neck with his fingers. 'Thanks for all of that. I might come back to you about that school visit to Orford End. Could you check when it happened?'

'I'll try.'

She took him to the front door, her glasses swaying on her chest. She was flatfooted, with a solid tread. She stood aside to let him out. 'Let's hope you do better this time with finding out what happened to my sister. You can hardly do worse.'

He bought a can of lemonade on the way back to the car and drank it all. He was lightheaded and was glad that the car was in shade. He checked Twitter. There had been lots of positive replies to his tweet about Lyn, even if there was no information. He longed for a shower. Perhaps he'd stop off at the gym on the way home. Now he'd head back to the station, write up his notes and see if he could find a plumber. As he started the engine, his phone rang. It was Noah.

'Bro, can you help? I've fallen in the kitchen. Nothing broken. Such a pain for you. Sorry.'

CHAPTER 9

Grant Haddon had phoned the station to say that he hadn't met Lyn Dimas, but he 'sort of knew' Adam, because they'd attended the same school. Ali had made an appointment at Haddon's for late afternoon so that they could speak to Grant again, as well as his father.

Lewis Haddon's office was on an industrial estate on the outer reaches of the town. The sky was promising rain as Ali drove down an unlovely, soulless spool of roads dotted with carpet and furniture warehouses, a tile factory, several car and motorbike sales rooms, a pet food wholesaler, the local rubbish disposal centre and numerous other small businesses.

'Whenever I think being a cop is thankless, I consider working somewhere like here and I reckon I'm flying it,' Ali said.

'At least we have some trees outside, whatever the headaches,' Siv agreed. 'What's the worst job you've ever done?'

'Summer job as a bin man back home. It was baking hot for weeks and the pong was something awful, plus I was paired with a bloke who was as rough as a badger's backside.'

She was getting used to him, his easy manner, his cadences of speech and his sayings. 'Is a badger's backside particularly rough? I've never touched one.'

Ali grinned. 'How about you?'

'Worst job? When I was fifteen, I had a Saturday gig at a shop in town. It was called Hilda's Hobbies. It closed down — it's a Tesco Metro now. I wasn't allowed to operate the till, just stack shelves and sweep up. It was never that busy. The day seemed endless and I hated the boredom. I'd have preferred hard work. Mrs Addington was the owner. She'd grown to dislike the shop and was trying her best to run it into the ground. I remember I suggested that I could organise some origami workshops to drum up interest — and save myself from dying of boredom — and she reacted as if I'd offered to arrange strippers.'

Rikka used to drift in sometimes on Saturdays to tease Mrs Addington, who was a fussy, elderly woman who blushed easily. Siv's heart used to be in her mouth then. Mrs Addington didn't realise that they were sisters, and Siv preferred to keep it that way. She'd watch Rik closely in case she stole anything but the wool, bolts of cloth, buttons, coloured card, crochet hooks and embroidery sets didn't interest her. She'd amuse herself by asking earnestly, *Would you have any feldgrau mosaic tiles? Painted acorns? Jar lids shaped like pumpkins? Silver fabric with a gazelle design?* She would express deep disappointment and sigh heavily when a flustered Mrs Addington would have to confess that she didn't stock the item. Sometimes, Siv wondered if Mrs Addington had sold up because of Rik.

Eventually, she couldn't take the boredom anymore and jumped ship to the new McDonald's, where she flipped burgers and was run off her feet. Rik had become a vegetarian by then, so there was no danger of her loitering amid the meaty feasts and causing a nuisance.

Ali pulled in outside Haddon's as rain cascaded, firing off the tarmac like bullets. They hurried into the squat building and announced themselves. They waited a few minutes, while Ali did his usual scan of wall notices, arching his back, jaw jutting forward, hands in pockets. Siv picked up a glossy brochure and flicked through.

Welcome to Orford End, an exclusive new development in the historic and popular town of Berminster. Just eight houses, built to a high specification and boasting solar heating, en suite to every bedroom and fully integrated luxury kitchens. Convenient for the station and excellent local schools.

Reserve your plot now to avoid disappointment.

Siv wondered if buyers would still be queuing if they heard about the discovery of a body on the site. Those with an interest in the macabre might be attracted.

A tall, well-built man with a shock of sandy hair and a lively expression appeared, bringing a buzz of energy to the room. He introduced himself as Lewis Haddon in a strong, resonating voice.

'Come on through, sorry to keep you waiting. Grant will be along in about twenty minutes.'

They followed him into a long office. It held a large blond wood desk, filing cabinets, wall charts, a computer, printer, and a scattering of unmatched chairs around a low coffee table.

'We can sit down here.' Haddon indicated the table. 'Would you like tea or coffee?'

'No thanks.' Siv took one of the grey fabric-covered chairs and Ali sank into another.

'Well, this has all been something of a shock to everyone at the firm,' Haddon said. 'Terrible about that poor woman. How anyone could do that is beyond me. My lad Grant still hasn't got over it. He's had some nightmares.'

'It was a shocking sight. Maybe your son should see a counsellor,' Siv said.

He raised an eyebrow. 'Oh, that's not necessary. He'll get over it. The young bounce back, don't they?'

'It depends on the person,' Ali told him. 'Your son struck me as sensitive. He might dwell on what he saw.'

'I'll keep an eye on him,' Haddon said. 'He's at uni now, so he's excited about that and busy with all the schedules and timetables. It amazes me how much bureaucracy he has to wade through. I prefer dealing with bricks and mortar.'

'It was unfortunate for Grant that he didn't make it to London that day, as planned,' Siv said. 'The idea that he might have avoided the discovery could prey on him.'

Haddon shifted in his chair and grimaced. 'I don't understand why he just didn't go ahead to London on his own. I'd no idea that he was at Steiner's until he rang to tell me what had happened. I was stunned and terribly worried, of course. Well . . . no good crying over spilled milk. Have you any idea who killed that woman? Some maniac?'

'We're investigating, that's all I can say. Did you know Lyn Dimas or her family?' Siv asked.

'I've never come across them. I read about her going missing at the time. When Grant saw that she'd been identified, he told me that he'd been at school with Adam, although Grant was three years ahead of him.'

'You were at Steiner's in April, with Ivor Bass,' Siv said. 'Had you been there on other occasions?'

'Yes, once, just to assess the area. That was external. It was early last December, when Building Blocks contacted me to say that they were hoping to buy it and if they were successful, they'd like me to take on the work. I was there for about half an hour, just scoping the land. Depressing place, especially on a freezing winter's day, but I could see the potential and it was exciting. I told them that.'

'This company, Building Blocks. Have you done projects for them before?'

'Just one before, outside Brighton. That's how they operate. They're a big outfit. They scan for opportunities all over the UK, and when they saw that the Orford End land was for sale, they put in a sealed bid and it was accepted.'

'Would anyone from Building Blocks have visited the site?' Siv asked.

He shook his head. 'They don't operate like that. They collect data about an area and get an architect to consider the possibilities. Then they make a decision based on that.'

'So once they'd acquired Steiner's they contacted you to confirm that you'd subcontract for the building work?'

'Correct.'

'And before then, had you ever had any business at Steiner's or anything to do with the premises?'

If he understood why she was asking, he gave no sign of it.

'It had been left empty for years,' he replied. 'Quite a few people in town would have known that. There'd been stuff in the paper about it being a shame that Steiner's was an eyesore, left empty and deteriorating. People living around there worried that it attracted rough sleepers and vandals. You'd see reports from council meetings now and again, where people complained about it. I never had any business with Steiner's when it was still operating.'

Ali sat forward. 'How come you never wanted to buy it when the Steiner family still owned it and had it on the market?'

Haddon seemed surprised at the question but answered readily. 'We usually specialise in larger projects. Demand for those has dwindled in recent years, but there's always a need for housing. When Building Blocks came calling with money to spend, I decided to branch into that whenever I could.'

Ali asked, 'How many staff do you employ?'

'We have a core of twelve. Then we contract out as we need to electricians, carpenters, plumbers. Depending on the size of the build, we can have up to thirty people on a site,' Haddon told him.

'We need a full staff list of your core staff. Can you give us one to take away?' Ali asked.

'I can print one out before you go. Was that poor woman actually murdered in there?'

'We can't share that information,' Ali said. 'Where were you on the night of the twenty-eighth of July 2013?'

'I was expecting that question, so I checked my diary,' Haddon said promptly, as if he was a pupil who'd done well in a test. He picked up an iPad and made a show of scrolling through, taking his time. 'I was visiting a site at Bexhill during the afternoon. Then I had a meeting here at four. It finished about five thirty. I worked late, until around eight. I live in Bywater, so I got home about eight fifteen. Grant was out, staying over at a friend's. I had a shower and something to eat. Then I just watched TV and went to bed, probably about half ten, my usual time.'

'And your wife or partner?'

He narrowed his eyes. 'My wife died years ago. It's just been me and Grant since then.'

'Did you talk to or see anyone between five thirty and ten thirty?'

'Afraid not. We have a part-time admin — Jenny, who greeted you — and she'd have gone home at four. You'll have to take my word for it.'

'We rarely do that,' Ali told him. 'We'll need details of who was at your four o'clock meeting.'

Haddon frowned. 'Surely you can't imagine that I had anything to do with Ms Dimas's death? I didn't know her.'

'You don't have to be familiar with someone to kill them,' Siv said. 'We would like to take DNA samples and fingerprints from you as part of the investigation. I assume you've no objection?'

'Okay with me,' he said. 'I understand that you have your work to do, but have you any idea when we can take back the site? We'd like to progress with the project as soon as you give us the nod. I've got timescales and wages to pay. You'll appreciate that delays cost us. I expect Jenny could tell you down to the last penny.'

'Murder has its own timescale. It's still a crime scene,' Siv said.

'Right. But you will contact me as soon as?'

'We've just started the investigation,' Ali said coolly. 'You'll have to raid your piggy bank if necessary.'

Just as Haddon pursed his lips to retort, Grant came in with a hefty rucksack slung across his narrow shoulder, earbuds looped about his neck. He smiled at his son. 'Hi, how was your day?'

'Great, yeah.'

'Come and sit down, take the weight off.' Haddon turned to Siv. 'I'll stay while you chat.'

'We'd rather talk on our own, Mr Haddon. Grant's an adult, he doesn't need you to be present. Unless you particularly want your dad to stay with you, Grant?'

Grant shook his head. 'No, I'm fine on my own.'

His father hesitated, but got up and reached for his phone on the desk. 'Right then. I'll be in the outer office. I'll give you a lift home, son, if you can wait until about six.'

Grant nodded to his father. He was still pale but appeared more relaxed today.

'How are you doing now, Grant?' Siv asked.

'Okay. Well . . . I do worry about what happened. Dad's been great but it's all been a real headache for him. I mean, in terms of the business. It hits him financially if work gets held up.'

'Of course. You could have counselling if you want to talk to anyone about the shock you had.'

Grant shrugged. 'It's okay. But thanks anyway. Dad's been really good about it. When I first told him what had happened, he was cross with me for being on site that day. I suppose he was shocked and worried for me. He calmed down after a while. Dad can be a bit overprotective. I . . . I had leukaemia when I was a kid. I had almost a year off school, what with being ill and the treatment. They cured me, I recovered and I'm fine, but Dad worries.'

'Is that why you stayed at school until you were nineteen?' Siv asked.

'That's right. The cancer set me back.'

'I'm glad you got better, and that you've got a university place.'

Grant smiled. 'Yeah, it's terrific. Dad said that getting stuck in at Rother College was a good distraction after what happened at Steiner's and he was right. We went shopping for more stuff I needed and that was great. I can't help remembering Ms Dimas though. And Adam . . . I can't imagine what it's been like for him.'

'Thanks for contacting us about him,' Ali said. 'How well do you know Adam?'

'Not well. He was in Drama club at school for a while. That's where I used to see him. It was quite a big group — about thirty. We chatted now and again, that's all. He was kind of shy. He never mentioned his mum, although I heard she'd gone missing. I can't remember who told me that. It might have been a teacher.'

Ali said, 'So you never mixed with Adam outside of school, or with anyone else in his family?'

Grant shook his head. 'Just Adam, at Drama club. That's all.'

He was growing edgy, licking his lips and fingering one of his earbuds.

'That's fine, Grant,' Siv reassured him. 'It was very helpful that you got in touch with us. Ms Dimas went missing on the evening of the twenty-eighth of July 2013. You were thirteen then. Your dad told us that he was at home on his own that night, and you were staying at a friend's.'

'Dad said you'd probably ask me about that. I remember it because it was my friend Freddie's birthday. We had a party with a huge bouncy castle in the garden — only time I've ever been on one — and then I stayed at his house for a sleepover. Freddie's mum was my childminder back then as well. It was the summer holiday, so I stayed there the next day. Dad picked me up in the evening.'

'You didn't phone your dad at all that evening of the party?'

'No, no reason to.'

'Okay, thanks,' Siv said. 'That's all we needed. I hope uni goes well for you.'

Back in the car, Siv scratched her head. 'Now we have Lewis Haddon with no alibi for his whereabouts that night. Forensics will be interesting.'

'So far, there's no trace connecting him to Lyn.'

'No. Doesn't mean it isn't there, though.'

* * *

Noah was on the kitchen floor, wedged between the table and the cooker. He'd managed to pull himself up so that his head rested against the oven door. There was a smashed plate and mug, with bits of a cheese sandwich lying saturated in a pool of tea. He grimaced as Patrick came in.

'I'm a klutz,' he said indistinctly.

'You certainly are. Is anything hurting?'

'My pride.'

'Okay. Let's do the routine.'

It wasn't the first time he'd had to help his brother up. Noah fell regularly, attempting to reach for things, miscalculating distances, wanting to act independently, trying not to be a burden. Patrick understood his frustrations but it meant he was always on tenterhooks, wondering what was going on at home. Some days, he was resentful. Others, like today, he was overcome with pity and tenderness. He drew Noah's wheelchair beside him and made sure the brake was on, then put his hands around his brother's back, bent his knees and rocked and slid him to the wheelchair. He took a deep breath and lifted him in one go. Noah thumped down, grabbed the side of the chair with his good arm and Patrick sat down to get his breath.

'Just as well you go to the gym.' Noah gave his tentative, lopsided smile.

Patrick fetched two glasses of water, putting a straw in Noah's. The floor was sticky and the sink needed scrubbing. The house always smelled a bit ripe, like the niff from an animal's enclosure in the zoo. They had a cleaner, Melinda, who came for a couple of hours a week but she seemed to skim the surface. Patrick suspected that Noah distracted her and got her chatting, because he seemed to have gathered a lot of details about her divorces, her internet dating and the kinds of manicures she liked — *Sometimes she has a shellac but her favourite is paraffin wax.*

He put the water on the tray attached to Noah's wheelchair. His tousled blond hair was dingy and was sticking up on the crown. Patrick guessed that the carer hadn't had time to comb it. Noah smelled fusty because the shower was out of order, his breath was sour and there were tea stains down the front of his T-shirt. There'd been a time when he was always smartly groomed. He'd been the handsome one of the two brothers, toned and fit from running and surfing until the day a stroke felled him on the path to the headland. Now his body was slack and sliding to fat, his face chubby, his neck vanishing into folds of flesh. The right side of his face was askew, his mouth slanting.

'I'll make you another sandwich and tidy up. Then I'm going to ring a plumber.'

'Do I pong?'

'A bit. Want me to spray you with air freshener?'

Noah gurgled a laugh. 'Don't you need to get back to work? Won't they miss Hat-trick?'

'It's okay, it won't take me long.'

Noah took his state-of-the-art motorised chair to the living room. Patrick cleared up the spilled food, mopped the tea and wrinkled his nose at the full bin. He squirted bleach in the sink, opened the air vent at the top of the window, made a fresh sandwich and took it to Noah. He was watching a recording of *University Challenge*, pressing a pretend buzzer and calling, 'Hill, Imbecile College.'

Patrick checked the time. The guv must be wondering where he'd got to. He rang a plumber and left a message on voicemail, watching Noah as he answered the quiz questions. He was mystified as to how his brother could stand this existence, listening to the traffic grind its way to and from the coast while he read, tapped slowly on his iPad or watched

118

TV. He'd gone to a day centre for a while, but then declared it was a waste of time and depressing — 'I'm not a bloody vegetable.' A few of his friends kept up contact but others had drifted away. Ali came round every couple of weeks and had a beer, played cards or just chatted, mainly about rugby. He was good at easy banter, 'having a gas,' as he called it, and he always made Noah laugh.

Most of the time, Noah maintained a cheery front but lately he'd been quieter than usual, and there were nights when Patrick heard him crying in his room. He'd knocked on the door, but Noah had shouted at him to fuck off. There were days when Patrick was panicky, picturing Noah in the half-light of the silent house, always waiting, waiting, for someone to relieve his isolation.

His phone rang. The sarge. He hesitated, ignored the call, fetched a comb and the gel that Noah liked and styled his brother's hair. His mind wandered to Kitty Fairway. He'd interviewed her back in May at Halse woods, where she was a warden. She'd been flirty as well as gorgeous, and he'd finally summoned the courage to invite her out. She'd said yes. He'd just have to keep his fingers crossed that there wouldn't be a Noah-shaped emergency.

Noah glanced up at him. 'Can you lend me thirty quid until I get to the bank later this week?'

'Sure, is that enough?'

'Yeah. Just to tide me over.'

The sweet cosmetic scent of the gel filled the room and Noah gave a thumbs-up, yelling, 'The Balearic Islands, you idiots!'

CHAPTER 10

'Sivvi! Were you on your way to see me?'

In the blinding sunlight, she hadn't spotted her mother coming and wondered if Mutsi had been lying in wait in a doorway. She shielded her eyes, both against the glare and her mother's vibrant outfit.

'No, I'm going to see a podiatrist.'

'At your age?' Mutsi raised her Jackie O. sunglasses and gazed despairingly at her daughter's sturdy black ankle boots. 'It's not as if you wear fashionable shoes. I have problems from years of wearing high heels but you . . .' The way her voice trailed off spoke eloquently of how much her daughter's lack of style pained her. She turned one of her long, elegant legs, showcasing a navy stiletto, pointing her foot like the dancer she'd once been in a hazy, distant past.

'It's an interview, not a personal appointment.'

Mutsi was holding two carrier bags from Ormonde, Berminster's upmarket fashion emporium. She was a vision in an eye-catching lime-and-orange jacket and emerald blue jeans, with a bandana holding back her strawberry-blonde hair. Her lipstick and nail varnish shimmered in the same orange as her jacket. Siv stood in the afternoon glare, a dowdy caterpillar to Mutsi's blazing butterfly.

Her mother pointed to a six-storey block of flats across the road, an Art Deco building called Waterside. Her silver charm bracelet, laced with heart shapes, slipped down her slim wrist. 'That's me over there, top floor. Here, take one of these for me and we'll pop in. I've been dying to show it to you.'

Siv found herself holding a carrier bag with Coco de Mer lingerie poking from the top, the words *Divinely Decadent* just visible on the box. She was early for her appointment with Antonia Santos and she might as well get this over with. Mutsi was already leading the way, fluttering fingers at the traffic as she crossed the street.

The flat was modest — poky, even — but it had a wrought-iron balcony with long-reaching views across the harbour. It was painted white throughout and gleamed in the bright light. It smelled new and airy. On the dining table was the heavy red-and-white embroidered tablecloth that came from Mutsi's grandmother's house. It was one of the few things she'd hung onto during her circuitous, meandering life. Siv recalled that it was always the first item that would be unpacked when they moved into their latest, hastily arranged accommodation in a random selection of areas: London, Surrey, Oxfordshire, Berkshire and Biarritz. If there was no dining table, Mutsi used it as a throw. Siv had regarded its familiar, worn weave as a talisman offering the flimsy hope of permanence. She put her hand down and stroked its ribbed, rough surface.

'The place has just been completely refurbished with a new kitchen. I really love it,' Mutsi said. She showed Siv the bathroom with a deep Victorian-style clawfoot bath and then threw open the doors from the bedroom to the balcony. 'And this view!'

Siv followed her out and gazed at the pale, smoky horizon. The water in the harbour was a still, pale blue. These flats were sought after and expensive, and she was mystified as to how Mutsi could afford the rent. She'd spent most of her life scrounging, spending and racking up bills. On one of the rare occasions when she'd called in on Siv and Ed in Greenwich, she'd cornered him in the kitchen and asked if he could lend her a thousand pounds. He'd said no, and Mutsi hadn't lingered for a cup of tea.

'I've made so many new friends,' Mutsi was saying. 'This balcony is lovely for having early evening drinks. One of the couples I've met owns a little pied-à-terre in Paris. They've invited me there for a weekend.'

'Sounds lovely.' Mutsi was adept at colonising people, slipping across their borders and planting her flag before they realised what was happening.

'Have you heard from Rikka?' her mother asked.

'Not for a while.'

'I've emailed her but she never replies. She's horrible, just blanking me.'

Siv said nothing and watched a boat tack slowly into the harbour and berth.

'So, do you like my new home?'

Mutsi touched her lightly on the arm, a little stroke of the fingers. She had a concentrated energy, a force of will that Siv had always found difficult to resist. Ed had shielded her, handling her mother with an easy determination. These days, she was back to being trapped in Mutsi's full beam.

She moved away. 'It's lovely. How do you afford it?'

'That's a rude question. You should never ask anyone about their finances.'

Siv inhaled Mutsi's rich, subtle scent. Even in full sunlight, she was remarkably unlined, her skin fresh and clear, her hair glowing. Siv touched her own hair, a finger automatically reaching for a bald patch. 'That was never your attitude when you were on the phone to Dad, querying his salary and asking for more money.'

Mutsi looked at her over her dark glasses, then took them off and nestled them in her hair. 'That was different. Your father earned well and I had to struggle to raise two girls all on my own.'

Her mother's version of events never ceased to amaze her. 'Come off it, you weren't often on your own. I can recall at least eight "uncles" and the turnaround was so fast, I'm sure I've forgotten some.'

'Don't be spiteful. It makes your mouth turn down and causes wrinkles. What was I supposed to do, stay lonely and celibate? It was all right for your father, he was footloose and fancy free. He could do whatever he liked.'

'I can't imagine anyone less "footloose and fancy free" than Dad. As far as I could tell, he never had another partner after you did a runner on him.'

'That was up to him. I can't help that he was the most boring man on the planet.'

Siv remembered a hissed argument between her parents when her father had visited them in London. He'd closed the kitchen door but she and Rik could still hear them, once they'd turned the TV off. Her father's tone had been mild, even though his words had been critical and, as always, he had been no match for Mutsi, who'd made game, set and match.

This isn't a suitable place for the girls to live, on the top floor with no garden and near a main road. This flat seems so cramped. I give you enough money to afford something better than this.

It's none of your business where I live. You've come to take the girls out, not to snoop into my life and police me.

Don't be childish. Children need fresh air and grass to play on.

Oh, so you're the expert on children now, are you? You only see them for five minutes now and again.

You know that's not deliberate. I can hardly see them regularly when I'm living in Dubai, and keeping up with where you've taken them is work in itself. You never communicate, unless it's about money.

Don't preach, it's tedious. You're a great loss to the clergy. You'd have made a fine bishop.

I'm entitled to expect that the girls are properly cared for, in an environment where they can—

Oh, shut up! I left you because I discovered that you were the most boring man in England and you've not changed. You're not entitled to anything.

Does this have to be a trade in insults?

No, because you're leaving now. Sermon over. Amen. Have them back by six, will you? I have to go out at seven.

Who's babysitting?

No one, I'm leaving them on their own with boxes of matches and candles!

The last remark had been nearer the truth than her father would have liked. There had been a babysitter that evening, a fifteen-year-old girl with terrible acne who lived on the ground floor and who'd let her boyfriend in after Mutsi had gone out. They'd sat on the sofa and demonstrated French kissing to a fascinated Siv and Rikka, who'd watched them from the carpet.

Mutsi's voice cut across her memories.

'Anyway, I can afford to live here in some style and comfort because I have an income stream.'

Siv was stunned. Her mother hadn't had a job for years. In 1968, when she'd arrived in London from Finland, she'd been a dancer for five months in a touring production of *Hair*. She used to have a framed photo of the show, with her wearing a tie-dyed gauzy pink top with tassels and patched jeans, her arms lifted high in the air. She'd met Siv's father on a train while the show was moving from Nottingham and they'd married within a month at the Finnish church in Rotherhithe. Mutsi was already pregnant with Rikka. They must have made an unlikely pair — her father the bookish, unworldly scientist and her mother the long-legged, glamorous dancer from Arctic realms. Mutsi had pirouetted around him and he'd wandered into marriage, bemused and enchanted, like a character in one of Bartel's folk tales. When she'd had enough, she'd danced off to pastures new.

'You have a job?'

'I have a blog called *60Chic*,' Mutsi said airily. 'I have more than fifty thousand followers. It's all about my style and exercise and beauty routines — make-up and wardrobe tips for the mature woman. Write what you know!' She gazed out at the water. 'You could read it, get some tips yourself. That sickly shirt does nothing for your skin tone. That colour's called "gamboge" — Buddhist monks wear it.'

'Who's spiteful now?' *What an ideal occupation she's found. Making money out of talking about her favourite subject.*

Ed hissed in her ear. *She should have called her blog AllAboutMe.* She snorted back laughter. 'I have to go. I have a proper job to do.'

Mutsi stood with her back to the railing, arms stretched out, one ankle crossed over the other. She could have been posing for a glossy magazine photographer. *The style blogger who writes the hugely successful* 60Chic *invites us into her smart waterfront home.*

'Can't you ever just be kind to me, Sivvi?' she said.

The familiar brew of hurt and anxiety that her mother had served up to her over the years sideswiped Siv. She could taste it in her throat, bitter and lingering. Her scalp was tight. She reached a hand out to the cool iron rail to steady herself, glad of the solid metal. 'I don't trust you. You've never given me reason to. All my memories of you are of your back as you're vanishing through a door.'

She walked away fast, leaving the door swinging. She didn't want to be trapped in the confines of the lift, so she ran down the stairs. On the street, she walked over to the harbour wall, closed her eyes and repeated the mantra that one of the counsellors had given her after Ed's death. 'All is well, all is well, all is well.' It was a trick and a lie, but a handy one. She shrugged her jacket off to show more of her sickly saffron shirt, and headed for Brookridge clinic.

* * *

The clinic was down an alleyway, at the back of a health food shop. Siv sat in the waiting area on a sofa covered with a brightly coloured throw that she recognised as Corran's work. After London's anonymity, she was still adjusting to life in a town where people constantly crossed paths. Wheels within wheels. There was a smell like minty mouthwash in

125

the room, and a range of pamphlets about foot health. She picked one up and read about the importance of moisturising and nail filing. She could hear a man's rumbling voice and a woman's answering chuckle from behind the adjacent door.

She helped herself to water from a dimpled glass dispenser. Thin slices of lemon and lime bobbed inside. The water tasted delicious. It would be good to have one of these in the detectives' office, but no one would clean it and the fruit would grow mouldy. The round, squat glass in her hand reminded Siv of a set that she and Ed had been given as a wedding present. She'd no idea what had happened to them. Ed had never liked them, saying that they were too small to be useful, but she'd shoved them in the back of a cupboard, in case they might come in handy. He'd given her a long-suffering look that had said, *I get that you hang onto stuff because of your childhood but you've got me now.* He'd probably taken the glasses to a charity shop. She had a sudden sense that he was near and closed her eyes at the sad pleasure. *Have you turned up to keep an eye on Mutsi? I do hope so!*

Antonia Santos had a firm, cool handshake. She ushered Siv into a space that was a cubicle rather than a room. They sat on either side of the treatment table, which was covered in blue paper. There was no window. Siv couldn't have worked in this confined place all day, inspecting people's gnarled feet and ingrowing toenails.

Antonia was cheery and tall, with sallow skin, a heavy, firm chin and wiry dark hair drawn back in a bun. She pushed a trolley holding the tools of her trade into the corner to give herself more legroom.

'I'm so glad you've found Lyn, Inspector. It's awful, but at least now the family can hold a funeral.' She touched the hollow in her neck with a long, slim finger. 'Mind you, that might be a complicated affair, given the tensions.'

'Elaborate on that for me.'

Antonia cleared her throat. 'Hmm. I've been weighing this up since you rang. Some of my information has come through Mr Dimas senior — Joe. He's a patient, attends every couple of months for treatment. Lyn used to treat him and then . . .'

'Lyn was murdered. I want to find who did it. I've probably heard some of the things you can tell me already, but you should speak freely.'

Antonia smoothed the paper across the table. 'I worked with Lyn for almost five years. We were colleagues rather than friends. Friendly colleagues, that's how I'd put it. She was a loving mum — maybe a bit too focused on the kids at times. She needed to stop crowding Lily and give her space. Lyn was never confident in herself. She wasn't sure about her looks. I couldn't understand it, because she was slim and attractive, but some people — women especially — are always judging themselves and finding what they see in the mirror wanting. I've never been like that. Have you?'

It occurred to Siv that if she was a man, Antonia wouldn't be asking her. 'Apart from craving straight hair for a couple of months when I was fourteen, no.' She'd had a crush on her maths teacher, Ms Northam, who'd had fine, long blond tresses and an elfin face.

Antonia said, 'Maybe it's best to be a plain Jane like me, and accept there's not a lot you can do about your manly chin.' She laughed a light, musical ripple and stroked her jaw. 'Lyn worried about being over forty and lines appearing, that sort of stuff. She was convinced that her legs were too thick, so she bought these contraptions that fitted inside her boots to make her calves appear thinner. Like a corset for legs. They put me in mind of foot binding. She was kind of obsessed about her image and any signs of ageing. I'd say to her that unless she had the money and courage to have plastic surgery, then lines, crow's feet and a general sagging are inevitable. I've decided to wear my accumulation of years with pride.' She grinned and touched the sides of her eyes, which had spiderweb lines fanning out.

'I suppose her husband wasn't giving her much reassurance.'

'Too right. She was convinced that Theo was losing interest. I remember she said once that he'd started to treat her as if she was his mother. I'm not keen on bedroom talk but she mentioned one or two things that indicated their love life was moribund. The pieces fell into place when Theo came out. The poor man must have suffered terrible conflict.'

'So she had a husband who wasn't paying her any attention, and then she found out why and she was furious.'

'And then some! She came in here and tried to work, but she was all over the place. I had to tell her to go home. She was devastated and she believed she'd been made a fool of. When she did come back, she was distracted and tired. By then, she was obsessing about Lily and Pearce, the new boyfriend.'

'She wasn't keen on Pearce.'

Antonia rolled her eyes. 'She was poisonous about him. I'd dread having a coffee with her because she'd be reciting his sins. He was too old for Lily, he was encouraging her to forget about university and blighting her future, he was distracting her from her exam work, she was young and impressionable, reeling from the shock of her father's departure, he was leading her astray, et cetera, et cetera. I understood why Lyn was concerned, because Lily met Pearce soon after Theo left, but then maybe he was just what she needed. I've no idea because I don't know him. Joe Dimas likes him, but I wouldn't rely on him as a judge of character. I tried to suggest to Lyn that coming down heavy on teenagers never goes well, and often achieves the opposite of what you intend, but she wasn't listening. You can take a horse to water . . .'

'Going back to Joe Dimas, tell me about the wider family and what's happened since Lyn disappeared. I can imagine that people chat away to you while you're working on their corns and calluses.'

Antonia linked her fingers and cracked them. 'Love that sound. So satisfying. Oh yes, I'm a bit like a hairdresser, I get confidences and life stories. It's amazing what people tell you when they're being attended to and they relax. As far as I can make out, there's a triangle.' She took a roll of bandage and placed it in the centre of the table. 'That's Joe Dimas.' She put a nail file and metal dish down at opposite corners. 'The nail file is Theo, Adam and Monty and the dish is Lily and Pearce.' She drew imaginary lines with her finger between the bandage and the dish. 'There's lots of contact and affection from here to here, but the nail file stands alone. Joe Dimas is a deeply prejudiced man. I have to ask him to stay away from some of his favourite hate topics: gays, people who have too many children, those on state benefits, drug addicts. Pearce Aston sounds similar, given that Joe rates him, and I get the impression that Lily adores Pearce. I assume it's mutual. Lyn was right in that Lily hasn't done much with her life other than marry Pearce and work as his assistant.'

'What does she do exactly?'

'Pearce deals in computers, runs his own business. That's how they met — her school was having an upgrade. She works at home, taking orders for Pearce and bookkeeping. Joe is mad about Lily — always talking about her and praising her. He doesn't mention his son or grandson, except to comment that Theo and his boyfriend are trying to turn Adam gay and that the young man is a "milksop". I'd say that Joe regards Pearce as the kind of son he'd have preferred.'

'Did Joe Dimas get on with Lyn?'

'Yes, they seemed to have a good relationship — well, until just before she disappeared, anyway. He certainly took her side after Theo came out. The way he saw it, Theo had brought terrible shame on the family. He blamed Theo for Lyn going missing — said that he'd broken her heart. He and Lily reckoned that she'd committed suicide.'

'Was that your view?'

'It didn't seem likely. Lyn wouldn't have abandoned her kids. And she was so full of anger, she'd want to live to make sure she took it out on Theo and stop him from seeing them. Lyn was out for revenge, big time.'

That echoed what Theo had said about his wife. 'What did you mean about Joe's relationship with Lyn — did they fall out?'

'Not as such. He tried to get her to go easy on Lily and Pearce, but as I said, she wasn't having it. I overheard them having a heated discussion one day when she was treating him and afterwards, she was muttering that he should mind his own business. Lyn invited people to comment on her situation, but if she didn't like what she heard, she could bite your head off.'

'Did Lyn have any problems here at work — any disputes with patients?' The first investigation report stated that she'd had no issues at the clinic.

'No problems that I was aware of, and she'd have told me as we worked closely together. She was skilled at her job, very professional. She'd had some problems where she'd worked previously . . .' Antonia hesitated and then carried on. 'I remembered recently, she once mentioned in passing that standards there hadn't been as she'd have wished, and it was one of the reasons she'd left. I'd forgotten all about it until a couple of months ago when I saw something on the news about a whistleblower at a dental clinic.'

'So you didn't mention this in 2013?'

'No — I'd forgotten, as I said, and it was just a remark Lyn once made.'

'Where did Lyn work before she came here?'

'I'm not sure. She'd been a stay-at-home mum for a while, when Adam was little. Theo would be able to tell you.'

Antonia's next appointment had arrived. As she showed Siv out, she pointed at her boots.

'I like those. Good foot support.'

'Thank you. My mother doesn't rate them.'

'Mothers! What do they know?' Antonia laughed her rippling laugh, and beckoned to an overweight woman with puffy ankles who lumbered towards her leaning on a stick.

On her way home, Siv got a call from Steve Wooton.

'We found Lyn's DNA on the mattress at Steiner's. There was a smear of her menstrual blood and a couple of her hairs. Also, her fingerprints and saliva were on two wine bottles, one by the side of the mattress, one in the kitchen and also on a mug in the sink. The mug had contained wine from one of the bottles.'

130

'Any other matches?'

'Still checking. I should have all the results in the morning.'

She drove on, weighing this unexpected development. What on earth had made fashion-conscious Lyn go to a derelict building to swig wine, and had she willingly lain on the mattress or been forced onto it?

CHAPTER 11

The incident board was satisfyingly full.

'The DNA results take us a step further, but also widen our possibilities,' Siv said. 'Unless someone took empty wine bottles and a mug that Lyn Dimas had drunk from and placed them at Steiner's, which seems highly unlikely, she drank wine there. It seems weird from what we've learned of her, but that suggests she might have been hanging out in that dump. She was in contact with the mattress there and she leaked menstrual fluids onto it. Either she was abducted and held there, or she was having consensual sex, or she was raped. I wonder if she was menstruating the night she vanished. Lily might be able to tell us, although I'm not sure she took that much notice of her mum. Steve, any other results?'

He spoke in his usual rush. 'There was no one else's DNA on Lyn's underwear or her dress. That was a busy mattress — we've got DNA from eleven different semen residues, a few hairs and multiple traces of saliva and sweat. There are lots of fingerprints around the building, especially in the office and kitchen. All the core staff from the builders, including the boss, gave DNA samples and prints, and we found no matches for them. No one from Building Blocks ever came near the site, and the architect they commissioned visited Orford End but never entered Steiner's. I've checked all the results and none of the DNA or fingerprints match anything on the database. No arrests were made during the previous investigation, so there's no DNA from any suspects back then to compare with. Oh — the batch the mattress came from was made in 2012. It's available in lots of places, including online, but I didn't find an outlet selling it locally.'

'Let's focus on people now,' Siv said. 'We need to ask all the names on this board to volunteer fingerprints and DNA samples. I'll go through what else we have. When I spoke to Adam, he gave me two new pieces of information. One was that on the night she vanished, Lyn turned down Jeff Downey's invitation to his barbecue, saying she'd prepared a meal. She hadn't. Maybe she lied just because she didn't want to spend time with Downey, or maybe it was because she had other plans that she didn't want him to be party to.'

'Or maybe for both reasons,' Ali said.

'True. The second thing Adam told me was that before she left the house, his mum had brushed her hair out and used hair mousse. That suggests that she might have been meeting someone, and if so, someone she wanted to look presentable for.'

'So probably a man.' Patrick ran a finger around the rim of his coffee cup and flicked the side rhythmically.

'Seems likely,' Siv agreed. 'If that was the case, whoever this person was, she was willing to leave Adam on his own, but she wasn't expecting the meeting to take long, and surely not long enough to be drinking wine at Steiner's. Antonia, her colleague, told me that Lyn was image-conscious and worried about ageing. Adam confirmed that she'd been spending on clothes and make-up after his dad left. It's hard to believe that she would consent to have sex with someone at Steiner's, but we have to consider that she did. It might not have been on that night, of course. She could have been meeting someone there previously, and more than once. The likelihood is that she was abducted on the night she vanished and possibly raped before she was murdered.'

Ali screwed up his mouth. 'Why would Lyn have agreed to have sex at Steiner's? She could have afforded a hotel if she'd had an affair. She'd no need to go to that skanky dive. And there was no indication that she'd been seeing anyone.'

Siv shrugged. 'It's bizarre, but she drank and made contact with that mattress for some reason. Wine and sex quite often go together. The way her body was left tied to the fridge indicates that this murder wasn't carried out in a moment of anger or passion. It was planned. Lyn's killer wanted to humiliate her, even in death, and they assumed that her body wouldn't be found for a long time. We need to dig more into her history. Antonia Santos said that Lyn was low on self-confidence and her husband's lack of interest fed that. If she was feeling unattractive and vulnerable, she might have taken risks, sought out excitement.'

Patrick leaned forward. He'd pushed up his shirtsleeves and his angular elbows stuck out like blades. He'd cut himself shaving and his cheek was raw. 'I found a connection to Steiner's with Trudy, Lyn's sister.' He explained what Trudy had told him. 'I've asked her to check when she went to Orford End with her class. She said it was a while ago, before Lyn went missing.'

Siv stared at him. He looked tired and bleached, as if he could do with a fortnight's sleep, and his constant fidgeting got on her nerves, but he had a way of digging out information that she valued. 'Did Lyn know that Trudy had been there?'

'Trudy couldn't remember if she'd told her, but it was possible. These days, her loyalties lie with Adam and his dad. She can't stand Pearce Aston — says he's very opinionated — and she's not fond of her niece. Claims she's selfish and was unkind to her mother.'

Ali was contemplating the ceiling and scratching his scalp between his centre cornrows. He might have a soft belly and a jovial manner, but Ali was no pushover, and Siv had seen him sideswipe people with a sudden switch from kindly to a bracing tone.

He focused and glared at Patrick. 'Would Trudy recall who was in the school party she took there?'

'I can ask her.'

'Aye, I'd say you should, wee man. Maybe one of those pupils told Lyn about the place or remembered from that visit that it was a potential hideaway for a body. Then we'd have another link to work on.' He rocked backwards on his chair. 'I saw Monty Barnwell. He said nothing new. Told me about how Lyn visited the hospital and caused trouble, going on about AIDS. He was very understanding and forgiving about her. Maybe a bit too much, given that she caused him and Dimas such grief. I dunno, I didn't quite buy it. He and Dimas had big-time motives, guv. Lyn was badmouthing them, and with her gone, they've got the house and an easier life together. Home free.'

'And Dimas got access to his son again,' Steve pointed out. 'It'll be interesting to get their DNA samples.'

'Coming back to the builders, we should check all of their staff out, to see if any of them had a connection to Lyn,' Ali said.

Steve narrowed his eyes. 'Why? None of their DNA was on the mattress, just fingerprints in places, which can be explained by their presence there.'

Siv shook her head. 'Doesn't mean they weren't there with Lyn. You're assuming that whoever was on the mattress with her killed her. That doesn't necessarily follow.'

He couldn't keep the irritation from his voice. 'But she was hardly likely to be meeting one of those tabloid-reading gorillas from Haddon's.'

'Doesn't matter. We follow up on them and their boss, see if there's any link.' Siv smiled tightly at him. 'Let's consider alibis from people interviewed in 2013, because several of them have no other verification. Dimas and Barnwell said they were together, Jeff Downey and Trudy Kemp were each home alone. Antonia Santos was confirmed to have been with family, so hers is tight, as is Pearce Aston's, because he was at the prom from seven forty-five. Joe Dimas said he was at his church, St Demetrius, from seven thirty to nine thirty, planning a fundraising dinner with Pater Basil, the priest, who confirmed that to the previous investigation. Coming up to date, Lewis Haddon states that he was alone during the evening. His meeting at his office until five thirty checked out. We need all our forensic results soonish, Steve. One other thing. Antonia Santos mentioned that Lyn might have had problems at a clinic in Seaford, where she worked previously. I'll see what I can dig up on that.' Siv gestured at the board. 'Patrick, can you round up any fingerprints and DNA samples we don't have already and liaise with Steve. Check Haddon's background and any of his personnel who visited Steiner's. Ali, talk to Pearce Aston, go back to the flats where Barnwell and Dimas were living at the time, and speak again to anyone who was living there. We still need to contact Maria Steiner. I'll see Theo Dimas again, Jeff Downey and Joe Dimas. Steve — I doubt we'll need you at the next meeting and I'm sure you're busy. You can email anything of interest.'

Steve stood. 'Sure, whatever. After all, you're the boss.'

Siv sounded chilly. 'That's right, well spotted. Thanks, everyone.'

* * *

A fine drizzle was misting the air when Izzie Sitwell drove to work at Berminster Station. She'd checked the forecast, and saw that a pulse of rain would clear the South East by mid-morning, when warm sunshine was due. That was good, because fewer passengers complained when the weather was fine. No one had any inkling why. Maybe it was down to the fact that the trains usually ran on time in clement conditions, or perhaps people were just less grumpy.

Izzie could do without jabbing fingers and raised voices today and the familiar litany of, *Why is there only one ticket machine working? Why is the lift still out of order? Why are the toilets closed? What happened to the 7:54 to Victoria?* She wasn't in the mood for dishing out the usual bullshit, and she couldn't give the true reasons — *Because Bodgit & Scarper, the company who provide the machines, are cheap and crap. The part has to come from Hungary and the first idiot who came to check it placed the wrong order. The Victorian plumbing's knackered and there's no budget for the foreseeable to have it dug out. The driver rang in sick at the last minute and although I'm convinced he's lying, there's sod all I can do about it.* Her mum might tell people (embarrassingly) that she was Queen of Berminster Rail, but frequently she felt like a pretender to the throne.

She had staff performance reviews to do this morning and was hoping to be uninterrupted. She needed a clear head, but right now, she was anxious and muddled. As she neared the entrance to Orford End, she slowed the car. Maybe if she sat and mulled things over for a few minutes, she'd be able to focus. She'd done a mindfulness course last year but she hadn't been much good at it. When the course leader had said, *Sense the points of contact between your body and the chair. Be aware of your breathing and now visualise a cornfield or a beach at dawn,* her mind had roamed to monthly staff returns, or she'd wondered if the cod she'd cooked for last night's dinner had been a bit off. Busy Izzie, her mum called her, saying she had an active brain. She made it sound like an allegation.

She pulled in by the kerb and squinted through the drifting, grey rain towards the police tape. There was no one around. The steady rhythm of the windscreen wipers was soothing. She'd been shocked when she had heard about Lyn's murder. Like the rest of Lily's 'girls,' she'd been convinced that her mum must have committed suicide. Izzie had been so fond of Lyn. Sometimes, she suspected — no, knew — she'd liked her more than her own daughter had. Lily used to say such awful, cutting things. Izzie could hear her now. *God, she's so embarrassing and clingy — I wish she'd get a life and leave me alone!* Lily had been lucky to have such a caring mum — Izzie had once plucked up the courage to say so to her. And it had taken courage because Lily was Queen Bee in the Damsels. She could bite your head off if you crossed her. When Lily was good, she was very, very good and when she was bad, she was horrid. But on that occasion, Lily had just stared at her as if she was talking in another language.

Izzie's dad had died when she was eight, leaving just her and her mum, who then took to religion in a big way and was always out at services, Church fundraisers and charity events. Lyn had always been welcoming and warm. Even after the terrible stuff about Lily's dad, she'd remembered Izzie's birthday and bought her a shimmery top from Monsoon and cosmetics that toned with her brown skin. Izzie had called to the house several times a week after Theo left, even if Lily hadn't been in. Especially then, because once Adam was in bed, Izzie had had Lyn pretty much to herself, and the atmosphere was relaxed. When Lily was around, it had been unpredictable, with Lyn trying too hard. Sometimes it seemed as if Lyn was Lily's hostage, always trying to placate and please her.

On some evenings, Izzie had gone upstairs with Lyn while she'd tried on the new stuff she'd bought and they'd chatted comfortably. Izzie had recognised Lyn's lack of confidence and the way she tried to disguise it, because it was how she saw herself. Every day was a masquerade, hoping that no one would call your bluff. Lyn was pretty, and Izzie had told her so as she'd held up hangers. That had made Lyn smile, although she'd always gazed dubiously at her reflection in the mirror. Izzie had been studying Psychology for A level, and she'd grasped that Lyn was buying love because she missed it so much and her life was empty. She'd watched her in the soft light, trying to cheer herself up, wondering aloud, with that undercurrent of anxiety in her voice, if Lily would like an outfit. Then Izzie had thought that Lily was a right bitch. But she was also a powerful one and Izzie had liked belonging to the Damsels, so she'd navigated her way around Lily with care, like a ship's captain keeping a wary eye on icebergs.

Then there was Pearce. Izzie's hands grew clammy on the wheel. The group of friends had been giddy and transfixed by Lily's fast romance with the slim-hipped, muscly guy who was like a cross between Jamie Dornan and Tom Hardy.

They'd all eyed him when he swaggered into their study room to sort out their computers. He'd played to the gallery as he surveyed their ancient machines. *Wow, this stuff should be pensioned off! I need to get you amazing people up to speed.* Inevitably, it had been Lily who'd snagged his attention because, quite simply, she'd deemed that she deserved it.

When she'd believed that Lyn had killed herself, Izzie's doubts about Pearce had faded away. Not that she really understood what those doubts were. She'd gone to Lily's wedding, uncomfortable at betraying Lyn, who'd disapproved so strongly of her daughter's relationship. It had been a grand occasion in a sumptuous hotel overlooking the Channel. Seated among the beautiful flowers, sparkling crystal glassware and snowy linen, she'd listened as Pearce said that Lyn would always be missed. He'd gestured to the empty chair and place setting they'd laid for her, with her name on the card. The guests had been impressed and moved, listening to this handsome young man speak so eloquently about his missing mother-in-law. When he'd said, *If only she could be here with us, to share our special day,* Izzie had detected a note of sarcasm beneath the bland sentiment. Some people in the room had understood how much Lyn had disliked Pearce, and how appalled she'd been when Lily had said she was going to marry him. But maybe she'd been wrong, and Pearce was just trying his best to make things okay for Lily, who'd sat smiling up at him adoringly.

It was hard to decide about Pearce.

She just wasn't sure what she recalled or what she'd seen. Or thought she'd seen. It was all a bit vague, about Lyn and that night at the prom. They'd all been half-pissed by the time they'd left Lily's, because Rosie had been passing around bottles of cava while they'd been getting ready. Izzie's head was full of blurred images, as fluid as the rain sliding down the windscreen.

She didn't want to make a fool of herself with the police and she certainly didn't want to cross Lily. Lily still had the power to make you an outcast, and Izzie needed the Damsels as much now as she had back then.

One of the gang. One of the girls. On the inside, protected by the magic circle.

She drove on to work, to the safe ground of performance categories, attendance levels and customer involvement.

* * *

The coast road was breezy and bracing and the sun glowed between fleeting clouds. Ali tasted salt spray and had the illusion of wellness as he cycled along. His blood sugar readings had been well above his target range for over a week now, due to guilty pleasures like cans of Coke, croissants, white bread sandwiches, pretzels and key lime pie. He was due to see Marcy Keene, the formidable nurse at the diabetic clinic soon, and he didn't want to face her frown and wagging finger. Some men seemed to get off on women in nurses' uniforms, but they made Ali weak-kneed in a nerve-racking way. He found Nurse Keene — 'Keene by name, keen by nature,' she was fond of saying as she frowned at his charts — truly terrifying, and he had a childlike need to placate her. Hence he'd decided to bike to his interview with Pearce Aston. The only problem was that cycling gave him a terrific appetite and he'd crave all the bad carbs later. You couldn't win — life was always waiting to trip you up. He glanced at Patrick and Noah's house as he wheeled past and saw Noah's silhouette through the partly drawn curtains, facing the flickering TV screen.

Pearce Aston was installing new software at an antiques warehouse called 'Time After Time.' It was a huge old barn, filled with rows of curios. The musty smell reminded Ali of his mother's sacks of poultry feed. True to its name, it specialised in clocks, and Ali walked past lines of ticking timepieces ranked under a banner that said, *Enjoy Yourself — It's Later Than You Think!* He wasn't sure that chilling message would encourage buyers. Aston was in an office at the back, behind the main counter, clicking fast on a mouse.

'Won't be a min, take a seat.' He flashed Ali a quick smile before gazing back at the computer screen.

Ali sat and watched him. Aston was exceptionally hand-some, clean-shaven with a square jaw, an aquiline profile and dark, wavy hair. Too good to be true, Ali brooded, resent-ing his gym-honed frame. The tweed peaked cap was an annoying affectation. He wore the kind of suit that Patrick favoured, narrow trousers with a slim-fitting jacket. Not the type of outfit you could wear when you had a straining gut and flabby torso. Ali sighed and retied a trailing shoelace. Bending down must use a few calories.

Aston said, '*Yes!*' and flicked a switch with a flourish. 'I'm all yours,' he said breezily to Ali, as if he were bestowing a great favour.

'Will we be uninterrupted in here?'

'Sure. Ms Carstairs, the owner, is out this morning and she said it was okay to use this office. How can I help? It was terrible news about Lyn. Lily's still in bits.'

'Was it terrible — for you? You didn't like each other.'

Aston shook his head. 'Correction. Lyn didn't like me. In fact, in my opinion, she hated me. It wasn't mutual.' He had a cocky manner. He'd pulled a little footstool up, crossed his ankles on it, and sat with his arms along the sides of the office chair. He might have been granting an audience.

'Oh, I see. Tell me about how you got involved with the family.'

'I have already given this information.'

'So you have. But we have to investigate now with a body and new details.'

'What new details?' He flicked the brim of his cap.

None of your business. 'Quite a few, including forensics. You met Lily at her school in early March 2013, didn't you?'

'That's right. I'd started my own company, installing and upgrading software systems. I'm doing really well, built quite a reputation around the region. The contract at the school was one of my first biggies. I walked into a classroom and there was my beautiful Lily. We really clicked and started seeing each other.'

'It must have been difficult.'

'How?'

'Her dad had just left the family and they were in turmoil. She'd have been raw and upset, not necessarily a good time to start a new relationship.'

Aston gave him a supercilious glance. 'Really? You sound like an agony aunt — sorry, uncle.' He smiled smugly at his own joke. 'Lily was mad at her dad and very let down. I couldn't understand how he could do that to his family, except that, in my opinion, poofs are always flaky. I'm glad we fell in love and I could be there for her and support her. She'd have sunk into depression like her mum if I hadn't come along. She says that I'm her anchor in life.'

Ali was starting to enjoy this. Aston was in love with himself, and narcissists often proved to be garrulous in interview. 'Her mum seemed to have thought that if you hadn't come along, Lily'd have gone to uni and got a career instead of rushing into marriage.'

'I couldn't help what Lyn believed. If she was alive now, she might see things differently and even acknowledge that she'd been wrong, although she wasn't ever the type to eat humble pie. I hope that I'd have won her round in time.' He seemed satisfied with himself. 'We're happily married with our own house, and Lily runs a very successful business with me. It's growing all the time, so much that I might have to take someone else on. I bet Lily earns loads more now than she would have with some wanky degree in hospitality, which is what she'd been aiming for. I rest my case. Not that I have to explain my marriage to anyone, even you.'

He had a point but he was an insufferable wee scrote. Ali crossed his legs, knocking the footstool so that one of Aston's feet dropped to the floor.

'I'd like to hear about the time Lyn came to your flat and there was a row.'

Aston realigned the footstool and adjusted his shirt cuffs. His silver cufflinks were in a figure of eight with intertwined letters, L and P. 'Lyn could be very full on and nasty when she took against someone. She'd had one of her regular rows with Lily, and Lily had come round to mine in tears. Then Lyn rocked up, all guns blazing. I wouldn't have let her in, but she was hammering on the door and annoying the neighbours. I just let her shout herself out. She was demanding that Lily come home with her, but Lily refused and locked herself in the bathroom. Lyn called me all kinds of names, including some I wouldn't have expected a lady like her to come out with.' That smug smile again. 'She spouted ridiculous stuff, like she'd get an injunction or go to Social Services. As if! It was all pathetic, to be honest. In my opinion, she was on a real edge and the doctor should have done more to help her. She needed stronger antidepressants. Finally, she wore herself out and left.'

'Must have really riled you.'

'Yeah, but only so much. I mean, I could have done without it, but Lyn was having a kind of breakdown, and Lily and me were solid. You put up with all kinds of shit when you love someone.'

'Where were you the night Lyn vanished?'

'At the prom, with my Lily. I got there at a quarter to eight, and I was with her until I saw her and her friends off in the limo after midnight.'

'Have you ever had any dealings with Steiner's in Orford End?'

'Nope.'

'Did you ever hear Lyn or anyone else in the family mention it?'

'Nope.'

'Okay. A colleague will be in touch with you for a DNA and fingerprint sample. I assume you'll be happy about that?'

He didn't seem too thrilled. 'Why do you need to do that? No one asked that back when Lyn disappeared.'

'As I said, we have new details. We're asking everyone who was close to Lyn, or had any connection to the premises where she was found. Just part of how we investigate.'

'It can't be easy, solving a murder after all this time.'

'Police work's never easy.'

'Sure, but there won't be much evidence.'

'Maybe. Maybe not.'

Aston tweaked his cap. 'Okay, well, if it's necessary I'll give the DNA and fingerprints. Anything to help find whoever did this to Lyn.'

He sounded insincere, but then sincerity wouldn't be Aston's strong point. Ali left him examining the software he'd installed and cycled away into the sunshine.

CHAPTER 12

As Ali neared Patrick's house, he had an attack of conscience. He hadn't seen Noah for weeks. He slowed, turned across the road and parked the bike down the side of the house. He had the code to the key safe so let himself in.

'Hi there, Noah, only me.'

'Living room,' Noah yelled.

The hallway floor was laminated and grubby, with coffee-coloured splashes at the bottom of the stairs. Noah was in his wheelchair by the window, reading on his Kindle.

'Just calling by. Sorry I haven't been in for a while.'

Noah had a blank expression. 'No need to be sorry. It's not a duty.'

'No, of course it isn't.'

'Hmm. I don't need mercy visits.'

Ali felt wrong-footed. 'Okay.'

'Patrick ask you to come?'

'No, I invited myself. Mind if I sit down?'

'Help yourself, there isn't a queue.'

Ali pulled up a chair. The place was a right kip. The room smelled like overripe fruit and the carpet needed vacuuming. It was unlike Noah to be so cutting. If anything, he usually put too brave a face on his situation. He seemed tense and withdrawn and his hair was matted.

'So, how are you doing?' Ali asked.

'Oh, okay.'

'I was up at the antiques place on a new case.'

'That's good.'

'See the match last night? New Zealand were class.' Ali expected Noah to come back at him, saying that they hadn't been a patch on Wales and then they'd launch into the usual teasing, but he just shrugged.

'Yep, it was a good one.'

'What are you reading?'

'Fifty shades of being a vegetable,' Noah said with a joyless smirk.

'Good read?'

'Excellent. A page-turner. Hope there'll be a sequel.' He glanced out of the window.

There was an awkward silence. Ali began to wish he hadn't come. Usually, he and Noah had a good bit of banter. Something had changed and he was out of his depth. Maybe the man was in pain or just having a bad day.

'Can I get you anything?'

'Like what?'

'A drink? Something to eat?'

'No thanks. You a home help now?' Noah looked out of the window again.

'Right, whatever you say. Game of cards soon?'

'Sure. Whenever. Cleaner will be here in a minute.'

Ali wondered what the cleaner did, given the state of the house. 'You're sure there's nothing I can do?'

'Sure. You keep asking that. I do still have some functions. It's marvellous what I can do with my limited capabilities.'

'Whatever you say.'

'Good. Anyway, Melinda's just on her way.'

'That's the cleaner?'

'Yep.' Noah bit his lip. 'Actually, there is something you can do, as you seem so keen. Lend me a twenty? I'm a bit short of cash until I get to a hole in the wall.'

'Sure.' Ali took his wallet out and handed over a note.

'Thanks. Appreciated.'

'I'll be off then. See you soon.'

'Yeah.'

As he wheeled his bike out, Ali met a statuesque woman with burgundy cropped hair, dressed in jeans and a clinging white T-shirt. Her lipstick was fire engine red.

'Hi, are you Melinda?'

'That's me, hun,' she said, with a toothy grin.

'I'm Ali, a friend of Noah's. I just called in to see him. He seems a bit down.'

'Hard for him, isn't it? Stuck there on his ownio. Some days, he's a sad panda. I'll see if I can cheer him up. We get on ever so well.'

She blew a kiss at the window and fluttered her fingers. She had long, purple lacquered nails. They wouldn't cope with much cleaning.

Ali rode back into the traffic. He realised that he was starving and started imagining steak and kidney pie with mashed spud and thick lashings of gravy.

* * *

The tiny back room of the narrow terrace house in Chaucer Road was cramped and dim. The walls were decorated with a deep blue embossed paper and covered in hand-painted Greek Orthodox icons of Jesus, the Virgin Mary and various saints. There were rows of Byzantine images on metal and wood. Siv sat below a triptych of a bearded Jesus and two stern angels in vibrant reds and greens. An ornate brass incense burner hung in front of a black and gold Madonna and Child, emitting a complex scent of frankincense and cedar. Music played in the background, deep male voices chanting to an accompaniment of bells. It was as if she'd entered Joe Dimas's private chapel.

He might be about to start conducting a service as he sat opposite her, dressed in a black polo neck beneath a black suit, blending into the dark walls. Taking in his thick white hair, bony nose and ice grey eyes, she was put in mind again of a tall, brooding bird, this time a jackdaw. Elegant, but with a certain air of menace.

'What have you done with Lyn's body, Inspector?' He made it sound as if she'd hidden it somewhere.

'Lyn is still at the morgue. They'll inform her husband when she can be released for a funeral.'

'Some husband!' He made a noise in his throat and then wagged a finger at her. 'That poor woman, left to rot for years! You should have found her. Yes, you should have been more diligent. I suppose you're going to make the excuse that you didn't work on the investigation back then.'

'I wish we had found her, Mr Dimas. In 2013, there was no indication of any connection between Lyn and Steiner's to take the police who were searching there.'

'Tcha! And is there anything now?'

'Perhaps.'

He made the throat noise again, a rasp of disgust. 'Perhaps, perhaps, perhaps. Isn't that a song?'

His challenging style was tiresome and she could taste the cloying incense.

'Where were you the night Lyn disappeared?'

'With my priest at the church of St Demetrius. I got there just before seven thirty and I left around two hours later. We wanted to raise funds for our various charitable projects and we decided on a dinner. My son didn't bother to tell me that Lyn had gone missing until the next day.'

'Were you and Lyn close?'

'We got on well. She was a good wife, and a good mother and daughter-in-law, nurturing and caring. My wife died a long time ago, and it was a pleasure to have a homemaker like Lyn around. She always made sure I was invited to family occasions, and she'd pop in to see me with casseroles and such. A woman, a mother, is the backbone and the beating, constant heart of any family, the source of comfort and reassurance. How can two men, two *husbands* create a family unit? It's against God and nature.'

You haven't met my mother. 'So did Lyn turn to you after Theo left her?'

Dimas steepled his fingers. 'I would say we turned to each other. We spoke regularly. It's hard to describe how shattered and appalled we both were. Such a betrayal, such shame on our family. And of course, the children were badly affected. I suppose that working with the police, you have to be politically correct about such things, but I say that a man who leaves his family for another man is no man at all. He's a thing of corruption and weakness.' It was issued as another challenge and he clenched a fist as he spoke.

'I don't agree with you, and not through political correctness, but let's not get distracted. Lily seems very fond of you. What did you make of her relationship with Pearce and Lyn's animosity towards it?'

His eyes glittered in the gloom. 'That's the one thing that Lyn and I disagreed on. She became insistent and rather loud and shrill about it, in a way that's unbecoming in a woman.' He made a little moue of distaste.

Siv could see how Lily's traditional set-up with Pearce would appeal to him, with Lily playing the homemaker and baking Papu's favourite pastries. 'Lyn didn't listen to your views on her daughter?'

'Sadly, no, she wouldn't see sense. She got quite heated about it one day at the clinic, so I decided to stay away from her, give her some space. I never saw her again.'

'You sided with Lily.'

'I sided with common sense. I couldn't see why Lily needed to go to university, and as for her being too young — I was married at eighteen and it was the making of me. I can't begin to explain how much I still miss my dear wife, even after twenty-five years. Pearce is a fine man, a man's man, with his own company and great ambition. Lily introduced him to me and I could see how much they loved each other. I was sure that he could look after her. Marriage is a great institution, and I believed it would be good for my dear Lily, especially after her father turned out to be such a disappointment.' His expression softened as he spoke his granddaughter's name.

'Lyn had a lot on her plate, with Theo leaving, and then her worries about Lily. Did she talk to you about any other problems?'

'No. Those would be enough for anyone, don't you agree?'

'Yes. But what about her work? She treated you at the clinic. Did she have any problems there?'

'None that she mentioned to me.'

'Did you ever suspect she was seeing someone else?'

The incense burner sputtered and he glanced at it, tensing as if he might spark flames himself. 'Tcha! Of course not! Lyn was a decent woman. She wasn't going to betray her marriage, even if her husband had.' He jabbed an accusing finger again. 'I hope you're not going to start tarnishing her memory. What's the point of these questions? You must already have much of this information.'

He sat perched in his chair, as if ready to pounce. The man chilled her. He wouldn't be someone to cross. He might be in his early seventies, but he was lithe and fit. The rich air choked the room. Siv's head was woolly, her airways tightening and the ranks of icons seemed to be crowding in. She stared at the veiled Madonna and Child. The Mother of God had a jaded expression. She blinked and focused, returning Joe Dimas's sharp tone.

'We found Lyn's DNA at Steiner's. It indicates that she took part in sexual activity there — whether voluntarily or under duress, we can't say, or when it happened. Have you any idea why she might have been there?'

That stopped him in his tracks for a moment and his head darted back. 'That's shocking, but I have no idea how she got to that place. She never mentioned it to me. This is terrible. Does Lily need to be told that her mother was molested?'

'It may not have been molestation. We don't know.'

His eyes flashed. 'You don't know! You don't know! You're like a weasel politician, circling the issue, never getting to an answer!'

She could see where Lily got her taste for melodrama. 'Would you rather I made something up to keep you happy? Have you ever had any dealings with Steiner's Removals?'

'Never. I bought this house in 1969. I've had no need of a removal company, nor have I worked with one.'

'What was your job, before you retired?'

'I arrived in this country in 1967 and set up a business importing the beautiful icons you see around you. Many people collect them as works of art. That silver and gold St Nicholas by the window is rare, and worth thousands.' He gestured at the walls with satisfaction. 'I worked all hours, and was very successful for many years. My beautiful wife came here with me. We raised our son and he was a fine boy, mannerly and intelligent. If his poor, dead mother knew what had become of him . . . Although I miss her, I'm glad she didn't live to see the shame he brought on us.' He gazed longingly at the Madonna and Child. 'Is there anything else? I have a lunch appointment.'

'You haven't mentioned your grandson, Mr Dimas.'

He sat up straight. 'Tcha! Adam is lost to me, living with those perverts. I expect they're turning him into one of them.'

Siv's hands were clammy with sweat. She could achieve nothing more here. She'd already read the information he'd given her in the case files. She stepped with relief into the air and bright sunlight, her eyes smarting, the aroma clinging to her hair and clothes. Still, she'd smelled of far worse things after home interviews. In the car, she opened the windows and watched a van driver unload crates of shopping.

This area was called Poets' Piece and was slowly becoming gentrified. The house that Bartel was interested in was in Wordsworth Road. She was due to view it with him the following day, and might as well drive by it now. She stopped the car for a minute. The house was mid-terrace, shabby, and she could see that the windows would need replacing, but Bartel was practical and wanted a fixer-upper. There was a side entrance after every sixth house, leading to an alley that ran along the backs of the terraces. When she was fifteen, she'd gone to a wild party in a house somewhere along this road, where she'd smoked a lot of dope and had unmemorable sex with a boy she didn't even fancy that much. A neighbour who'd had enough of the thumping music had called the police in the early hours. She'd slipped out the back gate as they were coming through the front door. Her father had been too exhausted by Rikka's arrest for shoplifting that week to notice that she hadn't crept into the house until 3 a.m.

She recalled her father's constantly perplexed expression. He'd been living a quiet, academic life until two adolescent hooligans descended on him without warning. He'd done pretty well, considering, kept them healthy and more or less attending school apart from brief episodes of truancy. Rik had carried on shoplifting after her caution but she had never been caught again. Siv wondered if she was still at it, cruising the aisles of shops in Auckland, her deft fingers magicking items into pockets or bags. Old habits die hard.

Before she drove away, she rang Lily Aston's home number.

'Aston Software Solutions,' Lily said in a bright voice.

'Hi, Lily, it's DI Drummond. How are you doing?'

Her voice dropped. 'All right, I suppose.'

'Just a quick question, and it might seem strange, but do you remember if your mum was having a period the night she went missing?'

'Sorry?'

Siv repeated the question. 'Sometimes, mothers and daughters share that kind of information.'

'I've no idea. Why are you asking me that?'

'We've found some DNA evidence. It would be helpful to clarify.'

'You could ask Izzie Sitwell. She and mum were great pals. I could imagine them doing girly talk and sharing out tampons.'

Spiteful. Siv remembered the name 'Izzie' from the reports — one of Lily's 'girls.' Such a juvenile concept for grown women to be clinging to, and so suited to the vacuous Lily. 'Is Izzie one of your Damsels?'

'That's right.'

'Can you still be a Damsel if you're married?'

'What do you mean?'

'A damsel is an unmarried woman.'

There was a long pause while Lily computed this and then replied sulkily, 'It's just a name that we decided on when we were at school. We can call ourselves whatever we like.'

'Of course you can. I can be the Duchess of Berminster if I want. Can you text me Izzie's number?'

'Okay.'

'Thanks. Talk soon.'

* * *

Up the steps, in the door, open fridge, pour a glass of akvavit. Bliss.

Am I turning into an alcoholic? It wasn't the first time she'd asked herself that question. Before Ed died, they'd had a couple of glasses a week. Now she craved a nightly supply. She'd have to consider this situation properly but she was too exhausted to bother about it now.

She changed into Ed's sweatshirt and heated the tortilla she'd bought on the way home in the microwave. Then she slumped on the sofa. Her food was only just warm enough, but she didn't care. The visit to Theo Dimas had been hard going. She'd kept back forensic details because he was still a suspect, explaining only that DNA results indicated Lyn's presence and possible sexual activity at Steiner's. He'd sunk back in his chair.

'So, what — Lyn might have been seeing someone? Meeting someone? In that place?'

'That's one scenario. The evidence could indicate that. She may have been there before the night she vanished.'

He'd bent his head and gone quiet. When he spoke, his reaction hadn't quite been what she'd expected.

'What a rotten, hypocritical bitch! She gave me hell about falling in love with Monty, and went on about loyalty and respecting marriage vows. Yet she was sneaking off to see someone! All those things she said about me to the kids, and she was shagging in a crappy deserted building like some wayward teenager!'

He had a point and she could see how, after the damaging lies that Lyn had spread about him, that belief would bring him gratification.

'I've said that it's a possibility, not a certainty. I have to consider it seriously. Take me back to before you left — maybe a couple of years, if you can. That premises had been empty for some time. Did Lyn ever give any sign that she was seeing someone else? Unexplained absences, odd phone calls, anything?'

He'd shaken his head, stared at the carpet. 'Hang on . . . the previous summer, 2012, she was having facials and trying out different hair colours. Just one of those things women do.'

'And maybe you weren't that interested in what Lyn was doing. Would you have noticed if she'd been having an affair? You were seeing Monty by then.'

He'd had the grace to blush. 'You're right. I didn't pay her much attention. I wouldn't have blamed her for having an affair — but then turning on me if she had, as if she was innocent of playing away herself! Talk about two-faced — one rule for me and another for her! I just don't get it, though. Why would she agree to meet anyone in that abandoned place? Lyn was so . . . particular. She kept this house spotless.'

Maybe she'd felt abandoned and wanted to experience abandon. Misery had clouded Dimas's eyes. She'd steered him away from the topic of Lyn's double standards and asked about her previous workplace. He'd told her that Lyn had worked at a clinic called Foot Heaven in Seaford, but she hadn't been happy there. He had been vague about the reason, saying that she didn't rate the way it was managed and she'd had to write a report. She'd left when she became pregnant with Adam and decided to stay at home until he went to school. Then she'd got the job at Brookridge.

Siv had left him bewildered and drove home. Now she finished her tortilla, poured another drink and saw that she'd had an email from Rikka, a reply to one she'd sent weeks ago. Her sister contacted her infrequently. She'd always been unpredictable and enigmatic, but she was even more of a mystery woman these days. Siv had no idea what she worked as. She'd never had a career, but had dabbled in various alternative health interests. After she'd moved to Auckland, she'd mentioned aromatherapy, but there'd been no other reference as to how she made a living, or in fact to any details of her life. Siv knew better than to ask. Rik would flinch from direct questions as if she'd been invited to an interrogation meeting. She hadn't attended Ed's funeral, saying that she couldn't afford the fare back, but then Siv hadn't expected her to be there. Hers wasn't that kind of family. She read the brief missive:

> *Hi, Siv. Must be hard, having mad Mutsi living round the corner. Maybe you should move again and change your name. The cops can give people new IDs, can't they? Hope you're keeping Berminster crime-free and arresting lots of shoplifters! R x*

A true-to-form Rikka communication, saying almost nothing.

The evening was fine but chilly, so she fetched logs from the stack that Paul left her and stood for a moment, watching the glint of the river through the trees. A bright crescent moon lit the sky and smoke was drifting from Corran and Paul's tall chimney. Corran's goats were bleating and she could hear him faintly, chatting fondly to them and clattering the bucket as he fed them. He had four goats now and she'd been introduced to them: Judy, Ella, Barbara and Nina. They didn't sound as harmonious as the legendary singers. Corran had explained that they were highly intelligent. Their bleats carried a range of emotional tones, and they could register moods in one another's voices. He claimed that they had different calls when they were hungry or wanted to be milked. Siv could only hear a generic *maah*, but didn't doubt their intelligence. However, it didn't stop them having terrible breath, and she tried to make sure she stood upwind if she was near them.

Last year, the background to her life had been the hum of London traffic. Now it was this rural soundscape. How quickly a coin flipped. *Next thing, you'll be riding to hounds and calling, 'Tally ho!'* Ed laughed in her ear.

The brisk air nipped at her skin. She shivered, headed back inside and lit the wood-burner. The room soon smelled of smoky apples. She poured more akvavit, put her feet up on the stove, and wondered about Lyn Dimas choosing to hang out at Steiner's, her tinted hair and her cleansed skin glowing amid the garbage and broken furniture. Now that she'd built a better picture of the dead woman, she could understand more readily why Lyn might lower her standards and rough it. She'd had guts and a temper, as well as being a good mother and the reliable homemaker Joe Dimas had valued. Being the backbone of a family could become wearing if that family didn't seem to notice or appreciate your constant support. Maybe Lyn had never pushed any boundaries, and turning forty had made her willing to regress and transgress. Midlife crisis territory. She'd been aware of ageing and taken for granted, her husband had lost interest, and her daughter had been scathing towards her and found her embarrassing. Maybe drinking and screwing at Steiner's had been a way of saying, *Look at me, I can get down and dirty and be a rebel.*

It was a theory, and one worth bearing in mind, but if it was the case, whom was Lyn beautifying herself for and rebelling with?

Siv hadn't intended to, but ideas of self-enhancement led her to open her laptop and google *60Chic*. She found her mother's blog and was dazzled by a photo of her on a sun-drenched beach, dressed in a shocking pink-and-black-striped tunic, white jeans, pink wedge heels and a necklace of huge black beads.

> Hi, I'm Crista Virtanen and you might not believe it from my photos but I'm sixty-eight. I'm from Finland, but now I live in Sussex, UK. I started this blog because I want to be pro-ageing! Hey, age is just a number and we older women should EMBRACE it. Be proud and bring it on!
>
> Come on, all you girls of age. You've got miles to go and you've gotta look good in the sunset! Be badass and strut your stuff!
>
> I used to be a dancer (see the photos of me as a rock chick in *Hair*!) and I want to share with you how you can twirl and glide through your senior years.
>
> I'll give you loads of style tips, as well as some smoke-and-mirrors hints for distracting the eye from those difficult patches of crêpe-y skin or the unsightly bumps caused by gravity.
>
> As we used to sing in *Hair*: Let the Sunshine In!

Mutsi's first name was also Siv but she'd always used 'Crista,' her confirmation name. She'd gone by that name as a dancer, saying it was more attractive.

There were videos of Mutsi advising how to transition your wardrobe and build a capsule collection according to shape, talking about and demonstrating hydrating and moisturising, applying smudgy eyeshadow for a softer effect, curling eyelashes with a heated toothpick, the clever use of concealers and brightening the skin with lemon juice. She demonstrated dance exercises in a skintight leotard, and showed how to make highly nutritious and energising salads with broccoli spears, chicken, alfalfa and feta.

There were about thirty videos, numerous photos of Mutsi through the years, and page after page of her style secrets. The woman was incorrigible, and Siv had to admit grudgingly that she was attractive. She was waiting for a comment from Ed but none came. She slammed the laptop shut. She was edgy and raw. It was hard, being unsure of when Ed might murmur in her ear. She longed to hear him, but when he went silent, she was bereft again. Well, if he was going to absent himself for now, she'd contact someone who'd chuckle. She emailed Rikka a link to the blog with a one-line message: *Mutsi's new incarnation as third-age guru. The pensioners' Gwyneth Paltrow.*

She needed to escape into her folding zone. The design she was working on was laid out on the kitchen table. She sharpened her pencil and reviewed her drawing so far. She was designing a kusudama piece, a modular creation made of multiple units fitted together. A software programme would make the work easier, but she preferred to have a pencil between her fingers, and the intricate grey marks fanning out on the whiteness of the paper.

She'd started folding when she was eight, motivated by a need to block out Mutsi's confusing shenanigans with yet another 'uncle.' Her skill at maths meant that she was good at working out complex patterns. Concentrating on designs had helped to bring order to her chaotic childhood. This thing that she could do so well was just hers, and a world that she could enter at will. Paper creations were a crutch and a comfort for a transient girl, because if they were left behind during a rapid flit, she could quickly make new ones. Folding had become her therapy and salvation. Recently, she'd received some commissions and there'd been growing interest in her work. This modular creation was destined for an architects' practice in Ealing.

She worked quickly, absorbed, unaware that it was well past midnight. She didn't hear the wind rising, the frenzied yowls of two cats fighting or a fox barking on the other side of the river. When she was folding, she tuned out noise and was lost in a place where time was suspended. And while she focused on lines, creases and symbols, she forgot about her grief.

CHAPTER 13

Scott Darnley checked Mr Shakespeare's respiration and blood pressure. They were behaving nicely. He wondered if the man was any relation to the bard. He had a high forehead, so maybe he was. Scott might ask him when he woke up, minus his colon polyps.

He watched the flickering monitors while the surgeons finished up and listened to Gregorian chant, sung today by the monks of Buckfast Abbey. Brendan Edgeworth, the surgical registrar, always played it when he was operating. Scott found it soothing, but it had occurred to him that if a patient regained consciousness during anaesthesia — and it had been recorded — they might hear the melodic voices and assume they'd died and were listening to a celestial choir.

His mind wandered to Justin, who'd suddenly dumped him last month and hadn't replied to any of his calls, texts or emails. When he'd spotted Scott in the hospital car park or a corridor, he'd hurried away. After more than a year together, Justin's pathetic line, 'It's not working for me, I'm stifled, we both need to move on,' just didn't cut it. Scott wanted a proper explanation. He was entitled to more than a brush-off.

They'd just come back from a week in Barcelona when Justin had told him it was over in the taxi from the airport. And how cowardly was that? Announcing that in a public space and then just blanking him. He'd said there was no one else, but Scott had his suspicions. He'd seen Monty Barnwell talking to Justin a couple of times, once by the lifts and then outside the doors of the orthopaedic ward. They'd been standing close, heads bent. They'd been friends for a long time, so they definitely had history, but that had made him sick to the stomach. He'd had to brush away tears and wash his face in the loos.

It was hard too, because they worked in the same place, and news travelled fast in the hospital community, zipping along on the trolleys, travelling in the lifts and murmured over the steam rising from coffees. Scott had been aware of curious glances. Maybe colleagues had known about Justin and Monty long before he had. It was horrible that he might have been an object of pity without realising. In his head, he'd been playing a conversation that Justin and Monty might have had before Barcelona. *I owe him this holiday, Monty, and anyway, it's all booked. I'll make sure he enjoys the week and then I'll tell him it's over.*

Since then, Scott had been picking over the relationship, recalling slights both real and imagined. He realised how much he'd always given in to Justin, letting him take the lead and make decisions about what films they saw, where they went on holiday, which restaurants they visited. He fixated on it, fuelled by hurt and resentment. He'd been dwelling on a night some years ago, when he'd seen Monty and Justin outside the Flare Bar in town as he was driving past. Monty's arm had been around Justin then. He'd been heading to a date himself and hadn't paid much attention, but the news reports about Lyn Dimas's body had jogged his memory regarding that night, particularly one online that recounted Theo Dimas's alibi. He'd seen a paragraph that said that Mr Dimas was estranged from his wife, and had been at home with his new partner that evening.

That was interesting. The police might well have the same response.

He kept seeing Monty's arm draped around Justin's shoulder. Maybe they'd had an on–off thing ticking along for some time, and Monty had tired of Theo Dimas now and was keen on another relationship. The gay community in Berminster was a small pond to fish in. It was bad enough being dumped and ignored, but if Justin had done it because he was already involved with Monty, that was even worse.

Time to send Mr Shakespeare to recovery. Scott signed off and sent a text to Justin on his break.

> If you keep ignoring me, you'll only make things worse. You don't just discard love as if it never happened. I miss you so much. We can make a go of things if we really try. I've been reading about Lyn Dimas, Theo's missing wife. They found her body. The evening she vanished, I saw you with Monty Barnwell outside the Flare Bar. There are people who might be interested in that sighting. I don't want to cause any trouble for you. It's the last thing I want. If we can just talk, we can sort everything out. You've got forty-eight hours to contact me or I might make some phone calls.

He pressed 'Send' and bought a carton of fruit juice. If Justin ignored him, he might well do some sharing. He could make calls that would ensure that Justin would end up wishing that he'd not been such a total shit.

Knowing that he could do that, that he could take control for once, knocked the edge off his pain. Justin would find out what it was like to be hung out to dry.

He had no idea that his memories of what he'd seen outside the Flare Bar were leading him to draw both right and wrong conclusions.

* * *

Siv had decided not to speak to Jeff Downey alone. Instead she would take Ali with her. He was waiting for her in the car park eating a muffin, sucking on a cigarette and gazing at a bush of white snowberries.

'I used to love popping those when I was a kid,' he said. 'My dad told me they were deadly poisonous and never to lick my fingers when I'd touched them. I believed him for years, until Polly said it wasn't true.'

'Maybe that's what your dad believed. Maybe his dad told him the same thing.'

Ali shook his head. 'Nah, it'd be my dad's idea of a joke. Verbal and practical jokes, his regular comedy turns. It's just another way of bullying people, isn't it?'

'I suppose. Is that why you're worried and chain-smoking, because of your dad's jokes?'

'Nah. I'm at the diabetic clinic tomorrow. Dreading it.'

She didn't comment on the muffin wrapper because there was no point. He made his own choices. On the way to Downey's, she went over the brief meeting she'd come from with DCI Mortimer. He'd seemed more emollient than usual.

The sun was low in the sky and she pulled her visor down against the glare. 'Is Mortimer married?'

Ali loosened his shirt collar. 'Divorced a couple of years ago. It was bitter, but he kept the yacht, which made his face less like a wet week than usual.'

'I gathered that he's interested in sailing from the pictures on his wall, but I wasn't aware he had a yacht.'

'Well, it's more of a big boat but he refers to it as his yacht. It's a white and blue one called *Quicksilver* — moored in the harbour. Occasionally, he invites us all on it for drinks. In fact, be warned, there'll be an invitation coming up soon, because he does an annual Halloween bash. Fancy dress and all. Mortimer gives a prize for best costume — posh bottle of wine.' He shot her a mischievous grin. 'Something for you to look forward to.'

Siv's heart sank. 'Is the fancy dress compulsory?'

'Well . . . let's just say that if you don't make a bit of an effort, you get a glare that tells you you've let the station down.'

'I suppose Tommy Castles always dressed up.'

'Oh aye. Tommy was your man for a great costume. The last one before he left, he went as a very scary Count Dracula with fake blood and all. He won the prize.'

'Of course he did. And you? What do you wear?'

'I'm from Derry, the Halloween capital of the world, so I'm in my element. I've gone as a wolf and a zombie, but my favourite is a banshee.'

'Isn't a banshee a female spirit?'

'Now you're being picky. Of course, but I reckon spirits can be gender-neutral in these enlightened times. I believe in ghosts.'

She turned to him. 'Seriously?'

'Aye, I do. There's definitely a spirit world. I've encountered it from time to time. There was a witch burned near the walls in Derry and I'm sure I heard her wailing one night.' He hummed under his breath for a few moments. 'Do you . . . erm . . . I hope you don't mind me asking . . . Do you ever sense your husband is near?'

She was taken aback, but she found that she didn't mind the question because it came from him. 'Quite often. But I don't believe it's his spirit. It's my memory of him, giving him form.'

'Does it comfort you, when you sense him?'

'Mostly, but not always.'

He hummed again. 'Hat-trick loves the Halloween party. He was a vampire bat last time. Noah comes too, usually as a spider covered in cobwebs. I'm a bit worried about him, he seems down and I reckon that's affecting Patrick.'

'About anything in particular or just the hand that life's dealt him?' Noah had once told her that Patrick shouldn't have to care for him and he hated being a burden.

'Not sure. He's not exactly communicative.'

'Have you said anything to Patrick?'

'Haven't had a chance yet.'

She stared at the road as Ali navigated speed bumps, still unnerved about Halloween. Her team in the Met hadn't gone in for parties or dressing up — just drowning their tensions in the pub. She wondered if she could have diplomatic flu for the end of October. No, that wouldn't wash. She'd have to turn up. She felt a ripple of panic and then annoyance with herself. *Get over yourself — it's just a party, not an invitation to an execution.* She switched her focus to the coming interview. It would have been handy to have had forensic results before seeing Downey, but it was going to be at least another day until they arrived.

His house was called 'Dunnitall' and had fake ivy attached to a trellis growing in a plastic pot by the door.

She fingered the stiff, dusty leaves. 'Who grows artificial plants in the garden? What's the point?'

'Someone who likes fakery? Mind, it's only like people having that phoney grass.'

Downey was still in his office suit, a grey pinstripe. The top of his head was bald, but he had a circle of gingery hair like a tonsure below it. Just beneath his right eyebrow was a large, distracting mole.

'Come in, come in,' he said breezily. 'Welcome to my humble abode. I've just got back from a hard day at the coalface, going through business loan applications and trying to work out who's telling porkies. No rest for the wicked, eh?'

They sat in his living room. It smelled strongly of the black-and-white dog who was curled up on the sofa. The walls were covered in a bright purple wallpaper and the carpet had a busy orange-and-green floral design. Over the mantelpiece was a garish picture in yellows and pinks, of a bare-breasted Polynesian woman with an enticing smile, holding a mango out to the viewer.

'Can I get you a hot beverage and a bikky? I've some ginger nuts.' He tapped his head. 'I'm a ginger nut who eats ginger nuts!'

'We're fine, thanks.' Siv made introductions as Downey sat, pulling up his trousers at the knees. His shoes had shiny patent-leather toecaps.

He flashed them a toothy smile. 'I follow your DC on Twitter. He tells it like it is. You've landed a tough job, trying to find a murderer when the trail's gone cold. I have great respect for the police, especially when you have to deal with scumbags who do this type of thing.'

'Who said the trail's gone cold?' Siv asked.

'Well . . . It's been a while, that's all I meant. It's bloody awful, what happened to poor Lyn. A crying shame. Left in that building like that — I still can't believe it. She was a lovely neighbour, a good egg. So friendly and kind, always a cheery wave and a smile.' He sighed nostalgically.

If Downey got any oilier, he'd slither off his chair. Siv said, 'But not friendly enough to accept your advances, I understand.'

Downey grimaced but the barb slid off him. 'You've read stuff from 2013. I'm sure the gossips had a field day. A man living on his own is always a subject for tittle-tattle. What can I say? I'm a red-blooded male and she was a good-looking woman. Do I have to apologise for fancying her?'

'No, but tell me about it.'

He had a doughy, pliable face, one moment sad, then wistful, then wearing a little-boy grin. 'I was on my own and Theo had left. Lyn was very attractive and she was lonely. I wanted to cheer her up and tell her I appreciated her. I took her flowers and asked if she'd like to go out for dinner. She said no.'

'And that was it?'

'Absolutely. If she hadn't disappeared, I'd have left things a while and tried again. Faint heart never won fair lady and all that. But I backed off when she turned me down. She was nice about it, said it was too soon after Theo going. That told me I'd have to pace things and bide my time.'

That made Siv queasy, but he sounded as if he was proud of his tactical skills. 'What kind of general relationship did you have as neighbours?'

He puffed his cheeks out and laughed. 'Neighbourly, amazingly enough!'

'Tell me a bit more. How long had you known the family?'

'I was living here when they moved in, so about twenty years. My wife was still with me then. We passed the time of day, chatted over the fence, borrowed stuff occasionally . . . the usual things. I'm keen on my barbecues in summer, so they popped round for those sometimes. I was doing a barbie for my family that awful night, as it happens, so I asked Lyn if she fancied coming, but she said no. If she'd come with Adam, she might never have ended up dead in an abandoned building.'

Siv said, 'What happened to that barbecue in the end?'

His eyes crinkled, glancing from her to Ali. 'How do you mean?'

All his expressions seemed fluid and exaggerated. She was reminded of Morph, the plasticine model she'd watched on children's TV, who could change shape randomly. 'I've read that your daughter couldn't make it.'

'Oh, I see. That's right. She had a problem with her car battery. I put the stuff I'd cooked in foil and we ate it the next day, when she came with my grandkids.' He turned to Ali again. 'Does the sergeant ever get a chance to talk or have you put him on the naughty step for bad behaviour?'

Ali smiled. 'Am I bothering you?'

'Gosh, no! I'm honoured to be visited by two detectives. Always happy to help the police when I can. I almost applied to join the force when I was eighteen, but my mum wanted me to go into banking. She said it would be a safer, steadier occupation. I suppose she was right about safer, although the routine can be stifling, and I've always regretted not joining the boys in blue and serving the public.'

Was this guy for real? Ali put a hand over his heart. 'That's touching. So, tell me — you say you found Lyn attractive. Had you ever tried anything on with her before her husband left? Given that you're red-blooded and all.'

Downey adopted a wounded expression. 'Certainly not! I don't do infidelity, especially after my wife left me. It only brings heartbreak. It took me years to get over the split. The Dimases always seemed happily married and mad about their kids. I was gobsmacked when I heard Theo batted for the other side. Never saw that coming. Poor old Lyn certainly went through the mill with that.'

'You never got the idea that she might have been seeing some other red-blooded male?'

'Lyn having an affair? I never got that impression. Why — has someone told you she was?'

Ali ignored the question. 'Have you ever had any connection with Steiner's at Orford End, or have you ever been to the premises?'

'I'd never heard of the place until I saw the news report about Lyn's body.'

'So Lyn never mentioned it to you?'

'Never.' Downey smirked at Siv, pointing a thumb at Ali. 'Crumbs, can't stop him gabbling now he's got going.'

'How many times did you see Lyn the day she went missing?' Siv asked.

'Twice. I was in her house that day returning a strimmer, and I saw her outside in the evening while the girls got in the limo.'

'Did you go out at all that night?'

'I didn't. After my daughter rang, I put out the barbie and covered it because rain had been forecast. I folded my apron, stored the cooked food in the fridge, and watched a game show with a plate of bangers. I must have dozed off, because next thing, poor little Adam was banging on the door. Then all hell broke loose. When they said at Smart Mart that they hadn't seen Lyn, I started dreading that something bad must have happened.'

'What did you think had happened, when weeks went by and Lyn hadn't been traced?'

His expression morphed to tragic. 'I had no idea. Lily said she'd killed herself. I supposed that could have been the case. People do strange things when they've had the kind of shock Lyn experienced, with her hubby leaving in that way. At least my wife left me for a chap — not sure how I'd have taken it if she'd gone off with Victoria, not Victor.'

Siv stared at him, wondering about his glib manner. She sensed an unpleasantness under the cheery front, but any further questions eluded her.

'What a slimy dose he is,' Ali said once they were back in the car.

'He plays parts well. I bet he's the archetypal bank manager at work. The Dimas family say he was a scrounger and a pest. Pests don't usually give up as easily as he claims he did when Lyn gave him the brush-off.'

'He's interesting in an off-kilter way.' Ali shrugged. 'Maybe he wears a police uniform in the privacy of his own home. Could he have had a thing going with Lyn the year before Theo moved out?'

'And then she didn't want to pick up where they'd left off? Possibly.'

'He's no Adonis and she was a pretty woman. Why would she ever have bothered with him?'

'Need, wanting to be wanted, desperation, he was all that was on offer and he was attentive. Take your pick.'

'He could have done it, guv.'

'A spurned man? Certainly. But we have nothing concrete on him, unless forensics provide something.'

'All the clashing colours in that room gave me a headache. And that painting! He's got terrible taste.'

'If having bad taste made you a killer, we'd be arresting half the population.'

Ali sighed and started the engine. Siv watched the glowing sunset, wondering if Downey had once morphed into a murderer.

* * *

Bartel was tapping walls and window frames with his huge roughened hands, lifting corners of carpets and rocking back and forth on floorboards. These narrow houses had been built for smaller Victorians, and he dominated the room, blocking the light. He was wearing a khaki-and-cream body warmer with his jeans tucked into size-fourteen army surplus boots, a paramilitary guise. The estate agent kept giving him dubious glances.

Siv found the inside of the empty house in Wordsworth Road dispiriting and she understood why. Mutsi had trailed her and Rik through a few places like this, pitching temporary camp. It had been divided into bedsits years ago, and it had the forlorn air of a place where joyless, transient lives had been lived. The walls were mainly covered with a rough, dirty white woodchip. All the internal doors had locks and there were odd light fittings with dangling cords. A pocked dartboard hung on the wall of the upstairs room they were examining. She glanced out of the back window and saw a long, narrow garden filled with weeds, bins, burst rubbish bags, rusting ladders and bikes, an abandoned avocado-green toilet, an old-fashioned, high pram which might be worth a bit if it was reclaimed, and a life-size cardboard Wonder Woman.

'Can I see the loft?' Bartel asked. He wasn't at all fazed by the state of the place.

The agent was Violet Finch — 'Call me Vi' — a middle-aged, nervy woman. She eyed the landing ceiling without much hope. 'I've no idea if there's a ladder, I'm afraid.'

'No problem.' Bartel seized a chair from a room, stood it under the loft door and climbed up. He pushed at the rectangle above and it slowly shifted, revealing the end of a ladder. When he pulled it down, the air filled with a cold, fusty smell, clouds of dust and flakes of insulating foam. He took a torch from his pocket and headed up.

'Please be careful, sir!' Vi fluttered her fingers anxiously.

'It's okay, he works on roofs,' Siv said. They watched the ladder shake as Bartel's huge boots clamped on the rungs.

The agent leaned back against a patch of damp woodchip, then pointed at her. 'I saw you on the news. A report about the body found at Steiner's.'

'That's right. I'm a detective.'

'Dreadful thing. I'm amazed that place ever sold, but it's a disgrace that it was left to rot for so long. It was on our books for two years and there was only one sniff.'

'You've been in there?'

'Just the once, when I showed a prospective buyer around.'

'When was that?'

'I'm not sure. Quite a while ago.'

It occurred to Siv that this was an avenue they hadn't yet considered, and she was annoyed at herself. Scoping the background in a case like this was crucial. She still had lapses of concentration when her brain was foggy, and she lived with an undercurrent of worry that she'd miss something important. Ali was one hundred per cent dependable and thorough, but not a self-starter, and although Patrick had his moments, he often seemed distracted and she didn't entirely trust him. She listened to the ceiling vibrate as Bartel tramped above. 'Do you remember who the buyer was?'

Vi pursed her lips. 'It was a man, but I don't remember his name.'

'Would you still have records?'

'Gosh, no idea.' Vi flinched, as if she wished she'd never mentioned it.

'I'd like you to find out for me.'

Vi was even more disconsolate when Siv asked her to go to the station for fingerprinting and a DNA swab. 'You do appreciate that we need to eliminate people from the inquiry. It would be a great help.'

'Do I have a choice?' Her mouth turned down.

'Yes and no. I'd rather you did it voluntarily.'

'Oh, I see.' She put an anxious hand to her throat as more dust sprayed from the loft aperture.

Bartel appeared, looming above them in the dark rectangle, the torch illuminating his beard. He resembled a Nordic god, Odin or Thor, or a Viking who'd strayed from his longship. Bartel the Bald.

'There's a wasp's nest,' he said. He climbed down and gave the ladder a shove, then clapped his hands together so that bits of debris fluttered around. 'That'll do.'

Vi gave him a full-beam smile. 'The owner is open to reasonable offers and I'd say there's room for negotiation.'

'There'd need to be,' Bartel said. 'It's not exactly immaculate. A lot of work to do. I'll be in touch.'

They headed to the Horizon café at Minster Beach for a lunch of mussels and chips, washed down with icy beer. Siv had a great fondness for it, because it was where her father had brought her and Rik for a much-needed dinner on the day they'd arrived to live with him. He'd had only a couple of hours warning of their arrival. Mutsi was heading to Helsinki to marry a baronet who didn't care for children, and who had spotted that Rikka and Siv spelled trouble. He'd given her an ultimatum of 'It's them or me,' so Mutsi had despatched them on the train from Victoria with a bag each and no money, and phoned their father to say that they were on their way. *All we need are labels round our necks saying, 'Please look after these unwanted kids,'* Rikka had said gloomily. Siv had sighed. *At least Paddington had marmalade sandwiches for the journey.* In the Horizon café, they'd wolfed fish and chips and double helpings of banana cheesecake. The food had heralded the start of an unexpected, welcome life with proper, regular meals and, best of all, the same house to return to every day.

'I'll make an offer on that place,' Bartel said, 'but I'll leave it a couple of days. Make Vi sweat.'

'You've got specks of fibreglass in your right eyebrow from the loft. It needs a load of work.'

'Hmm. But that doesn't bother me. It's sound and the roof's only fifteen years old.' He ran a massive finger along his eyebrow. 'Do you reckon you'll buy a place here eventually?'

The question alarmed her, made her scalp itch and she was irritated at her reaction. *It's a perfectly reasonable enquiry from a friend, you idiot!* 'Probably,' she said, her throat dry. 'I'm fine where I am for now. I can't plan that far ahead.'

'No, and you don't need to. You're like a wobbly little kitten, finding your feet.'

That made her laugh. 'I've a favour to ask you.'

'You want me to solve your case, like last time, *madame*?' He grinned and dipped a chip in mustard.

'Will you come to a Halloween party with me on my boss's boat? Fancy dress.'

He sat back. 'Mortimer's throwing a party?' He was aware of her views about the DCI.

'Mm. Ali told me it's an annual thing.'

'You really want to go?'

She shrugged. 'No, but I don't have much choice. It's expected.'

'Ah, it's like that. Okay, I'll come and watch detectives at play while the fine line between the worlds of the living and the dead is at its thinnest. Could be fun. I can bring a flavour of Poland and recite from our famous poem, "Forefathers' Eve."' He put a hand to his chest and declaimed, '"There's milk, cake, sweet rolls, and fruit and berries. What is it you need, soul, to enter heaven?"'

She shivered at his deep, rumbling voice and the image of a soul lingering and waiting. She took a sip of beer and then looked out at the calm, milky sea. *You could go as a witch and put a hex on Mortimer,* Ed breathed in her ear.

Bartel bent and rubbed at his heel inside his right boot. 'Bloody new boots. Bloody blister,' he said. 'I'll have to get some of those special plasters.'

The sight of his enormous foot reminded Siv of her interview with Antonia Santos and something she needed to pursue.

After lunch, she headed off on her own for Cliffdean Point, where she walked for a couple of miles along the stony headland path, enjoying the mellow sun. She could see no one else and the solitude was like a balm. Swathes of faded mauve heather lay around her, and golden gorse waved in the light breeze. Terns and seagulls wheeled and shrieked across the waves, landing briefly on the shoreline. The sea far below was in a gentle mood, a dappled mix of sapphire, green and grey. In the distance, she could see the Bere Marsh nature reserve and the glint of its deep lakes. She tasted sea salt on the breeze and sniffed the evocative scent of autumn: wood smoke, leaf fall, the cooling earth beneath her feet. Well-being stole quietly through her and she stopped to raise her face to the warming sun.

Somewhere along here, Noah had been felled by a stroke when he was out running. He'd have been full of energy and life, his heart working hard, blood pumping, his bones and muscles invigorated, his skin tingling with salt spray. She wondered how long he'd lain, helpless, listening to the murmuring breeze, hearing bird cries, the warmth of the sun on his cooling muscles. There was a terrible and random cruelty in the way that such a young man had been struck down, but even more so in a place of such wild beauty.

She turned off the path, climbing upwards a little way and sat on a mound of scrubby grass, arms around her knees, amid clumps of golden samphire. Her phone interrupted her reverie.

'Hello, DI Drummond. It's Lewis Haddon here. Just a call to ask if you can indicate when Steiner's will be available for us to get on with the job.'

'I'm not sure, Mr Haddon. I'll check with colleagues and someone will update you.'

'Is that the best you can do?'

'Yes.'

'Are you getting anywhere with finding this killer?'

'I can't comment on that. I understand your frustration.'

'You really sound as if you mean that.'

'You catch more flies with honey than with vinegar, Mr Haddon. We'll be in touch.'

She tapped her phone against her chin and reflected on Lyn Dimas and the woman's rage at her husband's abandonment. She rang Izzie Sitwell and left a message for her. Then she googled details for the National Organisation of Podiatry and Chiropody and sent an email requesting information about a registered podiatrist.

CHAPTER 14

Grant Haddon and Adam Dimas were in McDonalds. Grant sipped a coffee while he watched Adam demolish a Grand Big Mac with fries, washing it down with strawberry milkshake. He'd been contemplating becoming a vegan for some time, and seeing Adam chewing and slurping on the greasy grey flesh, he decided he would, from today. His dad would moan and call him a 'plant muncher,' but then Grant was planning to move out once he'd done a term at uni. He and his friend Jamie were going to join up and find somewhere. There were loads of student shares around the coast and he'd saved quite a bit in the past year. He'd be able to afford it. Dad wouldn't like that either, he'd assumed that Grant would live at home while he did his degree, but that was a different bridge to cross. Dad was such a fusspot and so protective. Grant got that Dad obsessed about his welfare because it had been just the two of them for so long, and then he'd had the cancer diagnosis. But he needed to get out from under his father's intense focus. Jamie joked about his dad, and said that cancer hadn't killed Grant, but his father might manage to smother him with love.

Adam dug a fry into ketchup. He'd got Grant's email address through someone at school and had messaged him, asking to meet because he wanted to talk about his mum. Despite his reluctance, it was hard to refuse. If their positions had been reversed, Grant would have wanted to meet. He'd always seen Adam as a bit of a loser and had been sorry for him at Drama club, because he'd struggled to forget his inhibitions. Grant also needed to talk about what had happened at Steiner's. He couldn't discuss it with his dad, who'd been irritable for days when he'd found out that Grant had been there that morning instead of going to London as planned.

He'd almost sounded as if it was Grant's fault he'd found a body when he shouldn't even have been at the premises. ('For God's sake, why can't I rely on you to just do what you say you're going to!') Then his dad had maintained that it was best to put it down to experience and get on with things. 'Keep your mind on the bigger picture,' he'd urged. That's what his dad always said when he was uncomfortable and wanted to avoid a subject. It was a meaningless phrase. He kept worrying about his dad. He couldn't talk to him about the important thing that he so badly wanted to mention because if he did, it would make it seem as if he was questioning his dad and that wouldn't go well. But it was there in his head all the time now, niggling at him.

Adam sniffed and wiped ketchup from his chin with the back of his hand. He seemed sweaty and weird, and his eyes kept flickering. Grant wished now that he hadn't agreed to meet. He had no idea how to start a conversation, but Adam resolved that by tackling it head on.

'You found my mum, tied to a fridge,' he said.

'That's right. Did the police tell you about it?'

'Some of it, and my dad as well.' Adam guzzled his milkshake. 'I wanted to hear about it from you because you were there. Was it terrible?'

'Yeah, it was. I mean, it was a terrible shock. It wasn't your mum, really. It was her earthly remains.' Grant had mulled over how he'd say this and he was satisfied with his description.

'Tell me from the start,' Adam insisted. 'You went into Steiner's that morning and then what?'

Grant blinked and took a deep breath. 'That's right, we went to clear the place out. I went into the kitchen with a guy called Ivor. We decided to move the fridge first. It was a huge, old-fashioned thing. Ivor pulled it away from the wall and then I saw a . . . a figure attached to the grille at the back. We weren't sure what it was at first, but then we realised it was human remains. It was hard to believe. Then Ivor rang the police.'

'I've been researching what a body would be like after six years. I read an article about a woman who was found in her car in a garage. She was all desiccated and covered in spiderwebs and it said her face was like a mask. Was my mum all dried up like a mummy in a museum?' Adam had a clownish pink moustache from the milkshake. It made a strange contrast to the grim subject of the conversation.

Grant sipped his coffee and tried not to recall details of the awful figure behind the fridge. 'Yes, your mum's body had dried out. She still had hair. I'm very sorry. This must be terrible for you.'

'Have you had nightmares?'

'I'll always remember it.'

There was a silence. Adam chomped on a sliver of gherkin.

'I haven't seen her. Dad isn't sure, but he says I probably can if I want once she's at the funeral parlour. I don't know if I want to. She might be terrifying. I don't want bad dreams again.'

Grant was out of his depth. 'Well . . . that's up to you.' He could only hope that the undertakers would be able to make Ms Dimas more presentable. He had a vague idea that they used fillers and cosmetics, but it would be hard to make that withered thing remotely human again.

Adam fixed an intense, needy gaze on him. 'Dad wants her buried, but I'd rather she was cremated. In Wiccan wisdom, fire is a transforming element. It would be more like a proper ritual that way, and I could put cleansing herbs in her coffin. Then I could have some of her ashes and carry them around with me. It would be a way, a way of capturing Mum's energy and purpose, and keeping it with me for ever. She'd be able to guide me through life and guard me.'

Grant wondered if Adam had been unhinged by the discovery of his mother's body. He remembered a production of *Cymbeline* he'd been in and replied carefully. 'Okay. I don't understand Wiccan stuff. But burial or cremation, the same thing happens in the end. Shakespeare wrote: "Golden lads and girls all must, as chimney-sweepers, come to dust." That's kind of comforting in a way.'

Adam seemed to consider this. 'That sounds nice. Mum's hair was golden. But she was too young to come to dust. How could anyone do that to her? Just dump her like that? My mum never harmed anyone.'

Adam was staring at him as if he might have the answer. Grant could only shake his head. The sun was bright in a washed blue sky and he longed to escape into the streets, but he couldn't leave just yet. He wished again that he'd gone to London that day and had never witnessed those shrunken remains. He waited while Adam finished his meal, heavy with the burden of responsibility.

* * *

All the forensic results were back from Steiner's. Siv read through with a buzz of excitement, surprise and a large measure of bafflement. Had Lyn Dimas been having an unlikely threesome? She took the results to Ali and Patrick.

'We have one set of Theo Dimas's fingerprints on a wine bottle found in the kitchen sink at Steiner's, along with several of Pearce Aston's and Lyn's. Aston's and Lyn's fingerprints and saliva are also on the other bottle by the mattress. We already have Lyn's prints being on a mug in the sink. Aston's DNA was retrieved from the mattress.'

'Stall the ball!' Ali's jaw dropped. 'Lyn was there with her old man and Aston?'

'Possibly. It seems a strange combo. Just one set of fingerprints are all we have placing Dimas there, so that could be tenuous. The wine bottle might have come from the Dimas house and I suppose the mattress could have as well. We'll need to tease that out.'

'Maybe they were trying to pep up the marriage,' Patrick offered.

Siv said, 'It would explain Lyn's subsequent animosity to Aston, but if that was the case, surely Dimas would have objected to Aston's involvement with Lily. I suppose that he could have gone there on his own at some point for sex and left a wine bottle that Lyn and Aston touched subsequently. To my knowledge, Steiner's has never been a meeting place for gay men. Have either of you picked up on that?'

They both shook their heads.

'Okay, so if Aston and the Dimases had some kind of threesome, and Lyn and Theo later found him coming on to Lily, surely Aston would have been the one who'd end up tied to the fridge.'

'Perhaps Dimas and Aston were having the fling,' Ali offered.

'What, with Lyn watching? Hardly, and from what I've gathered, Aston is firmly hetero. I still can't square any of this with them being in that dump, but maybe we're about to get answers. We arrest them both. I can't wait to hear their explanations. We don't have any forensic matches from Steiner's for Jeff Downey, Joe Dimas, Monty Barnwell or any of the other named people. I'm having an estate agent's samples eliminated.' She explained about Vi Finch. 'Before we bring Dimas and Aston in, let's catch up on other tasks. Patrick, you first.'

He stifled a yawn. 'Trudy Kemp was rushed into hospital with a ruptured appendix a couple of nights ago, so no progress there. She was complaining about stomach pains when I saw her. She's been out of it, so I've asked the ward to call when I can talk to her. Nothing useful from Twitter.

I checked out the builders and nothing negative came up on any of them, or any link to Lyn.'

Siv frowned at him. Those results couldn't have taken him long. What had he been doing with his time? 'When you do catch up with Ms Kemp, ask her if she recalls anything about Lyn's problems at Foot Heaven, in Seaford. Ali, what have you got?'

Ali was drinking green tea. He hated the stuff, but it made him feel virtuous. Nurse Keene had told him off at the diabetic clinic. She'd scowled and waved his chart under his nose. 'I'm very disappointed. An intelligent man like you should be able to manage this better. I can't help you if you won't help yourself!' Every time he got scared, he took to a careful diet of fish, eggs, leafy vegetables and herb teas for a few weeks, before he relapsed. The next month would be long and miserable. He was relishing the chance to take out his suffering on Dimas and Aston.

He made a face as he swallowed, checking his notes. 'Aston's an opinionated piece of work and he seemed reluctant to give fingerprints et cetera. Now we know why. He said he'd never been to Steiner's. I checked back at the flat where Barnwell was living in 2013. It's a block of six. Three of the tenancies have changed since then, and the other three residents were out that night and couldn't offer any information. Maria Steiner lives in Lincoln now. She told me that she's only been to Orford End once, soon after her dad died, and she was pretty sure there was no mattress in the office then. She's never heard of Lyn Dimas. She's got a clean record and I verified her alibi for the twenty-eighth of July.'

'Right. You two, sort out our arrests. Patrick, a word before you do that.'

In her office, she watched him flop into a chair. 'Are you okay? You look done in. Problems at home?'

'Er . . . Noah had a fall. He's okay. Just been a bit worried about him.'

'You're sure that's all?'

'Yeah, guv.'

She could tell that he was holding something back, but if he didn't want to talk about his home life, there was no point in pressing him. 'Right. I need you to flag it to me if you're not pushed for work. We're not short of tasks.'

'Sure, course. Can I do an interview?'

She wasn't sure he'd stay alert. 'No, I'll do those with Ali. I want you to chase up Vi Finch, find out who she showed around Steiner's and when. And put pressure on the hospital to let you see Trudy Kemp.'

'I'm on it.'

'Good. Tell me as soon as Dimas and Aston are in the building.'

Her phone rang as he trailed out of the room.

'Guv, it's reception. A Dr Scott Darnley phoned in about half an hour ago, asking to speak to you. Said he's got important information about Lyn Dimas.'

She took the number and tried it, but it went to voice-mail. She left a message and then googled the name. Scott Darnley was an anaesthetist at Berminster General. His Facebook page had a profile photo of a hypodermic needle, and the most recent posts were of his holiday in Barcelona. Lots of photos of two men in tiny swimming trunks on beaches. She tried his friends list but it was protected. She wondered if Darnley knew Monty Barnwell and googled him. He wasn't on Facebook or other social media. She rang the hospital and was informed that Dr Darnley wasn't on shift until 2 p.m. She left another message for him and then nipped upstairs to update Mortimer.

She found him cleaning the glass on his pictures with a cloth. A pleasant lemony smell met her as she stepped through the door and told him of the pending arrests.

'Sounds very odd but promising,' he said. 'It's hard to see why a couple like the Dimases would be in a run-down place like Steiner's, but perhaps slumming it was a way of trying to keep the marriage going. Keep me updated — it would be good to get this one cleared from the books. Bring me evidence, DI Drummond, hard evidence.' He cleared his throat. 'Oh, by the way, there'll be an email invitation to all staff tomorrow for my Halloween party, on my yacht. I don't go in much for this kind of thing but it's become a bit of a tradition. It's a chance to get everyone together.'

'Thanks, sir. Ali told me about the party.' Mortimer appeared less wizened than usual and his hair was different. A bit longer and a lighter colour. He'd got new glasses, too, round tortoiseshell frames. Very on trend.

'Ah, yes. The sergeant's a great one for a party. He has that tremendous Irish sense of bonhomie. It's in his DNA!'

She'd have to remember to tell Ali that and watch his eyes narrow. 'That picture's familiar, sir. I'm sure I've seen that lake before somewhere.'

'Really? It was a present from a friend. It's a little forbidding, but the colours are lovely. If that's all for now, I'm expecting a visit from HR.'

Back in her office, she tried Darnley's number again, but it went to voicemail once more. She reread records of interviews with Dimas and Aston and printed off the forensics. She was ready with ammunition.

* * *

They started with Theo Dimas. He'd opted for a duty solicitor, a young woman with a tight expression. Her lips compressed even more when Siv gave her vague disclosure about evidence, mentioning only forensics. Dimas had a startled manner and was perspiring.

Siv poured him some water. 'Mr Dimas, you've been arrested on suspicion of involvement in the murder of your wife.'

'It's absolutely untrue. I had nothing to do with it.'

His solicitor shifted in her chair. She'd have advised him to say, 'No comment,' but from what she'd seen of him, Siv expected Dimas would find that difficult.

'Where were you on the evening of the twenty-eighth of July 2013?'

'Mr Dimas has already told the police that on two occasions, in 2013 and recently,' the solicitor said.

'I'd like him to tell me again.'

Dimas was wearing bright green-and-yellow braces today. They brought a discordant air of jollity to the tension in the room. He fingered one strap. 'I was at home with my partner, Monty Barnwell.'

'In Mr Barnwell's flat?'

'That's right. We had a meal and watched football.'

'Did you contact your wife that day?'

The solicitor leaned towards him but he shrugged at her. 'I've nothing to hide. I'm telling the truth.' He sounded defiant. 'I didn't talk to or see my wife. The first I heard about a problem was when Mr Downey rang me.'

'Mr Dimas, I've been reading and hearing a lot about how vicious your wife was to you after you went to live with Mr Barnwell. She was bad-mouthing you, telling your children, your family and friends that you had AIDS. She went to the hospital and was verbally abusive to Mr Barnwell in front of staff and patients. That's correct, isn't it?'

'Yes.'

Siv injected warmth into her voice. 'You must have been very angry when Lyn acted like that. Those were terrible slanders that she heaped on you.'

He responded to her caring tone. 'I admit I was angry. Who wouldn't be, faced with that kind of onslaught? I was worried for my kids and I missed them. Surely you can understand that?'

Suspects who appealed for sympathy were usually the easiest ones to crack. 'You hadn't seen your children for months, had you? Lyn wouldn't let you. Lily was old enough to be a law unto herself but you must have been dreading divorce proceedings, and the fight that Lyn might put up to keep you from Adam.'

'That's right.' He rubbed his eyes.

Siv's tone grew stern. 'And then when Lyn went missing, you were able to live back in your own home with your son and eventually your partner moved in. Her disappearance solved quite a few problems for you, and let you forge ahead with a new life without ongoing harassment and the perils of the divorce court. Some might think that was a neat outcome.'

Dimas jolted in his chair and grimaced at the solicitor. She gave him an 'I told you' stare before she glared at Siv. 'Inspector Drummond, I object to your implications. My client moved back into the family home in very difficult circumstances in order to care for his son. That was his duty as a father.'

'Okay. Doesn't mean it wasn't handy, though.'

Dimas dug deep and found some bottle. 'I resent what you're saying, what you're implying. I was doing my best for Adam and I tell you again, I had nothing to do with Lyn's death.'

Siv switched to a conversational style. 'Mr Dimas, have you ever been to Steiner's, the premises at Orford End where your wife's body was found?'

'No, never. I've told you that.' He sipped water thirstily.

'Do you drink wine?'

'What?'

'Wine. Do you drink it?'

'I suppose . . . Yes . . . I drink wine. Why?'

'What kind of wine do you like?'

'I don't understand . . .'

'You don't have to answer,' the solicitor reminded him.

'Red. I drink red.'

Siv sat back. Ali opened his folder, took out a photo of the wine bottle and passed it across the table. 'Do you recognise this?'

Dimas picked the photo up. 'Why should I recognise a wine bottle?'

'Examine the label. Take your time.'

Dimas scrutinised it pensively and passed it to the solicitor.

'What's your point?' she snapped.

Ali ignored her. 'Any ideas about that bottle, Mr Dimas?'

'Pass. The label says "Hermandad Malbec."'

'And is that a wine you drink?'

'Sometimes.'

'Okay. You see, Mr Dimas, that bottle was found in Steiner's. It bears your fingerprints, and yet you say you've never been there.'

Dimas reeled as if he'd been smacked. He snatched up the photo again. 'I haven't. I've never been there.'

'So you say. You see our difficulty, though — that bottle was there with your prints on. It's a hard one to square.' Ali sat back and sighed.

Siv tapped the photo with her pen. 'I need to ask you again. Have you ever been to Steiner's premises?'

He was frightened now. 'No comment.'

'Mr Dimas, we're just trying to work out what happened to your wife. We have evidence that she might have been at Steiner's before the night she was killed. When I visited you, I explained that we've found her DNA there. That included on a mattress. One possibility is that she might have agreed to sex with someone. Of course, she might have been kept there forcibly. She also drank wine there, including from a mug.'

'A mattress . . . What? I still can't believe that Lyn would go to a place like that.'

'She did, either willingly, or because she was forced. I'm sure you want us to find who murdered her. You might have been at Steiner's for some other reason. It would be best for you to tell us.'

'No comment.'

'For example, did you go there to find a man to have sex with? You must have been seeking relationships before you met up with Mr Barnwell, or even after you did.'

He sounded offended. 'Absolutely not.'

'This puts us in a difficult situation, given the forensics . . .'

'Christ's sake!' He put his head in his hands. 'This is madness! Are you saying that I went to *Steiner's* to drink wine and have sex with Lyn? Why on earth would I do that?'

Siv poured more water for him and offered some to the solicitor, who appeared to be sucking lemons. 'This is hard, Mr Dimas. If you can try to help us understand what's been going on here . . . Did you go to Steiner's at some point with your wife and perhaps Pearce Aston, too?'

'Aston? That waste of space? What are you talking about?'

'I'm talking about forensic evidence. Did you, Lyn and Aston have some kind of involvement there?'

'No!'

'When did you first meet Pearce Aston?'

'First? I've only met him *once* and that was enough for me.'

'When did you meet him?'

He held his braces tightly in clenched hands like a man clutching a lifebelt. His face had gone puce. 'It was in the spring after I'd moved out. I can't tell you when, exactly. I was in Sainsbury's in Bere Place and he and Lily were coming towards me. I reckon Lily would have ignored me if she could have, but it was difficult, because we were face on in the aisle. I said hello and they both muttered back, and then he pushed the trolley on fast and they were gone.'

'That's it?'

'Yes, that's it! I'd never seen him before that, and I've never met or seen him again, except in some of the photos that Adam brought home from the wedding. You know full well that there's no contact between us!' He stared hard at her and then back at the photo. 'Hang on, hang on!' He picked it up again. There was a long pause. 'I belong to a wine club. I've ordered a dozen bottles of this one from time to time. I'd have touched the bottles when I was taking them out of the case. That means my fingerprints would be on them, wouldn't it?'

'How do you explain the bottle being at Steiner's if you've never been there?' But he had a point. Lyn Dimas could have taken the bottle from home.

The solicitor had scented the problem. 'I'd say that's for you to establish, Inspector. If this is all of your forensics, then after what my client has freely told you, it's not much. That bottle could have been in his home and if so, he'd have handled it, therefore his fingerprints would be on it. Anyone could have taken it to Steiner's, maybe even when it was empty. Someone could have taken it out of his rubbish bin!' She threw her pen on the table and folded her arms.

It was best to cut her losses. Siv ended the interview and asked them to wait. She and Ali went out into the little courtyard garden and he immediately lit up.

'Hell's bells, guv!'

'Well, it was always a possible explanation and a likely one. We've no other forensics placing him at Steiner's. Lyn could have taken the bottle from their supply. I checked out the label on the other bottle. It's a cheaper Spanish red, possibly Aston's contribution. We can examine Dimas's wine club history, but we're stymied with him for now. Thing is, I believe him. He was lying about something in there, but not about Steiner's.'

Ali blew out a gust of blue smoke. 'Aye, I agree. It's unlikely that he killed her but there's something sneaky about him.'

'We'll bail him pending further enquiries and let him get home to Adam. Best crack on with Aston now.'

'He and his solicitor are preparing a statement. A weaselly wee move and, having met him, it doesn't surprise me. He must have realised that forensic evidence from Steiner's would include him.'

Siv wrinkled her nose. A prepared statement could make questioning trickier, because the suspect could just refer back to the written account. 'Well, he'll be pressured because he doesn't know any details about what we've got. Let's see if we can raise his temperature.'

CHAPTER 15

Pearce Aston wore his peaked cap at a jaunty angle. He sat so close to his solicitor, Nicci Cornlow, that he was almost in her lap. She'd agreed to read out his statement for the tape.

Siv held up her hand. 'Just before you do that, could I ask you to remove your cap, Mr Aston?'

He gaped at her, flashing gleaming white teeth. 'What for?'

'Call me old-fashioned if I say courtesy.'

He shrugged, flicked the peak and removed it, fluffing up his waves. 'That okay for you?'

'Thank you.' Siv didn't care about the cap, but it was a small initial victory, putting him in his place and marking that she owned the room.

Nicci Cornlow had a slow, flat delivery as she read out the statement. Given whom Aston was married to, it held potentially explosive content but she might have been reading a shopping list.

> 'I had a brief affair with Lyn Dimas between
> April and August 2012. It started when we met
> at the gym. I was living in a flat with two other
> people and she was married, so we either made

188

love in one of our cars or we met up at Steiner's, on a Sunday afternoon. I knew the premises was empty because I'd seen a story in the local paper about the place, saying it was dreadful that it had been left abandoned. I bought a cheap mattress and took it there to make it a bit more comfortable. We'd spend an hour or so, having sex and chatting. That's why police will have found forensic evidence relating to me there. I finished the affair in August 2012, because Lyn's marriage was in poor shape and she'd started to get clingy. She was lonely and wanted us to see more of each other. That wasn't a good idea and I didn't want a long-term relationship with her. She was upset about me ending things, but she didn't try to stay in touch.

'In March 2013, I met Lily Dimas when I was upgrading the computers at her school. I didn't realise at first that she was Lyn's daughter and by the time I did, I was in love with her. I phoned Lyn to tell her before she found out. She was furious and she wanted me to stop seeing Lily, but I said I couldn't and I wanted to marry her. That's why Lyn was so against our relationship. I just tried to keep out of Lyn's way after that.

'I had nothing to do with Lyn's disappearance or her death, and I had no contact with her in the weeks before she vanished. I was with Lily at the prom the night of the twenty-eighth of July 2013, from 7.45 p.m.'

Aston seemed satisfied when she finished reading, as if that wrapped everything up nicely.

'If your statement is true, you've been lying a lot, Mr Aston,' Siv said. 'You lied in 2013 and when Sergeant Carlin interviewed you recently.'

'It is true now. Every word. Cross my heart and hope to die.' He spoke emphatically, making a cross on his chest.

She wondered if his flippancy was down to crassness or because he was innocent. 'As the saying goes, be careful what you wish for. When you were at Steiner's with Lyn Dimas, was anyone else with you?'

'No, come off it . . . Why would anyone else be with us?'

'More than two can get together for sex and there is evidence that a number of people used the place.'

He raised his brows. 'Maybe you like that kinky stuff. Not my thing.' He seemed pleased with his riposte.

'But your thing is taking the woman you're romancing to a squalid dump and your idea of luxury is a cheap mattress on the floor.'

'In my opinion, it was handy and a safe, anonymous place to go. At least we could stretch out. Have you ever tried having sex in a car? It's very hard to get comfortable. Lyn was well up for it when I told her about Steiner's.'

'Did you see anyone else when you were there?'

'No — although I can't swear there was never anyone else around because we'd be a bit absorbed. Lyn found it exciting, going there. She got off on being a bit of a rebel.'

'Every woman's dream.'

He stiffened a little. 'Sneer if you like, but that's just the way it was, okay? That's the truth of it, whether you like it or not.'

'Thing is, when people are caught out in a lie, it's hard for us to tell when they've switched to the truth, however much they cross their hearts.'

'Mr Aston had his reasons for not speaking the truth, Inspector, as you must realise,' Ms Cornlow said. 'He hadn't expected to fall in love with Ms Dimas's daughter. He didn't want Lily to find out about his previous relationship with her mother. He didn't want her upset.'

'Very touching. Very gallant. I'm not sure I buy that.'

'There's no need to be sarky,' Aston said. 'I'd never have had the fling with Lyn if I'd known I was going to meet Lily. I'm not some kind of dirty perv.'

'Mr Aston, would you say that your wife has been upset during the years since 2013, wondering what had happened to her mother?'

He fiddled with his cap. 'Yeah. Course she has.'

'So you've been happy to sit back and let her and her family suffer.'

'No, I have not! In my opinion, I've done everything I can to help Lily through it. You ask her. She's always saying she couldn't have done it without me.'

'I'm sure Lily does say that. But then, she's been unaware of your previous romance and the information you've been hiding from her.'

Ms Cornlow leaned in. 'We've dealt with that, Inspector. Mr Aston was protecting his wife.'

'And yet he was adding to her torment and prolonging the agony, as far as I can see. If that statement is true.'

'What do you mean? That's a horrible thing to say.' He pleaded with his solicitor, 'Is she allowed to say that? Isn't it slander?'

Aston might be full of bullshit, but he wasn't too bright. The solicitor must guess what was coming, unless she was as dim as her client. Siv said coldly, 'Mr Aston, if you'd told the police in 2013 what you've now stated, they'd have searched Steiner's and they'd have found Lyn's body. Her family would have been spared a lot of pain. All your actions here have been selfish, so don't try to tell me that you were lying for Lily's sake.'

'It never occurred to me that Lyn might be at Steiner's. Why would she be there after we'd called things off? I told you, I was only trying—'

'Oh, do cut the crap. If Lily had found this out before your wedding, she'd probably have refused to marry you.'

'No, that's not right. Lily's devoted to me. We'd go through fire for each other.'

'Come on! You'd been having sex with her mother on the floor of a derelict building! Hardly what the bride wants to hear before she heads to the altar to marry the man of her dreams! Seems to me you'd have turned from her dream man into her nightmare. Maybe you will now, when this comes out.'

He tugged at the front of his hair. 'Lily won't find out, will she? What's the point of dragging up something that's in the past?'

'Her mum's murder must feel very present for her.'

Aston bent his head and muttered to himself. Siv sat back and Ali took over. He launched in conversationally. 'So tell me, Mr Aston, when you and Lyn Dimas were snuggling up at Steiner's, did you have wee picnics and such?'

'What do you mean?'

'Well, it wasn't the most upmarket venue for a tryst. Maybe a wee drink helped the mood along, made things a bit cosier.'

'You don't have to add to your statement,' his solicitor advised.

Aston touched the paper, as if the statement was a lucky charm. 'We drank wine sometimes, yes.'

'Nice. Did you bring it along? White, red, rosé? Plonk or something classier?'

'We both liked red. I bought a bottle once or twice, I can't remember exactly. Lyn brought a bottle from home once, expensive stuff.'

'How many times did you have sex at Steiner's?'

'Half a dozen, maybe more. I can't remember exactly. Then, as I said, Lyn started wanting to meet more often and I got cold feet. Are you getting off on this or something? I've made a statement. You've got the information.'

'And that covers it? A woman was murdered in a place where you used to meet her. A couple of paragraphs doesn't cut it.'

The solicitor pointed to the statement. 'Mr Aston has told you what he can.'

Siv picked up the paper. 'I wonder if this is just another load of lies. What's the truth here, Mr Aston? You concealed crucial information in a serious investigation, which resulted in a body remaining undiscovered. I'll have to consider charging you with perverting the course of justice. That could mean a prison sentence.'

'Hang on!' He grabbed his cap and screwed it up between his fingers. 'I've made an honest statement — I've tried to help you here.'

'That's true, Inspector. Mr Aston has cleared a path for you.'

'Hardly. We're done here for now. You can wait while we consider charges.'

Aston shifted as if he was going to throw himself into the solicitor's arms and weep. Cornlow pulled her chair further away from him.

Siv and Ali headed upstairs and sat in her office, going over what they had.

'Did he really reckon that his crappy little statement was going to make us go away?' Ali asked.

'He's not the brightest and I'm not sure his solicitor is either. The statement rings true to me, and the forensics support it. He has an alibi for the night Lyn disappeared.'

'Aye. But he had a motive for killing her, given her opposition to him and Lily. Maybe she'd threatened to tell Lily if he didn't clear off the scene.'

'Would she have told Lily? I'm not so sure. She was desperate for Lily's approval, and if she'd revealed what she'd been up to with Aston, she'd have dobbed herself in and lost the moral high ground she was holding about Theo leaving.'

Ali said, 'Fair point, but she wasn't necessarily clear-headed, was she? Anger with Aston might have overwhelmed her. After all, he'd dumped her and then moved on to her daughter. She was already worried about her age and being unattractive. She might have given him an ultimatum.'

'All of that is true, but once again, he has an alibi.'

They both sat mulling this over.

Siv said, 'Aston's story about the wine supports what Dimas told us. We can put him on the back burner for now. We'll charge Aston with perverting the course of justice, and give him bail. That'll flatten the peak in his cap.'

Ali rubbed his hands together. 'That's class. I'm a happy man.'

Her phone rang. 'Guv, it's reception. We've got a Lily Aston here, shouting the odds about her husband. She's demanding to speak to you.'

'Okay. She'll have to wait a bit. I'll try not to be too long. Stick her in an interview room and offer her a hot drink.' She rang off. 'Lily's going to need something stronger than tea or coffee. I'll have to tell her about her mum and her husband. That's something to relish.'

'Want me with you?'

'No, you get on with processing Aston. Mind you, *in my opinion*, I doubt that he'll have a home to go to once we release him.'

* * *

Theo Dimas had just got through the front door, his head reeling, when his phone rang. He was astonished to see that the caller was Lily and he almost didn't answer. He didn't need any more grief right now. But she might be in trouble or needing to talk about Lyn. When he picked up, she launched straight in without any greeting.

'Why have the police arrested Pearce? What have you been saying to them?'

'I wasn't aware that they had arrested him. They've been questioning me today.'

'He rang and said they'd arrested him at work and they were taking him to the station. I'm going there now. I suppose you've been slagging him off, telling lies about him.'

'Of course I haven't. Why would I do that?'

'Because you hate him, just like Mum did.'

'I don't hate Pearce. The police did mention his name when they were asking me about Steiner's, but I've no idea why.'

'According to you. You're not exactly famous for your honesty, are you? You're a cheat and a liar. I don't believe a word you say.'

It was on the tip of his tongue to tell her what the police had said about Lyn and what they'd found at Steiner's, but he bit back his anger. Now wasn't the time and place. 'What I've told you is the truth.'

'Yeah, well, I'll find out what's going on when I get to the police station.'

'Do you want me to come with you?'

She snorted. 'Not likely! You'd just make things worse. While I'm on the phone, I'm warning you that I don't want to see that awful man at my mum's funeral.'

'What man?'

'Monty. He caused misery for Mum. I don't want him turning up, pretending to be sympathetic. As if he gives a toss.'

He was so weary. 'Let's not do this now, Lily. We're all raw. You're grieving for Mum but . . .'

'Yeah, I am. Unlike you and that shit Monty. If he dares to turn up at the funeral, I'll spit in his face and throw him out. You won't want that.'

There was no point in arguing with her. 'I'm truly sorry about your mum, Lily. Rowing with each other isn't going to help.'

'You've been told. I've got every right to say I don't want him there. Papu and Pearce agree with me. He's the last person Mum would've wanted at her funeral, so he can piss off.'

Having thrown in her final, undeniable winning card, she rang off. Theo glanced at the clock. Adam would be home in the next hour. Shaken by the conversation, he made himself a strong black coffee laced with brandy and sat in the kitchen. His phone pinged with an email and he wondered if it was going to be Lily again, berating him, but he saw that it was from Scott Darnley. Theo wasn't that familiar with the man, but he didn't like what he'd seen of him. Scott had come round a couple of times with Justin and he'd been spiteful about a lot of the people he worked with, criticising their mannerisms, habits and relationships. Theo wondered what Scott said about them as soon as he was out the door. He read the email.

> Hi, Theo, I was very sorry to hear about Lyn and I wanted to offer my condolences. This must be a difficult time for you. I really don't want to add to your burdens, but I needed to get in touch. I hope that you and Monty are well and happy, but I have my doubts. Are you always sure of where he is and who he's seeing? I don't want to worry you or name names, but I've seen him hanging about with someone. Just wanted to give you a heads up. The last thing you need at the moment is to be let down by your partner.

Theo put his phone down and stared into space. He hadn't wanted to disturb Monty at work, so he was unaware of the day's events yet. Sometimes he sensed Monty's dissatisfaction, but he didn't want to believe that his partner was being unfaithful. After a glorious, passionate start, their relationship had been bombarded by persistent and harrowing difficulties. Monty found Adam hard work. The two had never bonded as he'd hoped they might, and the atmosphere in the house was often awkward. There were times when he was exhausted at being the fulcrum of the seesaw, trying to maintain balance. Monty had had to ride a lot of resentment and insults from the Dimas family, and perhaps in the end it had proved too much.

He reached for his phone and read the email again. It was vague and typical of Scott's vindictive style. He hadn't sensed that Monty's attention had strayed elsewhere but then again, he hadn't suspected that Lyn had been having an affair. Had he or Monty annoyed Scott Darnley in any way? He couldn't understand why else Scott would have sent such a message, unless he'd really seen Monty acting suspiciously.

He made himself another strong coffee and waited for Adam to get in from school. His heart was thudding.

CHAPTER 16

Lily's fists were in tight balls, her eyes flashing. Fury blazed off her in waves. She had a friend with her — a Damsel, presumably, a pale, willowy woman called Tasha. Siv took them into an interview room. Tasha wiped her chair seat with a tissue before sitting. Siv didn't blame her.

'I want to see my Pearce,' Lily insisted. Her loose hair was flicking furiously.

'In a while. He's been arrested and we've interviewed him.'

'He'd better have had a solicitor!'

'He did.' *Not that it did him much good.*

'What's he been arrested for?'

'I'm sorry to have to tell you this, but it's in connection with your mother's murder and perverting the course of justice.'

'*What?* Don't be stupid! Pearce didn't have anything to do with that!'

'That's what he claims, but he has been lying to the police. He's made a statement that proves he's lied.'

Lily tensed. 'What the fuck are you talking about? This is driving me mental!'

Tasha put a hand on Lily's arm. 'Try to stay calm, Lily. Maybe the inspector can explain.'

Lily shrugged her off angrily and shot her a death stare. 'Calm! My husband's banged up in a cell! He must be terrified!'

Siv intervened. Lily was about to lose face, big time, and although she was a pouty madam, she was, in her own limited way, grieving for her mother. 'I'm going to give you some information now, Lily. It won't be easy for you. You might want to hear it alone.'

'No, I want Tash here as a witness in case you try to twist things.'

Tasha nodded solemnly. They were alike, slim and with short puffa jackets over ripped jeans. Maybe the Damsels had a dress code. Both wore smoky eyeshadow and pale lipstick.

'Have it your way.' Siv gave a brief summary of Pearce's statement, leaving out details such as the mattress and the wine. 'I'm sorry to have to tell you this, Lily.'

Tasha gasped, her hands flying to her face. Lily froze in her seat. 'It's not true,' she managed to whisper.

'I'm afraid it is. We have it in writing and Pearce volunteered the information. It explains why your mum was so against your relationship with him. If it's any comfort to you, he claims that he didn't realise when he first met you that you were Lyn's daughter, and then he protected you from finding out about his affair with your mum.'

'He's put it in writing?'

'Yes, with his solicitor. It was his choice.'

'He can't have . . .'

Siv heard the doubt in her voice and saw her eyes change from hot anger to cold. 'I wouldn't tell you this if it wasn't what Pearce has stated.'

'Him and my mum. They were doing it for months in that stinking place?'

'Yes, that was one of the places they met.'

'Pearce . . . and Mum . . . But she was so *old*! How could he *do* that?'

Siv was bemused at her take on it. 'Well . . . it happens.'

'OMG, Lily,' Tasha breathed. She was hugging the arms of her jacket. 'You poor thing!'

Tasha was gaping at Lily with suppressed excitement laced with a hefty hint of enjoyment. It was all very well being a tragic figure for your friends, but not when it turned into *schadenfreude*. The Damsels would be busy on social media later.

Lily rocked in her chair and bashed the table with her hands. Then she started screaming. 'I don't . . . I can't . . . No, he can't . . .'

Tasha tried to put an arm around her shoulders, but Lily smacked her hard in the face with the back of a hand before continuing to scream. Tasha started crying loudly and holding her scarlet cheek. The racket was terrible. Siv pressed the call button and asked a startled male constable to fetch a female colleague. Then she spoke quietly to Lily, asking her to calm down and insisting that she take a drink of water.

'For God's sake, do be quiet,' she said to Tasha. 'It was a smack. There's no blood. We'll get you checked over.'

When things had calmed and Tasha was holding ice to her cheek with Lily snuffling quietly, Siv told the female constable to contact Joe Dimas and tell him his granddaughter needed his help. She checked the time. It was after 7 p.m. and she was hungry. She was about to pop to Gusto for a sandwich when Ali appeared in the corridor.

'Guv, were you trying to get hold of a Scott Darnley?'

'Yes. He's an anaesthetist at Berminster General. He'd left a message saying he had info about Lyn.'

'Well, he's in the hospital now, but as a patient. He was beaten up this afternoon and he wants to talk to you.'

'I'd better get over there. Have you sorted Aston?'

'Yes, charged and released on bail. I told him his wife was here but he didn't hang around. How did it go with her?'

'Major drama. The Aston homestead won't be a happy one tonight.'

* * *

Theo's head was aching and muddled when Adam came in. All that caffeine wasn't good for his blood pressure. He made his son a hot chocolate and they sat at the kitchen table. He was still trying to get his head around the interview with the police and recall it moment by moment. It was difficult, because shock seemed to have paralysed his memory. Inspector Drummond had said something about a mattress, but he wasn't sure what now. Why had they talked about Pearce Aston? He was confused and worried. Lyn must have taken that wine to Steiner's, but what on earth had made her go there? The questions piled up in his mind. None of this made sense.

He longed for Monty to arrive so that he could share the tension, but he was also rattled by the email from Scott and unsure whether to mention all these details to him.

He told Adam about the police interview. It hurt his heart to do it, but there was no point in concealing things. Except the one thing he had to keep hiding. He had his fingers crossed on that.

Adam sipped the hot chocolate that he'd topped with pieces of white meringue. They were like snowy mountain peaks streaked with mud. 'The police are saying Mum was . . . was seeing someone at Steiner's?'

'That's what they said, that she might have been. I'm sorry.'

'What, she left me alone that night because she was meeting someone?'

'It's not clear. Not necessarily.'

'I don't believe it. Mum wouldn't do that.'

'Maybe the police have got it wrong.'

Adam frowned. 'But why did they arrest you?'

'Because my fingerprints were on a wine bottle they found there, the kind of wine I buy by the case. I was never at Steiner's, Adam, and I made that clear to them.'

Adam gazed into his drink. 'Why did they mention Pearce?'

'I've no idea. They've got forensics, but they didn't give details.'

'Just about the wine bottle.'

'That's right. Your mum must have taken it there. That's the only explanation.'

'So . . . so does that mean Mum knew the person who killed her?'

'I suppose that's possible.' The smell of the milky chocolate was turning his stomach. He put a hand on his son's. 'We've just got to get through this, Adam. It's going to be a tough time ahead so we have to help each other out.'

Adam withdrew into himself. He fell silent and spooned the soggy meringue from his mug. Then he got up and headed to his room. The door slammed. Theo took his mug and washed it out. His guilt about Adam was limitless. Before he'd left the family, Adam had been an outgoing, mischievous boy, always on the go and full of curiosity. Now Theo was terrified that his son was going to relapse into the depression and isolation that had overwhelmed him after Lyn had vanished. He'd hardly spoken for a couple of years, apart from repeating that irritating phrase of his: 'Catchungcatchungcatchung.' Neither a therapist nor the educational psychologist had made any difference. In the end, they'd suggested it was best to let Adam take his time, and he had. He'd lost friendships and he struggled with schoolwork. 'Inertia' was the word that summed him up. Adam couldn't take any more shocks, which was why it was important to keep the lid on the Justin situation.

Theo poured himself a glass of wine and took a long gulp. He heard Monty come in and went to greet him, relieved that he'd be able to talk freely about what had happened. Monty was pale and tired. He stood against the living-room door, staring blankly at Theo. He had a large plaster on his right hand.

'I've been such a fool, but I had to do something,' he said. 'Get me a huge brandy, will you?'

* * *

Patrick sat in the car with his phone, puzzled. He'd signed into his bank app to check his salary payment and the balance on his current account. He saw that five hundred pounds had been withdrawn from the account four days ago with the code 'ATM.' He hadn't made any withdrawals recently. In fact, he couldn't remember when he'd last used his card. He'd been too busy and had used cash for any small purchases. He checked his wallet, relieved to find that his bank card was there.

He rang the bank, and a cheery woman confirmed that the withdrawal had been made with his card and PIN number at an ATM at Wesley's garage near Minster Beach. Did he want to enquire further about this transaction? He was about to say yes, when an unpleasant idea snaked into his head. Only one other person had his PIN — Noah. He said he'd leave it for now. He sat, tapping his phone. Noah had his own bank account for his disability benefits. Occasionally, he used Patrick's card details if he was buying things for the house online. A couple of times recently, he'd asked for a sub until he could withdraw cash himself and that was unusual. When Patrick was at home, he usually left his wallet on the kitchen counter. A number of carers came and went from the house, but he honed in on one person in particular who lived in a mobile home near the beach.

His phone rang, making him jump. It was Vi Finch, the estate agent.

'I've gone through our old records, like your inspector asked me to. It took me ages! They'd been archived on our server.'

'Have you got a name for me?'

'Yes, I showed a gentleman called Barry Marlin around Steiner's.'

'Date, please?'

'Hang on. It was on the twentieth of May 2010. Mr Marlin made an offer, which was accepted, but then he pulled out. I can't remember why. People do. They're always messing us around.'

'Have you got an address for him?'

'No, afraid not. We'd have got rid of the paperwork when he dropped out of the purchase.'

Patrick ended the call and made quick notes. He needed to get to the hospital and catch up with Trudy Kemp, before the guv chewed his ear off. On the way, he stopped at his bank ATM and changed his PIN. He had no idea how he was going to broach the subject with Noah, but he couldn't leave it. In the meantime, his wallet would stay in his pocket.

He found Trudy Kemp sitting beside her bed, pale but snug in a dressing gown patterned with roses, and marking a pile of exercise books. She raised her red-and-purple glasses when she saw him.

'Whatever you do, don't make me laugh. It's unlikely, but the wound hurts like hell.'

'It wasn't indigestion, then.'

'No. More like exploding guts.'

'When are you going home?'

'Tomorrow, I hope. I've walked up and down for them satisfactorily and my temperature is okay.' She pointed at the cabinet next to her bed. 'I've got something for you. I'd found a folder about that trip to Steiner's. A colleague brought it in earlier. It's got the date and a list of the pupils who came along. Can you get it so I don't have to twist around?'

Patrick took a buff-coloured folder from the cabinet and glanced through. There were lesson plans, photos and drawings of the exterior of Steiner's and a sheet of lined paper with a list of names, dated 14 February 2010. He scanned them but they meant nothing.

Paul Bison
Bethany James
Nat Olawego
Karim Patel
Tim Stafford

'Would Lyn have known any of these pupils?'

'Doubt it. Can you make sure I have all that stuff back when you've finished with it? I was going to photocopy it but then my abdomen went into meltdown.'

Patrick assured her that he'd keep the contents safe. 'One other thing. Lyn used to work at a place called Foot Heaven in Seaford, before Adam was born. Did she ever mention having problems there?'

Trudy shifted in her chair and winced. 'I don't remember anything. Mind you, I took a sabbatical and went travelling for a year before she had Adam, so I might not have been around.'

Patrick wished her a speedy recovery and headed home so that he'd be around to check on the plumber.

At home, he was pleased to find that there was a new power shower. The evening carer was already in the wet room, helping Noah. He had a quick word with the plumber, paid her and put a pasta ready meal in the oven. The carer, a young man called Dmitri, stopped briefly at the door.

'Is everything okay with Noah? He's been very quiet the last couple of weeks.'

'He hasn't said there's anything wrong.'

'Okay. Well . . . we usually have a bit of a laugh, but not recently. Anyway, back tomorrow, got to rush.'

Noah wheeled into the kitchen, damp and fragrant. 'Thank goodness. I needed that. I was starting to hum. What's for dinner?'

'Pasta with meatballs. Remember I'm going out tonight.'

'Oh yeah. You're meeting Kitty-cat.'

'I'll help you to bed before I go, if you want.'

'No, that's okay. I'm going to watch a film.'

'Dmitri said you've been quiet recently.'

'Have I?'

'That's what he said. Ali mentioned it, too. He said you seemed a bit down when he called by.'

Noah glared at him. 'Am I supposed to entertain visitors, then? Is that my role in life now — the cheery wheelchair cripple who puts on a brave show, so that people can breathe a sigh of relief when they leave and say, "Isn't he marvellous, the way he copes and never complains?" Or maybe I should be free amusement on demand. Why don't we go the whole hog and get me a job in a freak show? I could appear with a bearded lady and juggling midget. At least I'd be earning a living.'

Patrick choked up but he attempted a light tone. 'Don't be daft, bro. People are fond of you. They care.'

'I'm grateful, I'm sure. So good to be patronised. I appreciate that people *care*.'

When Noah was in this mood, there was no way through. Patrick needed to have a shower himself before they ate dinner. He set the timer for the oven. Noah was flicking through the free newspaper on the table.

Patrick coughed. 'Erm . . . bro, talking about funds for living — you're not short of money, are you?'

'Me? No. I'm not exactly a big spender, living large while you're at work. Why do you ask?'

'I just wondered if you'd needed some money from my account and forgot to tell me.'

'No.'

'I checked my bank account today and someone took five hundred pounds out at the beginning of the week. I can't work out how that's happened.'

Noah glanced at him and then focused again on the paper, angling his wheelchair so that he was facing away. 'No idea. Did you tell your bank?'

'Yeah. Someone used my card and PIN at a garage near Minster Beach. I wondered about the carers, but even if one of them had lifted my card, they wouldn't have had the PIN. You haven't accidentally given it to anyone, have you?'

There was a long, awkward silence, broken only by the hum of the oven fan.

'How would I "accidentally" do that? You must take me for a complete moron,' Noah muttered.

'Of course I don't. It's a lot of money to lose. I can't afford it.'

'I'm sorry about that. Must have been a nasty shock. Will the bank reimburse you?'

'I haven't asked them to investigate it yet. I wanted to check with you first. I've changed my PIN.'

'Right. That's sensible.'

Patrick stared at the back of his brother's head. He couldn't grasp something here. He went to shower, worried and guilty, too, because he was going out on a date while Noah was stuck inside.

* * *

Siv found Scott Darnley in a cubicle in A & E, sitting on the side of a bed. Despite his battered appearance, she recognised him from his photos on Facebook. He had puffy lips, grazes on his chin, a cut over his right eye with stitches in, a swollen, bloodied nose and his right wrist was in a support bandage.

She pulled a chair up beside him. 'Hello, Dr Darnley. We've been trying to get hold of each other. You've been in the wars.'

'Yes, Inspector, but I survived the ambush. I contacted you because I realised that I might have some important information that I should advise you about.'

'Did that something lead to you being attacked or was that a coincidence?'

He cradled his wrist. 'I can't say, in all honesty, but I don't believe that the two things are connected.'

First lie. Some people started fibbing early, some waited until the going got trickier. 'You'd better tell me what happened to you.'

He spoke nasally. 'Someone attacked me this afternoon. I was putting my bin out. There's a communal, fenced area behind my house. I'd just unbolted the gate to it when they came at me. I didn't stand a chance.'

'What time was this?'

'Just after two thirty.'

'So, broad daylight. Did you see your attacker?'

He shook his head and touched his nose gingerly. 'No. It all happened so fast. It was a man, but he was wearing a balaclava so I couldn't tell you anything about him. He was there and then he was gone.'

A man with a balaclava in the middle of the afternoon. She didn't believe a word of it. 'What did you do after your attacker left you?'

'I managed to get indoors and clean myself up, but I needed stitches and an X-ray on my wrist. I called a cab to bring me into A & E.' He sounded impatient and moved on the bed so that he was directly facing her. 'But this isn't why I asked to see you.'

'Okay. I can get a constable to take a report about the attack.'

'No! You're not listening. Don't they teach you listening skills in police training? They must be crucial.'

'Go on.'

'I can't be bothered reporting the attack. Probably just some lowlife on the prowl. I wanted to speak to you about the evening Ms Dimas went missing.'

She sat back. 'I'm all ears, Dr Darnley.'

The whites of his eyes were bloodshot and yellowy. He blinked rapidly. 'I read about Lyn Dimas's body being found. I know Theo Dimas slightly, and also Monty Barnwell, his partner. Monty works here. There was a press report online about Lyn, recapping the night she went missing and saying that she and Theo had separated and he was at home with his partner. Then I saw the police appeal for information on Twitter. It's a very good way of engaging with the public, by the way.'

'Thank you. I'll pass that on to the detective who runs it. So did the appeal help to jog your memory?'

'It did, yes. I recalled that I saw Monty and Justin Desmond, another doctor who works here, that night in 2013. I was driving past the Flare Bar in town and I saw them outside, on the pavement. Monty had his arm around Justin's shoulders. Justin looked upset and he was holding his chest, as if he'd been sick or maybe hurt.'

The Flare Bar was the oldest and still the most popular gay bar in town. 'What time was that?'

'I was off on a date, and we met up about eight thirty, so it must have been just after eight.'

'Did they see you driving past?'

'I doubt it. Monty had his head bent to Justin and as I said, Justin seemed unwell.' He coughed and held his jaw, wincing.

'Why didn't you come forward and tell the police this in 2013?'

'I'd forgotten all about seeing them outside the bar that night until a couple of days ago. You see, I wasn't that friendly with them at the time so they didn't really register with me. I noticed them in a corridor here together a couple of days ago, and I suppose that jogged my memory, as well as the online stuff.' His manner was meek and mild now, but he couldn't conceal a mean edge to his voice. 'Is it useful information to you?'

'Possibly.' She wondered what his angle was. 'Are Mr Barnwell and Dr Desmond aware that you're telling me this?'

'I haven't mentioned it to them,' he said.

'Are you sure you don't want to report this serious assault?'

'I'm quite sure, thank you.'

'You should, and I'd urge you to, but it's your decision. If you change your mind, contact the station. Also, as soon as you're better, I'll need you to make a formal statement about what you've just told me.'

'Of course.' He placed a finger on his chin. 'I hope I haven't got Monty and Justin into any trouble. I'd hate for that to happen.'

From his sugary tone, she reckoned that was exactly the outcome he wanted. 'You're right to have given me this information.'

'Thank you, that's reassuring. Can you keep me updated about what's happening regarding this?'

'It doesn't work like that, Dr Darnley. I'll be in touch with you again if I need to clarify anything.'

When the inspector had gone, Darnley sat back on the bed and smirked, even though it hurt his jaw. Despite his injuries, it had been a worthwhile and satisfying day. He flicked open his phone and emailed Justin.

I hope you weren't in on it, but Monty Barnwell attacked me today. I'm not a pretty sight. A detective inspector, no less, came to see me in A & E. I told her I didn't recognise my attacker, and I don't want to report it. I did tell her about seeing you and Monty that night in 2013. I had to do the right thing about that, because Monty and Theo lied to the police back then. Justin, I'm doing all of this for you, for us. I love you so much. So much that I'm willing to let your friend beat me up. I don't even care if you planned it with him. That's real, selfless love, Justin. You'll never have anyone else who'd do that for you. Please, just talk to me. We can sort things out. I don't want to have to change my mind about reporting a crime. I don't give a damn about Monty, but I honestly don't want to get you into any trouble. You're a terrific doctor and you don't need Monty jeopardising your career.

You can rely on me to have your back, always.

Love and hugs, Scott.

CHAPTER 17

Siv drove straight to Theo Dimas's house to challenge the broken alibi and see if Barnwell bore signs of a fight. Her throat ached for a glass of cold akvavit but she had to make do with a dubious coffee from a machine at a garage. She phoned Ali en route and told him what she'd discovered.

'I don't recall that a Dr Justin Desmond has been mentioned before. Does the name mean anything to you? Did Barnwell refer to him when you talked to him?'

'No. Seems like Dimas or Barnwell, or maybe both of them, could have killed Lyn if they hadn't been together watching footie.'

'It opens up their account of the evening.' She just couldn't see Dimas as a killer and if Barnwell had been with Justin Desmond, that didn't place him at Steiner's. 'Darnley's got an agenda regarding Barnwell and Desmond. I'd say that Barnwell attacked him because he told them that he'd recalled seeing them in 2013.'

'Medics having punch-ups? That's a new one on me.'

She was amused at his naivety. He was in awe of the medical profession, probably because his health needed regular monitoring. 'They're just human, and subject to the same emotions as the rest of us. Maybe you imagine they'd be more likely to inject each other with nasty drugs when they fall out.'

'Well . . . just saying. Want me to meet you at Dimas's?' He sounded eager.

She could tell that he must be home alone and keen for company, but she wanted to tread carefully with this situation. Adam would be at home and he'd already had to deal with his father's arrest. Ali could sometimes be a bull in a china shop — or, as Bartel would say, an elephant in a porcelain factory. 'It's okay. I'm going to go in softly to start with.'

'You sure?'

'Yes. I'll call if I need back-up.'

When Theo Dimas opened the door, he seemed unsurprised to see her late at night.

'I need to speak to Mr Barnwell. Is he in?'

Dimas led her through. The living room was subtly lit with two lamps and cosily warm with the heady scent of brandy. Monty Barnwell seemed anything but cosy. He was a big man squeezed into a small armchair and his nose dominated his strained face. There was a hum of tension in the air — the two men had been arguing.

'Is Adam in?' Siv asked. She didn't want him involved in this conversation.

'He's upstairs, plugged into his headphones,' Dimas told her.

She sat in a chair opposite Barnwell. 'I've just come from the hospital, where I spoke to Dr Scott Darnley. I believe you're both acquainted with him.'

They murmured in agreement. Dimas crouched back into a cushion on the sofa.

'Dr Darnley was attacked earlier today and had to be treated in A & E. Do either of you know anything about that attack?'

They both shook their heads.

'Is he okay?' Barnwell asked, his voice sounding forced.

'Walking wounded. Rather like you, Mr Barnwell. What happened to your hand?'

'I hurt it in the kitchen when I was cooking.'

'Did Scott recognise his attacker?' Dimas asked.

'That's an ongoing inquiry,' Siv lied. Let them fret about that. 'I'm here because of other information that Dr Darnley gave me. Mr Barnwell, do you know Dr Justin Desmond?'

'Yes.'

'We both do,' Dimas said.

'Just professionally, or socially as well?'

Barnwell went to speak, but Dimas cut across him.

'Hold on, shouldn't Monty have a solicitor?'

'Sure. I was hoping to keep this informal for now, but if you want to come to the police station, Mr Barnwell, we can do this there and get you a solicitor.'

Barnwell frowned and gave Dimas an annoyed glance. 'I'm fine here. I'm fine with informal.'

'Good. Tell me about Dr Desmond.'

'We both work at the hospital, so I see him there and we have a drink or a meal now and again. Theo's met him through me.'

'You're friends?'

Barnwell paused. 'Justin's come here for dinner sometimes, and we've gone to his.'

'Have you ever been partners?'

'No. We're friends. Gay men can be friends. We don't all shag each other just for the sake of it.'

'It would help if you can try to answer without the aggression. And do you socialise with Dr Darnley?'

'Now and again.'

'Where? At the Flare Bar?' She dropped the name in deliberately and saw Dimas flinch.

'Sometimes, if he happens to be there. He's not a friend, as such. Scott's been here with Justin, for dinner.'

'Are Scott and Justin partners?'

'They were. They split up recently.'

That placed a piece of the jigsaw. Barnwell was doling out information in small segments, trying to play cat and mouse. She wondered if Darnley had been lying to her about seeing Desmond with Barnwell, taking revenge on an ex. But if that was the case, why would Barnwell have beaten him up?

'Why did they split up?'

'Just not compatible, I suppose. I've not been party to the details.'

'Would you tell me again where you were on the evening of the twenty-eighth of July 2013? I'd like the truth. If I don't get it, I'll arrest you and you'll definitely need a solicitor.'

Barnwell licked his lips and stared at his hand. There was a faint thud from upstairs and the sound of water in pipes. Dimas cleared his throat. They were making an effort not to glance at each other.

Siv let a full minute pass and then sighed. 'It's been a long day. I can sit here for hours, but I really don't want to. I'd remind you how serious this is. I'm conducting a murder inquiry.'

Dimas stood. 'This nightmare can't go on. Scott's been talking. Just tell her, Monty.' He took a step towards his partner, made a pleading gesture with a palm extended. 'Just tell her, or I will.' He sat down again.

Barnwell gave a slight, weary shoulder shrug. 'Okay, okay.' He swallowed and leaned forward, head down. 'Justin rang me the evening Lyn vanished, at about half seven. I was watching TV with Theo. He was terribly upset, barely coherent and needed help. Justin used to have a drug dependency. He'd started using at medical school to help with the stress and long hours. I'd been supporting him with it, trying to get him to access help and kick the habit. If he'd been found out at work, he'd have been reported to the GMC and probably suspended. It would have been a huge disruption to his career. He's clean now, but back then, he was using, mainly cocaine. He'd met a dealer outside the Flare Bar, in the side alley. There'd been an argument about the price and the dealer had pulled a knife, cut him across the chest and left him on the ground. Justin wasn't badly wounded, but he was bleeding and shocked. I managed to calm him down enough to tell me what had happened and I went to meet him.'

'What time was this?'

'I was alarmed so I left immediately, just after twenty to eight. Justin didn't want me to take him for medical attention because questions might be asked or the police involved, and then he'd be in real trouble professionally. I took him back to his home, patched up his superficial wound, made him a strong coffee and stayed with him until he was calmer and okay.'

'What time did you get home?'

'Around half ten.'

'So you've been lying all this time about that night.'

'But don't you see?' Dimas interrupted. 'Monty couldn't say where he'd been, because then Justin would have been in terrible trouble. He lied to protect a good friend who's a dedicated doctor.'

Siv snapped at him. 'Pity that Lyn didn't have anyone protecting her so keenly that night.'

Dimas reddened. His face was a mask of misery. 'That's a bit low.'

'I can go a lot lower when I'm fed bullshit. Which brings me back to you, Mr Dimas. Instead of being at home with your partner watching football, we now have several hours when you were alone at the time when your wife went missing, with no one to verify your whereabouts.'

'I've told you the truth. I stayed in. I watched the football. I was terribly worried about Justin, and waiting for Monty to call to tell me how he was.'

Siv turned to Barnwell. 'Did you phone Theo from Dr Desmond's?' *Not that I can believe you if you say you did.*

'I phoned him once Justin was calmer, around a quarter to ten, to tell him that things were okay and I'd be home soon.'

'That still leaves over two hours unaccounted for,' Siv told Dimas.

He bit his lip. 'I was at the flat, that's all I can say. Jeff Downey rang just after Monty called, to tell me about Adam and how they'd been out searching for Lyn. I didn't kill Lyn. I'd never have harmed her.'

'I'm sorry I lied,' Barnwell said. 'I did it with good intentions.'

Siv was about to speak when the door handle rattled and Adam burst in, red-eyed. He stood in fleecy pyjamas, trembling and breathing heavily. Siv wondered how long he'd been listening.

'Can't you leave my dad alone? He's done nothing wrong and all you're doing is telling horrible, filthy lies about my mum!' He jabbed a finger at Barnwell. 'You, you fucking liar! You're just causing trouble as usual and making everything worse. I bet Dad got arrested 'cos of you! I heard you arguing earlier. Sounds like you've been seeing someone else, after everything Dad put us through to be with you.' He choked, and then battled on. 'My mum was murdered and you've been protecting some fucking druggie and making my dad help you. Mum hated you and I hate you! I always have. I hate your sweaty fucking skin, the rancid casseroles you make, your hideous bonsai collection and the way you poke your big fat nose into everything. Why don't you fuck off out of our lives?'

'Adam . . .' Dimas stepped towards his son but Adam pushed him hard in the chest, sobbed loudly and ran upstairs.

Siv stood. 'I'll go now. You need to see to Adam. Mr Barnwell, I want you to come to the station tomorrow to make a statement. I'll have to verify what you've told me with Dr Desmond. If I find you've carried on lying, I will arrest you. Mr Dimas, I'll be in touch. In the meantime, don't forget your bail conditions.'

* * *

Adam waited until he heard his father and Monty go to bed. He crept downstairs, found his father's phone and checked through recent emails and texts. He forwarded the email from Scott Darnley to himself.

He padded to the kitchen and loaded a plate with chunks of strong cheddar cheese, pork pie, crisps, cake and biscuits.

Back in his bedroom, he sat on his bed and ate greedily, spraying crumbs, while he finished watching *Toy Story*. He'd played it several times a week since his mum had vanished, because it was the film she should have sat and watched with him that night. They'd seen it together a dozen times, snuggled up on the sofa with the soft throw tucked round them. She'd always dug him in the ribs and giggled whenever Buzz Lightyear misunderstood a situation. He cried every time he played it.

His life was full of *shoulds*. He should have gone to the shop with Mum that evening and kept her safe. He should have realised sooner that she'd been gone too long and maybe then he could have saved her. He should have phoned his dad instead of running to Jeff's. His dad had asked in a hurt voice, *Why didn't you call me instead of involving that pest next door?*

Adam carried all these *shoulds* around with him like stones in his pockets. Every day he needed to cry and be miserable. He had no right to be happy because his mum had gone and been murdered while he'd been watching TV. That was why he isolated himself in his room every night, repeatedly watching *Toy Story*, *Bambi*, *Ghost* and *Lion*, and any other film he could find that featured loss and grief, preferably loss of a parent. He sought out despair because it was all he deserved and, in an odd way, he found comfort in it. *Bambi* was the film that always made him sob the most. Every time the hunter killed Bambi's mother, he held his pillow against his face.

Now they were saying that his mum might have been shagging someone, maybe even the person who'd killed her. He didn't believe it. His mum would never have been messing with some other bloke. She wasn't like that. He was filled with a useless, draining fury.

Toy Story ended. Adam lay on his stomach and peered under his bed. His curse jars stood in a line of pent-up hostility. He hoped they were working their dark magick. The one thing that injected energy into his life was his enduring loathing of Monty. That fuelled his days. If he hadn't interfered

217

in their lives and taken Dad away from them, Mum might still be here. Tonight was the first time he'd let rip with the loathing and it had been good. Almost as good as making the curse jars. A bit like hope.

Adam had heard everything tonight from the sentry step. He'd heard Monty tell Dad that he'd attacked Scott because he was threatening to talk about what had happened at the Flare Bar, and Dad saying that he must be mad, what had he been thinking? Then Dad had said, *Have you been having an affair?* Monty had told him not to be dramatic, and then they'd both started shouting and it was just like the bad old days, with Mum and Lily rowing. He'd heard the DI say, *Pity that Lyn didn't have anyone protecting her so keenly that night.* She'd called it, all right.

Adam could have told DI Drummond that he'd heard Monty say he'd beaten Scott up, but he was going to hang onto that information for now. It might come in useful.

He lay back against his pillows. The awareness of the jars secreted beneath him, and the sense that their power was growing and expanding in the silence and the dark, brought him immense pleasure. He opened his laptop and was pleased to find Chimera online. He'd already told her about his mum's body being found.

> Chimera: How is your world of sorcery over there in England, Adam dearest?

Tears sprang hot in his eyes when he read the endearment and his anger spilled out.

> Adam: It's all a bit crap. Dad got arrested. The police are saying my mum might have had an affair, but that's a lie. Monty was in a fight today with a doctor he and my dad are friendly with. The detective was here again. Monty lied to the police about his alibi for the night Mum went missing. The detective threatened to arrest him

if his new alibi is false. Also, he's seeing someone else. I'm worried he'll break my dad's heart.

Chimera: Now, Adam, I can hear that you're in a lot of turmoil. Try to calm yourself. You do see what's happening here? Forces are slowly surrounding Monty and caging him. This is how your curse works, steadily but surely. His suffering increases daily. You're winning but you must keep your courage.

Adam: He's been saying horrible things to Dad about me again.

Chimera: Sticks and stones, Adam dearest. Trust this: you will prevail.

Adam: I created a new curse jar.

Chimera: That's good. You're adding to the power. You should now cast a protection spell for yourself, to counter Monty's evil and the awful lies about your mom. These are very difficult times for you and I want you to keep yourself safe. I'm very conscious that your mom would want that too.

She told him how to cast the strong protective spell. It was simple enough. He had to write his name and put the paper in a box with four pieces of black glass and a sprig of pine needles, then padlock the box and store it somewhere safe.

Adam: I'll do it tomorrow.

Chimera: Make sure you do. I made my own for you some time ago, to keep you safe but now you must have one near you. I've got your back on this, dearest one. Merry Meet Again.

He closed his laptop. He heard Monty's heavy tread to the bathroom and the sound of him peeing long and heavily. He sounded like a horse in a field. Adam stared into the dark, recalling how Mum had torn into Monty, calling him 'a despicable pervert.' He shivered with excitement. Dad had said that he definitely wanted Mum to be buried. He wondered if he might be able to place a curse jar in her grave or even better, with her in her coffin. He pictured tucking it in beside her, prompting her to help him from the world beyond. He'd chat to Chimera about it tomorrow night.

Adam was tired but too worked up to sleep. He nibbled the remaining crust of his pie and pressed 'Play' for *Bambi*. His chest tightened and his breath quickened as the blue, misty forest appeared and drowsy birds started to wake.

* * *

Chimera did live in Idaho, in Twin Falls, but her name was Adele Leigh and she was fifteen, highly intelligent, of a curious, spiteful disposition and bored at school. She found dispensing the spells and charms that she herself had googled immensely entertaining. The English boy was one of her more fascinating 'clients' and she was riveted by his painful story about the gay dad, the missing, now murdered mom, the nasty boyfriend and the weird sister. She'd got a real kick when he'd told her that his mother's body had been found. What an intriguing, terrible family triangle he had! She found it crazy and diverting. It was like tuning in for the next episode of some reality trash on Netflix. And Adam was so gullible and gratifying to tease! Sometimes she desperately wanted to type, *You do realise that 'chimera' means 'fantasy,' you dumb kid?* and one day she would. But not just yet, while there was still so much fun to be had.

As she finished typing *Merry Meet Again*, she was unaware that her father had entered her bedroom and was standing

220

behind her, observing the screen. He'd been worried for some time about her internet use. Now he snatched up her laptop and scanned the forum comments with growing horror.

He confiscated the laptop indefinitely, closed her account and grounded her for a month.

Chimera's magick was no more.

* * *

Siv was cloudy-headed and twitchy when she arrived at the station the next morning. She'd woken from a vivid dream that her wagon was slipping down the meadow and teetering on the edge of the river. She was inside, unable to open the door. Mutsi stood on the riverbank in a silver evening dress and stilettos, watching and shouting that this wouldn't be happening if her daughter had been more grateful.

As she reached her office, she heard that a Ms Sitwell was in reception, asking to see her. She briefed Ali and told him to find Justin Desmond and check out Barnwell's story. Then she opened a window, stuck her head out and took deep breaths to try to reset her agitated brain.

Izzie Sitwell wore a smart black skirt and jacket. She had a tight, thin face and an expression that seemed to tremble on the edge of tears. 'I got your message and . . . Well, after last night, I wanted to see you as soon as possible. I've told work I'll be in late.'

'After last night?'

'Tasha rang me. She told me about Lily and Pearce. Lily's told Pearce she never wants to see him again and she's gone to stay with her grandfather. She's in bits.'

'I see. Have you spoken to Lily?'

'No. She sent us all a message, saying she needs time alone. I can't believe that Pearce did that — had a thing with Lyn. I can't believe it of *her*.'

The young woman was distraught. Lily hadn't reacted like that when she'd heard about her mother. 'Were you and Lyn close?'

'Yes, really close. She was such a nice woman and very kind to me, always. I'd never have expected her to behave like that. Lily's said she doesn't want any of us to talk to her about it. Usually, we all meet up on Friday night for a drink and a chat but she's cancelled this week.'

The Damsels might be about to fragment. 'So, have you got something to tell me?'

Izzie fiddled with her watch strap and peered at her with tiny, liquid eyes. She had a soft voice. Timid, almost. 'It's about Pearce. About the night Lyn vanished.'

'Okay. That was the night of your prom.'

'That's right. I'm not sure, but I might have seen something that . . .' Her voice trailed.

'Take your time. You were at Lily's house, getting ready that afternoon.'

'That's right. Then we . . . the Damsels all arrived at the prom together in a limo. We went straight into the school hall, except for Lily. She said Pearce would be arriving any minute, so she'd wait outside for him.'

'What time was that?'

'About twenty to eight. Anyway, the rest of us went in. Loads of people were arriving and the hall got packed. It was chaotic in there and I was talking to friends. After a while, I needed a pee and I'd started to get a bit queasy. We'd been drinking during the afternoon and I wasn't used to it. I went to the loo. It was along a corridor near the entrance. When I was heading back, I thought I saw Pearce just coming in through the outside door.'

'How long were you in the loo?'

'About ten minutes, maybe a bit more. I wanted to be sick, but I got better after I drank some water.'

'What time was it that you saw Pearce arriving?'

She frowned. 'I can't be *sure* it was Pearce. It was just the back of his head and I was still a bit funny and wobbly, you see.'

'Okay, but the time?'

'There's a clock just above the hall door, and I remember noticing it and thinking that Lily wouldn't be best pleased because it said just after half eight.'

'When you went into the hall, did you see Lily and Pearce?'

'Gosh, no, not right away . . . It was so crowded and the music was loud. I just started dancing and drinking. I hoped that if I had some more booze, I'd forget the nausea. Big mistake! I was horribly sick when I got home and I had the hangover from hell the next day. I saw Lily and Pearce a bit later that evening. They were up near the stage, sort of wrapped around each other and kissing.'

'How come you didn't mention this in 2013?'

'I don't . . . I wasn't sure that it had been Pearce at the door and I didn't want to cause trouble.' She worried at her watch strap again. 'I suppose I am now, aren't I? Will Lily find out that I've told you this?'

'I can't comment on that at present. Are you frightened of her?'

Izzie blinked. 'She's forceful, and I like my friends . . . the Damsels.'

Siv judged she'd be better off finding herself some new friends, but gave her a moment. 'So, back in 2013, you were unsure about saying anything regarding Pearce.'

'That's right. We all believed that Lyn must have committed suicide, because Lily seemed so sure about that. Then Pearce and Lily were getting married and I didn't want to spoil that for them.'

I bet you feel safer coming forward now, because Lily's status has wobbled. 'I've got a question for you. Did Lyn Dimas have a period the day of the prom?'

Izzie squeaked, 'A period? What a funny thing to ask!'

'There's nothing funny about murder.'

'No, sorry . . . Of course not. I didn't mean . . .' She paused. 'It's unlikely, because Lyn had said she might be having an early menopause.'

'She told you that?'

'Yes, one night when I was round there, about a fortnight before she went missing. We had beans on toast together after Adam went to bed. Lily was out with Pearce. Lyn was worried that she might never have another relationship. She told me she hadn't had a period for a couple of months and if it was the menopause, she'd be over the hill and no one would want her. She was ever so upset about it. I said that it might just be stress and anyway, there are all kinds of things that can help with the menopause these days.'

Siv couldn't help picturing Mutsi, who must be post-menopausal. It didn't seem to cramp her style. Maybe she was pumped full of artificial hormones. 'Thanks. I'd rather you didn't tell anyone that you've been to talk to me, or give any details about that prom night and what you saw.'

'What I *think* I saw,' Izzie protested, but she was clearly relieved at the instruction to stay quiet.

'Exactly.'

'Why did you ask about Lyn's periods?'

'It's a detail.'

'You'll find who killed her, won't you?' She stood, clutching her slim briefcase with a trembling hand.

'We aim to, yes.'

'I miss Lyn. She was lovely. I don't understand why she got mixed up with Pearce. She didn't value herself enough.'

CHAPTER 18

Ali was back from seeing Justin Desmond.

Siv told him what Izzie Sitwell had revealed, including Lyn's concerns about the menopause. 'So, if Lyn hadn't menstruated for a while, that blood on the mattress might have been from her meetings with Aston earlier that year. If Izzie is right about seeing Aston arriving at the prom, he'd just about have had time to kill Lyn and get there. He's such a bloody liar. If he didn't kill Lyn, I hope he gets at least a couple of years for perverting the course of justice. What's Desmond like?'

'I saw him at home. He was so jittery I was worried he might have a heart attack. He confirmed Barnwell's account of the meeting at the Flare Bar. Said Barnwell took him home and stayed with him for a couple of hours. He was dead worried in case we'd come after him for previous drug use. I told him it was the least of our concerns. He was scathing about Scott Darnley, said he's pathologically jealous and clingy and won't accept that their relationship is over. He had the cheek to ask me if I'd tell Darnley to back off. I told him I don't work in personal protection. So, Barnwell's in the clear, but not Dimas, who was either home alone or out strangling his wife. Are we getting Aston back in?'

She glanced at her watch. 'Yes, right now. Can you go and get him? Where's Patrick this morning?'

'He rang in, said he needed to deal with some urgent personal stuff and he'll be here asap.'

'Problems with Noah?'

'Not sure. Something about his bank.'

* * *

Patrick knocked on the door of the mobile home. He didn't understand why he was so nervous, except that Melinda Foster was the kind of confident older woman who always made him feel as if he was still in short trousers. He'd been trying to remember how they'd come by her as a cleaner. Maybe Noah had met someone during one of his brief forays to a day centre who'd recommended her. Patrick rarely saw her. She had a cocky, shrewd manner that he didn't much like, but Noah had always sung her praises.

He knocked again more loudly. The curtains were drawn. He saw one twitch and caught a glimpse of her maroon hair. When she opened the door, she was tying the belt on a frilly lemon dressing gown. A stale wave of fug, beer and tobacco fumes hit him, along with the distinctive, salty smell of sex. Without her make-up, she seemed older, worn. Her hair was flat and tangled.

'Yeah?' she said.

'We've met a couple of times. I'm Patrick Hill, Noah's brother.'

'Right, hun. Noah okay?'

'He's fine. Can I have a word?'

She looked behind her and shrugged. 'Hang on a minute.'

She closed the door. Patrick waited, listening to the rhythmic wash of the sea. These seaside caravan parks always seemed ugly, desolate places, perched by the coast as if they were clinging onto dry land. Someone nearby was frying breakfast and the scent of bacon made his stomach rumble. After a couple of minutes, the door opened and a ferrety-faced man came out, yawning and pulling on his jacket. He avoided Patrick's eyes and hurried away.

'Come on in, hun,' Melinda said.

Inside was hot, cramped and messy. Bras and pants were drying on an electric heater and dirty crockery was piled high in the sink. A radio was on, a chat show with music. Melinda sat on the unmade bed and gestured for him to sit on a window seat. She'd put on a slash of lipstick and a pair of furry slippers decorated with spaniel faces and brown bobbles for noses. She lit up a king-size cigarette and smiled at him.

'To what do I owe the pleasure, hun? Hat-trick's your nickname, that right? According to Noah, you're a smart detective.'

He noted the mockery and decided to cut straight to the chase. 'Someone took five hundred pounds from my bank account a couple of days ago. They used an ATM at Wesley's garage, just over the road from here.'

'That's rotten.' She took a long pull on her cigarette and hooked an ashtray nearer. Then she cocked an ear at the radio, where two men were cutting across each other in a heated discussion about parking restrictions. 'Parking in Berminster is a bloody nightmare! What's my council tax paying for? If I had my way . . .'

Patrick interrupted her. 'Yes, it is rotten that someone stole from me. Thing is, Melinda, Noah's the only person who has my PIN and it wasn't him.'

'Okay. So?' She rolled her cigarette end on the ashtray and ran a hand through her hair. Her gaze was hard and unflinching.

'I reckon it was you. You took the card from my wallet and Noah gave you the PIN, although why he'd do that . . . Maybe you persuaded him.'

'That's quite an accusation. Although, being a cop, I suppose you're used to barging into people's homes and accusing them.'

'I didn't barge in.'

She scratched a shin with the toe of a slipper. The spaniel nose waved in the air. 'Hmm, okay. I'll give you that. You and Noah have nice manners. He's always a gent.'

'Was it you?'

She laughed. 'Oh come on, hun, you can't be that green behind the ears.'

Patrick sat forward on the narrow brown seat. 'If it was you and you give me the money back, I won't take it any further. But I don't want you working for us.'

She pursed her lips, her face sagging. 'What does Noah say?'

'He said he doesn't know anything about it.'

'Well, then. There you go.' She crushed her cigarette end and lit another.

'I can take this through official channels,' Patrick said. 'I've checked and there's CCTV by the ATM. It can all get formal and nasty. If you're going to steal, best not to target a cop.'

She closed her eyes for a moment. 'If I'm guilty, then Noah must be, too. Complicit, isn't that the word?'

She'd have prepared for this. 'Not if there was coercion.'

She laughed, throwing her head back and then glanced at him with something approaching sympathy. 'Coercion!' She pulled her dressing gown around her neck. 'You are so, so green,' she said softly. 'Haven't you ever wondered why I don't get time to do much cleaning at yours?'

'Judging by this place, you don't seem too skilled at it,' he said.

'Ouch! You've got some claws after all, hun. That's good. Maybe you haven't realised this, but Noah gets ever so lonely on his ownio and he's a young hetero man, after all. There's only so much pleasure you can give yourself . . .'

She winked at him and it dawned on him. 'He's paying you for sex?'

'Well done. It's more interesting than cleaning. Do you mind?'

'Is that why he needed the money — to pay you?'

She laughed. 'Oh, no.' She waved a finger from side to side and then hummed along with Dusty Springfield's song, 'You Don't Have to Say You Love Me.'

'I'm crazy about these golden oldies, could listen to them all day. Hun, I'm not talking about money. You're not tripping me up that easily. But I can assure you, there's been no coercion. Just a mutually beneficial bit of trade. Before you start chucking accusations at me, I reckon you need to speak to Noah again. Plus, you need to stop sticking your head in the sand, hun. There you are, off to work every day, suited and booted and my poor old panda is stuck in that house, sighing and wanking and bored out of his skull.'

She put her head to one side, with an expression of genuine compassion. Despite the heat of the caravan, Patrick was chilled.

'You see,' Melinda carried on, sounding almost kindly, 'Noah told me that he's been depressed since he had that stroke. He reckons he's cluttering up your life. He hates all the interference and pity. I get that — I couldn't stand it myself, it'd drive me mental. I can see you don't approve of me, hun, but at least I cheer him up and take his mind off his troubles for a while. I may not be much good with a hoover, but I have my talents. I'm a bloody social service, me! If you sack me, your brother's back to having to please himself, all alone on his ownio. Now if you don't mind, I've a living to make and another client to get to.'

Patrick stood by his car, staring at the sea. Before the stroke, Noah had had lots of girlfriends. No one permanent, but he'd never been short of a companion. He'd been gregarious, fun and generous. Women liked him. Since the stroke, he and Patrick had discussed all kinds of subjects, but never sex. What could either of them say? It was difficult, embarrassing. No wonder Noah had been uncomfortable when he'd talked about the missing money. How much had his brother been parting with over the months? And how on earth was he going to broach this with him?

* * *

Pearce Aston was back with his solicitor. There was no prepared statement this time. Perhaps they'd decided it hadn't worked that well before. He was unshaven and he'd abandoned the peaked cap today.

'You didn't waste any time ratting on me to Lily,' he said as soon as Siv and Ali entered the room.

'She turned up here to see me,' Siv said. 'What did you want me to do — lie to her? She's been lied to enough, surely.'

'She's left me. She said she's never coming back,' he said, self-pityingly.

In my opinion, that often happens when someone feels betrayed, Siv was tempted to say, but she needed to press on. She let Ali start the tape and the formal interview.

'Mr Aston, we have new evidence about you on the night of the twenty-eighth of July 2013. Could you tell us again where you were that evening?'

'With Lily, at the prom.'

'What time did you arrive?'

'Around a quarter to eight.'

'Are you sure about that time?'

Ms Cornlow butted in. 'My client has already told you this, several times.'

Ali said, 'True. He's told us lots of things several times, most of them lies. We have new information from a witness who says that Mr Aston arrived at the prom at just after eight thirty, forty-five minutes later than he claims.'

'Who? Who's this witness?' Aston appealed to his solicitor. She put a restraining hand on his arm.

'We're not revealing that,' Siv told him. 'What's your response?'

'No comment.'

'That's a shame, because we can only be suspicious and assume you're lying again. That's right, isn't it, Ali?'

'Unfortunately, that is the case,' he agreed.

'You see,' she continued, 'Lyn Dimas might have been killed between seven thirty and eight thirty, when you were apparently not where you claim to have been. Are you sure you don't want to add something?'

'No comment.'

'You leave me with no alternative but to charge you on suspicion of Lyn Dimas's murder.'

'No way! You can't do that! I never touched Lyn!'

'May I have five minutes with my client?' Ms Cornlow asked.

'Sure, but no more than that.'

In the corridor, Ali said, 'He did it. He's lower than a snake's belly. It would have solved a lot of problems for him and cleared the path with Lily.' He'd used a new wax on his hair and was surrounded by a faint and pleasant aroma of coconut.

'Anyone can kill if they're desperate enough, but he just doesn't seem the type. He's well up himself but he doesn't strike me as vindictive.'

'Can't wait to hear what hokum he comes out with next. Right, I'm away for a quick gasper.'

Ali sauntered off to the courtyard and Siv rang Patrick.

'Just on my way in, guv.'

'Are you okay?'

'Yeah. Just some financial stuff to sort. Be there in ten.'

'Good, because I want an update on information from Trudy Kemp and Mr Marlin. You have got some for me?'

'Yeah, sure.' He sounded vague.

Back in the interview room, Aston was perspiring and Ms Cornlow's expression indicated that she was less than pleased with her client.

'Mr Aston would like to change his statement.'

Ali smiled. 'Thank you. Mr Aston, can you take us through that evening of the prom, from when you left work.'

He folded his arms and stared at the wall behind Ali's head. 'I left work at six and I went home, showered and got changed. I left home just before seven. I stopped on the way to the prom because I needed to visit someone. I have an Aunt Tammy who has severe mental illness. She's schizophrenic and she lives in special accommodation. I'm her only close relative and I help her out a bit financially. Her support worker had called me that afternoon, saying Tammy had had a psychotic episode and she'd asked for me. So, I called in there to check on her. I was there for about half an hour. Longer than I'd expected. I headed to the prom and got there about half eight. That's why I was late.'

Ali stared at him. 'Did you tell Lily where you'd been?'

He shifted uncomfortably. 'No. She doesn't know about Tammy.'

'Why's that?'

'Lily's . . . a bit funny about people with mental health problems. She doesn't like talking about them. She finds the whole subject scary and she'd worry about genetics . . . if we have kids. And she'd object to me funding Tammy. So all in all, it seemed best not to mention her.'

'Where's this accommodation?'

'Glenside House. Her support worker is Lou Bryant. She can confirm I was there.'

Siv took over. 'Let's hope so. Why did Lily lie for you, and tell us that you arrived at the prom at seven forty-five?'

'When we found out about her mum, in my opinion it just seemed best to keep things simple. That's what I told her and she agreed. She was a bit fed up when I got to the prom. I told her I'd been held up at work and then we were drinking and dancing and everything was okay.' He put his hands out, palms up. 'I had to fib about what time I'd arrived because I didn't want Lily finding out about Tammy.'

'So many things you wanted to keep from Lily,' Siv said. 'We'll need to check this new version of events. You're still on bail, Mr Aston.'

When Ali had turned the tape off, Aston smiled at them.

'I'm in the clear now, though, about Lyn, aren't I?'

Ali stood, pulling up his trousers. 'Depends on what Lou Bryant has to say. If she doesn't confirm your story, you might be right back in the murk.'

'Nice one,' Siv told him in the corridor.

'Blokes like him, I can't stand them. Always dodging and weaving and lying. Lily's a lying wee toerag as well. Maybe that's because she was worried about what he'd been doing.'

'She was happy to live with the suspicion that Aston might have had something to do with her mother's disappearance?'

'Well — there was no love lost between her and Lyn.'

'Hmm. I reckon she didn't want to rock the boat of romance or lose face. What a pair. They deserve each other.'

'Bit harsh. She's younger and seems like she's easily influenced by him, her family life had gone to pot and it sounds as if he'd hemmed her in. And she's found out plenty about him now.'

'You're a softie,' Siv told him, 'and Lily's tough as old boots. She'd have you for breakfast. Can you chase up this Lou Bryant right away and then at least we'll be sure if we've got to the bottom of Aston's lies.'

Lily phoned her as she went upstairs. She launched in abruptly with no hello.

'That bastard Pearce — he lied about the night of the prom and he made me lie too.'

Siv acted surprised. 'Really? What's this lie?'

'He was late getting there to meet me. He didn't arrive at a quarter to eight. It was after half eight. He told me he'd been delayed at work.'

She paused on the stairs, leaning against the wall. 'I see. Why did you lie about that and back him up?'

'When Mum had gone missing and the police were asking us questions, he said . . . he said that it would only make things complicated if your lot found out that he'd been late. He said the police twist things and it was best to keep it simple, otherwise he'd be hounded and it might not be good for business. I wish I hadn't agreed with him now.' There was a sob in her voice.

'Did you believe he'd been delayed at work?'

A telling pause. 'Of course. He often worked late.'

'You don't sound convinced. Do you suspect now that Pearce murdered your mother?'

There was a gasp. 'What do you want me to say? It's as if I've been married to a stranger all these years. It's not fair, you asking me that.'

'It's a reasonable question, given the lies your husband has told.'

'Yeah . . . well . . . it's no good asking me.'

'Let's leave it there for now. Are you with your grandfather?'

'Yeah. I haven't told him about this yet. He's gone a bit wobbly, with everything that's happened. It's all too weird.'

'It's difficult for everyone involved. I'll come and see you soon.'

'Do *you* reckon Pearce did it?'

'I can't comment on that, Lily. It's an active investigation. I'll inform you and your family as soon as there's anything concrete to tell you.'

CHAPTER 19

They sat around the incident board the next morning. Patrick was flicking at his tie and eager to go first, so Siv let him. She could see he wanted to show that he was on top of things and pulling his weight in the team. She needed to check that he was.

'Right, first of all, I got info from Trudy Kemp. She doesn't remember Lyn mentioning a problem when she worked at Foot Heaven, but Trudy was away travelling back then. I've written up the names of the five pupils she took from Minster Academy to recce the outside of Steiner's and Orford End in general. That visit was in February 2010. The pupils were all around sixteen at the time, so they'd be mid-twenties now. As far as Trudy could tell, Lyn hadn't met any of them. I've checked and none of their names featured in the 2013 investigation. I rang Theo Dimas and he'd not heard of them, and said that he couldn't recall Lyn or Lily knowing any of them. Lily didn't attend Minster Academy.'

Siv scanned the names.

'Lily might be familiar with any of them through other contacts,' she said. 'I need to see her again so I'll ask her. What about Barry Marlin, the prospective buyer for Steiner's?'

Patrick tapped his pen against his thigh. 'I got hold of him. He lives in Rochester now. He confirmed that he'd been interested in the place in 2010, but withdrew his offer because he couldn't get outline planning permission for flats. He was staying with friends in Suffolk on the night Lyn vanished — they've confirmed.'

Ali stood and crossed Marlin's name through on the board, then did the same for Pearce Aston. 'I spoke to Lou Bryant, the support worker at Glenside House. She told me that Tammy Aston has paranoid schizophrenia and she's lived in supported accommodation at Glenside since 1999. She confirmed that Pearce Aston visits his aunt regularly. Ms Bryant went back through Tammy Aston's care record. She'd called Aston on the afternoon of the twenty-eighth of July 2013, because Tammy was unwell and asking for him. Amazing though it might sound, he has a calming effect on her when she's going through a bad phase. Lou Bryant was there when he visited, and confirmed the times he gave from their signing-in book.'

Siv reached for her coffee and surveyed the board. There were red dots beside the dwindling number of names with no confirmed alibi. The coffee was rich and warming but it couldn't stop her worrying that they were getting nowhere fast. She had a picture of herself sliding backwards down Bartel's glass mountain.

She pointed at the board. 'Let's recap. Lyn Dimas had been in a bad way for months after her husband left. She was highly emotional, prone to arguing with people, angry with Lily and Pearce, and was lonely. She'd discovered that her daughter was planning to marry a man who she'd had an affair with. She made an effort with her appearance before she went out that evening, ostensibly to the shop. It seems that she didn't intend to be out for long and she didn't take her car. So, it's unlikely that she planned to go to Steiner's that night, although she was familiar with the place. Also, it wouldn't have held pleasant memories for her, given that Aston had ended their romance. She might have had sex with her killer, consensual or forced, before she was murdered, or someone she'd never had sex with might have strangled her.

We can't be sure that the murder took place at Steiner's.' She gulped coffee and continued. 'We now have four names up there without confirmed alibis for the twenty-eighth of July: Jeff Downey, Theo Dimas, Trudy Kemp and Lewis Haddon. Lyn didn't like Downey, who'd tried it on with her and she was furious with her husband and tormenting him — no love lost. However, we have no information to indicate that Downey or Dimas had ever been near Steiner's and no forensics placing Downey there. Theo Dimas says that his fingerprints are on the wine bottle because he unpacked it at home, and I can't see that we can challenge that statement. There's no evidence that there was any antagonism between Trudy and her sister. Lewis Haddon had been to see Steiner's, but he says he never entered the premises until the visit in April with Bass, and we have no connection between him and Lyn. And again, we have no forensics connecting Trudy or Lewis Haddon to Steiner's, and none of the forensics we have matches to anyone else in our lists of names or the national database.'

Ali was leaning against the window, arms folded. 'We can't rule out Theo Dimas and Downey. Either of them might have killed her, and especially the husband.'

'You've always fancied Dimas for it. I'm not so sure.'

'We've been chasing our tails, got half the DNA in town and we've got sod all,' Ali muttered.

Patrick added, 'Hard to see where we go, guv. It's all a dead end.'

'Not necessarily, and I can do without negativity in the ranks.' She smiled but her voice was sharp. This case was important to her, and not just because a woman had been murdered. Tommy Castles, Mortimer's golden boy, had failed to find Lyn's body. It would be satisfying to solve a crime he'd flunked, and to watch Mortimer's face when she told him. 'I keep coming back to the way Lyn's body was left hanging to rot away slowly in a deserted place. Her killer realised that she probably wouldn't be found for some time, and they needed to demean her, even in death. Almost as if killing her wasn't revenge enough. That's a strong emotion and very personal.' She wondered, too, if the person who had strangled Lyn had known about her use of Steiner's for an affair, and had left her there as a kind of punishment for her transgression. She gulped back her coffee, stood and picked up a marker pen, quickly creating a list on the board:

- Was Lyn planning to meet someone when she went out?
- How did she end up at Steiner's?
- Do any of the names on Trudy's list link to Lyn?
- What was the problem she'd had in her previous job?

'These are our outstanding questions. The first two might be answered if we find anything useful from the last two. Can you deal with those names from Trudy between you? Check out where they are now, if any of them have form, where they were on the night Lyn went missing, and if there's any crossover with her. Did any of them visit her clinic? It's time-consuming, but see them in person if you can. Ali, tell Aston and his solicitor he's off the hook on suspicion of murder, but he still has the charge of perverting the course of justice. I'll chase up on Lyn's previous employment and see Lily Aston. Anything else?'

Ali and Patrick stared at the board, silent. She decided to interpret it as determined focus.

'Good. Crack on, then.'

She was back at her desk when Patrick tapped on the door.

'Guv, can I have a word?'

'Sure. Take a seat.'

He edged in and sat, rubbing his thumbs together. His colour was high and he had pink blotches on his neck. 'Erm . . . it's difficult. I'm not sure whether or not to ask you.'

She couldn't imagine what was making him so embarrassed. Maybe he wanted a reference for another job, or to discuss promotion. 'Don't ask, don't get, Patrick.'

'Right. It's . . . it's about Noah. I'm really worried about him.'

'I see.' Her heart sank. She'd never been much good at managing other people's personal problems. She didn't lack empathy, but worried about how to respond in the right way. Her weird upbringing seemed to have left her without the necessary emotional codes. 'Is Noah unwell?'

'No — no more than usual. It's . . .' He fiddled with his shirt cuffs and then sat up straight. 'I've been worried about him because he's seemed down and irritable recently. I found out that he's been paying the woman who cleans our house for sex. Her name's Melinda Foster. I've no idea how much he's been giving her, but it's been leaving him short of money. He's been borrowing from me now and again. Melinda took my bank card and he gave her my PIN. She drew money out of my account at an ATM, five hundred pounds. When I asked him about it, he denied it and got very chippy. I visited Melinda. She told me about the relationship and said that if I do anything about the theft, she'll refuse to visit again and Noah will be mortified. She went on about how lonely and frustrated he gets, which is true. She described herself as a social service.' He paused, puffing his cheeks out.

Siv spoke gently. 'Did you tell Noah you'd talked to Melinda?'

'Yeah. It was grim. He accused me of spying on him and refused to talk to me.' It had been a terrible scene. Noah had gone white with anger and yelled that Patrick had no right to intrude in his personal life. He'd shut himself in his room.

People were always surprising and mysterious. Poor Patrick was scarlet now, and there was desperation in his eyes. It must have taken all his courage to speak about the matter. Siv was blindsided but tried to concentrate as he carried on.

'I was going to talk to Ali, but then I reckoned that Noah would be even more humiliated if Ali heard about this. He's got his pride and they have, well, a blokeish friendship. They don't talk about personal stuff. I'm at a loss and he's giving me the silent treatment. It's awful because really, it's his personal, private business and I've no right to be involved. I don't *want* to be involved . . .' He sighed.

His mother died soon after Noah had the stroke and he's been left to cope with a daily, heavy burden. The exploitation angered her. Noah was a bright, engaging man and this Melinda was abusing his vulnerability. 'Of course Noah's entitled to a private life, but the reality is that he has a disability which renders him susceptible, and makes it difficult for him to act autonomously. It's clear that he's being abused. If this Melinda was trading as an honest sex worker, she wouldn't be persuading Noah to let her steal from you. I've no idea what the going rates are in town, but it suggests that hers are inflated.' That brought a weak smile from him. 'I'd bet that Noah's really guilty about this. He's had to be underhand, and Melinda has manipulated him. They've both involved you by stealing from you. That crosses a line.'

'Yeah. It's such a mess and it's like anything I say to Noah is a criticism.'

'I get that, but Noah is an adult and he can make his own decisions. He made a bad one about your card and PIN. If he wants to be treated with respect, he has to show you some, apologise, and pay you back. Noah can't have it both ways.'

Patrick didn't look convinced.

'Have you sacked Melinda as your cleaner?'

'Yes. I told her to get lost on that front. Doesn't stop her visiting Noah when I'm not in.'

'Does Noah have any other friend who could talk to him about this? It would take the pressure off you.'

Patrick shook his head and then said imploringly, 'Would you talk to him, guv?'

'Me? Patrick, I don't —'

'It's a big ask and an imposition, guv, but he really likes you and respects you. He says you don't talk down to him. I just can't discuss this stuff with him, even if he'd let me. It's too embarrassing and it's like I'm treading all over his life.'

She found it hard to imagine that anyone found her easy to talk to. She'd never been the type to encourage intimacies and she'd pulled the drawbridge up since Ed died. But she could sense Patrick's desperation and she liked Noah.

'Leave it with me. I'm not promising anything.'

'Okay. Thanks, guv.'

When he'd gone, she turned back to her murder inquiry. She'd had no response to her email to the National Organisation for Podiatry and Chiropody, so she rang the London number. She mentioned her previous email, expressed her displeasure at not receiving a reply, and asked to speak to someone concerning a murder investigation. She listened to a stunned silence and then gave her phone number to a woman who promised that she'd get a call back in the next fifteen minutes.

She crossed to the window and stood contemplating the handsome museum edifice across the road and Noah's circumstances. Life had dealt him a cruel blow, yet he usually spoke of his situation with a dry, forthright wit. He had two words tattooed in red on the backs of his hands: *No* on the right and *Pity* on the left. She recalled speaking to him earlier in the year, when he'd told her that Patrick shouldn't have to care for him. Noah carried his own burden of guilt. She could only imagine the current tension between the brothers. She needed Patrick back on an even keel and focused on his work. That wasn't going to happen while he was fretting about Noah. If empathy wasn't always one of her virtues, pragmatism was.

Back at her desk, she opened her laptop where she spent five minutes scouring websites and noting phone numbers. She made a couple of calls, asked questions and took down details. Not part of her usual investigative work, but it added to her familiarity with market forces in Berminster.

Hey, Sivvi, if anyone looks at your search history, they might get the wrong idea. Ed made her jump. He'd never spoken to her at work before. How would she cope if he was going to start calling by when she was on duty?

You can't start chatting to me when I'm at work, it's not fair, she told him. Her phone rang and she paused before answering, but her office was silent again. She shook her head to clear it as she picked up the call. It was a Hassan Kibet from the NOPC, apologising profusely for not replying sooner.

'Your email was forwarded to me, but we've recently had our first child and I've been somewhat distracted.'

Given his reason, it would be churlish to press the point. 'Thanks for getting back to me promptly today. I'm investigating the murder of a Lyn Dimas. She died in 2013. She was a registered podiatrist, working in a clinic in Berminster. I believe that there was a problem in her previous workplace in Seaford, a clinic called Foot Heaven. This would be before 2004. I'd like to establish what the concerns were.'

'How do you spell that surname?'

She told him and he asked her to hold for a minute while he searched for Lyn. She glanced outside at Ali and Patrick as they headed to the car park, Ali with his easy, loping stride, a blue wisp of cigarette smoke hovering above his head like a wraith, and Patrick bobbing up and down beside him, tapping his phone screen as he walked.

'I've found Ms Dimas's registration record. It's been suspended and says that she's missing.'

'Not anymore. We've found her body. She was murdered.'

'Oh my goodness. Well . . . I'll get that amended. I can see that there was an issue about a complaint in 2002.'

'Can you tell me what that entailed?'

'I'm afraid that I can't right now. It's a protected file, and I'll have to go through a senior manager.'

'How soon can you do that?'

'I'll try to get access this afternoon.'

'Make sure you do. I need this information urgently so you must come back to me today.' She had a sudden sense that this might be important. 'Please stress that this is a murder inquiry.'

As she left the station to see Lily Aston, she passed a muscular, sinewy man in reception, dressed in jeans, Aran jumper and walking boots. He struck her as an off-duty soldier. He was leaning sideways against the desk, chewing gum and chatting easily to a uniformed colleague. As she walked past she was aware of his insolent, assessing glance.

* * *

Ali and Patrick had talked to Karim Patel, who was an accountant and Nat Olawego, who was a househusband. They had varying degrees of recollection of the school trip to Orford End with Ms Kemp. Neither of them had heard of Lyn Dimas or any of her family and both had said that they'd never had any reason to return to Steiner's. Olawego had stated that he would have been at home that night because it was his dad's birthday and there was always a party. Patel had checked his electronic calendar and said that he'd been at university in Bournemouth. Paul Bison had been drowned in a boating accident in 2012.

They'd been unable to trace Tim Stafford and the reason for this became clear when they talked to a chatty Bethany James, now a florist. She was a rotund little woman with a broad smile, wearing a bright yellow apron and fingerless mittens. Her shop, Blooming Lovely, was empty and she was keen on their company, commenting that she'd only had one customer since she'd opened that morning.

'I blame Brexit for the downturn in business. People don't buy flowers when they're worried if they can pay the bills, or they get those dull but cheap bunches in the supermarket. Half-dead before you get them home, most of those. I suppose a beautiful, fresh bouquet is a luxury when you're hard up, but I'm worried about staying afloat if this carries on much longer. If I didn't have weddings and funerals to supply, I'd be in a worse state. I call it my "match and despatch" business.' She tied an intricate knot in a length of white ribbon and attached it to a bowl of pink-and-white amaryllis.

'I can see it must be hard for you,' Ali agreed. 'We're investigating the murder of Lyn Dimas, and talking to anyone who might have visited Orford End.'

'Gosh, yes, I read about that. Poor woman. Her family must be in bits. You found her at that deserted place, didn't you? Steiner's. It used to be a removals firm.'

'That's right. Had you come across her or her family? Ms Dimas was a podiatrist in town. Did you ever have treatment at her clinic?'

'No, I never met her or her family. I've had trouble with my teeth — bloody painful wisdom tooth that's given me awful jip — but so far, my feet have been fine, which is just as well as I'm on them all day. I read that Lyn Dimas had two children. It must be terrible for your mum to vanish and then her body to be found years later. I hope you find the scum who did it and put him away for life. They never do get life these days though, do they?'

Ali avoided opening up any discussion of the penal system. It was a favourite with the public and a minefield. 'Ms James, we're trying to find out where Lyn Dimas went on the night she died in 2013. Some years ago, you visited Orford End on a school trip with your geography teacher, Ms Kemp. Can you cast your mind back to the other pupils you visited with that day? We've talked to some and we found out that Paul Bison died. We'd like to speak to Tim Stafford.'

It was chilly in the shop, and Bethany had a trembling drip at the end of her pudgy nose, which she brushed away with the back of a mittened hand. Within seconds, a new one appeared. They stood among the buckets of blooms, trays of pot plants and ready-made bouquets while she talked away in a circuitous monologue. Ali liked interviews where you pressed someone's button and set them off, but he could see that Patrick was wide-eyed at her dripping nose as she rattled on.

'I really liked Ms Kemp. She was a good teacher and keen on her subject. Fire in her belly, that one. I got a B in Geography A level, thanks to her. She comes in now and again for flowers and we have a chat. She tells me about the economies at Minster Academy, and how it's all about records and league tables these days. Asters and freesias are her favourite flowers. That was terrible about Paul Bison. Goodness knows why he went out in a boat without a life jacket when he couldn't swim. Mind, he was always larking around and a risk taker. One risk too many. The lifeguard tried to save him, just off Minster Beach, but it was too late. He should have been more careful. We've been warned all our lives that there are strong currents there, but some people never get any sense.' She gazed into the middle distance, shaking her head.

'And Tim Stafford?' Patrick prompted. He stuck his hands in his jacket pockets to try to keep warm.

'Oh, he was such a sad boy, was Tim,' she said, trimming rose stems. 'We used to call him "Staffy," after the dog breed, because he had a habit of hanging his tongue out. He had a funny home life. It was a private fostering situation. I'd never heard of one of those before he told me. His foster dad was his uncle. Tim always put me in mind of that Keats quote — "alone and palely loitering". He was a weedy, bony kid and he never seemed to have any friends. He'd just hang around. He wasn't too bright and he struggled with schoolwork. He could be a troublemaker, too, and sneaky with it. He had a talent for telling tales, starting arguments between people and then standing back to watch the fallout. I heard that his foster parents kicked him out soon after we left school. I saw him sleeping rough in town a couple of years ago. He had a sort of makeshift camp outside the empty BHS store on the parade and he was begging. He had a bedside table by his sleeping bag and a bookshelf with a reading lamp on it. That was bizarre because he'd no electric supply. I remember how sad it was, like a pretend bedroom in the street. I gave him a fiver, but he didn't recognise me. He was sort of skeletal. I haven't seen him around for a while. It crossed my mind that he might have died. People do, don't they, when they live on the streets. They get TB, hepatitis and all sorts, and a strong breeze could have blown Tim away.'

'Any idea where his foster parents live, or their surname?' Ali asked.

'Their name was Stafford, too. Not sure of the house number, but I remember it was on Chiltern Drive, near the park end.' She sniffed and dabbed again at her nose. 'Sorry it's cold in here. I'm used to it. I try to keep the heating bills down and the flowers stay fresher for longer in a cool environment.'

Ali bought a bunch of chrysanthemums, gerberas, orange lilies and mixed berries for Polly. Bethany threw in extra free foliage, 'Because I wouldn't want to do your job for all the tea in China.'

The flowers sat on the back seat of his car now, filling it with a sedgy, fresh scent and moistening the air. Patrick looked up Stafford and found the address in Chiltern Drive while Ali leaned out of the driver's door, puffing on a cigarette and phoning the St Helen's soup kitchen. Berminster didn't have a homeless shelter, but the vicar at St Helen's had started the kitchen a couple of years ago, and she allowed rough sleepers to stay in the church overnight.

'They've met Tim Stafford,' he told Patrick, 'but they haven't seen him for months. The woman I spoke to said Tim sometimes goes on the road, moves on to check the pickings in other places.'

'If he's been homeless for a while, he might have kipped at Steiner's.'

'That's true, or he might have been hanging out there as a teenager and seen Lyn there with Aston. We could do a trawl of rough sleepers in town, but it might be quicker to talk to the Staffords first.'

'Okay. Chiltern Drive's south-east of town, near Stoneydown Park.'

Ali glanced in the rear-view mirror as he started the car. His hair was straggly and needed replaiting. 'I'm like an owl peeping out of an ivy bush,' he muttered.

Patrick rubbed his chilly hands together. 'It was bloody freezing in that shop. No wonder she doesn't have many customers. They'd get frostbite.'

'I didn't notice it that much. Mind you, compared to you, I'm well-padded. There are advantages to carrying some heft instead of being a skinny-ribs. Did you see Tommy Castles at the station?'

'Yeah, just to say hello. He said he has a few days off and he's walking the coastal path. He'd been hobnobbing with Mortimer.'

'Hmm. Probably arranging lunch at the yacht club. I wonder if the guv saw him.'

'Would it bother her?'

'I'd say so. It'd bother me if the bloke who'd wanted the job I'd got was sniffing around his old hunting ground, and hanging out with my boss.' Ali glanced across. 'What are you wearing for the Halloween do?'

'Skeleton costume for me, and Noah's planning to be a bat. How about you?'

'Haven't decided yet. Maybe a púca. It's an animal from Irish folklore, a bringer of bad or good fortune. So I might go as an evil hare.'

Patrick laughed. 'You'd better get a wiggle on, it's next weekend.'

'That's what Polly keeps telling me. Been meaning to ask, how's Noah doing?'

'Yeah, okay. He's just had a bit of a blip.'

Ali started humming in his melodic voice, one of those sweetly haunting Irish airs that he liked. Patrick watched the flying grey clouds, glad that he'd asked for the guv's help but worrying that it would make Noah even madder when he found out. *Damned if I do, damned if I don't.*

CHAPTER 20

Lily Aston had perked up and was firing on all cylinders. She was out of place in her grandfather's dim living room, her skinny ripped jeans and low-cut, tight T-shirt at odds with the sacred icons and formal, religious ambiance. Joe Dimas was dressed in black again, but with a dark-grey polo neck. He seemed somehow frailer and his shoulders sagged inwards. He sat perched close to and just behind Lily, his hard eyes glinting back and forth between her and Siv.

'Let me make sure I've got this right,' Lily said. 'Now you're saying you don't suspect Pearce of killing my mum?'

'That's right. He has a verified alibi for his whereabouts before he turned up late at the prom.'

'So, where was he? Shagging someone else after he moved on from Mum?'

'That's for him to explain. You'll have to talk to him.'

'Not bloody likely!' Lily folded her arms. 'How come it took all this fuss and aggravation for you to find he had a proper alibi?'

She made it sound as if the police had been harassing an innocent man. 'You'll find it was Pearce who caused the aggravation by lying consistently and repeatedly.'

'Wait a minute,' Joe Dimas said. 'What's this about Pearce being late at the prom? That's the first I've heard of such a thing.' He tapped Lily's shoulder but she shifted away from him.

Siv didn't see why she should withhold the truth. He'd have to find out, and Lily clearly didn't want to tell him. 'Both Pearce and Lily lied to the police in 2013 and during this investigation. They said he arrived at the prom at seven forty-five but in fact, he turned up at gone eight thirty. When we found out from another source that he'd lied, we were suspicious. After wasting a lot of our time, he told us that he'd had to see someone after he left work and before he arrived at the prom.'

'Some slag, I expect,' Lily said. Then she worked out what she'd heard. 'Hang on, you mean someone else told you he arrived late?'

'That's right.'

'Who was it?'

'I can't divulge that and it's not relevant to our inquiry now.'

Joe Dimas was frowning. 'But why did you lie for him, Lily? You shouldn't have done that.'

'Oh, leave me alone, Papu. I've got enough on my plate without you on my case. Like she said, it doesn't matter now.'

'Lying to the police is a serious matter,' Siv said. 'If I didn't judge it to be a waste of time and resources, I'd charge you with perverting the course of justice. Pearce still faces that charge and he could go to prison. I'm only letting you off because I believe he put pressure on you.'

Lily flushed. 'I don't care what you charge that fucking prick with. You can bang him up for ever, for all I care. I never want to see the lying shit again.'

Dimas flinched as his granddaughter swore and glanced at the Madonna. 'Tcha, Lily, language! Our Lady is listening.'

'*Lily, language!*' she mimicked. 'Our Lady had better get some ear muffs. I'll call him worse than that before this is over. I'm going to a solicitor tomorrow. I'm going to get every penny

I can from him, the house, and half the business. Tasha read up about it and her mum's a solicitor so I'm up to speed with my rights. And he can fuck off out of the house that Papu's money helped buy and find somewhere to stay while I divorce him.'

Dimas muttered to himself, '*Theé mou, voítha me*,' and closed his eyes with an air of defeat. He must be crushed by what he'd been hearing about Pearce, the man he'd respected and chosen to favour over his own son. It might be best if Lily went home and her husband camped elsewhere. This setup couldn't last for long and Siv suspected that there'd be no flaounes baking for some time.

'There's another reason why I wanted to see you, Lily. Ever met any of the people on this list?' She scrolled to Trudy Kemp's list on her phone and showed it to Lily. Her grandfather peered at it over her shoulder.

'Nah. Who are they?'

'This is a photo of one of them, Tim Stafford. How about him?'

'Nah.'

'How about you, Mr Dimas?'

Joe Dimas shook his head.

'They're a group of pupils who once visited Orford End with their teacher, Trudy Kemp.'

'Auntie Trudy?'

'That's right.'

'Well, they mean nothing to me. She's a right bitch anyway, siding with Dad and Monty and betraying her own sister. She's got no loyalty, has she, Papu?'

Her grandfather shook his head and reached out to touch the feet of St Nicholas.

'Your aunt's been very unwell and in hospital,' Siv said. 'Ruptured appendix.'

Lily's mouth turned down. 'Who gives a fuck?'

'Lily, please, I must beg you, don't speak like that. Have some respect,' Dimas urged.

'Oh, stop banging on, Papu. Get off my case. My life's turned to shit, okay?' She sprang up and left the room, leaving the door swinging. The sudden draught caused a dense billow of sickly incense from below a triptych. Dimas rose, leaned against the back of a chair, and then saw Siv to the front door. He put a hand to the frame, as if needing support.

'I'm sorry about Lily's bad language, Inspector. I've never heard her talk like this before. She's not herself at all. She's had a succession of terrible shocks. First her mother's body was found, and now Pearce's appalling betrayal has been revealed. I'm in shock myself, discovering that Lyn was having an affair and meeting Pearce at Steiner's. I can't believe it. I've always held that young man in such high esteem, supported him both emotionally and financially. I worry about what will happen to Lily. Anything I say, she snaps at me.'

'Murder invades and taints the lives of all those associated with the victim. As you say, Mr Dimas, Lily's had a number of shocks. It will take time. She still has her mother's funeral to come. I'm sure your support is invaluable to her, whatever she says.'

Ali phoned with an update as she got into her car, saying that he and Patrick were about to call on the Staffords. Hassan Kibet called her back as she reached the main road and she pulled in to speak to him.

'I've accessed the complaint record,' he told her. 'Lyn Dimas made an allegation about a colleague. It's quite complex and, of course, there are confidentiality issues. I wondered if you might be able to meet in person to discuss it. Our office is in Islington.'

She deliberated. She'd finished folding her kusudama model and needed to take the piece to the architects in Ealing. She always took completed work in person, not trusting the risk of damage to delicate sculptures by delivery drivers. If she went to London to see Hassan Kibet, she could also make her delivery. She agreed to meet Kibet the following morning and drove on as the heavens opened, heading for the coast road. She'd rather speak to Noah while Patrick wasn't around. She'd also rather interview the most hardened criminal than make this visit, but she'd agonise over it if she didn't try to help and she wanted to get it over with as soon as possible.

* * *

Clement Stafford had died a couple of years ago and, from the offhand way his widow told them, she wasn't too sad about his demise. Esme Stafford sat opposite them in her bright living room. The beech-framed sofa and easy chairs looked new, as did the pale apricot paint on the walls and the leaf-patterned window blinds. She was in her sixties, with a heart-shaped face and trim figure, and she wore a purple tunic over black leggings. Her silvery hair was cropped short and her large hoop earrings were inset with tiny diamonds. Her manner was frosty. She didn't offer drinks and made it clear that she couldn't tarry.

'I have a t'ai chi class at four. I don't see how I can help you about Tim. I haven't seen him since just after Clem died. Tim didn't come to the funeral, which was no surprise and a huge relief, but he called here afterwards, asking if Clem had left him anything. I didn't want to let him in, but he was unusually meek and mild, it was pouring rain and I had a friend here. I told him Clem hadn't left him any inheritance. I've no idea why Tim had got it into his head that there might be one, not after what he'd done to us. He hung around for about an hour, asking if I had any photos of his mother. I gave him an album with a few in. We never had many — she wasn't the type to send photos. Then I gave him a hundred pounds to get rid of him and one of Clem's winter coats, a handsome woollen Burberry. He took off and that's the last time I saw him, thank goodness.' She wrinkled her nose. 'I worried I'd have to fumigate the place after he'd gone.'

Ali had told Patrick to lead on this interview. He smiled, hoping to mellow the atmosphere a little. 'Do you have any idea where we can contact Tim?'

His attempt failed. She gave him a cold stare. 'Are you really old enough to be a police officer?'

'Just answer the question, please.'

'No. He could be anywhere. He's probably in a squat or sleeping in a doorway. Tim is a mass of self-destructive impulses and if anyone tries to help him, he'll bite the hand that feeds. He made my life miserable for years. I don't want to see him or have anything to do with him.'

'What did he do to you?' Patrick asked.

'What didn't he do, more like,' she replied tartly. 'Clem persuaded me to let Tim come and live with us when he was ten. He was Clem's sister's kid. She wasn't married and never named Tim's father. She was a hopeless woman, always in and out of jobs and in debt. Then she got a job as a travel rep, based in the Greek islands. She couldn't have Tim with her — or so she said — so she asked Clem if we'd take him in. It was supposed to be a temporary arrangement but of course, she was just trying to find a way to dump Tim, and Clem was soft as butter. I wasn't keen. Tim was a strange, morose boy, sort of detached and slow on the uptake, but Clem wanted to give his sister a chance so Tim landed here. His mother visited now and again, but more and more infrequently. She sent dribs and drabs of money towards Tim's upkeep, but then that dried up, just as I'd predicted. She died of a pulmonary embolism on Rhodes when Tim was fourteen. He was uncommunicative and difficult to get on with, never showed us any affection but he became impossible after that. He was a slow learner at school and he truanted regularly. There were lots of rows and he'd stay out late, or not come home at all for a couple of nights. The rows continued and then on his eighteenth birthday, he blew a fuse with me when I told him he needed to pull his socks up and find a job. He started throwing stuff. Clem stepped in and Tim punched him in the face. That was it. I told Clem he was an adult and he had to go, so we gave him his marching orders.'

'When was that and where did he go?' Patrick asked.

'It was May 2012. I've no idea where he went. I suspect that Clem used to see him sometimes and give him money. As long as he wasn't here, I didn't care. When he turned up after Clem died, it was the first time I'd seen him since the day he left, and I sincerely hope it was the last.'

Patrick was starting to feel sorry for Stafford. 'You haven't asked us why we want to find Tim.'

She gave a dry laugh. 'Well, as you're police, I assume he's committed a crime, which wouldn't surprise me at all. It amazes me that he hasn't already been jailed. I don't care why you're after him, DC Hill. I never wanted him here in the first place, and I always said he'd end up in trouble of some kind. Now, is that all?'

'Not quite. Did you know a woman called Lyn Dimas, or any of her family?'

She tapped her chin. 'Lyn Dimas. She's that podiatrist woman who went missing. Her body's just been found. I went to her a couple of times at the clinic when I had heel pain. It was years ago. The problem went away after treatment and it's never come back. Tim saw her once, I remember. He had an obstinate verruca.'

Patrick asked, 'Do you recall when Tim saw her?'

'Not exactly, but it wasn't that long before we gave him his marching orders, because Clem got a verruca just after he left, probably from one of the disgusting towels Tim used to leave lying around.' Her eyes became saucers. 'You don't think Tim killed her, do you?'

'We're making lots of enquiries, Mrs Stafford.'

'But my God, if he's a suspect . . . might he come after me? You read about these disturbed young men becoming violent. Thank goodness I wasn't on my own that day he called here! Should I change my locks?' She was eyeing the room with a hand to her throat, as if she expected Tim to leap out at her from behind a sofa.

Patrick glanced at Ali, who scratched his neck. 'Does Tim have a key to this house?'

'What? No . . . no. I made sure we took his keys back the day he left.'

Ali reckoned that it was best to be on the safe side until they found out what they were dealing with. If Tim Stafford was their killer, he was capable of extreme violence and his foster mother wasn't exactly on his Christmas card list. 'Mrs Stafford, you said that your husband might have met up with Tim after he left here. He might have given him a key, or Tim could have stolen one. Clearly, you've had problems and disagreements over the years. You're probably not in any danger, but it might be best to change your locks.'

'Yes, I see. Goodness. Well, that's put bit of a damper on the day! I'm not sure I'll be able to focus in t'ai chi after all this!' She spoke as if they'd called round just to inconvenience her.

They rose to leave. Ali paused, and asked Mrs Stafford if she had a photo of Tim as an adult.

She tutted. 'Oh, somewhere probably. Not that recent, but there's a school one of him when he was seventeen. Do you need it now?'

'It would be helpful and if we take it away, we probably won't need to come back.'

That decided her. She made a fuss of searching through a drawer, muttering to herself as she took out photo albums and flicked through them. After a couple of minutes, she took a photo from its sleeve and handed it to Ali.

'There,' she said. 'I warn you, he doesn't look much like that now. He's even skinnier and you'd need to add long filthy hair and a scraggy beard.'

Back in the car, they scrutinised the photo of a scrawny youth with ear studs, hooded eyes and acne scars on his forehead. He gazed furtively at them.

'He didn't smile for the camera,' Patrick said.

'Not much to smile about, from the sound of it.'

'What a cold woman she is.'

'She doesn't radiate kindness,' Ali agreed. 'Mind, if she's telling it like it was, she had to put up with a lot for years. Sounds as if Tim is a mess.'

'The way she described him, he might be autistic.'

'As the guv always says, let's not jump to any conclusions. We need to find him. The acne scars are a handy distinguishing mark, but the years of rough sleeping might have altered him. Can you start ringing around homeless hostels in other towns? Try Hastings and Brighton, for starters.'

* * *

Siv dashed through torrential rain from her car, waving at Noah, who was gazing out of the front window at the deluge. She waited in the porch while he opened the door and followed him in, hanging her dripping jacket on a hall peg. He was pasty and little pouches of fat rippled over his shirt collar. His eyes were dull and guarded as he turned his chair to face her. She needed to make this quick and straightforward, to spare his blushes.

'I'm not going to ask how you are, Noah. Patrick's told me you've had a rough time. He's explained about Melinda and the money.'

He stared out at the rods of rain. 'He'd no right to do that.'

'He's worried. He doesn't know I'm here now. *You'd* no right to steal from him.'

'Have you come to arrest me?' He sounded defiant, angry.

'Hardly. You're not exactly a major criminal. Noah, I don't want to intrude on your personal life.' Although taking in the messy room, with its discarded plates, half-empty cups and teetering stacks of magazines and books, his life could do with a clear-up.

He laughed unhappily. 'That's what people say just before they wade right in. I can hear the unspoken "but". People usually behave in one of two ways around me. They either tread on eggshells, as if I'm Berminster's Stephen Hawking, the intelligent but tragic man imprisoned in his body, or they act cheery and talk to a point somewhere over my head while they patronise me. Both approaches are excruciating and piss me off.'

She wasn't having that. 'I've never behaved to you in that way.'

'No, you haven't.'

'Sounds like Melinda hasn't, either. I suppose that she's just treated you like you were any young man. I bet she seemed like a breath of fresh air.'

He flashed her a surprised look. 'That's right.'

Siv held his gaze. 'But she's a chancer. She ripped you and Patrick off, so that doesn't work so well. She might be a laugh but she's bad news. You need to take control and shop around, just as you would for anything else you wanted. You've let Melinda play you. That's as bad as being patronised. You should be pissed off at her, not at your brother.' She reached into her pocket and handed him an envelope. 'I did some market research and got you information, names and contact details for women working in town who you can phone. They offer services with a clear payment tariff and they'll visit you. I bet that when you check, you'll realise that Melinda was overcharging.'

He stared at the envelope and then took it with his good hand. His eyes were moist. 'Melinda made me happy. She was a friend and fun. She's a laugh, took my mind off all this for a while.' He gestured at the room.

'Of course she did, and why shouldn't you want that? But she did it by pressurising and cheating you. Has she been near you since Patrick sacked her?'

He shook his head. 'I keep calling her but she doesn't answer.'

'That's what I expected. She's blown her chances. She wasn't a friend, Noah. She gave you sex for money, which can be an honest trade, but not with Melinda. She exploited you and Patrick. You need to face up to that. You'll find she's not the only woman you can have fun with. Get a grip and don't let anyone take advantage of you. I have to go now. I have a murderer to find.'

He bit his lip. 'I've been an idiot. Thanks for this. Sorry you had to get involved in my problems.'

'That's okay. Do me a favour, tell Patrick we've spoken and then you can both forget I ever came here today.

Actually, do me a second favour and say sorry to Patrick. He only talked to me because he was at his wits' end with worry.'

She was at the door when he called her name. She turned.

'Just . . . I'm so selfish. I haven't even asked how you are.'

'I'm doing okay,' she said. 'That day-by-day thing.'

'See you at the Halloween party?'

'Oh, God. Yes. That. I haven't done anything about it yet. Haven't got a clue what to go as.'

He raised a finger, a gleam back in his eyes. 'Lightbulb moment. Want me to order you a costume online?'

'Would you do that?'

He grimaced, then laughed. 'I can make time in my hectic schedule. Any preferences?'

'Just nothing too fussy, something I can sling on at the last minute, and no more than fifty pounds.'

She ran to the car, relieved that was over, avoiding puddles.

* * *

Noah watched her drive away, closed his eyes and listened to the thudding, hypnotic rainfall. He took a couple of deep, shuddering breaths and was calmer than he'd been in months. Patrick seemed a bit nervous of Siv, but Noah couldn't understand why. He liked her candour and the way she didn't tiptoe around him. Now and again, a shadow crossed her strong face and then she'd reach a finger to her scalp or rub at the scar by her eyebrow.

He turned the envelope over a few times and then opened it, scanning Siv's clear but hurried notes. His phone was perched in its holder, attached to the arm of his wheelchair. He pulled it towards him and dialled some numbers.

CHAPTER 21

Siv woke at 5.30 a.m. after a restless night and found that her eyes were wet with tears. She opened the window wide and lay for a while, breathing the moist dawn air and listening to the river murmuring. The trees rustled softly in the breeze, dropping their leaves. The prospect of visiting London had triggered kaleidoscope memories of a life interrupted. In shards and fragments of jumbled dreams, she'd walked through Greenwich again with Ed, watched a juggler in Covent Garden and laughed as he indulged in his weekly struggle to insert the duvet into its cover. He'd been so real, she'd reached out to touch him, but his side of the bed was empty now.

Ali had called her the previous evening, to tell her about Tim Stafford's connection to Lyn. They'd discussed the possibility that he could have camped out in Steiner's when he was missing from home, and once he'd taken to the streets at eighteen.

When she surfaced from dreams, she fretted about finding him. Homeless people who didn't regularly use formal support could stay under the radar for years. She was holding the strings to numerous kites that were snapping in the wind and tugging her in myriad directions.

She showered, dried her hair and arranged it in the tousled style a hairdresser had shown her to hide her bald patches. There were only two now but she was conscious of them and tweaked strands of hair for concealment. She dressed city smart in a navy suit and white shirt, made tea and toast and ate with her feet up on the wood-burner, which was still warm from the night before. She'd already boxed the kusudama model, and was ready to go as soon as she'd rinsed her breakfast things. This little wagon was so easy to maintain, she wouldn't mind living here for ever.

She left at half six, driving slowly along the rutted lane that led to the road. She waved back at Corran as he emerged to see to the goats, wrapped up in a padded jacket. They were Alpine goats, used to cooler climates, but he started to feed them extra rations in the autumn and had a plentiful supply of hay laid in. They started bleating as soon as they heard him approach.

The morning was drenched with cloying mist and she needed the windscreen wipers. The bare trees and dying vegetation signalled winter's fast approach. She wondered if it would be dank and misty like this at Halloween, encouraging notions of spirits and wandering souls.

Bartel had phoned to tell her that his offer on the house had been accepted and that he had decided to attend Mortimer's party as a wodnik, a wicked water spirit who drowned swimmers, and kept their souls trapped in his teapot for ever. She'd laughed and commented, 'Who'd have credited that a teapot could be used for such evil purposes?' When she'd asked what a wodnik looked like, Bartel had replied darkly that because she'd mocked, she'd have to wait and find out.

She was pleased about his house purchase. He'd been living in rented accommodation for years but he was a homebird, a nester, and now he'd have a permanent roost. She'd have described herself in the same terms before Ed died. After her uncertain childhood, she'd craved stability and order. Now, she wasn't sure how she saw herself. Maybe she'd become one of those birds that stayed on the wing and never built a nest.

She made good time until she reached the outskirts of London, when traffic slowed to a crawl and it took an hour to reach Islington. She parked at the NOPC office with half an hour to spare, found a café and had a coffee while she phoned Ali.

'The alibis we got from Patel and Olawego check out,' he told her. 'No luck tracking Tim Stafford in Brighton or Hastings, so we're going to trawl further along the coast. We're checking hospitals as well.'

'We need him. Make sure you and Patrick consider every possibility. Also, get Patrick to tweet about him.'

'He already has, didn't need to be told.'

Hassan Kibet had a tiny office on the ground floor of a modern block. He had a thick, matted beard, appeared tired and dishevelled and was putting a tie on as he greeted her. He offered coffee, which she declined and opened a Thermos cup for himself.

'Hope you don't mind the third person in the room.' He pointed beneath his desk.

Siv hadn't noticed the tiny baby asleep in a carrycot and barely visible inside a quilted bag.

'I don't need to worry about confidentiality,' she said. She imagined Mortimer's face if one of his staff arrived with an infant. The NOPC must be an enlightened employer.

'I don't make a habit of bringing him to work, but my wife is exhausted and a bit down. It was a long labour and a difficult birth. I wanted to give her a day when she can just stay in bed or do whatever she likes. He's not due a feed for a while, so we shouldn't be interrupted.'

'I'm sure your wife will benefit from the rest.'

'Yes . . . Anyway, you haven't come all this way to hear about my childcare arrangements.' Kibet seemed embarrassed by his domestic confidences and became businesslike. He took a folder from his drawer. 'I've made you a copy of significant documents. Obviously, you can request the complete file if you find you need to.' He handed Siv a small, stapled collection of papers.

She started to flick through. 'Can you talk me through the highlights?'

'Of course. In 2002, Lyn Dimas was practising podiatry in a clinic called Foot Heaven in Seaford. During March of that year, she contacted us to say that she was concerned about another podiatrist at the clinic, a Tilly Hemmings. She expressed the view that Ms Hemmings lacked skills and sometimes caused minor injuries during treatment. She informed us that earlier that year Ms Hemmings had cut a patient's foot when she was dealing with ingrown toenails. The patient had fibromyalgia and other health problems. He complained to Ms Dimas when Ms Hemmings told him not to worry. Ms Dimas told the practice manager, but her other concern was that the manager wasn't dealing with these issues when she raised them, and it had got to a point where she had to contact us. A week after the cutting incident, the patient developed a serious infection, which didn't respond to antibiotics. It led to gangrene and ultimately, partial amputation of his leg below the knee. He consulted a solicitor, who advised that there had been a breach of duty that may have constituted clinical negligence. Ms Hemmings was suspended from work. The case went to court and clinical negligence was proven. Ms Dimas didn't have to attend court, but she provided a statement about her various concerns regarding Ms Hemmings, and her view that the clinic had ignored and mishandled them. The patient was awarded damages and Ms Hemmings was subsequently removed from our register.'

'So she wouldn't have been able to practise as a podiatrist again?'

'That's correct. I wasn't working here at the time, but a colleague who was involved in interviewing Ms Hemmings after the court decision said that she was very emotional. It was sad, because she was a single parent with two children to support, but after a court case like that, we really had no other option.'

'What happened to the practice manager?'

'He was reprimanded but allowed to continue practising with extra training in complaint handling. I've seen a note on his file that he died of a heart attack in 2011.'

So, Lyn Dimas had been involved in a colleague losing her career. This issue should have been tracked down in the first investigation. 'Do you know what happened to Tilly Hemmings subsequently?'

The baby gave a tiny whimper and shifted. Kibet bent down and lightly stroked his head. 'No. We closed the file after she was officially deregistered. I suppose she found some other employment.'

Siv saw that there was an address for Ms Hemmings in Seaford. 'I would appreciate the full file in the next couple of days. Thanks for your help.'

'Does this have something to do with Ms Dimas's death?'

'I'm not sure at this point, Mr Kibet.' She glanced down and saw that the baby was kicking. 'I'll take these papers for now and leave you to your son. Feeding time is approaching.'

She had an hour to spare before she was due in Ealing, so she bought a tea and sat in the car, sipping and searching for Tilly Hemmings. The first hit was a local newspaper report on a coroner's inquest from October 2006.

> A verdict of suicide was returned on Matilda Hemmings of Seaford, East Sussex. Ms Hemmings, 44, died from an overdose of sleeping tablets. The inquest was told that she had suffered depression since losing her job as a podiatrist. Ms Hemmings had been unable to secure other long-term employment because of her battle with mental health issues, and had accrued large debts. Her family reported that she worried about how she would pay these off. She left a note, indicating that she was taking her life. Ms Hemmings leaves two children aged 15 and 23.

Here was yet another strand to unpick. Someone might have held Lyn responsible for Tilly Hemmings's death. She emailed Ali a link to the article, explaining what she'd discovered: *Can you find out who her children are and, if they're still reasonably local, arrange for us to meet with them tomorrow.*

She drove on to West London at a snail's pace and was relieved to find that the architects in Ealing had an empty parking spot for visitors. She unpacked the sculpture in the director's office, enjoying the reveal as she lifted it carefully from the packing material. The director expressed delight, touching the piece carefully, and told Siv that they had another office in St Alban's, whose manager was interested in discussing a project with her. Siv agreed to talk to him and watched while her work was displayed in the window. She experienced the usual frisson of sadness when a piece left her hands for good. It was like losing a little part of herself. A couple of the architects insisted on buying her lunch. She hesitated, aware of the need to press on with the investigation, but she reckoned that she was entitled to eat and accompanied them to a sushi bar where she downed delicious seafood ramen.

She was on the road back to Berminster at two thirty when Ali phoned.

'Death is stalking us, guv. Tilly Hemmings has one surviving child now. Her daughter, Posy, killed herself in December 2012 — jumped from a multistorey car park. Her son, Clive, still lives in Seaford. He agreed to meet us there tomorrow morning.'

'Did you mention Lyn Dimas to him?'

'Yes. He confirmed that he'd heard of her. I explained that we'd found her body and he went very quiet, so I said we'd leave it there until tomorrow. Still no joy with Stafford.'

* * *

Clive Hemmings finished dusting, plumped cushions, altered the angle of a chair and stood in the centre of the sitting room. He smiled with satisfaction. All was orderly and gleaming. Over the weekend, he'd taken everything from the shelves and wiped all the surfaces. He could afford a cleaner, but he didn't want anyone else in his home and such intrusion had too many disadvantages. Some of the homes where he tutored had cleaners and they all brought their own odours with them, which they left behind when they'd finished: cigarettes, unwashed clothes, sweat and cheap perfumes, to name a few. He was cursed with a highly sensitive sense of smell and he was happiest in a neutral environment. All his cleaning materials were non-perfumed. He breathed in deeply now, enjoying the smell of . . . nothing.

His mother and sister had been chaotic, noisy and messy, cluttering their tiny, two-bedroomed house. He and Posy had had to share a bedroom until she was a teenager, and he'd hated waking up in his bottom bunk to the smell of her fuggy breath drifting from above like a noxious miasma. Her cheap Superdrug cosmetics, her relentless tide of clothes and magazines, and her habit of spraying air freshener around the room had suffocated him. When Posy turned thirteen, his mother had put a bed in the utility room off the kitchen for him, where he swapped his sister's aromas for lingering food odours of onions and meat. Other boys talked about wanting gadgets. He'd longed for his own airy, neat room and dreamed of the day that he could have a front door that was his alone.

He'd always been detached from his mother and sister. He'd been fond of them in his own way, but he'd never wanted the casual intimacy that he noted among other families. It made him curl into himself, like a hedgehog. He told himself that he'd been born weird. After Posy died, he'd sold their house. It had been neglected for years and had needed a lot of work, but he'd made enough on the sale for a deposit on this one-bedroom flat beside the sea. His neighbours were older, retired people and that suited him fine. They were quiet and courteous and left him alone, apart from an occasional greeting on the stairs. Having this solitary, inviolate space to himself was a joy.

He stepped to the window and straightened a blind. His routines were important and, this morning, the police were disrupting them and causing anxiety. Usually, he swam between nine and ten in the private basement pool, when it was empty, but he'd had to forgo the pleasure today. He'd been a chunky, fat-faced boy, but he'd shed that surplus weight as soon as his mother had died and he'd taken control of his diet. He liked to keep to his ideal weight of eighty kilograms and stepped on the scales every morning before swimming. Any change in schedule caused him stress, as did the prospect of the conversation to come. He'd been surprised that the police hadn't turned up when Lyn Dimas had vanished. When he'd read that her body had been found, he'd anticipated that they might yet come to his door.

In the kitchen, he quietened his nerves by carefully laying out a tray for his visitors and grinding coffee beans. The bell rang promptly at ten, and he opened the door to a tall, smartly dressed woman with a sombre expression and a stocky man in a leather jacket. She made introductions, and he asked if they'd take their shoes off in the tiny hall, which they did, and showed them in before going back to the kitchen.

* * *

Siv and Ali waited for coffee. Hemmings had seemed tense, so Siv had accepted the offer. Sometimes, the small rituals of hot drinks helped to relax people. There was a delicious smell of fresh coffee beans. Ali was standing by the picture window that faced the sea, hands behind his back, feet apart. Farmer's feet, broad and capable, solid on the earth. He'd told her that his parents were farmers and she pictured him coming from a long line of well-built people who strode their acres of wheat, corn and barley and could forecast the weather from the sky.

When she glanced down, she saw that he had a large hole in the heel of his right sock. She'd wondered if Hemmings had asked them to remove their shoes in order to put them at a disadvantage, but now she saw the spotless room, she realised that he was probably just house-proud. His flat was on the fourth floor of a wide block, just metres from the seafront. Today, the early mists and rain had cleared quickly and the sky was an intense blue, with far-reaching visibility.

There was just one photo in the room. Siv reached for it. It was of a woman with two young children. The chubby boy in it had curly red hair, a snub nose, glasses and prominent front teeth. She was puzzled, as he was nothing like Hemmings. She showed it to Ali, who muttered that they'd better double-check they had the right man.

'Great view you have here,' Ali said to Hemmings as he came in with a tray.

'It is lovely. I wondered if I might get used to it but it's always a real surprise, every time I walk in.'

'I'd waste a lot of time if I had that view.'

'Why would that be time wasted?' Hemmings sounded perplexed. 'Gazing at the natural world must always be beneficial, surely. But maybe you're an external, doing person, rather than a mindful, being person.'

Ali was a stranger to philosophical discussions about human nature. He didn't wonder about existence. As far as he was concerned, we all found ourselves on the planet and the mess we managed to make was quite enough to deal with, without questioning why we were here. He gave Hemmings a baffled glance and sat down.

Hemmings served the cafetière of coffee with a jug of warmed milk, a separate one of cream, a bowl of brown sugar cubes and a plate of thin, spiced biscuits. The ceramic crockery was a stylish matching set in pale green and cream. There were green paper napkins by the biscuits. Siv regarded the tray with appreciation and a dash of suspicion. This kind of hospitality was unusual, and she wondered why the man had gone to so much effort.

The room was elegantly and simply furnished with cream leather easy chairs and a low ash table, reflecting the classiness of the refreshments. Hemmings fussed over the coffee. Siv refused biscuits while Ali accepted two and set about dunking. Everything in the room seemed somehow manufactured and brand new, as did Hemmings himself. He was of medium height and slim in spotless, smart black chinos and a grey shirt that were as immaculate as if they'd just been unwrapped. His thick, black hair was swept back smoothly from a high forehead, his skin was clear and curiously matt, his eyes were an astonishing cerulean blue and his perfect teeth had to be veneers.

'Is your coffee okay?' He sat back with his knees together.

'Fine, thank you,' said Siv. 'I'm sorry about your mother and your sister, Mr Hemmings.'

'Please, call me Clive. Thank you. I've had difficult things to overcome.'

'As Sergeant Carlin told you on the phone, we came across your late mother's name in connection with a murder inquiry. Did you know that we'd found Lyn Dimas's body?'

There was a brief pause. Hemmings sipped his coffee and placed the cup back carefully in its saucer. 'I read about that, yes.'

'And were you aware that she'd been missing since July 2013?'

'I heard that on the news at the time.'

'Presumably, you knew that Ms Dimas and your mother had worked together in Seaford?'

'Yes, I did.'

'We've received information about a professional complaint that Ms Dimas made concerning your mother, and her subsequent loss of employment as a podiatrist. I understand that this might be painful, but can you tell us about your mother's death?'

He put his cup on the table and folded his hands together on his knees. Tension radiated from him.

'I was fifteen when it happened. Posy, my sister, came home and found Mum dead in bed. I was devastated, because I was downstairs, doing homework. I hadn't even realised that

Mum was in and had taken an overdose. I got in from school and called her, but when there was no answer, I assumed she was out somewhere. She often went for long walks.' There was a tremor in his voice and he swallowed hard.

Siv was still puzzling over the photo and pointed to it. 'Is that you, with your mother and sister?'

'That's right. I was eleven when that was taken.'

'What happened to your red hair?' Ali asked.

Hemmings smiled. 'I can see that you can't equate the child in the photo with me. That's exactly how I wanted it. I was never happy with my appearance. My mother always overfed me and I spent my childhood being called names because of my hair, my weight, my goofy teeth and sometimes, if the bullies ran out of ideas, my glasses. "Fatso", "Fatarse", "Rustbucket", "Rabbitface", "Specky" and "Firebunny" are just a few of the insults that came my way. After my mother died, I went on a strict diet and as soon as I had money of my own, I had my nose remodelled, my teeth capped, I have my hair dyed and wear coloured contact lenses.'

This was a new take on the meaning of a self-made man. Hemmings must have suffered terribly to alter himself so drastically. 'What's your line of work?' Siv asked.

'I'm a private tutor, maths, mainly. Why is that relevant? Oh — maybe you're wondering how I could afford the cosmetic work. Tutoring is well paid if you're good and in demand, and I am.'

'Can you tell us about your mother's connection to Lyn Dimas?'

He seemed to withdraw into himself for a few moments and then focused on her with his remarkable eyes. 'Maybe it would be easiest if I show you my mother's suicide note.'

He rose in one swift movement and glided from the room before she could reply. She and Ali sat in silence until he returned. A window was open a little and they could hear the surge of the incoming tide. He came back with a sheet of notepaper and handed it to Siv. She read the note and passed it to Ali.

I'm being a coward, but I can't go on. Since I lost my career, I've been lost. Posy, look after Clive. You'll both be happier and better off without me hanging around and depressing you both. I hope that woman who caused all this and didn't care who she was hurting is pleased with herself. Sorry.

Hemmings gestured at the note. 'My mother always called Lyn Dimas "that woman", so we did too. I gathered that they worked together, but I didn't really understand much about the trouble when it was all happening and the subsequent court case. I could see that Mum was terribly upset and she'd lost her job. She completely lost the plot after that.'

'Were there any family or friends around to support her?' Ali asked.

Hemmings stared back at him. 'None — just like always. My dad left when I was three and went to Ottawa. He didn't support us. Mum worked really hard to get a qualification and a career while she brought us up alone. It was a three-year degree course and money was tight — she had a real struggle paying the mortgage. After she qualified, she got a good job and income at Foot Heaven and things were much better for us financially. Then she saw it all go down the drain when she was barred. She got one or two menial jobs, as a care assistant in a nursing home and then on a checkout at a supermarket, but she got sacked from the first because she'd turn up late, and she left the shop because she couldn't stand the monotony. Posy told me all the details after Mum died. She said that Mum had been treated harshly because of a mistake, and that if Lyn Dimas hadn't stirred it all up, the patient she accidentally wounded might never have gone ahead with a legal case.'

That's one take on what happened, Siv reflected, *but hardly fair on Lyn Dimas, who seemed to have acted from genuine professional concerns. And a man had lost part of a leg.*

'How did you react to Lyn Dimas, Clive?' Despite his permission, she saw his flash of surprise at her use of his name.

'I'm not sure what you mean,' he said.

'Were you angry with her? After all, she'd caused your mum a lot of misery and hurt.'

'I suppose I was angry for a while, but I had to get on with my life and my studies.'

'Why did your sister commit suicide?'

'She didn't leave a note, but Posy never got over Mum's death. They were very close and Posy was guilty that she hadn't done more to help her. She worked really hard to pay off the debts Mum had left, and it wore her down. I regretted not having done more to help Posy after she died. I was busy completing my degree and I just didn't realise how depressed she must have been.'

It was a sorry tale, although considering the emotions he was describing, his tone was bland. Hemmings appeared to be direct and open in relating events, yet his information could well mean he'd have a motive for taking revenge after losing both his mother and sister. He was too intelligent not to realise that, but his gaze was steady.

Ali shifted in his chair. 'Could you tell us where you were on the evening of the twenty-eighth of July 2013?'

'Not offhand, given that it was six years ago. I was tutoring by then and a lot of my work is in the evenings, so that's probably what I was doing. I don't have a diary from back then. I upgraded my laptop to a different system a year ago and the diary didn't migrate.'

'Have you ever been to Berminster, and in particular to a place called Orford End?' Ali asked.

'The answer to both parts of that question is no.' Hemmings added a splash more milk to his coffee and sat back.

'Did your sister have a partner at the time when she died?'

'She didn't mention anyone. Certainly, no one contacted me about her funeral. But I was at uni and doing some tutoring to cover my fees when I wasn't studying, and she was working in Lewes, so we weren't spending a lot of time together.'

There was some undercurrent running beneath the conversation, but Siv couldn't decide what it was. This room was too much like a stage set to present a scene, with Hemmings sticking to a script.

She took out Tim Stafford's photo and passed it to him. 'Do you recognise this man? His name is Tim Stafford and he's currently homeless.'

'Stafford? No. I meet a lot of people because of my work, you see, but that name doesn't ring a bell. You do see the odd homeless person in Seaford, but we don't have as many as the bigger seaside towns.' He handed back the photo. 'Would you like some more coffee?'

'No, thank you. Did you kill Lyn Dimas?' Siv didn't often ask the bare, bald question in an informal interview but there was an opaque layer here that she wanted to cut through.

Hemmings put a hand on his chest, as if he was swearing an oath. 'No, I didn't kill Lyn Dimas. I can see why you'd believe I had a motive — I would if I was doing your job — and I realise that's where your questions have been leading, but I didn't harm her. There's been enough death around my family without adding to it. I realise that it would be better for me if I could give you an alibi, but I can't.'

Siv asked if he'd give a DNA sample and fingerprints and he agreed without hesitation. When he showed them out, she could almost hear him exhale with relief.

* * *

They sat on the sea wall opposite his flat, buffeted by the salt breeze.

'He's like one of those Ken dolls. Sort of plastic. He was wearing foundation,' Ali said, lighting up.

'He certainly has a flawless complexion.'

'Must be odd, to grow up looking a certain way and then change your appearance so radically. I wonder if he gets a shock when he sees himself in the mirror? Maybe I should have liposuction on my belly and dye my hair, get rid of the premature grey.'

Siv laughed. 'Polly likes you the way you are. It was strange in there. There was something going on and it was more than plastic surgery. He lied, but I'm not sure what about. I'm sure he recognised Tim Stafford. His hand twitched when I asked him.'

'He was tense all the way through. Lyn Dimas's actions led to both his mother and his sister committing suicide. He'd have had good reason to murder her and he can't tell us where he was the night she went missing.'

'He's joining that club with others. But he wasn't bothered about us taking DNA. He's a curious mixture of strung out and yet apparently honest. He baffled me, and I don't like that.'

'Guv, even if we do find out who killed Lyn — and I reckon it's now a long shot — we might never have enough evidence.'

'That's what keeps me awake at night.'

Ali glanced across as she sighed and rubbed an eye. She was so pale. Some mornings, she seemed hung-over, although she never smelled of alcohol. He'd noticed her drinking a lot of water first thing. He had an image of her alone in her wagon, getting bladdered, and anxiety knotted his guts.

* * *

After the police had gone, Clive Hemmings opened two windows wide and let the chilly breeze flow in. The sergeant had reeked of pungent cigarettes. It would take a while to eliminate the smell.

He took the tray to the kitchen and washed the dirty crockery by hand, taking time over each piece. He had a dishwasher but rarely used it, convinced that it harboured bacteria. He threw the uneaten biscuits away because the sergeant's fat fingers might have touched them.

He rubbed soapy suds through his hands, recalling the day his mother died. He'd panicked and lied then, to Posy and the police, and he'd lied today. He'd known his mother was at home. When he'd got back from school, he'd gone to her bedroom and seen her lying under the duvet. He'd heard a little groan, and he'd backed out of the room, not wanting to wake her. It was better when she was asleep, because then she wasn't moping around downstairs, sighing and staring out of the windows. When she cried, which she often did, she would drape herself around him and he hated the sticky heat of her body and her gulping sobs. That day, he'd had chemistry homework and had been eager to tackle it without her bothering him, so he'd crept downstairs, set out his books at the kitchen table, turned on the radio and studied for two hours until Posy had come home, gone upstairs and started screaming.

The autopsy had said that his mother had died between four and five that afternoon, during which time he'd been sitting in the room below, working on equations. The police had told him it wasn't his fault but then, they didn't see through his lies.

In a way, he counted himself a murderer. A murderer by omission if not by deed. When he'd been told his mother was dead, his first excited reaction was that now he could have her bedroom. He was aware that if anyone had been able to read his mind, they'd have been horrified. He hadn't felt guilty about Posy, because it wasn't an emotion he experienced, but he was aware that it sounded good to say it. He should have been guilty and ashamed about his mother and Posy, and if he wasn't so weird deep down, he probably would have. He'd enjoyed erasing the old Clive and seeing a different, reshaped face. He could pretend that some of his weirdness had vanished with the surgery.

He'd told two lies today. He wondered if his visitors had noticed. His body language was well controlled, but he'd read that the police were trained to spot tells. The woman, Drummond, had that ability to sit very still and focused and it had unnerved him. He dried each piece of crockery and put it away in the cupboard. He wondered why the police were searching for Tim Stafford, remembering the way he'd stunk the house out when Posy had found him wet and hungry, begging outside the station, and had brought him home for a hot meal. She'd always been a soft touch. A bleeding heart, attracted to waifs and strays.

He'd seen Stafford leaving once and had confronted Posy about it. She'd promised it wouldn't happen again, but she'd given Stafford shelter and fed him a couple of times. When he came home, he could always smell those lingering traces of filthy clothes, damp and poverty lurking below the air freshener she'd plugged in. He'd denied knowing Stafford because he didn't want the police coming back here, cluttering up his life and there was nothing useful that he could tell them about him, other than that he was a sad loser.

He dried the work surface and rubbed the chrome mixer tap until it sparkled. Then he stood back, pleased with his efforts. When he went back to the living room, the intrusive smells had almost gone. He hoovered up the scattering of biscuit crumbs dropped by the messy sergeant.

He didn't expect that the police would be back, but if they did return, they'd learn nothing more from him. That woman had deserved to die.

CHAPTER 22

Tim Stafford checked the time. He'd been dozing all afternoon, tucked up in two sleeping bags. He was warm enough,
despite the chilly breeze snaking through the broken window,
but his legs were stiff and his nose was icy. It was half five and
he heard his stomach grumble. He dug into his pocket and
checked that he had enough for a burger and chips. He could
get a free soup and sandwich from the St Hugh's outreach
van later in the evening, but that was at least three hours
away, and he preferred to keep away from the do-gooders if
he could. They were always asking nosy, nagging questions.
He craved a plate of hot carbs now, drenched with salt and
vinegar. He salivated, anticipating the savoury hit.

He sat up and coughed chestily, then removed his woolly
hat and scratched his head. He reached into the scarred desk
with names etched into the top that served as a bedside cabinet, and took a slug from a bottle of lemonade. The fizz
had gone, but at least it washed the fur and phlegm from
his mouth.

Tim had decided to give up on London, where he'd mis-
takenly hoped that a homeless person might come by more
freebies. He'd left the city and had been camping out for a
couple of weeks in this empty school in St Leonard's. A street

sleeper in Brighton had shown him a website about abandoned places, and he'd found Westhaven on there. It was on the coast, not that far from his usual haunts. A link led him to a YouTube video some kids had made of themselves exploring the building. One of them had gone to school there, and she'd whooped with amazement as she'd found her old classroom, the same room where Tim was now living.

The first time he'd entered, he'd approached carefully, because other people, including homeless, would probably be using it, and things could get territorial. He didn't want a repeat of the bad experience at Steiner's. There had been two women hanging out in the least damaged parts of this building, one in the head teacher's study and one in a storeroom, but they seemed peaceable and said they didn't mind if he took over Room Three as long as he didn't bother them.

In its heyday, Westhaven had been a handsome Edwardian red-brick building with mock Tudor cladding above the front windows and a deep veranda with wooden railings running along the front. It had opened as a school in 1908, and had continued as an educational establishment with a succession of owners through the years. In 1988, it became an independent sixth-form college, but closed for business in 2003 after the company that owned it went bankrupt. Now, it was more derelict than Steiner's. Lead had been stripped from the roof so that parts of it had collapsed, only two sash windows were still intact, and vandals had smashed and flooded the toilets.

Tim had no idea that he was sleeping in the Classics room, where pupils had once learned Greek and Latin in preparation for their Oxbridge applications, and the teacher had inspired her pupils with her love of Plato's comic poems. He hadn't noticed the sign over the door, *Condemnant Quo Non Intellegunt* and it wouldn't have interested him much if he'd understood it. He was using two damp, speckled copies of Caesar's *Gallic Wars* and a tatty paperback of Homer's *Odyssey* to prop up the broken chair he threw his clothes on. Despite the decay and damage, the room retained some of its handsome features: parquet flooring, high ceilings with ornate friezes above the picture rails, central sunflower roses, elegant cornices and stained glass in some windows. Tim was fascinated by patterns and he liked the herringbone design of the floor. He'd cleaned a large square around his sleeping area, exposing the warmth of the wood, where he'd lie tracing the oak blocks and lines with a finger.

Tim's experience of school had been hazy and overwhelming. He'd spent a lot of time truanting to avoid the chaos, noise and indecipherable pages of information — and to spite his foster parents. When he had attended, he had been more interested in the shapes made by interconnecting triangles, the configurations of rivers on the map of the UK, and the details of the geometric designs on his form teacher's ties. He was just about literate, but that was all his teachers had managed to do with him over the years. Tim had passed through the education system with staff who lacked the training and time to recognise Asperger's syndrome, and would have been short of resources to compensate if they had.

His hunger was growing. He unzipped his sleeping bags, wriggling out like a pupa shedding its skin, and put on his Burberry coat. It was covered in muck and smelled terrible, but it still kept the cold out.

He stuck his hands in his pockets and walked, head down, towards the town centre, imagining crispy fried onion rings. He might get a double portion of chips and bring some back for breakfast. The evening was dank, with a thin, cold mist drifting from the sea and he coughed as it crept into his lungs. Two giggling girls ran past him, dressed as witches and waving wands. One of them had to hold onto her cone-shaped hat and she called to him as she flashed by. 'Trick or treat?' He stopped for a moment and stared after her, realising that it must be Halloween.

He trudged on, passing houses with glowing, ghastly pumpkins in the windows and fake, wispy cobwebs tracing the glass. He laughed, his chest rattling. He'd plenty of genuine cobwebs. Thick, furry ones in Room Three.

A car behind him slowed and he heard the purr of a window opening and a voice. 'Is that you, Tim?'

He turned, alert and ready to bolt, and peered through the dusk. He'd had enough run-ins with people over the years to get nervous when approached. He made out a smiling, familiar face, and he relaxed.

'I haven't seen you for ages. I thought it was you, I recognised your walk,' the voice continued.

He waved. 'Hi, what brings you here?'

'Just passing through. This is an amazing coincidence. How are you?'

'Oh . . . just going for a takeaway.'

'Well, hop in and I'll give you a lift. It's a rotten evening for walking.'

He didn't need to be asked twice. He slid into the warmth and comfort of the passenger seat and sat back. The car smelled of mints and leather. His driver's voice was low and soothing, the way it had been that last time at Steiner's, when the old guy with the dog had got angry and come at him with a broken bottle. He'd avoided the place after that, reckoning it had bad karma, because another time when he'd gone there, he'd nearly tripped over the couple in the office. He'd had a shock when he'd recognised the woman half-naked on the mattress he'd kipped on the previous week, and the muscly guy beside her wearing just boxer shorts and opening wine. He'd got out of there quickly, before they saw him.

'This weather's a bit like it was that evening we first met, outside Steiner's,' the driver said. 'You had a nasty cut from that broken bottle. Seems ages ago now.'

'Yeah. I was just remembering that. You gave me a tenner and a plaster.'

'So I did. I could see you'd been rattled. Have you ever told anyone about meeting me that night?'

'Nah.'

'What about what you saw inside Steiner's that other time? Those two on the mattress — ever told anyone about them?'

279

'Nah. Too much hassle.'

'I don't blame you. It's hard enough being homeless without making life even more complicated. Comfy?'

'Yeah, lovely and warm.'

'Good. Sit back and enjoy it while you can.'

The car surged forward through the deepening night, while the thickening haze licked at the windows.

* * *

Patrick had left Siv's Halloween costume on her desk with a note. *This is from Noah. He decided you're a wood sprite. Thanks for the help, guv. We're doing okay.*

It was a light, gauzy costume in many shades and layers of green, calf length, with a headband of mosses and acorns. At home, Siv put it on, deciding that she passed muster, albeit rather tall for a wood sprite. She was hunting for black tights and flat shoes when Bartel sent an email.

> Just a chilling little story to put you in the mood for tonight.
>
> A peasant's wife and children died of the plague and he fled to the forest. He fell asleep and was woken after midnight by a great noise of music and dancing. He was astonished and delighted as he heard joyful pipes and drums approaching, but his heart froze in fear when he saw a crowd of spectres, dancing beside a high black wagon with the plague sitting on top. Everything the ghastly company met on the road changed into a spectre and joined them. The peasant was terrified. He seized his axe and struck at a spectre, but instantly it became a tall woman who spat fire. Then the peasant saw that even the trees, the owls and plants were changing and joining the awful harbingers of death. He fell senseless on the ground, and when he woke in the

morning, all his belongings were broken or burnt. He knew that death had sent him a warning, and hurried from his own country to a land that was free of the deadly sickness.

She replied, *You've certainly put me in the mood. See you at the harbour.*

The story had made her shiver. When she looked out of the window into the murky, damp night, she was glad to see the glow of Corran and Paul's light from across the meadow. The wind was rising and sighing around the wagon, teasing at the door and windows as if it was trying to find a way in. Scraps of dark cloud drifted across the dull moon's face. She had a fleeting sense of foreboding and shook her head impatiently, blaming Bartel and his unsettling tale. Time to fix a smile and mingle.

At the harbour, the wind was gusting, the boats rocking at their moorings. Salt spray stung Siv's cheeks and she held onto her headband as she saw a vision with a long, grey beard carrying a staff and covered in large slimy scales approaching.

'I hope none of your boss's guests get seasick,' Bartel said.

'You're . . . astonishing.'

He waved his staff. 'Ah, your British irony. Astonishing good or bad?'

'Oh, good, of course. Are those scales made of rubbery stuff? They're disgusting.' She touched one. It was damp and sticky.

'Behave, or I'll trap your soul in my teapot. We'd better get inside or your flimsy layers might blow away. Which boat is it?'

She frowned into the wind. 'Just along there, *Quicksilver*.'

'Smile, you're going to a party, not an execution!' Bartel struck his staff imperiously on the ground and strode towards the boat while she scurried after him, head down against the next gust, her flimsy skirts flapping.

Inside *Quicksilver*'s large cabin, there was a tight crowd and all was warmth, light and noise. Paper bats and huge spiders hung from the ceiling and a tango played, a tune with dark, insistent rhythms. The raw night outside was held at bay in the clink of glasses and hum of conversation. Now and again, the boat lifted almost imperceptibly, the only sign that the weather was bad-tempered. Bartel went to the makeshift bar in the corner to find a beer while Siv accepted a glass of wine from Patrick, who was dressed as a skeleton. Beside him was a flame-haired woman in a Bride of Dracula outfit, who he introduced as Kitty.

Siv asked, 'Where's our host?'

Patrick pointed with his thumb. 'He's with his new lady friend in the other room, helping her fix her costume. Seems very smitten with her.'

She sipped her wine. The cabin was fitted with grey leather seats, ceiling to floor walnut shelves and cupboards, with dimmed spotlights inset into the ceiling. She'd never have considered Mortimer as a sailor, reading charts and tides, battling the elements, and couldn't equate his narrow fingers and manicured nails with a mariner's hands. He seemed like a man built for more domestic, small-scale activities such as golf or bowls. She gazed at the weird and wonderful characters thronging the cabin. Noah waved to her from a corner, raising his bat wings in greeting. She spotted Ali, dressed in shaggy brown fur with a hare's ears, a horse's mane and a long tail. He was gazing longingly at the table spread with food, a finger to his lips.

'Bet you he takes one of the chocolate brownies,' a voice said at her side.

She turned to see a man dressed as a grey wolf with tall, pointed ears. He wore a sleeveless black leather jerkin over ripped black jeans, with thick fur covering his chest and arms. Amused eyes glinted through his facemask.

'Two, probably,' she replied.

'Just as well Polly's not here yet. If she sees him, there'll be trouble. Could you just push this sleeve up for me? I'm struggling with my claws and I don't want to spill this excellent beer. It's hard enough trying not to dip my whiskers in it.'

She put her glass down and pushed at the elastic over his right wrist, freeing his fingertips from the pointed black claws. 'That okay?'

'Great, thanks. What are you, some kind of elf?'

'I'm a wood sprite,' she said, mustering her dignity. 'Isn't it obvious?'

'Can't say it is, whereas I'm clearly seeking Little Red Riding Hood.' He took a draught of beer. He had a sturdy, square jaw and his teeth were large and even.

'What big ears you have, Grandma,' she said.

He stroked his whiskers and grinned. 'Is the big guy you came in with your partner?'

She preferred men who didn't vacillate when it came to acting on attraction but this was intrusive. 'Bit nosy,' she said.

The wolf man laughed. 'Just a polite enquiry.'

'He's my friend.'

'He'd like to be more than that. I've seen the way he looks at you.'

'Maybe you need an eye test.'

'Okay, I can see I've stepped over a line. How are you doing with the Dimas murder?'

She stared up at him. She couldn't place him and didn't recognise the silky voice. 'I can't discuss a case with you.'

'What, not even with a colleague?'

'Who are you?'

He put his paw out. 'DI Tommy Castles.'

She could hardly refuse a handshake. He had a strong, hairy grip. His claws scraped her skin lightly and she had to control a tremor. She was annoyed at her disadvantage and the way he'd ambushed her. A wood sprite would be a walkover for a prowling wolf. Bartel probably had a tale about such an encounter.

'Good, steady hand,' he said. 'So, how's the investigation? I hear you've ruled out Barnwell and Aston.'

'That's right. We've got some new leads, including information you failed to pick up on.'

'Really? What information is that?'

'About Lyn Dimas and problems at her previous workplace.'

'Is that why you were rushing out of the station the other day?'

She recalled the figure leaning against the desk and gathered that he'd been doing his homework, and that she'd been set up. 'Possibly.' She eyed him. 'I hear you're not happy in your new job. Is it a case of a too early promotion or just the wrong time and place?'

He put his head to one side. 'Don't make too much of station gossip. What's your take on that creepy neighbour, Jeff Downey? I reckoned he might have been behind Lyn's disappearance but we had no evidence.'

'We still have no evidence regarding him.'

'Right. I hear you've got a tight little team, just Ali and Patrick. Ali's okay, although his fitness must be questionable. I expect you find Patrick a tad flaky now and again, what with his phone addiction and his home situation.'

She wondered if Mortimer had primed his bosom buddy to explore weaknesses and find ammunition. If so, they were both despicable and deserved each other. 'As you say, we're a tight team. If you're fishing for me to criticise colleagues, I'm not up for that.'

He held up a paw. 'Hey, no need to be so defensive, I was just interested in how things are going.'

She was about to reply when she was distracted by the sight of Mortimer in a Gomez Addams striped suit, leading a woman costumed as Morticia. Her long, clinging black satin dress had lace sleeves and a grey lace veil and the curtains of her long, black wig obscured her face. Mortimer straightened his bow tie and handed his companion a glass of champagne.

'The boss has done okay for himself with his new woman, she's a stunner. It was time he moved on from moping over his divorce.' Castles raised his glass towards Mortimer as he approached them with his partner.

Siv stared through the assorted strange and outlandish figures with their horns, cloaks, fake blood, fangs and hideous make-up. Bartel was leaning on his staff, talking to a woman in a black-and-silver cat suit. His scales glowed eerily in the low lighting. The boat lurched in the wind and her stomach lifted queasily. The woman at Mortimer's side was slowly raising her veil to reveal crimson lips and kohl-rimmed eyes with a familiar glint in them.

'Welcome aboard,' Mortimer was saying. 'I'm glad to see that you two have met at last. This is Crista Virtanen. Crista, this is Siv Drummond.'

'Lovely to see you again, Crista,' Castles said.

'Mutsi! What are you doing here?' Siv realised that she'd almost shouted and that Mortimer was frowning.

Her mother gave a dangerously sweet smile. 'Will invited me, of course. I do like your costume, Sivvi. Very airy-fairy, although you might blow away.'

Siv recognised that gleeful, complacent air. Mutsi always had it when she'd acquired a new romantic interest. Someone had pressed a volume switch, and the voices in the cabin suddenly grew into a clamour. Siv couldn't breathe. She remembered the painting on Mortimer's office wall. *It was a present from a friend.* She realised that it was of Lake Keitele, in central Finland, painted by Akseli Gallen-Kallela, and she'd seen it in the National Gallery.

'You've met before?' Mortimer asked, bewildered.

Siv's phone rang. She dug in her bag and moved towards the door. A zombie had just opened it to come inside and she pushed past him, stepping on to the cold, bracing deck. She leaned against the rail. The call was from the duty desk at the station.

'Guv, sorry to interrupt the party. Colleagues in Hastings have been in touch. A man's been attacked on the beach at St Leonard's. Head wound and unconscious. He's been identified as Tim Stafford. They said you've been trying to find him.'

'That's right. Thanks. I'll contact them now.'

She stood gazing at the dancing, shimmering harbour lights and took deep gulps of salty air. She shivered. Through the cabin window, she could see Mutsi standing close to Mortimer, a hand on his arm, her lips moving near his ear. He was nodding, his arm about her waist.

This was bad, and she could be confident about one thing: it was going to get worse.

CHAPTER 23

Adam got home from school and dumped his bag in the hall. His phone rang as he headed to the kitchen. He saw Lily's name on his screen, and he answered with the upbeat tone he always used with her to mask his unease.

'Hi. How're you doing?'

She snapped, 'I expect you can guess. Have you heard about our cow of a mother or has Dad kept the awful truth from his little boy?'

He sank onto the bottom stair. 'Dad said that the police reckoned Mum had been at Steiner's, that she might have been seeing someone there. I don't believe it.'

'Well, you should! She was screwing Pearce there.'

He leaned on to his knees. 'Pearce?'

'Yes, my darling husband. They had a thing.'

'That can't be right. Mum and Pearce?'

'It's true. Pearce confessed at the police station after they arrested him and questioned him *the second time*. He's a fucking cheat and a liar and I'm divorcing him.'

He rubbed at the carpet with a finger. It was gritty and soft at the same time. 'I don't understand.'

'You mean you don't *want* to understand. You need to grow up and get a grip. I can't make it much clearer! Mum was shagging Pearce. She was a common slag. They were at it for months before Dad left.'

'But Mum didn't like him!'

Lily laughed. 'On the contrary, dimwit, she liked him rather a lot!'

'Hang on . . . Were they seeing each other when he was with you?'

'He claims not, says they'd finished by then because Mum was getting too serious about him, but he's such a liar, he'd say anything to try to get out of this.'

Adam pictured Pearce's muscly arms lifting his mother and securing her with rope. 'Did he kill her?'

'The cops say not. He's supposed to have an alibi, although I wouldn't believe anything he says. I don't care anymore about who killed her. She deserved it. You can tell Dad I'm not coming anywhere near her fucking funeral. I stayed at Papu's but I'm back home now. Pearce has moved out.'

'Where's he gone?'

'Some woman's letting him kip where he's working. An antiques place. He's probably shagging her too as payment. Come round soon. I hate being here on my own. Tasha offered to stay for a bit but I don't want her around all the time, she gets on my nerves. In fact, you could move in, if you like. It'd be good for you to get away from the gay mafia.'

She rang off. He put his head back and looked up the stairs, seeing his mother in her lemony dress, leaning against the wall.

He stood and walked slowly to the kitchen, stunned. No way was he going to stay with Lily. She only wanted him there for convenience, and as soon as he did something to annoy her, which wouldn't take long, she'd start complaining. He put two slices of bread on a plate and took chocolate spread and peanut butter from the cupboard, layering the bread carefully on each side before pressing the heavenly sandwich of deep and golden browns together and slicing it in half.

His dad had left a proof copy of Mum's funeral service by the bread bin and he picked it up. There was a photo of her on the front, from when they had been on holiday in Brittany. She was smiling, sun-dappled and bronzed. He flicked through the pages. There were songs by Annie Lennox, David Bowie and lastly Shakira singing her favourite, 'Try Everything'. He remembered Mum dancing around this kitchen to it, shaking her hips and laughing. Now it seemed that she'd *tried* Pearce. What a total skank. He screwed the paper up hard and threw it down.

He'd just taken a huge bite of the sandwich and turned to sit at the table when he saw the curse jars, stacked on the top. One of them was open. The paper with Monty's name was on the table, amid a scattering of thorns and chilli flakes. There was a note.

> Adam, we need to talk. I found these under your bed when I was vacuuming. I've no idea what they mean or what you've been doing but it seems deeply unpleasant. I've sent a photo of them and a message to your dad. We'll both be home about 9 p.m. and then you need to explain what's going on.

He sat down heavily. The bread was like a solid lump in his mouth. He swallowed and stared at the note. That bastard had no right to go in his room. He continued eating automatically, taking huge bites, even though the sandwich was making him sick. He wondered if the curse was now weakened, or even cancelled. He had an overwhelming need for Chimera's warmth and reassurance. He ran upstairs, grabbed his laptop and returned to the kitchen. He groaned when he saw she wasn't online. He clicked 'View members' and saw with disbelief that she had left the forum. He clicked again and got the same outcome.

He was dizzy. He filled a glass with water and drank it down. Why had he never got any other contact details for her? He sat and googled 'chimera' but all he found were definitions and links to Greek mythology. Tears came then. He was bereft, stranded, alone. No more *Merry Meet Again*.

His mother had left him alone. Betrayed him. The night she'd gone missing, she'd abandoned him, probably to go and screw someone. She'd never intended to watch *Toy Story* with him. His stomach somersaulted and he rushed to the toilet, where he vomited repeatedly and then sank back on the hard floor tiles. He curled into a ball, his cheek on the cold surface, and lay there for what seemed a long time, drifting in and out of awareness.

When he roused himself, he returned to the kitchen and read Monty's note again. A cold fury seized him. Who did this sneaky fuckwit think he was, prying into his things and demanding explanations? He shredded the note, letting the pieces drop to the floor. Then he ran and attacked the bonsai collection, ripping it apart in a frenzy, sending the soil, branches and leaves spinning through the air. When he'd finished, he trampled on the debris and ground it into the floor. He threw the curse jars one by one against the wall, watching shards of glass fly all over the room.

He sat, panting and staring at the chaos. His head was like a steaming pressure cooker. He put his hands to either side of his skull and pressed hard.

Everyone was lying and treating him like a child, invading his privacy and deceiving him. Now Chimera had taken off without a goodbye. How could she do that to him when they'd had such a close friendship? His dad had walked out on him and his mother had lied to his face and snuck off into the night as if he didn't matter. Lily had told him to grow up. Well, he would. He'd start acting like all the shitty grown-ups who infested his life and did whatever they liked, not caring who they hurt.

He was going to make a start right now.

He spent a few minutes on his laptop, packed some things he'd need in his rucksack and left the house.

* * *

Siv stood at the spot where Tim Stafford had been found. She studied the photo that a responding constable had taken of his skinny body. He was sprawled face down on the shingle, the back of his head a mass of matted blood and hair. Stafford was in hospital now, and in a critical condition.

She sent the photo to herself, handed back the phone and scanned the area. This was the furthest stretch of beach from the town centre, unlit and well away from the seafront hotels and cafés.

She turned to DS Shaw, a small woman whose glasses dominated her face.

'Who found him?'

'Dog walker doing the nightly stroll.'

'How did you identify him?'

'He had a CitizenCard on him. Various charities give them out to homeless people these days. They're useful in shops and night shelters.'

'Any phone?'

'Not on him. Just the ID and a wallet with a fiver in.'

'I'd say the wound was made with a blunt object.'

'Could have been a rock from around here. We've not found anything yet. It's difficult in the dark.'

The wind was whipping in from the sea. The tide was out, but Siv could hear the angry waves crashing landwards. She pulled her coat tightly around her. She'd driven straight from the party and was still wearing her wood sprite costume beneath it. She'd never been less suitably dressed for a crime scene. Ali had wanted to come with her, but she'd said there was no point and he might as well stay at the party. Truth was, she couldn't bear company after Mutsi's ambush.

'Posh coat he had on — or it was once. A Burberry,' DS Shaw said.

Siv recalled Ali's report of the interview with Esme Stafford. 'His foster mother gave it to him to get rid of him.'

'Poor bloke. I suppose at least he was warm and fed. I'd say he was eating the takeaway when he was hit.'

The photo showed a box with a half-eaten burger and chips not far from his feet. Even in the gusting sea air, Siv could smell the vinegar on the abandoned chips. He'd have been distracted, head bent, an easy target. He was a pathetic sight in the photo, his bony frame encased in the voluminous coat.

She wasn't needed here and she didn't intend to linger, but she'd wanted to see where Stafford had been attacked. He might well have stayed at Steiner's and he was linked to Lyn Dimas. He might have killed her. Now someone had tried to crush his skull. If he was guilty of Lyn's murder and died of his injuries, that would be a kind of rough justice.

She asked to be kept informed of his progress and the investigation, and walked back along the rough shingle. It was hard going in her flat pumps and she turned an ankle a couple of times. She picked her way more carefully. The last thing she needed at the moment was a sprain. She climbed the steep path that led to where she'd parked, still hearing the insistent thudding of the sea. Inside the car, she turned on the engine and the heater, directing the warmth at her feet.

The wind had chased the clouds away and a crescent moon lit the dark swell below. A white yacht moved silently across the horizon, like a ghost ship. Many ships had lost their way off this coastline over the centuries, or had been lured onto the rocks by smugglers, and there were stories of sightings of old sailing ships, lit by lanterns, silently riding the waves. Siv recalled a teacher at school who'd sworn that she'd heard the cries of drowned sailors on Minster Beach. She must tell Ali about that, he could add it to his fund of ghostly apparitions.

Siv was more concerned with living hauntings than dead ones. She put her hands over her eyes, reflecting on that scene on *Quicksilver*. Mutsi must have known about Mortimer's job. She was playing games as usual, manipulating information for her own enjoyment. How she must have anticipated that moment of surprise at the party, and enjoyed her daughter's horrified expression! If Mortimer took exception to the way he'd been treated, things at work were going to be sticky. Her only hope was that although he wasn't a stupid man, he was a vain one, and Mutsi had exceptional, well-honed talents for playing up to a man's conceit. She wondered how many people at the party had noticed what had happened. Castles certainly had and she was sure he'd love to spread the gossip.

Let them get on with it. They deserve each other, Ed murmured.

Easy for you to say. I was humiliated in front of Mortimer and that bastard Castles.

Maybe Mortimer was even more embarrassed than you. There's nothing you can do about it, so park it for now.

That had been one of his favourite sayings. He'd been good at putting aside what couldn't be resolved, his mantra being that if you left things alone, they often sorted themselves out. She listened, holding her breath, but he'd gone. Her feet were toasty now. She opened her window a little and listened to the restless, moaning sea. If Tim Stafford wasn't their killer, he might have been assaulted because he had information about Lyn Dimas. She was annoyed that they hadn't found him before his attacker.

Her phone rang and she saw that it was Ali. She didn't answer. It was gone midnight and there was nothing more to be done for now. She texted him and Patrick to say that Stafford was in hospital, and they needed to be in the office first thing tomorrow, the weekend suspended with so much work to do.

She just wanted to go home and lock the door. Shut out the living and the dead.

* * *

Siv was out of sorts the next morning. Her stomach was queasy and she couldn't face breakfast. Bartel had emailed her first thing. He'd made her smile, even if it was mirthlessly.

Famous ambushes: the sack of Rome by the Visigoths, the Battle of Trenton, the Battle of

France, Pearl Harbour, Crista on *Quicksilver*. I met her. Wow. Hope your boss can handle her type of dynamite. I can only sympathise. You weren't exaggerating. Here when you need me and btw — isn't Crista quite a bit older than your boss?

She emailed back, *Thanks for sharing the pain. Crista the cougar.*

She called Patrick and Ali into her office. They were both bleary and hung-over. Patrick had nicked himself shaving and was drinking a tall glass of water and popping aspirin. The sight of them reflected her own fatigue and irritated her.

She glared at them. 'Tim Stafford is stable, in an induced coma while they do brain scans. Why didn't we find him?'

'We trawled loads of places, including Hastings and St Leonard's,' Ali replied. 'He moved around a lot, all over the south coast. None of the homeless organisations had seen him recently. Several said that he often went off the radar, especially if anyone tried to find out anything about him. He must have been lying low somewhere.'

'Not low enough for his attacker, apparently. Stafford might not be our killer but the more I weigh this up, the more I'm convinced that this assault is somehow linked to Lyn.'

'We've no evidence of that,' Patrick said. 'Street people are vulnerable and subject to violence.'

'Yes, I am *aware* of that, Patrick. We've no evidence, full stop. Just call it a hunch. Tell me all the places where you *did* manage to confirm any sightings of Stafford.'

Ali opened his laptop. 'We went along the coast from Hastings to Bognor Regis. A lot of centres we contacted were a bit vague about timings. Stafford was seen in Worthing and Hove last year, here in town and in Eastbourne earlier this year but then we drew a blank after June.'

Siv pondered the geography of this case, and pictured the locations of people they'd interviewed. 'Does Seaford feature in Stafford's ramblings?'

Ali checked. 'Yes. Last sighting we found there was in 2017.'

'So he was probably there on other occasions. Patrick, contact DS Shaw at St Leonard's. Make sure we get Stafford's DNA cross-referenced with results from Steiner's asap. I want to find out if he was ever there. Ali, get hold of Clive Hemmings and ask again if he or his family knew Stafford. That would be an interesting connection. I'm sure he lied about something when we saw him.'

As they were leaving, she called Ali back. She forced a smile. It wouldn't fool him. 'Did anything much happen at the party after I left last night?'

He gave her a measuring glance, then leaned against the back of a chair. 'Mortimer and Crista vanished for a while. Tommy Castles made sure that word got round that she's your mum, and that seeing her with Mortimer gave you a nasty shock. She and Mortimer reappeared about twenty minutes after you left. No major drama. Except, I suppose, for you. You didn't realise your mum and Mortimer were an item?'

'No, I didn't. I'm over the moon. No doubt everyone at the station has heard about it by now.'

'Probably. Does it matter? I mean, I can see it could make things awkward with Mortimer, but in this kind of place, there are lots of family links. People are used to it.'

Ali had a point but he didn't mind living a public life with little concept of privacy. When he spoke of his background, she got the impression of a busy, packed household where the door was always open and neighbours dropped by constantly. 'We'll see. Depends on the family involved.'

'You've never mentioned that your mum lives here.'

'That's right. You'll find that odd, but I have my reasons.'

'Sure. Your business, guv. I erm . . . I gather you don't get on with her.'

'You gather correctly. How old is Mortimer?'

'Just turned fifty.'

Eighteen years between them. Maybe Mutsi wouldn't be able to maintain the pace and they'd fizzle out. But she had years of insight into her mother's strategies. When Mutsi had homed in on Mortimer, she'd have weighed up his status and assets, both financial and personal, and the prospect of a secure future. She'd be prepared to put in the hard graft.

Ali said, 'Anything I can do?'

'No. Yes — get me some evidence.'

She rose and stood at the window after he'd gone. The Japanese maples across the road now boasted a colour palette of fiery hues, but the leaves were thinning and the pavement below was a carpet of red and burnt orange. She watched a road sweeper clearing the fallen leaves from the gutters, rendering them into a brown sludge that symbolised the state of her brain at present. Doubt gripped her. Had she made a mistake, leaving London with its blissful anonymity? After Ed's death, Berminster had appealed because it was familiar. Her memories of living here with her father were comforting. The downside was that it was a place where the grapevine worked swiftly and efficiently.

She forced her mind back to the job. Without forensics or other evidence, getting any kind of grip on this investigation was like trying to grasp smoke in her hand. Her door vibrated as Ali barged through it, waving the banana he was eating.

'Guv, Pearce Aston and Adam Dimas are both in hospital. Aston has a superficial knife wound and Adam has mild concussion and bruising. Uniform are dealing with them. According to Aston, Adam turned up last night at Time After Time, the antiques place, with a knife. Aston's been staying there because Lily's back at home and he's had to move out. Adam managed to stab him in the shoulder before Aston overpowered him and knocked him out.'

'That doesn't surprise me, he's a fit guy and Adam wouldn't be quick on his feet.'

'Aston managed to call an ambulance.'

'Lucky for both of them. Is Theo Dimas with Adam?'

'Aye. He's seen Aston as well.'

Siv rested against the window ledge. 'What a total mess this is. I bet Lily's been talking to Adam, and making sure he has all the details about their mum. She's a piece of work. I'm sorry for Adam. He's young and he's had a lot to deal with.'

'Yeah, his bread falls butter side down. Talking of food, d'you want a banana? I bet you could do with a bite to eat.'

'Hmm? No, that's okay.'

She turned again to gaze at the trees as he left. The road sweeper was moving on and the pavement was bare and stark. More leaves would fall soon, laying a new carpet. Her mind dwelled on Adam's troubles and she wondered how Theo Dimas would react to this latest blow. She ran through recent interviews permeated by loss, shock and anger and reviewed the reactions she'd witnessed, and the latest connections in this tangle of people. Young men and their grieving fathers, young men lacking fathers, young men with overprotective fathers. She recalled Grant Haddon sitting in his father's office and speaking of his childhood illness.

She stood motionless, catching her breath and leaned her forehead on the windowpane as she turned over the germ of a possibility. Could it be true? Was it even relevant? She picked up her phone, rang Grant Haddon and had a brief conversation. When she'd finished, she found Clive Hemmings's previous address, snatched up her bag and hurried from the office.

'Are you heading to Seaford to see Hemmings?'

Ali was putting his jacket on. 'Aye, he's at home today.'

'Good. I'm hitching a ride and I'll explain why in the car. I'm ravenous, I'll have a banana now.'

CHAPTER 24

On the way to Seaford, she told Ali about her conversation with Grant. 'I remembered that he said he'd had almost a year's illness with leukaemia, and that it had delayed his schooling. It struck me that he might have had private tutoring. When I rang him, he confirmed that he had a tutor for six months in 2012, and his name was Clive Hemmings. Hemmings used to go to their home in Bywater, but Lewis Haddon once gave him a lift home to Seaford when his car broke down.'

'Okay, that's interesting, but where does it take us?'

'I'm not sure, but let's consider the cross-threads here. Hemmings believes that Lyn Dimas's actions caused his mum to kill herself, and impacted so much on his sister's mental health that she committed suicide. He has no alibi. Grant was at school with Adam, and we now discover that he was tutored by Hemmings, who lives in Seaford. Tim Stafford was in Seaford, and he was treated by Lyn Dimas. Stafford might well have hung out at Steiner's and could have seen Lyn there.'

'Sure, I can see that you're playing with degrees of separation, but that doesn't connect Hemmings with Lyn, other than through his mother. He had a strong motive to kill Lyn, but that's all we have.'

'Bear with me. If we find that Hemmings lied to us and did know Stafford, and if we can link Stafford to Steiner's forensically, we can bring Hemmings in for questioning. Stafford could have told him about seeing Lyn at Steiner's. That could have given Hemmings the idea of killing her there. That's a number of "ifs", but I'm sure that he's concealing something.'

Ali tapped the steering wheel and pursed his lips. 'It's a long shot but I don't dislike it. What we really need is for Stafford to wake up and start talking.'

'Even if he regains consciousness, he might have brain damage. Go easy on Hemmings when you see him, I don't want him alarmed. If he still denies meeting Stafford, don't press it. I'm going to knock along Hood Lane, where the Hemmings family used to live, see if anyone recalls seeing Tim Stafford at their house.'

It was a bright, chilly but calm day after the winds of the night before. Hood Lane was a street of terraced houses with neat front gardens, many of which had been paved or gravelled. It had a settled air, and Siv was pleased to see a number of handrails by front doors, indicating older residents who had been around for a while and might even take an interest in their neighbours. Several houses had smoke curling from their chimneys and there was a sweet smell of cherry in the air at number nineteen, but the young woman who opened the door had only lived there for a year. She mentioned that Esther Walsh at fifteen had lived there 'like, for ever — in fact, she might have been *born* in that house.'

Siv rang the bell at fifteen but there was no reply. She read the black-and-red notice on the door:

POLICE & TRADING STANDARDS NOTICE
NO JUNK MAIL
NO MENUS

NO FLYERS
NO CHARITY COLLECTIONS
NO SALESPEOPLE
ADDRESSED MAIL ONLY
THANK YOU

She worked her way along either side of twenty-one. There were few people in. None of them recognised the photo of Tim Stafford. She had the beginnings of a headache, the kind that starts behind the eyes and works its way to the temples. She was about to cross the road when a taxi drew up outside number fifteen, and a tiny old woman wearing a blue denim jacket, navy jeans and rainbow-striped plimsolls hopped out, hefting two full shopping bags. She waved to the driver, calling to him to behave himself and adding, 'If you can't be good, be careful!'

Siv approached, holding out her ID and asking if she could have a word.

'What about? If it's about my grandson and his parking, that's nothing to do with me.' She stared up at Siv with impudent green eyes.

'It isn't. I want to ask you about the Hemmings family who used to live at number twenty-one.'

'Well, you can, but you'll have to come in because my feet are killing me. You're young and supple, take a bag while I get my key.'

Siv followed her down a narrow, dark hall. The shopping bag was as heavy as if it contained bricks. She blinked when Esther opened the door into an extended kitchen. It was flooded with light from the skylights in the roof. Esther balanced with one hand on a counter while she shucked off her plimsolls and flexed each foot carefully. Her feet were dainty and bare, her toenails scarlet.

'What they don't tell you about getting older is that it hurts,' she said ruefully. 'I'm eighty-six!'

Her saucy air made her seem younger. She was upright, her silvery backcombed hair standing up like a dandelion clock around her pert face. She peered in a round wall mirror that was circled with gold lettering, *You're Looking At The Best Gran In The World.*

'Just had my hair done. Like it?'

'It suits you.'

'Hmm, not bad. She wanted to do a rinse but I said no. I don't like too much messing about. Now, I just need to put the perishables in the fridge. You could stick the kettle on if you want to make yourself useful. I'm as parched as a woman lost in the desert.'

Siv did as she was bid, following orders to find the tea-pot and caddy. The tea was leaf, and she had to confirm that she understood to warm the brown earthenware pot.

'And it's three spoons, one each and one for the pot, and let it brew for at least two minutes before you pour,' Esther said bossily, making a racket as she stacked the freezer. 'See all this packaging! It makes you sick. If I were younger, I'd be marching with that Greta Thunberg and speaking truth to power. Mind you, a square meal wouldn't harm her. The strainer's in that drawer on your right, and there's biscuits in the tin just above your head. Nothing fancy, just digestives. Unless you're one of those faddy eaters, gluten free or whatever, in which case, you'll have to go without.'

'Digestives are fine,' Siv said, taking two mugs from hooks. They were both embellished with slogans, *You know you're getting old when happy hour is a nap* and *Age and treachery will always overcome youth and skill.*

'And the milk goes in the blue-striped jug,' Esther said. She handed Siv a bottle of semi-skimmed.

Siv was amused and obeyed. Esther might look as if a breeze would blow her away, but her impishness spoke of a robust core.

At last, they were seated at the table with tea and biscuits. Esther poured, setting the silver strainer on top of each mug. Only her hands, gnarled, crêpey and with a slight tremble, gave her age away.

'I prefer my tea this way. I suppose you just have tea bags like most people. I was reading that they're full of plastic. What about that, isn't it terrible what they put in our food?'

'It's a minefield,' Siv agreed. She stirred her tea. It smelled fresh and fragrant. Her head was pounding now, and she was starting to worry that it might take hours to navigate Esther's stream of consciousness and establish if she had any useful information. 'Would you have some pain killers?'

Esther laughed. 'I'm old, of course I have!' She went to a drawer and brought back a pack of paracetamol. 'You're a funny colour. Period pains? Now, that's one of the few benefits of old age, I don't have to put up with that anymore.'

'Just a headache.' Siv swallowed two capsules with the hot tea and took a biscuit. The sunlight was streaming through the skylight above, striking her eyes and she raised a hand to shield them.

Esther picked up a remote control and lowered the electronic window blind. 'That better?'

'Much, thanks.'

'I like the skylights, but they can make the place too warm. I have the blinds down all day in summer. Glad I've got this gizmo, I wouldn't want to be climbing on chairs. I was born in the room over your head, four o'clock in the morning and deep snow outside.'

Siv smiled and tilted her mug in respect. 'That's amazing. You've always lived here?'

'Baby to geriatric, that's me. Mind you, my parents wouldn't recognise the house now!' She paused to munch a biscuit and Siv made the most of it.

'Were you friendly with the Hemmings family? I'm really hoping that you can help me.'

Esther sat up straight. 'I lent Tilly a hand the day she moved in with the children, and I saw them taking her body out on a stretcher. That unfortunate woman. She wasn't one of life's copers. Oh, she tried, but she couldn't ride the storms. Posy took after her. Too soft, took things to heart too much. When you're like that, you get overwhelmed. What do you want to find out?'

'Tilly and Posy both committed suicide, and then Clive sold up and bought his own place. I've spoken to him.'

'He's a funny lad, always was. Sort of in a world of his own. I didn't recognise him when I saw him in town a while back. He said hello and I had to stare. He'd lost all the weight and done something to his face and dyed his hair. If he took pills, tell him I wouldn't mind some!'

'Did a man called Tim Stafford ever come to their house? This is him.' Siv took Stafford's photo from her bag and placed it in front of Esther. 'He took to living on the streets after that photo was taken, so he might have been worse for wear.'

Esther turned the photo from side to side and tapped it with a nail. 'I never caught his name, but Posy had met him. She'd made him something to eat one night when I called in. It was the summer before she died. Posy had found him on the streets and was sorry for him. She had a social conscience and she'd get very worked up about homelessness, saying it was dreadful that a wealthy country like ours had people sleeping rough. This chap was a miserable sight, all right, all damp and dirty. Talk about smelling ripe! You had to pity him, but I told her off about it afterwards. I said it was all very well being charitable, but no woman should invite a man into the house like that. She said she could see that he was harmless from his honest eyes. Some rubbish like that.' She tutted and shook her head. 'These girls won't be told.'

'Was Tim Stafford there more than once? Did Clive meet him?'

'Posy told me that she wouldn't tell Clive, because he was always keen on keeping the house spick and span and she was a messy sort. He was a bit obsessed that way. Worried about germs and always using hand gel, that type. He'd nag Posy about the cleaning. This homeless man was like germ central, so Posy would have been mopping up after he'd gone. She was the kind of woman who always wants to please people and keep them happy. "Please yourself first, because no one else will", that's what I say. Then she killed herself. She didn't have much of a life, putting up with Tilly's depression and then trying to make sure Clive was okay.'

Siv was disappointed. She'd been hoping that there would be a proven link between Hemmings and Stafford, a sighting of them together. She found a photo of Lyn Dimas on her phone and showed it to Esther. 'Did you ever see this woman around here, or visiting the Hemmings?'

Esther shook her head. 'Never seen her.'

A text popped up from Ali as she took the phone back. *On my way over, Hemmings still says he never met Stafford. I'll be outside.* She was about to thank Esther and take her leave, when the old woman poured them both more tea and stopped her in her tracks.

'I didn't see that coming, when Posy killed herself. I mean, I realised she'd been down about her mum, but she'd met a man she liked and things were on the up for her. You just can't tell with people, can you?'

'Who had she met?'

'Well, that I can't say. I saw her one morning about a month before she died, and she said she was seeing someone. It was early days, but she liked him.'

'No name?'

Esther shook her head.

'Did Posy indicate if he was local?'

'She didn't say. She told me that he was a good listener, very sympathetic, and she'd been able to talk about her mum and all the bad things that had happened.'

'Was Clive aware of this new man?' Siv remembered him saying that Posy didn't have a partner.

'No way, although she did say that she'd met this chap because of Clive. Posy was so careful around that brother of hers, very mother hen. She said she wanted to wait until she was sure the relationship was going anywhere before she told him. Hang on . . . I remember that Posy said the chap she was seeing lived on a steep hill in a village because when it was icy he had to be ever so careful on the roads.'

Siv thanked Esther and headed outside to Ali. 'How did Hemmings seem?'

'Same as last time. Adamant that he's never met Stafford. I'm not sure I believed him, but he wasn't giving anything away. How did you get on?'

Siv told him. 'From what Esther Walsh said, Hemmings could be telling the truth. Now we hear that Posy had a male friend.'

'Any identification?'

Siv's headache had almost gone and it was as if a mist was clearing. She paused for a moment, reordering her ideas. 'Posy told Esther about this man shortly before she died in 2012. She said she'd met him because of Clive Hemmings, even though Hemmings didn't know about him. Hemmings was tutoring Grant that year, in Bywater, and Lewis Haddon once gave him a lift home. Let's drive back via there. I want to see where the Haddons live.'

'Why?'

'I'm hoping that the house is on a steep hill.'

As Ali started the engine, Siv received a text from Patrick: *Guv, Tim Stafford's DNA confirmed on mattress and two mugs at Steiner's.* She read it to Ali.

'So Stafford could well be our killer,' Ali said.

Siv sank into silence. Adam Dimas was on her mind. She rang the station and checked in with the duty desk.

'They're dropping the charges against Adam Dimas,' she told Ali. 'Small mercies.'

'That surprises me. No love lost between him and Aston, is there?'

'Maybe Aston has enough on his plate, or he sees it as a way back into Lily's good books.'

'Surely she won't take that waster back!'

'Not if she's got any sense.'

She imagined that Lily, like her dead mother, would take no prisoners once slighted.

CHAPTER 25

Siv spent an evening designing and making origami acorns for her own amusement. She incorporated metallic paper for the tops, her mind roaming over the investigation and time-lines. The Haddons lived in a detached house in Bywater, set up a steep road. It would be a nightmare in icy weather. But plenty of people lived on hills. If Lewis Haddon had killed Lyn, proving it would be difficult.

The next morning found her in front of the incident board, correlating dates.

'A number of events pertaining to this case happened in 2012,' she said to Ali. 'We've got a general picture of them and to some degree, how they interconnect. Lyn and Pearce Aston had an affair, Grant had Clive Hemmings as a tutor and Lewis Haddon might have met Posy Hemmings because of that arrangement. Tim Stafford was thrown out of home in May, and at some point that summer met up with Posy Hemmings, who died in December. I want to talk to Grant Haddon again.'

Ali sounded confused. 'What can he tell you?'

'I'm not sure. I want to see if he's heard of Tim Stafford or Posy Hemmings, for starters.'

* * *

Patrick fetched Grant from university that afternoon and brought him to the station 'just to check a few things out'. Siv took him round to Gusto to get some drinks — coffee for her, fruit tea for him — and then back to an interview room. She'd said that she would talk to him on her own, keep things low key.

She watched him put down his rucksack and cup his tea in his hands. His black-and-white jumper was emblazoned with a silhouette of a man wrapped around a microphone and the legend, *Eat. Sleep. Performing Arts*. He wore a red-and-gold plaited wristband and played with it as he relaxed in his chair. That was good, because she reckoned that the next half hour or so might increase his stress levels. She pulled a spare chair over and put her feet up on it. 'How is it, being a student?'

Grant sank back, stretching his legs out. 'Great, thanks, full on. I've signed up to loads of societies.'

'I can imagine it's exciting. Thanks for coming to see me. We've made some progress with the investigation about Lyn Dimas, and I need to ask you a few more questions.'

He sipped his tea. The steam from it filled the room with a raspberry aroma, a big improvement on how it usually smelled.

She showed him Stafford's photo. 'Do you or your dad know this man? His name's Tim Stafford.'

'No. Who is he?'

'A homeless man, originally from Berminster. He was attacked on the beach at St Leonard's and he's in hospital with serious injuries.'

'Well . . . that's horrible. I don't recognise him, and Dad's never mentioned him.'

'When I rang you, you told me that you'd been tutored by Clive Hemmings, in Bywater. Did you ever go to his home in Seaford for tuition?'

'No. He came to our house. That was the deal.'

'How did your dad find him?'

'Sorry, no idea. A website, probably.'

'So did Clive drive to your house?'

'That's right. He had a little Fiat. He'd got it second hand and it wasn't that reliable.' He laughed. 'Clapped out, to be honest. Dad had to help him with it a couple of times. Like I told you, it wouldn't start at all one evening when Grant was going home.'

Siv said encouragingly. 'That was when your dad gave him a lift. Did your dad mention meeting Clive's sister, Posy Hemmings?'

'It was a while ago, but I don't remember that name.'

The questions weren't troubling him and his answers came easily, but he turned his wristband and looked at her curiously.

'What have Clive and his sister got to do with Lyn Dimas?'

'It's a bit complicated. Just bear with me for now. You're being very helpful. I suppose your dad's had some women friends since your mum died?'

Grant blinked at the change of direction. 'Erm . . . yeah. Well, actually only one. He went out with Val, but that was quite a while ago. She lives in the village, runs the wine bar. They're still friendly, but it didn't last.'

'I see. You don't recall that he was seeing anyone around the time that Grant was tutoring you?'

'No. But . . . Best to ask Dad.'

'Of course, and I will. Lyn Dimas vanished on the twenty-eighth of July 2013. Your dad was home alone, and you were staying at your friend's house.' She pretended to consult her notes because she could see Grant tensing. 'Freddie, that was it. Have I got that right?'

'Yeah, like I told you before.'

'Does Freddie live near your house?'

'Five minutes away.'

'And next evening when you saw your dad, how did he seem?'

'Fine.' Grant's right heel was tapping the floor. 'I don't get why you're asking me about this again.'

She took her feet off the chair. 'You said that your dad was very upset and angry after you discovered Lyn's body.'

'Yeah, of course.'

'Not just because of that discovery. Because he hadn't expected you to be at Steiner's that morning.'

'What are you getting at?'

'Grant, something doesn't add up. You see, we believe that your dad might have met Posy Hemmings, Clive's sister, and could have been seeing her. Posy killed herself. She was depressed because her mum had committed suicide, after Lyn Dimas was involved in her dismissal from her job. Your dad knew about Steiner's and that it was an empty premises.'

Grant was pallid.

'Your dad has no alibi for the night Lyn vanished.'

'My dad wouldn't kill anyone!'

'That would be for us to prove. I believe that Lyn's death and the attack on Tim Stafford are connected. Are you sure that your dad didn't seem upset in any way when you came home on the twenty-ninth?'

'I don't . . . I can't . . .' He was holding onto the sides of his chair.

She took out her phone and showed him the photo of Stafford on the beach. 'You saw Lyn's body. You saw what someone had done to her. This defenceless young man was attacked. You must, Grant. You must tell me if you can help.'

Grant flinched away from the photo, burst into tears and shielded his face in his hands. She placed a box of tissues at his elbow and waited, disliking herself. The car park fence was being renovated and the man repairing it had a radio on, tuned to a classical station. Bach played while she waited for Grant to compose himself.

At last he blew his nose and said, 'I nipped back home the night Lyn went missing. I'd forgotten my iPad. Freddie was asleep and no one saw me go out. Dad wasn't in.'

'What time was this?'

'About half nine.'

'You've never mentioned this to your dad?'

'No. No reason to.'

'But then it played on your mind when we came asking questions, and you realised that he'd told us he was at home that night.'

He sniffed. 'I didn't get why he lied. I tried not to think about it. What are you going to do now?'

'Speak to your dad and ask him.'

'He'll guess I dobbed him in.'

'If he has nothing to hide, why should it matter that you told the truth?' She could see that he was in shock. 'I want you to wait in here. Not for long. I'll send someone in to be with you and we'll take you home.'

In her office, she brought Ali and Patrick up to date. 'Lewis Haddon lied about being at home all evening on the twenty-eighth of July. I believe that he's the man Posy was seeing before she died. Esther Walsh said that Posy had told him all about her traumatic history. After Posy committed suicide, he could have been angry enough with Lyn to plan her murder. Steiner's was standing empty, so handy. Haddon may well have met Stafford through his connection with Posy.'

'We need to bring him in,' Ali said.

'Hmm, we do.' She hesitated, tapping her fingers on the desk. 'But what I don't understand is if Haddon did murder Lyn, and then found some years later that he'd got the contract for dealing with Steiner's, would he not have moved her body?'

'Maybe he wanted her found,' Patrick said.

'Maybe. And he didn't expect that his son would be working there that day . . . Even so, I'm not sure.'

'We'll get him in, guv.' Ali stood and beckoned Patrick. 'There's only one way to find out. Search warrant?'

'Let's talk to him first.'

She watched them go. She wasn't getting that adrenalin rush that came when she sensed a case breaking.

* * *

310

Mortimer was cautious, conciliatory, even, when Siv briefed him in his office later.

'We've interviewed Lewis Haddon, sir. He's told us that he was seeing Posy Hemmings, and that he met her when he gave her brother a lift home in 2012. They'd seen each other a couple of times, and Posy had told him what had happened to their mother after Lyn reported her. Clive Hemmings wasn't aware of their relationship. According to Haddon, he and Posy hadn't yet slept together. He says he was devastated when Posy killed herself, and that he didn't see it coming. He states that he's never met Tim Stafford, although Posy talked about him and how she'd helped him now and again. He admits that he lied about being at home on the night Lyn vanished. He now claims that he went for a walk along a footpath across the fields near his home, to get some air on an oppressive night. He didn't meet anyone. He said that he claimed to have been at home and denied knowing anything about Lyn because he didn't want to bring trouble to his door. He didn't see that what Posy had told him was relevant. He insisted that he'd needed to focus on his son, who'd had a terrible shock at Steiner's, and if he'd talked to us about Posy, he'd have been getting in deeper for no reason.'

Mortimer cracked the knuckles on his left hand. 'What do you make of it? Truth, lies or something in between?'

Siv recalled Haddon's angst during the interview and the way his voice had broken suddenly when he'd spoken of his son's distress. *My God, how I wish I'd never taken that contract for Orford End, it's brought nothing but trouble!* She spoke firmly. 'I'm sure he was telling the truth, and I keep coming back to why he'd have left the body there to be discovered by his own employees, let alone his son. He's given us permission to search his house and garage. Unless we find any forensics there, we have no evidence against him.'

'Better get on with the search, then.'

'Yes, sir.'

There was a pregnant pause. *He's the boss. It's up to him to say something.*

He moved his laptop an inch and fiddled with the edges. 'Well . . . regarding the party . . . clearly, we were both surprised.'

'Yes, we were.'

'Have you spoken to your mother?'

'No. We don't speak often.'

'Yes . . . well . . . that's as may be. Crista explained that she hadn't told me about your family connection because there are . . . *difficulties* between you, and she didn't want to contribute to any problems in the workplace. Understandably, she was anxious that it might cause embarrassment. She was terribly upset when she believed she'd done the wrong thing. I've reassured her that we're all adults and not to worry about it. No one's committed a crime!' He gave a forced laugh.

Siv almost pitied him, imagining Crista's glistening tears and the wheedling, little-girl voice she employed when she was manipulating and web-weaving. Then she thought of Mortimer's friendship with Castles and the awful possibility that he could become her stepfather, and steeled herself.

'It did cause embarrassment,' she said. 'It certainly achieved that.'

'Yes . . . Anyway, that's over and done with. Crista . . . your mum, told me how close you and your husband were. She's concerned about how you're coping. She's worried that you're isolated, out where you live, and that you're not mixing socially. If there's anything I can do to help . . .' He fumbled to a halt.

Siv was furious. Mutsi was busy with her spade, digging at the foundations of her life. If Mortimer was going to start being paternal and caring, she'd have a meltdown. Sod him and sod Mutsi. 'I'm doing fine, thanks. I'm the best judge of that.'

'Of course. I'm . . . well, I'm very fond of your mother and I hope that we can continue to work professionally. I can tell that she cares deeply about you.'

Despite her anger, she had to suppress a grin. There he was in the web, dangling helplessly. She'd bet that his new glasses, hair shade and upgraded style were down to Mutsi's influence. A Mortimer makeover. 'I hope that I'm always professional at work, sir. Thank you for clearing the air. Now, I must get back to the team.'

He coughed nervously and tapped at his laptop. On her way downstairs, she got a call from DS Shaw at St Leonard's. Tim Stafford had regained consciousness. He'd named his attacker and had managed to give a few other crucial details. When she heard the identity, she was winded. She leaned against the wall and let out an exclamation of surprise. Then she hurried to her office, all plans about Lewis Haddon shelved.

CHAPTER 26

A storm was hurtling across the Channel. The wind was whipping the last leaves from the trees planted by Victorian builders at Poets' Piece. Only the sycamores were holding on defiantly, with leaves that seemed to have been tie-dyed in yellows, reds and browns.

'A sycamore can bleed to death if it's pruned in the spring.' Siv said.

'Why's that?' Ali asked.

'It's when the sap is strongest.'

'Aye, right. Polly says my sap is strongest in the spring.'

'Too much information, DS Carlin.'

They were both processing this latest development and attempting to defuse their tension. Ali turned into Chaucer Road and parked. They sat silently for a moment.

'It doesn't mean he killed Lyn,' Ali said.

'Oh, I think he did. Why attack Tim Stafford otherwise?'

They'd been focusing on the wrong Dimas.

Stafford had named his attacker as a man he called Papu.

'When I first met Joe Dimas, a chill went through me,' Siv said. 'He's a man who deals in absolutes. A fundamentalist. He places great faith in marriage and in women as nurturers and caregivers, at the centre of family life. That's why he was so keen for Lily to marry, and so scathing about his son abandoning the traditional family unit. When I came to see him, he was well prepared. He spoke about his admiration for Lyn and a woman's role in her family. I can remember his words because he was so eloquent: he said that a woman, a mother, was "the backbone and the beating, constant heart of any family, the source of comfort and reassurance." So he must have had a terrible shock when he found out that Lyn had sought her own comforts elsewhere. We still might not get him for her murder, though, with no evidence.'

'And then there's his alibi,' said Ali. 'We need Patrick to get back to us.'

Siv had sent Patrick to St Demetrius, to speak to Pater Basil. He rang, sounding breathless, as she stepped from the car. She got back in and put him on speaker.

'Guv, Pater Basil is an ancient guy, unwell and about to retire. I tried to talk to him about Joe Dimas, but I couldn't get any sense from him and to be honest, I'd gauge he can't recall what happened yesterday, let alone six years ago. I've spoken to a Pater Nicholas, who's been brought in to work with him for a while at the church. He's told me that Pater Basil has had memory loss for some time, going back years. Parishioners have been concerned about him. He had a diagnosis of dementia last year. Pater Nicholas knows Joe Dimas, says he's a highly influential church member and that Pater Basil has been very dependent on him, relied on him for a lot of day-to-day decisions. Guv, it sounded to me as if Joe Dimas could have got the priest to agree to anything and if he's confused, he might have believed the alibi he gave was correct.'

'Thanks, Patrick. We'll take it from here.' She frowned at Ali. 'We should have double-checked that alibi.' This was exactly the kind of slip that worried her these days.

'Even if we had, we couldn't have proved it wasn't tight. The priest only had the dementia diagnosis last year. Don't sweat the small stuff, guv. We can still use what Patrick's told us to rattle Dimas.'

They went up the path to the front door. 'Take deep breaths, it's like an incense-filled church in here,' Siv said.

Joe Dimas seemed unperturbed by their visit and, although still unyielding, in better spirits than the last time Siv had seen him. Perhaps, despite his adoration of her, having Lily around all day, every day, had proved onerous and he was relieved that she'd flounced home. He led them into the sitting-room-cum-chapel. Ali gazed around in astonishment at the splendid icons and votive candles. Today's incense smelled of balsam fir, woody and pungent.

'Sit down,' Dimas said. He was dressed in his customary elegant black. 'I suppose this is about Pearce and Adam. I went to the hospital and spoke to Pearce. I hope I persuaded him not to press charges. I was bracing in my language, I can tell you. It's the least he could do for us, given the way he's behaved. We've had quite enough drama in the family, and Adam is too weak a character to cope with court appearances.'

They sat crammed in the small, claustrophobic space.

'The charges are actually being dropped, but that's not why we're here,' Siv said. 'For starters, we've come about a man called Tim Stafford. I asked Lily about him last time I was here, and I showed you both a photo. You said you didn't recognise him. Are you sure about that?'

'Stafford . . . No, I'm afraid I don't.'

He stumbled on the name. It wasn't much of a lie. His heart wasn't in it. She forced sympathy into her voice. 'You must be terribly tired,' she said. 'So much has been happening in your family, and you're not a young man. I believe you do know Tim Stafford. He's told us that you attacked him on the beach in St Leonard's. He calls you "Papu". I suppose you gave him that name because the first time you met him, you took care of him, as a grandad would. Unlike the second time, when you tried to kill him.'

He rallied and made an effort. 'Tcha! I don't understand. Who is this man?'

Siv shook her head. 'You picked him up in your car on Halloween and attacked him on the beach. He didn't die and he's identified you. We'll be crawling all over your car for forensics, Mr Dimas, and believe me, we'll find traces of Tim Stafford. You might as well tell us the truth.'

Ali pressed the point. 'The truth about Stafford and what you did to Lyn. Stafford told you about seeing Lyn with a man at Steiner's. You've been carrying a terrible burden.'

Dimas tensed. 'I have an alibi for the night Lyn went missing.'

Ali waved a finger. 'Pater Basil has had memory problems for years. He's been very reliant on you. Your alibi is a tad wobbly.'

'Pater Basil will back me to the hilt.'

Siv shook her head. 'Hardly, in his current state of health. All of this must be eating into you. Your conscience must be keeping you awake at night. When I saw you again after Lily came to stay with you, you seemed frailer because of all the turmoil in your family. But now I'd say that you only learned the identity of the man who'd been with Lyn at Steiner's when Lily told you. That must have been an awful shock on top of all the others you've been absorbing.'

Dimas's head sank down to his chest. Siv pictured a scales, with a full confession hanging in the balance. They sat in silence, listening to the incense burner hissing.

Siv said, 'It's over, Mr Dimas. We will charge you with the assault on Tim Stafford. I believe that you have confession in your religion. Tell us about Lyn.'

Dimas looked up with longing at the Madonna and Child and crossed himself, right to left. 'The Greek Orthodox term for confession is *metanoia* — repentance.' He knelt in front of the Madonna, his head bowed. 'To cure your soul, you need four things. The first is to forgive your enemies. The second is to confess thoroughly. The third is to blame yourself. The fourth is to resolve to sin no more. God, who is most compassionate, will forgive you.'

'That's handy,' Ali said. 'Maybe it's Tim and Lyn you should be asking for forgiveness.'

317

Dimas stood, holding onto his chair for support. 'Not here,' he said. 'I don't want to speak of this here.' He gestured at the icons. 'I don't want them to witness.'

'That's fine. We'll go to the station,' Siv told him.

He stood and listened while Siv charged him. He picked up a book, the cover embossed with a double-headed eagle, and slipped it into his pocket. He then took a long rope of wooden prayer beads from beside his chair, twisting them through his fingers as they led him to the car.

He didn't speak on the way to the station. He declined a solicitor, refused a drink and sat in the interview room, perched on the edge of his chair. His white hair was brushed back high and thick, like a crest.

When Siv went to start the interview, he held a hand up, staring with his hostile grey eyes. He kissed his prayer beads and said, '*Theé synchórresé me.*'

Siv asked, 'What does that mean?'

'"God forgive me." You can switch your machine on now and just let me talk. You can ask me about anything I've missed at the end.'

He clutched his prayer beads, speaking slowly and clearly. He sounded as if he'd expected this day to come and had rehearsed. 'I was driving past Orford End one evening in June 2013. It was the feast of St Jude, and I was on my way home from a church service. I saw a young man running up the road. He was distressed, ragged. I stopped the car and asked if he was all right. He said that he was homeless and that he'd been hoping to sleep the night in Steiner's, but a man living in there had attacked him with a broken bottle. He told me his name, Tim Stafford. He had a cut on his hand, where he'd defended himself. I had a first-aid pack in the car so I gave him a disinfectant wipe and a plaster.

I drove him into the town centre, where he wanted to wait for the mobile soup kitchen. He was a talkative young man. Perhaps he enjoyed company when he could get it. While I was driving, he chatted away. He told me that he'd never go back to Steiner's again, because he'd had bad luck in there. He described a couple he'd seen in there the previous year, half-naked, on a mattress, drinking wine. "They were getting down and dirty," was how he put it. He said that the woman was called Lyn Dimas, and she'd once treated him for a verruca. I asked him if he was sure and he was quite certain. He said he'd been surprised that someone like her would be slumming it. I was so appalled, I could hardly keep the car on the road. Tim didn't recognise the man who'd been with her, and he said he crept back out without them seeing him.' Dimas pressed his beads to his lips and continued. 'As if that wasn't enough, Tim went on to tell me that he'd heard bad things about Lyn Dimas from a woman called Posy, who lived in Seaford. This Posy was a kind woman. She'd given him some hot meals in her house and they'd talked a lot. He said she was very depressed. She'd told him how Lyn had worked with her mother in a podiatry clinic, and had made a fuss about her mum making a mistake. It had cost Posy's mother her job and she'd killed herself as a result. Then Tim heard that Posy had committed suicide. It affected him badly, because not many people had shown him kindness. He got quite dramatic about it, and said that Lyn had blood on her hands.

'I gave him some money and left him in town. Then I drove to the harbour and just sat there for a long time. I was shaking with shock. After a while, I went back to Orford End and parked outside Steiner's. I sat, staring at that awful place. My son had abandoned his family, and now I'd been told that my daughter-in-law, who I held in such high esteem, had been having a tawdry affair in that squalid building. She'd already become unpleasantly shrewish towards Lily, and was generally behaving in a loud, unfeminine way that I found distasteful. As if that wasn't enough, she'd made terrible trouble for those two women, Posy and her mother. Tim was right — she'd caused their deaths as surely as if she'd killed them herself. My son's betrayal had been bad enough, but to find that Lyn had been disporting herself in that way, behaving adulterously and shaming motherhood . . .

'Finally, I went home. I did nothing for a week. I was ill, as if I had a flu. I tried to pray but the words wouldn't form. Nothing was sacred anymore — not marriage or family. There was no loyalty, no trust. If we don't have those, we have nothing, we're worse than the beasts of the earth. I'd supported Lyn to the hilt when Theo left her, given her comfort, and this was my reward, to find that she was a whore! I rang and asked to see her. When she came to my house, I challenged her. She blustered and said that Stafford was lying, that it was untrue, but I could tell from the shock on her face that it was all a front. In the end, she admitted it. She wouldn't tell me who the man was. As you said, I didn't find that out until Lily told me. Lyn said that the affair was over, and she begged me not to say anything for the sake of the children. She turned on the tears. She was pathetic, trying to justify what she'd done, saying that Theo had been distant and that she was entitled to love and affection. As if that's what she'd been getting with her fancy man! I told her that she was entitled to nothing in this life. We have duties and responsibilities and we ride out difficulties with steadfastness. I agreed not to tell the children — they were innocents and guilty only of having unfit parents. When I asked her about the family in Seaford, she tried to say that all she'd done was to ensure professional standards were met. Two women dead, and there was no humility, no remorse! I told Lyn I didn't want to see her again. I threw her out.' He stopped and cleared his throat.

'Have some water, Mr Dimas.' Ali poured him a beaker.

He took a sip, eyes still lowered, and whispered in Greek again as he fingered his beads. 'It all preyed on my mind. I couldn't see a way forward. My son was a useless husband and father, but Lyn was worse because she'd betrayed her sacred role in her family. She'd behave like that again and bring even more shame. She was trying to stand in the way of Lily's marriage, and what would Adam's life be like with a mother who'd turned out to be the worst kind of slut? She was a toxin, a contaminant in my family, and I decided that she had to die. This was the only solution. If she was out of the way, I'd be able to bring Adam here to live, raise him as a proper man, give him the guidance he needed. I never anticipated that Theo would step up and claim him, form a family with his paramour — that came as a real shock. And Lily's path in life would be eased without her mother constantly berating her.

'I rang Lyn and told her I needed to see her about something important. I said that it wouldn't take long. She didn't want to meet me, but I guessed that she would, because she was so frightened that I'd reveal her dirty secret. We agreed on the evening of Lily's prom. I did have the meeting with Pater Basil, but it was the twenty-seventh, the night before. He was confused and I was sure I'd be able to persuade him that we'd met on the twenty-eighth.

'I went into Steiner's late that afternoon and checked that no one was there. I picked Lyn up at the end of her street. She'd made herself up and put scent on. Thinking that she could still persuade me with her feminine wiles that she was worth a second chance! Tcha! She expected that we were going to talk in the car, but I said that there was something in Steiner's that she needed to see and deal with, something that could give her away. I'm not sure that she believed me, and she said that Adam was on his own, but she didn't resist when I said that we wouldn't be long. When she stepped out of the car, I kissed her on the forehead and told her I was making my peace with her. I put my driving gloves on and made sure that she went through the door in front of me. I had cord from my garage in my pocket, and I strangled her with it. I was going to leave her on the mattress. That would have been fitting, in keeping with her filthy activities, but of course that meant she would be found reasonably quickly. It occurred to me that if I tied her behind the fridge, it might be years before anyone discovered her and the more time that passed, the more likely it was that the police wouldn't be able to establish who had killed her. People might even say that she'd run away, or killed herself. I found the rope and left her tied there.'

He kissed his prayer beads, sat back and glared at them. He was defiant, calm.

'And what about Adam?' Siv said. 'Weren't you concerned that he'd been left alone?'

Dimas pursed his lips. 'I knew that he'd phone someone or go next door. It would do him good to be self-reliant. I can see the way you're judging me. I did what had to be done.'

It was irrelevant but Siv couldn't resist probing. 'How did you react when you found out that Pearce was the man Lyn had been meeting at Steiner's?'

'That was a terrible kick in the teeth. I'm surprised that my heart hasn't given way.'

'You weren't tempted to punish him as the other guilty party?'

'Tcha! He's pathetic, behaving in that way. But young men are weak vessels, easily tempted, and Pearce wasn't married at the time. He couldn't predict that he was going to meet Lily. Lyn was still the one at fault. I've explained that to Lily. Although she's distressed, I hope that she'll forgive her husband and take him back.'

'I see.' Siv rarely ran out of words in interviews but she couldn't summon up anything else to say to this man. She made a gesture to Ali.

'Tell us about Tim Stafford,' he said.

'I saw his name on that list you showed Lily and recognised his photo. Then I read that you were appealing for information about him. I hadn't seen him since that night I met him running away from Orford End, but I worried that if you found him, he might remember talking to me about Steiner's and Lyn, and then I could be in real trouble. I couldn't let that happen. I had no personal animosity towards him. My church conducts services once a month for the homeless and I've met a few of the people who sleep around town. I talked to a man called Slugger. He often camps out in the doorway of the betting shop on Sheep Street. He told me that he'd seen Tim Stafford in Hastings recently, and that he was heading for St Leonard's to check out a deserted school called Westhaven. I searched online and found it. I decided to drive around the area. I didn't need to go to the school. I struck lucky that night when I saw Tim walking along the road. I gave him the money for a takeaway. Then I suggested a stroll along the beach while he ate it. I picked up a rock and hit him. I thought he was dead, but I'm not as strong as I used to be. I'm annoyed with myself now. My motto has always been, "If you're going to do a job, do it properly".'

He drew himself upright, closed his eyes and moved his bony fingers across his beads as his lips moved soundlessly. It was as if he was alone in the room. Siv wondered how he now made sense of the outcome of his actions, but they had what they needed and she was sick of listening to his dry, factual account of his cruel judgements.

* * *

She sat with Ali outside in the little courtyard, under a watery sun.

'The world according to Joe. Old-fashioned man with old-fashioned values,' Ali said as he lit up.

'The family patriarch, making the rules and exacting punishment for transgression. But not for the men, only for the women.'

'That's because you're supposed to be above reproach. Pure and incorruptible.'

'Thank you. Maybe I should have scrutinised Joe's numerous prejudices more closely. It's too easy to dismiss someone who comes out with such bigotry. Easy to forget that they can act on it.'

'There was nothing pointing to him and we had an alibi on record. Luckily, most bigots only talk the talk . . . unless you come from my neck of the woods, where some have made a career out of acting on their intolerance.' Ali blew smoke rings into the nipping breeze.

'Did you come in for much crap, back in Derry? Stupid question, I suppose.'

'Oh aye, given my skin colour and the fact that I have a Catholic mummy and a Proddy dad. But as Jane Eyre said, "I have no tale of woe".'

'You're a Bronte fan?'

'Aye, big time. Their daddy was born in County Down so we kind of own them.' He smiled at her, his brown eyes kindly, giving Siv a little lift after the bleak interview. He sucked the last lungful from his fag. 'You can go and tell Mortimer now that we've got a win.'

'I can. I will. I just want to savour it for a bit longer. Then I'll go and see Theo Dimas.' That Finnish saying came back to her, 'My family is my strength and my weakness.' She'd be bringing heartache to the Dimases' door once more.

'I'll go and sort out Joe, make sure we've relieved him of his prayer beads before he goes in a cell. They're long enough to hang himself with.' He got up, stretched, exposing an expanse of soft, brown belly, hitched up his trousers and ambled away.

Siv checked her phone and saw that she'd had an email from Tommy Castles.

Hi, the party got a bit interesting! We sort of got off on the wrong foot. Wondered if you'd like to have a drink some time. I'm in town fairly regularly. So, let's hook up.

Ed whispered, *You should meet him. He's just your type, totally honest and with no axe to grind!* She laughed. It would be good to be a fly on the wall when Mortimer told his protégé that they'd found Lyn's killer. She'd pay money to be that fly. For now, she needed to go upstairs with her news.

THE END

ALSO BY GRETTA MULROONEY

**DETECTIVE INSPECTOR SIV DRUMMOND
SERIES**
Book 1: THESE LITTLE LIES
Book 2: NEVER CAME HOME

THE TYRONE SWIFT DETECTIVE SERIES
Book 1: THE LADY VANISHED
Book 2: BLOOD SECRETS
Book 3: TWO LOVERS, SIX DEATHS
Book 4: WATCHING YOU
Book 5: LOW LAKE
Book 6: YOUR LAST LIE
Book 7: HER LOST SISTER

Thank you for reading this book. If you enjoyed it, please leave feedback on Amazon or Goodreads, and if there is anything we missed or you have a question about then please get in touch. The author and publishing team appreciate your feedback and time reading this book.

We hate typos too but sometimes they slip through.
Please send any errors you find to
corrections@joffebooks.com.
We'll get them fixed ASAP. We're very grateful to eagle-eyed readers who take the time to contact us.

Made in the USA
Columbia, SC
09 November 2023

25851476R00198